Also by Cheryl Brooks

CAT STAR LEGACY
Maverick

THE CAT STAR CHRONICLES
Slave
Warrior
Rogue
Outcast
Fugitive
Hero
Virgin
Stud
Wildcat
Rebel

MYSTIC

CAT STAR LEGACY

CHERYL BROOKS

sourcebooks
casablanca

Published by Sourcebooks Casablanca, an imprint of Sourcebooks, Inc.
P.O. Box 4410, Naperville, Illinois 60567-4410
(630) 961-3900
Fax: (630) 961-2168
sourcebooks.com

Printed and bound in the United States of America.
OPM 10 9 8 7 6 5 4 3 2 1

For all my buddies in the Indiana chapter of RWA.
Thanks for keeping me going!

Chapter 1

IN A VISION, AIDAN HAD WATCHED HER FALL, DISAPPEAR-ing through a fissure in the rock as the ground gave way beneath her, her screams reverberating through his mind like the tumbling roar of an avalanche.

Although most people would've dismissed it as a dream, he knew the terrifying vision for what it was: a portent of a future event, which was not uncommon among his kind. Therefore, she hadn't fallen—yet. The trouble was he didn't know whether he was supposed to prevent the accident or rescue her after she fell.

He'd spent the last week flying over the cliffs, his keen eyes searching the jumbled boulders for any sign that she'd ever been there. Thus far, he'd found noth-ing. No trace of any life aside from the cliff-dwelling condors and the assorted rodents that were widespread in the remote mountains of Rhylos.

But the vision… He'd seen it four times now. This was the right place. He was certain of it. More certain, perhaps, than he'd ever been of anything.

He skimmed over the plateau before swooping down over the edge of the cliffs—jagged rock fit only as a nesting place for the huge condors, which had been named for an extinct Terran species. Some said they looked similar, and, having seen pictures, he agreed. However, these birds were even larger than the original condors had been, and they defended their nests with a ferocity few avian species could match.

His vision had been maddeningly vague. He should've at least known why she was there. Was she studying the condors? Or was she simply trying to find their nests in order to steal the eggs? He couldn't think of any other reasons why anyone would venture so far from civilization to this, one of the few uninhabited regions of the planet. Neither of those reasons seemed important enough to warrant a vision. Visions came when they wished; he had no control over their timing or their topics. The only thing he could control was the wind, enabling him to don a pair of wings and create updrafts strong enough to carry him aloft.

Only Valkyrie, the Avian clone, knew of his flights. Val would've hidden his own talent if he'd been able to remove his wings, but his were as much a part of him as his other limbs. No genetic manipulations could undo what had already been done to him.

As Aidan flew back up the cliff face, a flash of light on the plateau caught his eye—the effect of sunlight on metal. Something was moving down there. Something he'd only seen because of his vantage point high in the sky.

And there she is…

How he'd missed her before he couldn't imagine, especially on the open mountainside, unless it wasn't quite as open as it appeared. As she climbed up the edge of the plateau as though ascending a staircase, the air crackled around him like a thousand tiny lightning bolts. The moment had come.

He flew lower, hovering effortlessly, letting the wind do the work while he studied her approach. A backpack and other accoutrements were strapped to her upper body. Everything she wore—from her wide-brimmed hat, leather jacket, and khaki trousers, down to a pair of dusty boots suitable for climbing—was the same color as the rocks, causing her to blend in with her surroundings in a manner that seemed strangely covert.

A visual sweep of the plain revealed no speeder or other conveyance nearby. Had she hiked into the wilderness?

When she looked up, his eyes met hers—huge, expressive, and brown—with an impact that nearly caused him to fall out of the sky.

In the split second before he shouted a warning, she slipped from view, leaving nothing behind beyond a puff of dust that feathered away to nothingness even as he plummeted toward her, his heart pounding like a drum. He chastised himself as he flew; he'd assumed he was there to save her when, in all probability, he'd actually been the cause of her misstep.

A condor's harsh cry made him alter his route from the plateau where she'd disappeared down to the opening in the cliff face and the cavern into which she had undoubtedly fallen. He soared through the opening just as he'd seen the condors do. Unfortunately, he'd only come prepared to rescue her, carrying a knife, a length of rope, a sling made of leather straps and carabiners, and a comlink. He hadn't counted on having to get past an angry condor with murderous talons and a razor-sharp beak.

Correction. Make that two condors and a nest full of eggs. At least he assumed there were eggs in the nest. He couldn't see for sure, although given the female's protective stance, he deemed it a safe bet. "Son of a *bitch*."

Fortunately, the female seemed disinclined to move from her position on the nest. The male, however, was already advancing on the woman's crumpled body. Against the far wall of the cave below the crack in the plateau, she lay unmoving amid the rubble that had fallen with her. A soft moan told him she still lived.

No doubt the condor, which was easily twice her size, intended to change that.

Focusing his attention on the huge bird, he created a gust of wind with a sweep of his arm, sending the condor fluttering to the side of the cave where his nest and mate were situated between two upright slabs of rock.

Undaunted and angrier than ever, the condor hissed and began stalking toward him. Aidan really didn't like the idea of killing or even injuring the bird, but he might not have a choice. Taking advantage of the bird's position, which was now between him and the mouth of the cave, he created another gust that sent the bird flapping out into the open air.

One glance was enough to inform him that this woman was quite small. Val could've carried her easily. Never having flown with more than his own weight, Aidan wasn't sure he was up to the task. His own physical strength wasn't the only factor. The wings and their harness were sturdy but not unbreakable. Not for the first time, he wished his wings were a part of him the way Val's were, although when it came to sitting and sleeping, wings large enough to enable a man to fly tended to get in the way.

Upon reaching her side, he recoiled immediately when he spotted what he took to be a snake but was actually a leather bullwhip.

He almost laughed aloud. "Who do you think you are? Indiana Jones?" Upon closer inspection, her outfit was exactly the same as that worn by the fictional archaeologist. For trekking through the mountains, such garb was quite practical, although the resemblance to "Indy" ended there. She was small and undeniably female, with shiny black hair that had been braided back from her face and pinned into a twisted knot at her nape. His gaze swept over her exotically beautiful face, taking in the rich brown of her skin, the fullness of her lips, and the lovely arch of her brows.

"No," she murmured. "I am Sula." Her eyelids fluttered, and she let out a gasp. "Are you an angel, come to take me to Raj?"

Given his feathered wings and long, golden curls, her assumption was reasonable enough, although not many people believed in angels anymore.

"Hadn't planned on it," he replied. "Who's Raj?"

Her attempt to raise her head must've triggered more pain or had simply been too much of an effort, for she lapsed into unconsciousness. He folded his wings and detached the sling he'd brought, grateful that she'd fainted. This maneuver would undoubtedly be terrifying and—depending on her injuries, which, he could see at a glance, included a break in her left lower leg—excruciatingly painful. Moving her was risky; leaving her where she lay meant almost certain death.

A wingbeat drew his attention to the opening in the cliff face. Mr. Condor appeared to have recovered nicely and had returned for another round. Aidan's response was to summon up the wind and literally blow him away.

He'd brought along a few basic supplies, but his

vision hadn't included treating a broken leg or fighting off enraged condors. Fortunately, Mrs. Condor remained on her nest, providing Aidan with the opportunity to scavenge for something he could use as a splint. He found a large piece of a bamboo-like material, which he was fairly certain he could split lengthwise down the center with his knife.

That was, until he found a spearhead that had been chipped out of stone.

Although he'd never heard of such a thing on Rhylos, apparently a primitive culture had once lived there. A glance at the cave walls revealed crude drawings of condors similar to the two he'd been dealing with. The drawings appeared to be fairly old—scuffed in some places, quite clear in others—and depicted strange beings brandishing spears to drive the birds from the cave. Primates with elongated heads and surprisingly short arms...

Rhylosian cavemen?

Possibly, although they were unlike any species he'd ever seen. Someone's idea of a joke, no doubt. To the best of his recollection, Rhylos had no indigenous primates. Unless they'd died out long ago.

After splinting her leg with the bamboo and fastening it in place with her bullwhip, he rolled her onto the leather sling and then snapped it onto his wing harness. To support her head, he made another sling from her own scarf—the only item of her clothing that was colorful rather than drab—and tied it so her head wouldn't fall back as he flew. He didn't have to fly her very far— just out of this cave and away from irate condors—but he certainly didn't want her to wind up with a broken neck in the process.

Mr. Condor returned, somewhat befuddled and as dangerous as ever.

"Persistent fellow, aren't you?" Aidan muttered before blasting him out of the cave one more time.

Standing upright with Sula in his arms took surprisingly little effort. Clearing his mind as he made his way to the edge of the cliff, he let the sling support her weight, then raised his hands and produced a strong updraft. As the wind whipped past him, he tapped the control to spread his wings and stepped out into thin air.

Unfortunately, he'd overestimated the increase in weight, and the two of them shot up into the sky with enough force that he was sure his wings would snap— along with a few of his ribs. The harness squeezed the air from his lungs, and he fought desperately to inhale. Passing out now would be fatal. He focused on reducing the wind speed to tolerable levels, only managing to gulp in sufficient air just as his eyesight began to dim. Air flowed back into his compressed airways, and his vision cleared.

The male condor gave chase for a while before flying back into the cave. Evidently, it had decided that, however tasty they might appear, Aidan and Sula simply weren't worth the trouble.

In truth, the condor could have caught them fairly easily, because unlike a bird's wings, Aidan's weren't very effective at creating forward thrust. Although he could manipulate them to a certain extent, flapping them was so tiring that he'd developed a sort of swooping flight pattern. Using his control of the wind, he would rise high enough to allow him to glide forward and downward, letting momentum and gravity create the thrust. Flying alone was difficult enough; he'd never tried to fly carrying a living, breathing passenger. If she were to awaken and begin to struggle, maintaining altitude would be tricky, if not impossible.

During his flights over the area, he'd spotted a likely site to rest or set up camp if necessary. Greener than the surrounding terrain, the nook was an oasis of sorts, complete with soft grass, a few small trees, and a spring-fed pool. He might have to compete with the local animals for the water, but unless there were condors defending the territory, he was the largest critter around.

He kept his eyes peeled for any type of vehicle Sula might've used to travel out so far. That he never saw anything didn't mean nothing was there. Even with his keen eyesight, he couldn't see through rocks. If she'd left her speeder beneath an overhang, spotting it from the air would be highly unlikely.

He stumbled as he landed at his chosen campsite, thanking the gods that Sula was still unconscious. There would come a time when being out cold would be detrimental; for now, he was grateful.

Strangely enough, he had no idea what she planned to do—not with her life or whatever had set her on a path into the wilderness. With most people, he had some inkling of their desires, their dreams, and occasionally, their fate. He hated that. Hated knowing things about people that they didn't know themselves. Such knowledge was unnerving, and for that reason, he didn't pass on the information. Timelines were significant. He didn't want to be responsible for messing them up.

This one, however, was different. He felt as though he was already a part of her timeline, somehow entwined with a woman he'd never met until today. Fate had obviously brought them together. Was he only there to save her and send her on her merry way? Or were they destined to remain together forever?

Raj…

She'd hoped an angel would take her to someone named Raj—a man's name, surely. A lost love, perhaps? He could feel the sadness and the sense of longing in her. The hope that she might be reunited with someone she'd loved.

Clearly, she'd had no premonitions that a Zetithian "angel" named Aidan Banadänsk would save her and go on to become an important part of her life.

He'd never had anyone like that in his life. He had roamed the galaxy with his family and never found a single, solitary soul to complete him, to give his life purpose or joy. His gifts had set him apart from everyone he'd ever met, even the family he loved. That it hadn't driven him insane was a wonder. His sister, Althea, had a similar problem, although she'd finally realized that the one man whose emotions she couldn't read was the one destined to be her mate.

He'd had a vision about Sula. Not a premonition. There was a difference. The one was chiefly visual and a Zetithian peculiarity. He could deal with that. Such visions were infrequent and didn't necessarily involve the people around him. The other was pure Mordrial, allowing him to glimpse the future of anyone he met and also to push his consciousness ahead a few seconds. Quite often, he felt nothing beyond a sense of foreboding or elation upon meeting someone new, while other readings were visceral and terrifying. Readings among friends and family usually concerned only the near future, whereas shaking the hand of a stranger often showed him their ultimate and sometimes horrific fate.

Kneeling on the soft, fragrant grass, he attempted to release her from the sling without worsening her injuries—or thinking about what would've happened to her if he hadn't been tormented day and night until he finally solved the vision's riddle.

Had he saved her for himself or for some greater purpose?

Time would tell. This was one outcome he couldn't predict.

As he removed her backpack and placed it like a pillow beneath her head, something about her stirred the depths of his soul, bringing his own destiny into question. For perhaps the first time in his life, he was annoyed by his inability to know what fate had in store for him. Of all the people he'd ever met, the only two whose futures were as murky as the fogs on Taelit Ornal were himself and now Sula.

However, before he could speculate on her future, he had to ensure that she had one.

———

An angel wouldn't have asked who Raj was. An angel would've *known*.

Then again, he hadn't said whether he was an angel. He'd only claimed he wasn't planning to take her to Raj.

Pain soon expunged any doubts from Sula's mind. Had she been on her way to the afterlife prior to being reincarnated into another form, she doubted the body of her current life would've troubled her quite so much.

Therefore, he was no angel—certainly not like any angel she'd ever heard about.

Nor was he like any living being she'd ever seen. A man with pointed ears, feline eyes, and enormous wings? Unless the wings weren't real. They'd certainly looked real when he'd been sailing through the sky above her. Plenty of black and gray white-tipped feathers, arranged row upon row like those of a bird. Or was she confusing him with the birds in the cave? In the short time before she'd passed out, she'd seen drawings of them on the cave wall, being hunted by primitive humanoids. She'd finally found the evidence she'd been searching for.

The question was, could she ever find it again?

The warm sunshine beating down on her face was proof enough that she was no longer in the cave. She wasn't lying in a pile of stones, either. The ground beneath her was relatively soft, and a gentle breeze carried the fragrance of fresh, green grass to her nose—a smell quite unlike the dank odor peculiar to caves, particularly those inhabited by birds.

Her leg still pained her, although she could tell that it was at least lying straight. The initial shock of the break that had brought on her fainting spell had passed. She was thirsty, almost to the point that her tongue seemed cemented to the roof of her mouth. An attempt to moisten her lips failed.

Within moments, a hand slipped behind her head, and a cup was held to her lips. As the cool water soothed her parched mouth, she recalled doing the same for Raj in the last hours of his life.

Dear, sweet Raj. So intelligent, such a promising student, and the one man she would never forget. The love of her life—or rather, the *lost* love of her life—and she'd had to watch him die.

She'd been helpless to prevent his death or even ease his suffering. The aftereffects of the disease were nearly as bad. Within hours, even his body was gone; nothing remained of him aside from the clothes he'd been wearing and a pile of dust that was soon scattered by the wind.

Surrounded by an eerie silence, she'd returned to their ship. Purely out of habit, she'd gone through the decontamination process. The scanner proclaimed her to be free of disease, although she hadn't been sure she could trust even that. She and Raj had gone through a similar process prior to their departure, and yet Raj had been among the first to fall ill. They'd had minimal contact with the natives, observing rather than interacting with them directly. Granted, they'd barely begun their study before Raj began to feel sick, but on the whole, the natives had seemed industrious and intelligent and appeared to live together in relative harmony. Rather strange in appearance, perhaps, but that was to be expected.

Not nearly as strange as her rescuer. Despite being somewhat afraid to take another look, she opened her eyes a teensy bit.

The wings were gone.

So they weren't real after all.

The long golden curls remained, as did the peculiar eyes. Rather than the usual dark, round pupils, his were vertical slits that emitted a soft, golden glow. His ears came to a point like those of a storybook elf, and a pair of straight brows slanted up toward his temples.

"Glad you're awake," he said. Then he smiled, revealing his sharp fangs.

A scream had nearly left her throat when she remembered something from her studies that caused her to gasp instead—a textbook description of a nearly extinct species of feline humanoids.

"You're Zetithian."

Chapter 2

"I'm impressed," he said, and judging from his tone, he actually meant it. "Most people have never heard of us."

Sula had heard of them, all right. After learning about the sexual abilities of Zetithian males, she and her classmates had joked that they would dearly love to hook up with one of them someday.

Of course, that was before she met Raj.

"I'm working on a PhD in anthropology," she said. "I've probably learned something about every humanoid species in the known galaxy."

"Then I'm doubly impressed, although I'm kinda surprised we made it into a textbook." He arched a brow. "Or are we listed as extinct?"

"*Nearly* extinct," she replied. "Definitely on the endangered list."

A smile touched his lips. "We're working on fixing that."

"So I've heard," she said, not bothering to keep the dryness from her tone. According to her textbook, Zetithian children were nearly always born in litters of three, and the males could mate with any number of different species and still produce triplets that at least had the appearance of purebreds. The prevailing theory was that, along with their dominant genes, Zetithian semen acted as a fertility drug, triggering multiple ovulations. Perhaps the Zetithians' most unusual and endearing trait was that they weren't simply monogamous—they truly mated for life. Perhaps "hooking up" with one of them wasn't possible after all, at least not in the usual sense.

"So tell me, Sula, why would an anthropologist be exploring an uninhabited region that only a condor could love? Or were you searching for a man with wings? If so, I believe I can point you in the right direction. My friend Val has *real* wings. But you didn't have to come all the way out here to find him."

She tucked her upper lip firmly between her teeth. Revealing her suspicions would do him no good and might even get him killed. Only this time, no bounty would be paid on his body as there would have been in the past. He would simply disappear, never to be heard from again.

Like Raj…

She couldn't even tell Raj's family what had happened to him. Nor did she know how much they already knew. Having already been targeted once since she'd left Ecos, she had opted to keep moving. Their ship was a research vessel belonging to the university, which meant that selling it required her to deal with some rather shady characters. And while she'd somehow managed to come out of that adventure unscathed and had since managed to remain incognito, this particular man had pegged her costume almost immediately.

Her natural curiosity got the better of her. "Indiana Jones? I didn't think anyone would remember him."

If he wondered why she hadn't answered his question, it didn't show. Still smiling, he sat back on his heels. "You're discounting my upbringing. I grew up on a starship owned by a woman who's a huge fan of Old

Earth culture. I probably know more about what went on a thousand years ago than I do about current events."

She frowned as she recalled that much of her life had also been spent studying the past. However, none of that study had prepared her for the mess she'd gotten herself into. "I know the feeling."

Partly. She certainly hadn't grown up on a starship. If she had, she wouldn't have had quite so much trouble flying the *Dalb Explorer* to Rhylos. Fortunately, the onboard computer and the autopilot were both very helpful, although she still had a hard time believing she'd actually done it. Raj had been much better at such things than she.

Tears filled her eyes at the thought of him. He'd been gone for almost a year now, but the wound still seemed fresh. Even if she hadn't loved him, his had been such a wasteful, needless death.

"I'm sorry," he said quickly. "Was I too rough?"

His meaning wasn't immediately clear. Too rough with what? Moving her? Time seemed out of sync somehow. What happened in the past was intruding into the present, then retreating to leave confusion in its wake. "No. I'm okay." She dashed her tears away with a grimy finger.

"Here," he whispered. "Let me do that." He cupped her face in his palms and dried her tears with an unexpectedly gentle touch, almost as if he could feel the pressure of his thumbs on her face from her perspective. "That's better."

"Thank you." Her reply was even less than a whisper. More of a moving of her lips, not trusting her voice not to crack.

"No problem," he said. "Now we need to figure out

how to get you to a hospital. I can fly you part of the way, but—"

She put up both hands. "No hospitals." Desperation triggered the break in her voice she'd feared. "Please."

Narrowing his eyes, he folded muscular arms over a broad chest, which she realized for the first time was bare and appeared to be every bit as powerful as his arms. "Mind telling me why? Or is it the same reason you're doing an Indiana Jones impersonation out in the middle of nowhere?"

"Yes, I suppose it is." She racked her brain for every particle of information she could recall about Zetithians. Their sexual prowess overshadowed several laudable traits, the most significant being their inherent honesty.

He could most likely be trusted with any confidence, although part of what she'd already done fell outside the law on almost any world. Then again, this *was* Rhylos, and as the slogan went, *Anything goes on Rhylos*. There were laws, however.

"That's all you're going to say?"

She drew in a deep breath, which, surprisingly, didn't cause her any pain. "For now."

"Something illegal?"

"Not entirely." She hadn't technically *stolen* a starship, even though the one she'd sold didn't belong to her in any manner other than possession being nine-tenths of the law. She bit her lip again, determined not to say anything further.

He glanced skyward as though seeking strength from the heavens. "So I'm supposed to leave you here to provide food for the condor chicks?"

"I'd much rather you didn't."

"Wasn't planning to. No point in rescuing you only to abandon you to your fate." His gaze made a sweep of the surrounding area. "Don't suppose you have a speeder stashed somewhere nearby, do you?"

"No. I needed to save my credits for more important things."

He nodded. "Like food and clothing."

"Yeah. That stuff."

"And a good pair of boots. That is, if you walked all the way from Damenk."

She studied him for a long moment. "How is it that you can fly?" Zetithians might have sexual abilities that were second to none, but she'd never heard it said that they were capable of flight, even with artificial wings.

His eyes became shuttered, and where it had once been open and friendly, his posture now seemed guarded. "That's *my* secret."

She considered striking a bargain with him but ultimately decided she didn't need to know how or why he could fly. She only needed to know that he could. In her current predicament, she had no choice but to trust him. Coming at a time when she'd concluded she couldn't trust anyone, this realization shook her.

I already should've died several times over.

Raj was dead. Her only reason to go on living was to prevent further deaths. That was if her suspicions were correct, and she was fairly certain they were. In the weeks following her escape from Ecos, she was haunted by Raj's last words: "This is how they did it, Sula. It's happening again." Those words were more than enough to start the wheels turning in her head, perhaps to the point of imagining conspiracies where none existed. Granted, she might be suffering from latent paranoia, although considering everything she'd been through recently, a touch of paranoia was not only to be expected, it was essential to her continued safety.

"I guess we're even, then."

"So it would seem." He slapped his hands on his thighs as though he'd made up his mind. "Okay, then. No hospitals—although you're placing an awful lot of faith in my ability to set a broken leg. You could end up with a limp for the rest of your life, if you're even able to walk again. The break of a long bone can also cause a fatty embolus. Or you could throw a blood clot to the brain. Either of those things could cause a massive stroke and leave you paralyzed if they don't kill you outright."

"Are you trying to scare me?"

He shrugged. "Just calling it as I see it. My mother has always been a healer. I've picked up a lot of knowledge from her. I'd take you to her if she weren't halfway across the galaxy at the moment. The other option is to take you to a Zerkan friend of mine. He could cure you pretty quickly, although their 'cures' are sometimes worse than the ailment."

Sula also knew a little about Zerkans. He was right, of course; the lasting effects of the cure probably *would* be worse than those of the injury. A transient limp was infinitely preferable to having glowing red pupils for the rest of her life. She glanced at her leg. "You're not giving yourself enough credit. From my perspective, it looks as though you did a fine job."

"I may have set it correctly, but I can't make it heal any faster than normal. Without further intervention, you're looking at six weeks in a splint." He peered up at the sky again. "The wind is picking up. If I'm going to fly you anywhere, we need to get ahead of the storm."

"What storm?"

He pointed eastward. "*That* storm."

Massive dark, ominous clouds boiled up from the lower plain, spitting lightning in every direction. She hadn't seen anything of the kind when she'd climbed up onto the plateau. "Oh my… How long was I out?"

"About three hours," he replied. "Listen, if Mom, hospitals, and Zerkan healers are out, exactly where *do* you want to go?"

The last thing she wanted was to annoy her rescuer—a strikingly handsome Zetithian man whose name she didn't even know. "I have no idea. Any other suggestions?"

"I could take you to my place, although that might be a bit presumptuous."

"Is it secret?"

"Not really. It's just a house in the Talwat district near where some friends of mine live. They run an orphanage in the brothel district. I work there sometimes. I could see if they have a bed for you."

"No, thank you," she said with a shudder. "I'd rather take my chances here than spend any time in an orphanage—especially one in the brothel district."

His brow rose. "It isn't that kind of orphanage. Trust me."

Trusting him would make her next move so much easier, if only she could bring herself to do it. On the other hand, she couldn't think of a single viable alternative. "I probably shouldn't be too picky, especially when it doesn't matter where you take me, as long as no one else knows where—or who—I am."

"Shouldn't be too hard. I don't even know your full name. Sula, you said?"

"I never should've told you that."

He chuckled. "I can call you Indy if you like."

"Never mind. Sula is fine as long as no one else knows I'm there."

Tilting his head to the side, he peered at her through narrowed lids. "You don't strike me as the criminal type. What the devil did you do?"

She shook her head. "It isn't about something I *did*. It's about something I *know*."

"Okay, Sula." He held out a hand. "Aidan Banadänsk at your service. And believe me, I can keep a secret with the best of them."

When she took his hand, Aidan fully expected images of her destiny to flow into his mind like a raging flood. Instead, he felt only the sort of things a man should feel when shaking hands with a beautiful woman who'd entrusted him with her life.

Most of those things, anyway. Without the scent of her desire, he didn't react sexually, which wasn't too surprising, considering how she seemed to feel about this Raj fellow—at least he *assumed* Raj was a fellow. For all he knew, that might be the name of some sort of god.

He wasn't exactly looking for a mate himself. His life was too complicated to bring anyone else into it. Even so, he would sooner betray his own secrets than betray hers, mainly because divulging his secrets wouldn't result in any real danger. At least not right away. However, he suspected that if her secret were to become known, there would be more than enough danger for both of them.

"Speaking of secrets, who's Raj?"

For a long moment, he thought she was going to ignore that question like she'd dodged most of the others he'd asked.

"Raj was my boyfriend," she finally said. "He…died."

"I'm very sorry for your loss."

Her complacent shrug seemed at odds with her bleak expression. "He died about a year ago. It still feels like yesterday."

Aidan had never lost any of his family or friends, let alone a lover—mainly because he'd never had one to lose—but that didn't mean he didn't understand the feeling. "I imagine it does." He hesitated before asking, "Does his death have something to do with why you're here?"

"In a way," she replied. "I'm not out to avenge his death, exactly. I'm just trying to find out *why* he had to die."

The plot thickens… "I take it he didn't die of natural causes."

She snorted with disgust. "If you can call the Scorillian plague natural."

A long moment passed before he realized his jaw had dropped. "The Scorillian plague? Seriously? How did he manage to catch that? I thought it had been eradicated."

"So did I," was her tight-lipped reply.

"You're sure that's what it was?"

Her firm nod conveyed no doubts whatsoever. "Unless there's another disease that reduces a body to dust in a matter of hours."

"If there is, I've never heard of it. I can't imagine where or how he would catch it." He fixed her with a quizzical gaze. "But I'm guessing you know—or at least have your suspicions."

She drew in a long breath, then blew it out as she shook her head. "I've already said too much. I don't want to put you in any danger."

"Thanks, but we'll worry about that later. Right now, we need to figure out where to go. If you don't want to stay at my house or the orphanage, I have other friends who can be trusted."

To his surprise, she actually smiled—an expression that changed her from suspicious and wary to something far more approachable, perhaps even charming. "Like the one with *real* wings?"

"Yeah. Being something of a recluse, Val doesn't encourage visitors, so you'd be safe from prying eyes. Aside from his ability to fly, he's also the best computer hacker you'll find anywhere. His expertise might come in handy with your quest." He hesitated. "But if you want his help—or mine—you're going to have to trust us."

Her dark-brown eyes clouded with doubt. "Why would you want to risk your life for a cause you know nothing about? Especially one that doesn't even affect you directly?"

"Oh, Sula," he said, chuckling as he patted her hand. "That textbook of yours didn't include many details about Zetithians, did it? Our species was persecuted to near extinction and our planet destroyed, so we know what it's like to be the underdog. Now that we've removed the threat to our own kind, fighting injustice is what we do." With a grin, he added, "Some of us, anyway."

"So what are you? Some sort of vigilante?"

"Not exactly. I've been helping out at the orphanage ever since I came of age. Haven't been on any real adventures as of yet. But I have a few talents that might prove useful."

"You mean besides being able to fly?"

"That's right."

She still seemed doubtful, tipping her head to one side in a rather endearing manner. "What kind of talents?"

"I have...visions."

"Visions?" she echoed with a scornful snort. "Seriously?"

"Oh yeah. It's a Zetithian thing. Happens to us every once in a while—some of us more than others." For the time being, he deemed it best to avoid mentioning his Mordrial ancestry, although he might have to own up to his control of the winds eventually. His knack for fortune-telling was his deepest secret—an ability that seemed to have deserted him at the moment. "How else would I have found you?"

Chapter 3

SULA DIDN'T KNOW WHETHER TO BELIEVE AIDAN OR NOT. Granted, Zetithians were purported to be honest and trustworthy, but this sounded completely preposterous, and his roguish grin suggested he might be teasing her. Still, she couldn't argue with the incredible odds against him being in the right place at the right time—and she *had* seen him fly.

"You have a point."

He rolled his eyes. "At last, she believes me."

"It didn't take *that* long to convince me," she said with a withering glance. "Although I'll need further proof before I can fully credit you with having… visions."

If her lack of faith annoyed him, it wasn't apparent in his casual shrug. "There's plenty of anecdotal evidence to support my claim. No idea if anything has actually been documented since our planet was destroyed. Like you said, there aren't very many of us left, and even I'm not a purebred. My father is Zetithian, but my mother is…Terran."

The hesitation in his speech piqued her interest.

So…it's something about his mother…

She deemed it best not to prod him unnecessarily. At the moment, knowing his mother's ancestry was fairly low on her list of priorities. Keeping on his good side was much more important. She doubted he would leave her to fend for herself with a broken leg even if she were to anger him, but she saw no point in making her rescue more difficult than it already was.

"I'm Terran as well," she said. "Originally from Bangalore, in southern India."

He nodded. "I thought you might be. Believe it or not, I've been to India. Interesting culture." His gaze slid from her face to her boots and back again. "I notice you don't favor the native dress."

"I've been known to wear a sari on occasion, although they aren't terribly practical for field work."

His smile made her heart take a dip. "I don't suppose they are. They're quite beautiful, though. I've been all over the galaxy, and I've never seen fabrics that even begin to compare."

Heat prickled her face as though he'd complimented her directly. Why she should be so inordinately pleased by his appreciation of Indian fashions escaped her. She didn't know whether to agree or simply thank him. In the end, she opted to do both. "Thank you. I feel the same way, even though I haven't traveled as much as you have."

"Not that much, really. I should've specified the *known* galaxy, and only the major trade routes."

"Still more than I've done."

"I dunno... Rhylos is a long way from Earth."

"True. But aside from Earth, I've only been to two planets during the course of my studies." Three if she counted Ecos. However, she wasn't prepared to admit that just yet. "I went to university on Ursa Prime."

"Went? Didn't you say you were *working* on your doctorate?"

Ooh, he's quick. At this rate, he would have everything figured out long before her broken leg even stopped hurting, much less healed.

"My studies have been…interrupted."

"I see. Financial troubles?"

This was one lie she had no qualms about telling. "Something like that." She'd gone to Dalb University on a full scholarship. As matters now stood, going back there was out of the question.

Unless I have proof…

Closing her eyes, she did her best to think rationally, a task his proximity rendered difficult from a visual as well as a mental perspective. The sight of him was riveting, and not only because she viewed him through an anthropologist's eyes.

He was flat-out gorgeous. She'd seen attractive men before—Raj had ranked high on the list—but this guy cast the others in the shade. No wonder she'd mistaken him for an angel. Even with his alien features, he was too handsome to be real.

Am I still unconscious and dreaming all of this?

If so, she would recommend unconsciousness to—

No. That was silly. Besides, Raj had been the man of her dreams. She wouldn't be granted that sort of happiness a second time, even if she lived to be a hundred. In fact, the way things were going, she'd be lucky to make it to her next birthday.

On the other hand, luck or fate or visions had sent Aidan to her. As omens went, he struck her as a pretty good one. She should take him at his word and make the most of him—and the help he offered.

"Okay, Aidan. You can take me wherever you think

is appropriate—except a hospital, of course. I have no desire to stay here and become condor food."

"That's more like it." He hopped to his feet. "It'll be dark soon. We could wait until morning, although going in under the cover of darkness would probably be best."

"Go in where, exactly?"

"Damenk," he replied. "My house to start with. And don't worry about security. Zetithians are something of a novelty, even on this crazy planet, so we have to take precautions to ensure our privacy. You'll have plenty of time to recover without being bothered by anyone." He grinned, once again revealing his fangs. "Unless you decide to let Giklor heal you."

"Your Zerkan friend?"

"Yeah. I won't tell him you're staying with me. He's kinda persistent that way. Dearly loves to heal people. Gets off on it, actually."

She cleared her throat. "I believe I'll pass."

"Suit yourself," he said. "Although you might change your mind after a few days. Waiting for a broken bone to heal can get old real quick. Not that I mind if you stick around for a while."

"You know what they say about fish and uninvited guests. After three days, they both start to stink."

"I don't think you'll stink even after three months," he declared. "I've never had a houseguest before—not a stranger, anyway—so this'll be a new experience for me. And you aren't uninvited. Unexpected, perhaps, but not uninvited. I promise to take excellent care of you."

She arched a brow. "Is taking care of me part of your vision?"

"Nope. That's just me being a nice guy."

A giggle slipped out, a sound she hadn't made in a long, long time. "A nice guy with nothing better to do?"

"Maybe. But those are your words, not mine."

———⁓⁓⁓———

Aidan had actually been a bit nervous about what Sula might say when she woke up. Most of the fortune-telling stuff came within moments of meeting someone. Touch, in the form of a hug or a handshake, accelerated the process. He'd taken to avoiding physical contact whenever possible. Other times, he forced himself to go ahead with it simply to get the "reading" over and done with. Sadly, knowing someone's fate tended to affect how he related to them. Being ignorant of Sula's destiny was as refreshing as it was unusual. Talking to her affected him the way flying did, lifting his spirits and brightening his mood. While it was true that not everyone's destiny was disheartening—some were hopeful and fulfilling—the bad seemed to outweigh the good, leaving him with a rather pessimistic outlook.

Sula was different. She might be doomed to face a ghastly end, but having been spared that knowledge, his soul wasn't being dragged into the depths of despair. Some people did that to him. They were losers no matter which way they turned, and their misfortunes affected Aidan almost as though they were his own. He'd seen a number of things he wished he could unsee. Too bad this was one instance when a peek into the future would've been useful, perhaps even welcome.

The vibes he picked up from his friends and family differed from the impressions he received from strangers. Those with close ties generated sporadic readings that tended to reflect short-term events, whereas strangers' impressions tended to reach further into the future. Into which category would Sula fall? Perhaps, given enough time, she would affect him the way his family did.

The only hitch was, for that to happen, he would have to be near her on a daily basis—a situation he didn't mind in the slightest.

She intrigued him far beyond what ignorance of her future should have evoked. This puzzled him until he realized what made her so different.

He was attracted to her—attracted in a way no woman had ever affected him in all of his twenty-six years. Sure, he'd met loads of women throughout his life, traveling from planet to planet with his family and that of Captain Jacinth "Jack" Tshevnoe, but he'd never fallen in love with any of them. Jack was a trader with a wanderlust that even a Zetithian husband and nine children couldn't cure, with the result that they never stayed in one place long enough for Aidan to form an attachment with anyone. His mother, Tisana, had a similar affliction, and their two families had roamed the galaxy together aboard the starship *Jolly Roger* even before he and his littermates were born.

He didn't regret his upbringing. However, the only girl he'd known while growing up was his sister, Althea, who, being an empath with Zetithian, Terran, and Mordrial ancestry, was unlike any other girl in the galaxy. The rest of the children born aboard their ship were boys. The girls they met in spaceports thought Zetithian guys were hot, but any relationships were brief and superficial at best. Aidan's insight into each girl's future caused him to shy away from most of them, and since there were four other available Zetithian boys who were fairly close to him in age, the girls rarely had any need to pursue the one who wasn't interested. Because he and his brother Aldrik had similar coloring, he wasn't even the only blond.

A restless movement from Sula returned his attention to her. "Do you want more to drink before we go? Something to eat, maybe?"

"I have some food in my backpack, but I'd better wait, or I might end up losing it to motion sickness."

"Hadn't thought of that. I was more concerned with causing you pain."

"I'll be okay," she said. "Just don't drop me."

"Wouldn't dream of it." He tugged on the leather sling, which was still underneath her. "This thing is pretty sturdy, which means you won't fall unless I do." He paused as he remembered she'd been unconscious the last time they'd flown together. "I should warn you I don't fly like the typical bird. I use more of a rise and fall pattern, which could make you a little queasy, especially if you're feeling bad to begin with."

"You should probably carry me with my back toward you." Her eyes danced with mischief. "That way, I can see where we're going, and I won't throw up all over you."

He shouted with laughter. "My, how thoughtful." Still chuckling, he buckled on his wings as he nodded toward a small but sturdy-looking tree growing near the spring. "Think you could stand on one foot if you were holding onto that tree?"

She nodded. "I don't feel faint anymore."

The thought of holding Sula against him with her backside nestled against his groin sent Aidan's libido soaring off into space. Fortunately—or perhaps *un*fortunately—he wouldn't get an erection unless he inhaled the scent of her desire, sparing him the inevitable embarrassment that would result from his hard cock pressing against her bottom.

On the other hand, a raging hard-on would prove she was interested in him—or had at least forgotten about Raj.

No. It wouldn't prove either of those things. A woman's body could respond sexually even if she didn't want it to. The same was true of the males of most species.

I just had to be Zetithian.

Sometimes, being touted as the best lovers in the galaxy was a good thing. Other times, it was dammed inconvenient.

"Okay, then." Kneeling beside her, he placed her hat firmly on her head, then gathered her up in his arms, sling and all. "Let's see if you can stand without passing out."

Thankfully, Sula was able to stand, although she doubted she could've done it without Aidan's assistance or the tree for support.

She still hadn't completely recovered from the breathtaking experience of being carried by such a ridiculously sexy man. Her reaction might've been different if he'd been wearing a shirt, and the brown leggings he wore—although undoubtedly quite suitable for flight—left very little to the imagination. She should've closed her eyes instead of staring, but she couldn't bring herself to do so. Not with the expanse of hard muscle and tanned skin right in front of her face.

He draped the upper straps over her shoulders and

fitted the leather contraption around her waist and hips in a deft manner that seemed devoid of any romantic or sexual overtones. When he stepped around behind her, Sula blurted out, "How in the world did you ever manage this while I was unconscious?"

"With difficulty," he replied. "The hardest part was those last two straps."

She didn't have to ask which ones he meant. They were dangling between her legs. "I guess those are some of the more important pieces, aren't they?"

"Yep. They're what keep you from slipping out like an overripe banana."

She pressed her lips together but failed to keep the lid on her laughter. Her poorly timed moment of mirth loosened her grip on the tree limb, and she fell back against him. In the next instant, his arms snaked around her, pulling her against him hard enough to knock most of the wind out of her.

"You okay?" His lips were so close, his breath tickled her neck.

She nodded but signaled her discomfort with a wiggle of her hips and a tap on his arm. "Too tight," she gasped.

"Sorry," he said as he eased his grip. "Don't know my own strength sometimes. Just didn't want to have to set that leg again."

"No problem. I was a little startled, but I'm okay now."

"Good. Hang on to that tree while I get the lower straps fastened. Works best to snap them on first."

She didn't want to know how he knew that, although as businesslike as he was now, she couldn't imagine him taking liberties with her unconscious body. Oddly enough, a moment's reflection on such an occurrence didn't distress her as much as it should have. If he'd been the one to need rescuing, she wasn't completely sure she wouldn't at least have taken a moment to comb her fingers through his long blond hair. Although as tightly wound as his curls were, getting her fingers tangled in them probably would've brought him out of anything short of a coma.

He certainly hadn't messed with *her* hair, which was still braided and pinned as securely as ever.

As he reached for the infamous crotch straps, his fingers didn't even graze the fabric of her trousers. Come to think of it, he hadn't come close to touching her breasts when he'd grabbed her from behind.

He's either homosexual or the most gentlemanly gentleman imaginable.

Not that his sexual orientation mattered. He was simply her rescuer, like a firefighter or an emergency medical technician. Certainly not her knight in shining armor or a brooding, romantic hero.

Then again, he'd had a vision about her, and he'd obviously come prepared to rescue her and fly her to safety. He was taking her to his house. Maybe then he would—

No. If he wasn't interested in romance out in the middle of nowhere, he probably wouldn't change his mind after he took her home.

Why am I even thinking this stuff?

How could one man alter her focus so completely and in such a short time? She had an important mystery to solve and a lost love to avenge. She didn't need a new romance to complicate matters.

*He's Zetithian...*a species whose legendary sexual prowess was compounded by the fact that, as far as most females were concerned, they were irresistible. Aidan was all that and more. Dammit, he even *smelled* good.

Of course, he probably had women crawling all over him wherever he went, to the point that he needed a security system on his house to keep them away. He didn't need *her*.

"Hold onto your hat, Sula. Here we go."

While she'd been mulling—okay, *mooning*—over him, he'd been busy preparing to fly her to safety.

The wind picked up, seeming to arise from the ground beneath her feet. Aidan didn't flap his wings. Didn't need to. With the wind to lift them, they simply floated upward like a helium-filled balloon. As the wind grew stronger, they soared high above the plateau, swooping down the cliff face before rising again.

She twisted around to look up at him. "How are you *doing* that?"

"Guess I might as well tell you," he said, his tone conveying reluctant resignation. "In addition to my Terran and Zetithian blood, I'm also part Mordrial. I can control the wind. Watching Val gave me the idea to try flying. As you can see, it works—up to a point. However, I'd appreciate it if you didn't tell anyone."

"This is your secret?"

He sighed. "One of them."

Chapter 4

A MAN WITH SO MANY BIZARRE SECRETS COULD PROVE to be a valuable ally. Still, Sula wasn't completely convinced she needed Aidan's help—except for providing a place to stay while her leg healed. By that time, who knew what degree of trust or distrust might develop between them. She might decide she needed his continued assistance, which meant she would have to tell him everything. This mission was too dangerous to enter into without full knowledge of the facts as well as her suspicions.

Time will tell.

In the interim, she focused on the incredible adrenaline rush of actually flying with nothing more to support her than the wind and a man with a pair of what she hoped were very strong artificial wings.

"I know what you're thinking," he said. "The wing rods are made of a superstrong, lightweight titanium alloy. The harness is as sturdy as I could make it without adding too much weight. I tried several materials before opting to go with full-grain leather reinforced with a synthetic mesh. Synthetics don't break easily, but they aren't as comfortable as leather."

"Why natural feathers instead of fabric?"

"I suppose I could've used fabric—construction certainly would've been easier—but feathers just seemed the best way to go about it. Maybe I envied Val a bit." With a sigh, he added, "He has the most *amazing* wings."

"You do sound sort of envious," she admitted. "But then, he probably wishes he had your wind-control ability."

She felt as much as heard his chuckle. "Guess no one's ever satisfied with what they have. He probably wishes his wings were detachable. Although, considering his history, he might wish he didn't have wings at all. Sure, being able to fly is awesome, but it sets him apart from nearly everyone in the galaxy. There are only five others like him—they call themselves Avian clones— and they've each been genetically engineered to have wings, incredibly sharp eyesight, and a highly developed auditory sense. Unfortunately, those genetic modifications carry even more stigma than simply being clones."

"Which isn't a bit fair when you consider that the clones themselves—modified or not—didn't have any say in their own creation."

"No kidding."

Sula had studied the cloning craze from a few centuries back. The practice was rampant until lawmakers on most worlds decided it wasn't such a hot idea, partly because of the replicative fading problem. Make a copy of a copy enough times, and mutations were inevitable. They could be fixed, but gene editing was difficult, costly, and not always successful. The legal ramifications posed the biggest drawback. Was the clone a new person or merely an extension of the original? Dozens of inheritance and property-ownership clashes cropped up. In the end, outlawing the cloning of intelligent species seemed the easiest way to deal with the issue.

Once passed, those laws left the existing clones with no rights whatsoever. Even though that was changing, the taint remained, especially for those who had been created illegally. Sula suspected that Val and his fellow Avian clones belonged in that category. Add genetic manipulation on top of that, and it was no wonder Val didn't "encourage visitors."

As they soared past the mountains and down into the foothills, Sula began to wish she'd met Aidan under different circumstances. Having him fly her into the mountains would've been a whole lot easier than going in on foot. She could've explored dozens of cliffs and caverns in the time it had taken her to find the first one. Too bad his vision hadn't sent him to find her before she'd been foolish enough to break a leg.

Still, it wasn't every day a girl looked up and saw a freakin' angel flying overhead. The only things he'd lacked were the flowing white robes, which ancient artists might've added merely for the effect. She'd taken a few classes in art history before deciding on anthropology as her major, and she'd never seen a single angel depicted in leggings.

"We'll be landing soon," he said, interrupting her thoughts. He reached past her shoulder, pointing toward a grove of trees near a bend in the Unghela River. "My speeder is parked down there."

She chuckled. "You mean we aren't going to fly all the way to Damenk?"

"Nope. My flying ability is a secret. Remember?"

"I remember. Just teasing."

"Better laugh it up while you can. This landing might be a little rough."

As the ground seemed to fly up to meet them, Sula instinctively bent her left knee as far as she could without kicking Aidan in the shins.

After all, kicking one's guardian angel could have any number of dire consequences.

——✦✦✦——

Aidan had already landed with her once, so he'd had a little practice, with the result that this landing was much smoother than the first. Even so, balancing the amount of lift with the planet's gravitational force was tricky. He hovered just above the ground about a meter from his speeder before slowly reducing the wind speed to nil.

Sula clapped her hands as they touched down. "Way to go, Aidan. Didn't even feel a bump."

"That was one of my better landings. Damn near broke my own legs the first time I tried it."

"I guess practice really does make perfect."

"Sometimes." The trick now would be to get her into his speeder without hurting her.

Think, Aidan.

Using a tree for support had worked before. Hopefully something similar would work this time. "I'm going to carry you over to the speeder. We only have to go a few steps. Then you can hang onto the side while I get you unhooked."

"Sounds good," she said.

"Stand on your good leg for a few seconds." Aidan wrapped his arms around her and lifted her, doing his best to ignore the way her bottom bumped against his groin and how good she felt in his arms. He inched his way over to the speeder and popped open the canopy.

Her breath hissed through her teeth as he set her down.

"You okay?" he asked.

"I think so," she said, although she didn't sound terribly confident.

He would have to hurry. "Grab onto the door, and tell me when you're ready."

A few deep breaths later, she nodded. "Try it now."

Starting at her shoulders, he unfastened the carabiners and worked his way down to the crotch straps. "Okay, you're loose. Now, I'm going to pick you up and put you in the front seat, hopefully without bumping your leg."

After adjusting the seat to allow maximum leg room, he moved in behind her. She slid her arm around his neck, and he slowly lifted her before cradling her against his chest.

Her sharp inhale made him glance at her face—a glance that lasted far longer than it should have. The beseeching expression in her big brown eyes caught him unawares, affecting him on a primal, visceral level.

"You're doing great," he said, forcing a cheerful, encouraging note into his voice. That his words came out with a purr was completely unintentional.

"I'd forgotten about the purring thing," she whispered. "It's very...comforting."

"I'm glad you think so." Purring wasn't supposed to be comforting. It was supposed to be sexually stimulating—to Zetithian women, anyway. He had no business purring in such a situation. But if it calmed her, what did it matter?

He set her in the speeder as carefully as he could. Once she was settled, he was about to step back when she tightened her hold on him.

With a shy smile, she pulled him close enough to kiss his cheek. "Thank you. You're very kind. I'm sorry to be such a bother."

Aidan didn't know what to say to that. He'd been purring, and she'd kissed him. The only thing missing was the scent of her desire. If she knew Zetithians could purr, most likely she also knew that males purred to entice females. If, knowing that, all she could do was thank him for being kind to her, she obviously wasn't interested.

"Don't worry about it," he finally said. "I'm just here to help."

Aidan knew his appearance was pleasing to most women, even those who knew nothing about Zetithians. He'd met dozens of women in his life—some while traveling from planet to planet aboard the *Jolly Roger* and others encountered more recently on the streets of Rhylos—and he'd picked up at least a hint of desire from the vast majority.

Except the one he suspected he was about to risk his life for.

Figures.

Sula aroused something in him—a protective instinct or some other bond he couldn't identify. He didn't believe in love at first sight. He wasn't even sure this was love. But whatever it was, it was potent and undeniable.

And if he didn't push her to let his pal Giklor heal her, he'd have her as a recuperating guest in his house for six weeks. By then, she might feel a little something for him beyond gratitude.

Then again, the one woman whose future he couldn't fathom might also be the one woman who wasn't attracted to him.

Better call Giklor. Now.

—~~—

I shouldn't have kissed him.

The moment her lips touched his cheek, Sula remembered the significance of purring. Aidan might be the hottest man she'd ever run across, but her heart was still raw from Raj's death. The pain of a breakup was traumatic enough. Having your lover die in your arms left a much deeper wound.

The kiss had seemed so natural, though. And she hadn't exactly given him a passionate, tonsil-deep kiss. It was a friendly gesture, nothing more.

So why did she feel so embarrassed?

Interestingly enough, he seemed a tad self-conscious himself. Perhaps he hadn't intended to purr, or her textbook could've been wrong about why Zetithians purred. There might be other reasons that had nothing to do with sex.

She certainly hadn't imagined his blush. The type of heat that prickled her cheeks had also blossomed in his. In addition to that, he seemed to be taking an awfully long time to remove his wings and stow them in the rear compartment of his speeder. Or maybe he wasn't. Maybe that was simply how long it took for the task to be done correctly.

Aidan got in the speeder without a word, fired up the engine, and closed the canopy. She had several questions on the tip of her tongue but deemed it best to keep quiet and let him be the one to break the silence. For all he knew, she was ignorant of the nuances of Zetithian behavior. She didn't have to tell him she'd scored higher on that particular exam than anyone in her class—a perfect score, in fact. She'd even considered making Zetithians the subject of her master's thesis, and she would have if at least ten other students hadn't already chosen that topic. Her advisor had begged her to choose something—*anything*—else to research.

In the end, she'd chosen to study Norludians, a species that was about as far-removed from Zetithians as any she'd ever heard of. However, Norludians were interesting, if only because their reproductive organs shared structures with the digestive system as opposed to the urinary tract. For Norludians, oral intercourse was the real deal.

Feeling some minor discomfort behind her knee, she shifted the splint and winced as even more pain shot through her lower leg.

"I'm sorry," Aidan said, proving that he was nothing if not observant. "I should've propped your leg up with something."

"No. It's fine. It just hurt a little when I moved."

"I could take you straight to Giklor. He could get rid of your pain in no time."

"I'll think about it." She wouldn't, of course. Her leg would heal soon enough without having to swallow Zerkan spit. Or maybe it was more like vomit. There were supporters in both camps. Whichever it was, she had no interest in trying it. If she'd been on death's door, she might've felt differently, but not for a simple fracture.

If she were honest with herself, she actually welcomed an excuse to rest for a while. She'd been clambering about in the mountains for months and was exhausted, both mentally and physically. Besides, she'd finally found what she'd been searching for. Now all she had to do was figure out what to do with that discovery. Aidan had found her there once. Surely, he would remember how to find that same cave again.

Rhylos had indeed once been home to a species of primitive primates.

And now there were none.

That they'd died out naturally was a distinct possibility, although she'd only found archaeological evidence in one very remote cave. If there'd been other examples, she would've found them. For that matter, the first colonists to that world would've found traces of a lost civilization, and that information would've been documented. The entire planet seemed to have been wiped clean, like a murder weapon with no fingerprints on it.

"Will you be able to find that cave again?" she asked suddenly.

"I don't see why not," he replied. "Did you leave something behind?"

"My walking stick," she said. "It—it belonged to my grandfather. I'd hate to lose it."

"I didn't notice anything lying near you, although I didn't have time for a thorough search. There were some pretty nasty condors disputing the territory. I can go back there in a few days. Might need to move some rock to find it, though."

"No rush," she said. "It's not going anywhere."

At least she wasn't lying. Not entirely. She did have a walking stick, and while it had never belonged to her grandfather, retrieving it was as good a reason as any for returning to the cave, even though she might end up having to explain why a stick bought at an outfitter's store in Damenk had somehow acquired a significant amount of sentimental value.

I'll figure that out later.

By then, Aidan might have some inkling as to why she'd been traipsing through the mountains alone, which would make any explanations completely unnecessary.

I should tell him everything right now.

From the way he'd talked, he had friends who could help. She didn't have to do this alone. Still, the thought of putting even more people at risk kept her silent. What they didn't know wouldn't hurt them.

Knowledge might be power, but it could also get you killed.

Chapter 5

TAKING SULA TO GIKLOR WAS OBVIOUSLY OUT, UNLESS THE Zerkan were to drop by for a visit, which wasn't out of character for him. In fact, he'd been known to come knocking on Aidan's door in the middle of the night simply to have a chat, leaving Aidan to surmise that Zerkans preferred philosophical discussions to sleeping through the night. On the other hand, the possibility existed that Zerkans, being rather small with pale, almost translucent skin and a tendency to wear no form of clothing whatsoever, avoided sunlight whenever they could.

He'd never heard it said that Zerkans possessed the knack for knowing when a friend was in need. However, he suspected they might, in some manner, for those late-night chats tended to come at uncannily opportune times. Having a recuperating woman in his home seemed destined to be one of those precipitating events.

Aidan had met the Zerkan in a bar in Damenk when he and his brother Aldrik had gathered with the rest of the family to celebrate their sister's mating to Larry Tshevnoe. The little alien had approached the group after noticing that Larry's parents had each been treated by one of his species. Larry's father, Cat, had been healed by a female, as evidenced by Cat's glowing blue pupils, while Jack, his mother, had a reddish glow from having been bonded to Cat by a Zerkan male. This was, apparently, a peculiar enough circumstance to attract

Giklor's attention, after which he'd been drawn into the general conversation.

Jack had later commented that Zerkans tended to butt into other people's lives with very little provocation, but because a similar intrusion had led to her finding the kidnapped sister for whom she had been searching for six years, she couldn't find it in her to complain. Nor did she complain about being bound to her mate. If there had ever been two people more devoted—or suited—to one another, Aidan had yet to see them, although his own parents' connection appeared to be every bit as strong.

Thus far, such a relationship had seemed elusive for Aidan, mainly due to his own reluctance to share his secrets with anyone. Nor had he ever encountered a woman who wasn't interested in him sexually. Sula was different in that respect, a factor that he found intriguing, and he didn't believe it was because he was annoyed that she didn't find him attractive. He wasn't that vain—at least he didn't think so. Other women had been attracted by his appearance and his species' reputation as lovers, neither of which had any bearing on him specifically.

Luckily, this chance meeting—if, given his visions, it could even be called that—was more than a fleeting encounter. Like her missing walking stick, she wasn't going anywhere for a good long while. She might be able to get around with the aid of various self-help devices, but if his suspicions were correct, she had nowhere else to go.

Unless…

"Where's your campsite?" He shot her a quelling, sideways glance. "And don't tell me you don't have one. You didn't walk all the way from Damenk this morning."

"I don't, actually," she replied. "I keep moving."

"What do you do for food?"

"The same thing the condors do. I hunt rabbits and birds."

"Seriously?"

"It's easier than you might think. The little critters are everywhere out here. There are also edible fish in some of the ponds."

"How do you—"

"Catch them?" she scoffed. "Really, Aidan. You can take down just about anything with a wide stun beam."

He hadn't bothered to check her backpack for weapons. *My mistake.*

If she'd been more alert after she'd fallen, she could've easily defended herself against the condors. For that matter, she could've shot him out of the sky the moment she laid eyes on him.

He cleared his throat with an effort. "Guess I should be more careful."

To his surprise, she responded by giving him a light slap on the arm. "I wouldn't shoot at *you.*"

"That's good to know." But she *was* armed and had the potential to deal with anyone who posed a threat to her. In many ways, this information made Aidan feel better about her safety, despite not having the knack for setting her own broken bones. Or did she? She'd been unconscious when he'd applied the splint. For all he knew, she could've done a reasonably good job herself.

"Besides, carrying a pulse pistol is easier than carrying food around. I could've stocked up on dried foods in Damenk—and I do carry a few things—but this way, I can keep moving."

"Do you at least have a tent?"

She shook her head. "Adds too much weight. The temperatures are moderate, so I have no need for blankets or a bedroll." With a smile, she added, "Although I do have an inflatable pillow."

"Thank the gods for that," he muttered. Clearly, this woman had no qualms about roughing it—or being alone. Here he'd been congratulating himself for saving her life when in all honesty, his help had likely been completely unnecessary. "What would you have done if I hadn't gotten you out of that cave?"

She shrugged. "Lived on condor eggs for a while, I guess. They're pretty good if they've just been laid. I roast them in a small fire and chip off the shells when they're done. As for the birds themselves, the juveniles aren't bad, but the adults don't taste good at all—very stringy and tough. Still, in my position, I can't afford to be too picky."

"My, how…resourceful of you. Tell me, have you always been this self-sufficient?"

She shrugged again. "Not really. Lately, it's been more of a necessity than a choice."

"I see." She'd been living entirely off the grid, like some sort of nomadic hunter-gatherer. "Do all anthropologists learn how to live off the land?"

"Not directly. But you can't study primitive cultures without picking up a few of their everyday survival techniques." She chuckled. "Then again, most primitive people don't carry pulse pistols."

"Probably not." He waited a beat before adding, "You aren't going to tell me, are you?"

"Tell you what?"

He rolled his eyes. "Why an anthropology student is

roaming the mountains of Rhylos living on rabbits and condor eggs and doesn't want to seek medical attention even when she has a broken leg."

"What you don't know can't hurt you." The firm set of her jaw warned him that this was no dainty little woman who could be pushed around or tricked into divulging her secrets. She was as tough as, well, Indiana Jones. Or Jack Tshevnoe. From what he'd seen of Jack over the years, about the only difference between her and Indiana Jones was their gender.

"I disagree. It's better to be prepared to face danger when it comes than to be caught unawares. And just so you know, my offer of help still stands."

"I'll keep that in mind."

He tried a different tack. "Anyone who knows we've been together will assume you've told me everything."

"That's why I'd rather no one knew you found me."

"Not sure I can keep you a secret forever," he said. "You aren't exactly something I can stash in a locked drawer."

She huffed out a breath. "Look, I know it sounds crazy or at least unreasonable, but humor me, will you? For a while, anyway. Protecting myself is hard enough without having to worry about someone else."

"True," he conceded. "Although having someone to watch your back is pretty useful. I've been involved in a few harrowing adventures—most of them when I was a kid—and I understand the value of teamwork."

"Like I said, I'll keep your offer in mind." With that, she folded her arms, and her features took on an expression that informed him in no uncertain terms that the conversation, as far as she was concerned, was over.

He waved his arms in defeat. "Okay. I'll stop

hounding you. Let's just get you home, and we'll figure out the other stuff as we go along."

For one thing, he had to find a way to help a woman with some of her more intimate bodily functions without embarrassing her to death. While the idea of tending to her needs himself had its appeal, he seriously doubted she would see it the same way. Perhaps one of the older girls from the orphanage could help out. Sula would undoubtedly balk at the suggestion; if she feared for his safety, she would be doubly concerned over a teenage girl's well-being. The problem was which girl to ask. It couldn't be one of the Norludians. They were well known for their inability to keep a secret, and given what had happened to Raj, a Scorillian was also out of the question.

Then there was Qinta...

The Treslanti girl had arrived alone on the doorstep of the orphanage a few months back. No one had sent her; she'd claimed to have observed other children coming and going and deemed it a safe place to stay for a while. Since then, she'd been helpful in looking after the other children. Onca and Kim had even discussed hiring her as an assistant. If she was willing, she could stay at Aidan's house and help with Sula's care. He would even pay her a salary to make it worth her time. More important, with her species' ability to blend in with their surroundings to the point of invisibility, no one would ever know she was there unless she chose to show herself.

Not a bad idea for a dumb blond.

Aidan wasn't truly stupid, although compared to someone with Sula's level of education, he might seem that way. Throughout his formative years, he'd spent so much of his time and energy pretending not to have any

Mordrial powers that he hadn't bothered to do the one thing that made the most sense, which was to pursue a career of some sort. Even though he didn't really need the money, there were bound to be plenty of jobs that his fortune-telling ability would enhance. He just didn't know what they were—at least none that weren't illegal.

It was only when he realized that in the process of hiring Qinta he would have to explain why he needed her that his failings were highlighted once more.

The dumb blond strikes again.

However, despite the inherent flaws, he still believed it was a good plan. The details were a tad murky, but no doubt they would reveal themselves in time, as the solutions to most problems generally did.

Sula stifled a yawn as they flew into the outskirts of Damenk. "Pardon me," she said. "Must've gotten up too early this morning."

"It's been a busy day for both of us. How about I fix you something to eat, and then you can get some rest."

"Sounds great," she said. "I'm looking forward to eating something other than roasted condor eggs and rotisserie-style rabbit."

"Can't promise you much, but I *can* promise you I don't have anything like that in my house."

"Trust me, I'm not picky. Although I don't suppose you have anything other than water to drink, do you?"

"As a matter of fact, I do," he replied. "My house-keeping droid can make anything from lemonade to a margarita."

She sighed. "There've been times I believe I would've given anything for a glass of lemonade. You probably have running water too. I really miss that."

"Yep. Running water and electricity and everything. I even have a sonic shower."

This time, her sigh was more of a groan. "Ohh… That all sounds perfectly *wonderful*. You never realize how much you take those things for granted until you don't have them. *Especially* running water."

Quite honestly, Aidan wasn't all that anxious for her to hop in the shower, because her scent in no way repelled him—in fact, it had quite the opposite effect—and the urge to purr was growing stronger with every breath he took. He could almost feel her pheromones pinging his olfactory receptors, affecting him in a way no one else's scent ever had. Diluting them down would undoubtedly be for the best.

Too bad I can't open a window.

Aidan snatched onto the new thread in the conversation like a lifeline. "Speaking of which, what have you been doing for drinking water?"

"I fill up my canteen at any ponds I run across, and when there aren't any ponds, I have this cool gadget that pulls water right out of the air. It cost me a bundle, but it was worth every credit. The air is pretty dry in the mountains, so it takes a while to fill a bottle. Sometimes I think I'm recycling my own sweat. If I'd still been out there, I'd have been very happy to see that storm coming."

The mental image of Sula standing naked on the mountainside with rain sluicing down her body distracted him to the point that an alert sounded as he came dangerously close to sideswiping another speeder.

"Sorry about that," he said as he corrected his flight path. "The anticollision system won't let me run into anything, but it loves to fuss at me if it thinks I'm being careless."

"You say that like it happens a lot. Are you normally so careless?"

"Nope." Turning a corner, he aimed the speeder down the street, doing his best to focus on the way ahead rather than the increasingly desirable woman sitting next to him. She was too close, the speeder too enclosed. If she hadn't stressed the need for secrecy, he'd have slid the canopy back to let in more air. The lack of desire in her scent didn't matter one iota; she still smelled fabulous. At this rate, he'd be purring long before they reached his house.

Stealing a glance at her, he spotted a possible reprieve. "Want me to turn up the air? You've got to be burning up in that jacket."

"It *is* a little warm," she admitted.

He tapped the control as quickly as he could without appearing too anxious. Cool, fresh air flowed over his face and filled his lungs. "Better?"

"Yes, thank you."

"Let me know if you get too cold."

"Okay." She sounded somewhat meek, almost as if she'd seen through his ploy—but for the wrong reason.

As always, honesty was the best policy. "I don't mean to insinuate that you smell bad, Sula. To be perfectly frank, you smell too good. I just needed a little air."

—―⌇⌇―—

Sula hadn't forgotten the important role scent played in Zetithian interpersonal relations. However, never having dealt directly with a Zetithian male, she hadn't realized how much it would affect the way he related to *her*.

"I promise to take that sonic shower as soon as we get to your place. Are we by any chance getting close?"

"Almost there," he replied. His voice sounded odd, as if his throat hurt or was constricted in some manner. He cleared it with a significant effort. "I've been thinking. Maybe we need a female to help care for you. I could hire someone—maybe one of the teenage girls from the orphanage. There's a Treslanti girl named Qinta who might be willing, although I'm sure she would want to know a little something about you before she would agree to take the job. You wouldn't need to tell her everything, of course," he added hastily. "Although she strikes me as being fairly tight-lipped. If she isn't interested, there's also Abuti, who's about the same age as Qinta. Being Norludian, she probably isn't much good at keeping secrets, but we'd only have to tell her that you're a friend of mine from offworld who needs help for a while."

Sula was silent for several moments as the wheels in her head began to spin. Knowing what she did about Norludians, she probably couldn't trust Abuti with her given name, let alone her surname. She'd be a fool to tell her the real story. On the other hand, Treslantis tended to be a little on the dishonest side.

"I mean, all I did was find you," he went on. "I don't even know what you're hiding—other than yourself—so I can't blab about it to anyone else."

"What about *your* secret? Will you tell them you found me while you were out flying in the mountains?"

"No," he admitted. "But if we put our minds to it, we should be able to come up with plausible explanations for everything."

"I'm sure you're right," she said with a slow nod. "I'll think about it." As her gaze drifted to their surroundings, the size and style of the buildings made her gasp. "Oh my…"

"What's wrong?"

"Nothing," she replied. "You live around *here*?" The squeak in her voice made her want to smack herself. She hadn't exactly lived in a hovel while she was growing up; her parents both had well-paid, respected careers. Even though she had been living in dormitories for several years, she'd only been technically homeless since she left Ecos.

"Yeah. Just down the street a little." He turned his head to stare at her. "Is that a problem?"

"No. I-I guess not. I mean, no. It's fine. I just didn't expect the neighborhood to be so…grand."

To her surprise, he actually laughed. "You've obviously never been to the ritzy side of town. This area is pretty tame in comparison. When I bought the place, it was listed as a *modest starter dwelling, suitable for growing young families*."

She reacted with a snort. "Young families with a dozen kids, maybe."

"I bought it thinking I might have a family someday, and if you know anything about Zetithians, you know we tend to have children in litters of three."

"Yeah. I knew that. Just never thought about what it would be like to house a family that size in a 'starter' home." Sula was the third of her parents' four children. A Zetithian family could top that number with two pregnancies.

"Tell me about it," he said with a trace of sarcasm. "My mother only had two litters, which, given her Mordrial witch ancestry, was extremely rare. The witches of Utopia usually have only one daughter. The fact that my sister has five brothers is nothing short of a miracle. We lived on a starship with another Zetithian family that had three litters. All of them boys."

"I feel sorry for the girl," she whispered under her breath.

He apparently heard her, despite her mumbling. "She turned out okay. Took her a while to come to grips with her Mordrial side, though."

She gave him a wry smile. "She sounds a lot like you in that respect."

"I suppose she does." He heaved a sigh. "Until today, Val was the only one I'd told about my Mordrial powers, and even he doesn't know everything. I'm pretty sure my sister, Althea, has figured out at least part of it, although she's never come right out and said so. Being an empath, she probably sensed my desire for secrecy."

With very little warning, he banked the speeder into a sharp turn before coming to a stop beside one of the larger buildings. "We're here."

Chapter 6

SULA'S JAW DROPPED. "THIS IS A *MODEST STARTER DWELLING*?"

"It's just a house," Aidan said wearily. "No need to make such a big deal about it."

"Sorry," she said. "I guess I'm not used to the building styles on Rhylos. I grew up in a very nice house in Bangalore, but it wasn't quite so…"

"Ornate? Yeah. I thought it was a little over the top myself when I first saw it. Although compared to some of the others around here, it's actually kinda plain."

Plain was definitely not the word Sula would've chosen. Broad, shallow steps bordered a wide front porch that was spanned by six columns set between intricately carved arches. Beyond that was an arched entryway that wouldn't have been out of place on a cathedral. Numerous windows studded the facade of both wings of the two-story building, each of them framed with gilded molding carved with asymmetrical curves and S-shaped designs.

"It's an Old Earth style called rococo," he said. "Probably the sort of thing that made French peasants want to start a revolution."

Sula's background in ancient architecture being virtually nonexistent, she was in no position to argue. "I'll take your word for it." Nevertheless, after living in the mountains for months on end without so much as a roof over her head, the place looked like a palace. "You must really be rich." The words were out before she could stop them. Heat rose in her cheeks. "Please forgive me. I'm not usually so tactless."

"No offense taken," he said with a smile that warmed more than her cheeks. "A trust fund for surviving Zetithians was set up using the assets of the man responsible for destroying our planet. He had a ton of money, so we're all pretty well off." A soft chuckle escaped him as he waved a hand toward the house. "The design *is* a little pretentious, but the interior is more functional than fancy. Plus, there's plenty of room. You could have the entire second floor to yourself if you want."

"I think staying on the ground floor would be easier for both of us."

"True. Although if you're hiding from someone, I can't imagine a better place to do it." He shrugged. "I hardly ever go up there myself."

She took a good long look in every direction and didn't spot any assassins lurking nearby. Of course, if they were decent assassins, she *wouldn't* see them. They'd already bungled the job once. This time, they might send someone who actually knew how to shoot. She still had trouble believing the last guy had missed her. Twice. "Speaking of hiding, think we could go in through the back door?"

"That's the plan."

She was pleased to hear this, despite having felt so much safer when she was alone in the mountains. At least out there, she could hear someone coming from a long way off. In the city, there was too much noise and too many places to hide. Anyone walking along the street or standing inside a doorway could be gunning for her. Even Aidan had managed to sneak up on her, although she doubted many assassins would use the same mode of transportation.

He steered the speeder around to the rear of the building, which, not surprisingly, was also festooned with ostentatious ornamentation. After parking the speeder relatively close to the door, he turned to face her. "We can figure out where you're going to stay later. Right now, I just need to get you inside. Then I'll fix us some dinner. Dunno about you, but I'm starving. After that, you should try to get some sleep if you can."

She opened her mouth to comment and wound up stifling a yawn instead.

He grinned. "Apparently, that won't be a problem."

Aidan wished he'd been better prepared to care for a convalescent for an extended period of time, but he hadn't the first inkling that he would be faced with such a task.

Damn visions.

He still had hopes that she would allow Giklor to treat her. In the meantime, he felt he had to do more than provide her with food and shelter and pat her hand in comfort.

Splints, bandages, painkillers, even antibiotics… Not for the first time, he found himself wishing his mother lived nearby. She would know exactly what to do for Sula, and she would have the supplies with which to do it. Thanks to her influence, he did have a few herbal remedies on hand, but if there was a magic potion for mending bones, he'd never heard of it.

If Sula had been Zetithian, the splint and two or

three days of restorative sleep would've healed the fracture enough that she would've been able to walk by the time she awoke. For a Terran, however, about the best he could do was give her willow bark tea for the pain and chamomile tea to help her rest. Arnica cream applied to the tissue over the break might help with the bruising. Turmeric and pineapple were both good anti-inflammatories. He was pretty sure he had some turmeric in the spice rack, and pineapple was easily obtained from the local market. He also had a tube of Derivian ointment that would heal any minor cuts and scrapes practically overnight.

Guess I'm better prepared than I thought.

Following a brief survey of the surrounding area to prove there were no obvious onlookers, he popped the canopy and climbed out of the speeder. He hurried around to the passenger side and gathered her up in his arms as carefully as he could. As before, she put one arm around his neck. Her hand on his bare skin jolted his already alert senses, and he inhaled yet another whiff of her enticing aroma.

If she'd been sexually aroused, his cock would've swelled to its full size in a heartbeat. He felt everything but that. She was clearly right for him. Whether the reverse was also true seemed doubtful.

If I'm nice enough to her, maybe she'll kiss me again.

If she did, he had every intention of ensuring that his lips would be her target, even if he wound up with whiplash from turning his head too fast.

The back door of his house slid open as he approached.

"Don't you lock your doors?" she asked, sounding a tad apprehensive.

"Trust me, it was locked. The house, um, knows me."

"I see," she said. "Nice feature."

He nodded. "That's about the only upgrade I've made. It had a palm lock originally. Comes in handy when I'm carrying groceries—or damsels in distress."

Aidan was still working on getting the door to react quickly enough for him to fold his wings and glide in, but he'd caught a shoulder on it enough times to know he could run faster than it could respond. Flying in would've freaked the neighbors anyway, although they'd seen Val swooping around enough that they might assume it was him.

"I've never thought of myself in that light before." A short, sardonic laugh didn't entirely alleviate her grimace. "I've always been the independent type."

Clearing his throat, he allowed himself a slight smile. "I've noticed."

"No need to rub it in," she said, grumbling.

"Didn't intend to." He carried her through the kitchen and into the main sitting room. "You can rest here on the sofa while I get dinner ready. Can I get you something to drink?"

"A glass of lemonade would be lovely. Thank you."

He put her down on the sofa, thinking that if she made the "You're very kind" comment again, he was going to scream. Nevertheless, he lingered within kissing range as long as he could without being too obvious.

No such luck. Damn.

Perhaps if dinner was good enough, he might get lucky.

No pressure—ha!

Living alone, his meals usually weren't very remarkable. Edible and reasonably nutritious, maybe, but nothing designed to impress.

He could call for delivery. Damenk's restaurant district boasted cuisine from every corner of the galaxy.

No. Having food delivered was too easy. And she *was* from India…

Would she appreciate his efforts to produce authentic Indian dishes, or would she merely tolerate his feeble attempts?

He doubted she would ever be so ungracious. She would probably lie very convincingly while assuring him that his version of chicken korma was exactly like her mother used to make.

Might as well ask.

"What would you like for dinner?"

"Whatever you have," she replied. "I'm not exactly in a position to be choosy."

"You're my guest, so you can be as choosy as you like."

She smiled. "Believe me, anything would be an improvement over the stuff I've been living on."

He'd forgotten about that. "Something Indian, maybe?"

Her eyes widened. "You have an Indian restaurant nearby?"

"No—well, there *is*, but that isn't what I meant. I loved the food when I was in India, so I've done some experimenting. My chicken korma may not be the greatest, but I like it."

Her expression went from incredulous to misty-eyed in less than a heartbeat, making Aidan wish he'd remained within kissing distance. "That sounds absolutely wonderful."

Aidan had never had what he would call an attack of the warm fuzzies before, but he was certainly having one now. "I hope you enjoy it."

"I'm sure I will."

Her smile was so completely genuine, it altered the way his heart lay within his chest—a good feeling rather than the dip that organ normally took whenever he encountered someone with a disturbing future. That the meal he provided for her would be a step up from her more recent fare didn't matter. For a smile like hers, he would make this the best chicken korma outside the entire Indian subcontinent.

"I'll get that lemonade for you and be right back."

With a nod, he left the room before doing something stupid like kissing her senseless.

He returned to find her brushing dust from her jacket. She stopped as soon as he entered and handed her the glass. She took a long drink before asking, "Think I could take that sonic shower before dinner?"

"Absolutely. Just let me get the chicken in the marinade, and then I'll help you with that. I'll try to find something more comfortable for you to wear too."

Her smile faded slightly, and her gaze slid from his face to somewhere in the vicinity of his feet. "How are we going to do that?"

"Dunno exactly, but I'm sure we'll figure out something."

In Aidan's opinion, he couldn't get Qinta there fast enough. He didn't want Sula to be unnecessarily embarrassed, nor did he want to get himself into an awkward situation.

Normally, keeping his emotions under control was easily done—he'd been hiding them from his empathic sister for most of his life—but the feelings he had toward Sula were so new, he couldn't be certain of anything.

He could, however, help her out of her boots and jacket without causing either of them any untoward distress.

"In the meantime, I think you'll be more comfortable if we can get you out of your boots and jacket."

Her stiff nod suggested that even this minor adjustment was enough to cause her some embarrassment.

As she began to shrug out of the jacket, he helped to ease her arms out of the sleeves. Pebbled nipples pressed against the fabric of her gray T-shirt, proving that she wasn't wearing a bra. He studiously avoided staring, opting to fold the jacket and set it aside. She lay back on the sofa, crossing her arms over her chest, proving she was fully aware of the level of exposure, however minor it might be.

He started on her boots without comment. Unfortunately, this proved to be a source of further discomfiture.

"Careful," she whispered as he removed the first one. "My feet are kinda sore. It-it might help to wash them. If you could bring me a wet, soapy washcloth…" A beseeching look accompanied her request.

"I think I should be the one to do the washing," he said firmly. "Not sure you could reach that left one without messing up my bone-setting handiwork."

After an obvious and thankfully brief battle with her misgivings, she nodded.

"Be right back," he said.

Upon his return with the washcloth she requested,

plus a pan of water to rinse and a towel to dry, he lifted her right foot and removed her sock. The feet of some of the street kids they'd taken in at the orphanage looked worse, but Sula's were bad enough. Blisters in various stages of healing dotted her feet.

"Mother of the gods," he whispered. "How were you even able to walk?"

"I've learned to ignore the pain," she said with a shrug.

"You need to take better care of yourself," he scolded. "You won't do yourself or anyone else any good by letting your feet rot off."

She heaved a wretched sigh. "I know. They're actually better than they were. I didn't have time to break in my boots before I started, and some of my blisters had already turned into calluses by the time the boots began to feel comfortable. Then my socks started to wear out, and the blisters came back. Thicker socks would've helped, but I didn't realize the problem until I was too far into the mountains to turn back for better ones."

"When you go back into the mountains—*if* you go back—we'll make sure this doesn't happen again."

If the use of "we" bothered her in any way, it didn't show. A demure smile accompanied her soft "Thank you."

"In the meantime, I'll get your feet washed and put some Derivian ointment on those blisters. Should have you healed up in no time."

"Derivian ointment?"

"Oh yeah. My mother swears by it. Just wish it could cure a broken bone."

He wiped her foot as he spoke, keeping his eyes focused on his task rather than her grimaces as he washed some of the more sensitive areas. Already, he viewed causing her any pain with abhorrence and longed to give her only pleasure.

His thoughts drifted to how she would look if he ever made love to her, her eyes heavy-lidded with bliss, her lips curved in a sensuous smile.

He'd finished washing her foot and had it rinsed and dried before he realized he was purring. He saw no need to stop; purring didn't affect a Terran the way it would a Zetithian woman. Most humans interpreted it as an expression of contentment, the way they would feel with a purring kitten in their lap. Nevertheless, as he spread the ointment over her wounds, mere application progressed to a luxurious massage. The soft moan of pleasure that escaped her lips sent thrills racing over his skin. Purring even louder, he applied more ointment to enable him to continue far longer than was strictly necessary to achieve a therapeutic effect.

When he finally abandoned one foot for the other, he followed the same procedure, still not daring to look her in the eyes. Her scent had undergone a subtle change. Although not the stimulating aroma of desire, it was nonetheless pleasing to him, making him reluctant to bring such a delightful interlude to an end.

At last, he knew he couldn't keep going without seeming to take advantage of her situation, and he rose from where he sat at her feet. Gathering up the damp towels, he dropped them in the pan of water before stealing a glance at her face.

Her sweet smile made his heart swell within his chest.

"I've never known anyone so kind or anyone with a gentler touch," she whispered. "You missed your calling as a healer."

"Must be my mother's influence." With his voice still roughened by the remnants of his purr, he didn't trust himself to say anything further.

"Doesn't matter where it comes from," she insisted. "It's part of you now."

"I suppose it is." Not that it mattered. Almost his entire life had been spent harboring secrets, keeping to himself the portents that bombarded his brain and hiding his reactions to them. Something about Sula made him let down his guard, if only for the few minutes it took to bathe her feet. Now the walls began creeping up once more. Stiffening slightly, he gave her a brief nod and said, "You rest easy, and try to sleep if you can. I'll wake you when dinner is ready. We'll tackle the sonic shower after you've eaten."

A slight frown creased her brow as her smile faded. "Sounds good. Thank you."

"Give a yell if you need anything. I won't be far away." Far enough to escape her captivating aroma— one that conveyed gratitude as opposed to the warmer emotions that stirred within him and deepened with each moment he spent in her presence. He'd felt the connection the instant their eyes met while he hovered above her.

He had no business purring, whether she would respond to it or not. She was too vulnerable now. Not only was she injured, she had also suffered the loss of someone very dear to her. He might kid himself into believing he couldn't control the impulse to purr, but he knew he could. He always had. He'd drifted through life, aiding those in need while suppressing any desires of his own.

That was what he had done. What he had *always* done. This day was no different from any other.

Chapter 7

SULA DIDN'T KNOW WHAT SHE HAD SAID OR DONE TO ALTER Aidan's mood, but the difference was as real as the ache of her broken leg. The very last thing she wanted to do was to hurt him in any way, and she hated the idea of being the cause of his discomfort.

She reminded herself that she didn't really know him. His mood swings might have nothing to do with her. From what she'd observed, he seemed cheerful enough most of the time, but there was something else there that wasn't as obvious. Something lurking behind his eyes that betrayed his pain.

Perhaps he was lonely. The sheer size of his house was enough to bring out the latent loneliness in anyone. He claimed to have bought the place with his future family in mind, but was that the real reason? Did he like the openness and the fact that he could lose himself inside those walls? Or did the empty space only serve as a reminder of the family he *didn't* have?

To hear him tell it, his parents and siblings were scattered across the quadrant, if not the entire galaxy. Being similarly situated, she could easily understand how that might affect him. Traveling through space had always made her feel so isolated, so small and insignificant—a feeling that had increased in severity during the return trip without Raj.

After the horrors she'd witnessed on Ecos, with

death and desolation all around her and no power to stop it, almost anything would've been an improvement. The mountains of Rhylos had brought her solace, despite having traversed them alone. Then she'd met Aidan, for whom she felt an almost instantaneous affinity. She couldn't decide whether her feelings for him were the result of having been rescued by him or simply because he was the only intelligent being she'd encountered in months.

Whatever the reason, she owed him her life—a debt she could never repay unless she were to save him from certain death. Somehow, she couldn't see that happening.

She contemplated this as she sipped the blissfully cool lemonade he'd given her, hoping she'd been dehydrated enough that the inevitable result of taking in fluids didn't happen too quickly. He'd talked about hiring a girl from the orphanage, and in her opinion, the sooner he did that, the better. Aidan wouldn't have to pay the girl, either. Thanks to her frugal ways, Sula had more than enough credits to cover the cost herself. She was already staying in his house. He didn't need to pay her caregiver.

She set the glass down and closed her eyes, the constant ache in her leg making her regret her refusal of the Zerkan's treatment. Most of her reluctance lay in the aftereffects of their healing practices. As a Terran woman from India who was trying to keep a low profile, acquiring a pair of glowing red pupils was inadvisable. Then again, the strange eyes might serve as a disguise— until she'd been identified through some other means.

Sula still hadn't figured out how she'd been spotted the first time. She'd been in the commerce district shopping for supplies when she heard someone asking the clerk if he'd seen a woman fitting her description. After ducking out of the store as unobtrusively as possible, she ran down the street as fast as she could. She'd just turned the nearest corner when a pulse beam struck the stone exterior of the building across the street. After another beam hit the sidewalk beside her, she darted into the nearest shop, which, fortunately, had a rear entrance and was too crowded to allow her pursuer to get off another shot. She caught a glimpse of him—a tall, grim-faced Terran—as she ran out the back way. Upon finding herself in the midst of a street fair, she threaded her way through the throng and somehow managed to lose him. Although she barely had enough supplies for her journey, she concluded that remaining in Damenk any longer might prove fatal.

She'd found relative safety in the mountains, feeling more at home hiking across that barren, rocky terrain than she ever had in the city. At first, she'd done most of her traveling at night, sleeping during the day in any secluded nook she could find. Once she reached the higher elevations, she switched back to a normal routine, waking with the Rhylosian sun and only bedding down after it set. She'd always preferred to let her body follow the natural planetary rhythms rather than allow herself to be governed by the dictates of artificial timekeeping, and living off the land had struck a resonant chord with a deeper part of her character. Even the solitary nature of her quest had its appeal—until she'd been careless enough to break a leg.

Despite her willingness to go it alone, she might've asked for help if there'd been anyone available whom she felt she could trust. Aidan might be the right person for the task. He was proving to be more trustworthy with each passing moment, and a man who had visions would be a useful cohort in almost any endeavor. He hadn't exactly disagreed when she'd accused him of having nothing better to do than take care of an injured woman for several weeks, which seemed to indicate that he had plenty of time on his hands. As far as she could tell, he didn't even have a regular job. He'd only said he helped out at the orphanage from time to time, not that he was officially employed there.

Thus far, he struck her as an idle rich man who made a habit of volunteering to help the needy. Plus, unlike other wealthy people who tended to own planes or starships, he could actually fly. Some rich people might give their entire fortune to possess that ability—along with Aidan's incredibly handsome face.

The sudden heaviness of her eyelids made her wonder if Aidan had put a sleeping potion into the lemonade he'd given her. As she drifted off, she realized she didn't care if he *had* slipped something into her drink. Sleep was as welcome as he had been when he came to her rescue.

My hero…

Was the way to a woman's heart through her stomach? While Aidan had his doubts, he saw no reason to leave anything to chance. If she liked his chicken korma, that would be one step up in her esteem.

You idiot. You've already rescued her from hungry condors, set her broken leg, and brought her into your home. You even washed her feet. What more do you need to do to earn her favor?

Perhaps he should put on some less-revealing clothes. The tight, stretchy pants he used when flying were similar to the kind Val always wore, but if Sula's scent were to contain even a trace of desire, his resulting erection would be embarrassingly obvious. Plus, having honest-to-god wings, Val rarely wore a shirt. Aidan, on the other hand, didn't have that excuse and deemed it prudent to put on something more…normal.

Opting for a T-shirt and jeans, he dressed quickly and headed for the kitchen. After taking a peek in the living room and assuring himself that Sula was indeed asleep, he selected two chicken breasts from the stasis unit and cut them into chunks. After combining plain yogurt with the masala paste he always kept on hand, he stirred in the chicken and set the mixture aside to marinate. Since he planned to serve it over brown rice, he started cooking that first. He could've used one of his insta-cook appliances, but the old ways were still the best. Besides, with Sula asleep, he wasn't in any hurry.

While growing up aboard the *Jolly Roger*, Aidan had always enjoyed being the cook whenever his turn rolled around. It was the "cooking for one" thing that he didn't like. He missed the camaraderie of mealtimes with his family and Tshevnoe clan—the boisterous boys and the one solemn, empathic girl stuck amid the chaos. If he hadn't felt the need to shield every emotion his talent for fortune-telling triggered, he might've developed a closer relationship with Althea, the lack of which he deeply regretted.

Althea had never hidden her talent as an empath, nor

did she mask her ability to use the power of suggestion with many of the lower life-forms or her power over earth, which was her primary element. She hadn't needed to hide her control of fire, an ability that hadn't come to her until after she'd left the fold at the age of twenty-one.

There'd been times when Aidan wished he'd been a bit more forthcoming about his own gifts—if they could be called that. In many ways, he considered them to be more curse than blessing. In retrospect, he probably could've told Larry and Althea that they would eventually become mates. However, as with many of the more pleasant twists of fate, he preferred to allow those events to unfold without interference. Any meddling on his part usually backfired anyway.

A glance out the kitchen window proved that the storm had followed them from the mountains. Dark clouds scudded across a sky that had been perfectly clear when they'd arrived, accompanied by flashes of lightning and rumbles of thunder. Before long, rain pelted the glass in heavy, drenching splashes, making him very glad that Sula was already safe and dry inside his house, even if she was cooped up with a strange man she had no real reason to trust.

With a heavy sigh, he tapped the comlink that hung on the wall beside the window and said, "Call Onca at the orphanage."

Moments later, the image of an auburn-haired Zetithian man appeared on the viewscreen. Onca was in his midforties, but like others of their species, he looked much younger than his chronological age—one of the many perks of being Zetithian. "What's up, Aidan?"

Another long breath escaped him. "I've acquired a

female houseguest who has a broken leg. Think one of the older girls would like to earn a few credits as her caregiver?"

Not too surprisingly, Onca responded with a snort of laughter. "Let me get this straight… You have a female houseguest who doesn't want *you* to take care of her every need?"

"She's a little shy," Aidan explained. "We only met today."

"I see." Onca's doubtful expression suggested that he didn't "see" anything at all.

Explaining why Sula was staying with him was going to be harder than Aidan had imagined. "She didn't want to go to a hospital, and since she had nowhere else to go, I brought her home with me."

Onca's "Uh-huh" sounded even more suspicious, prompting Aidan to explain further.

"I-I…found her. In the mountains." As if the location made any difference. "Her business there is very… private."

Onca arched a brow. "A secret mission?"

"Maybe. She won't say exactly."

"I'm not sure—" Onca stopped as his eyes narrowed in a frown. "Wait a second. What were *you* doing in the mountains?"

"I go there a lot," Aidan replied quite truthfully. "It's very peaceful."

"I can't argue with that." Onca appeared to consider this for several moments. "The girl wouldn't be in any danger, would she?"

"None that I know of," he said—again, quite truthfully. "But there *is* a need for secrecy."

Onca still seemed hesitant. "I'll ask around," he finally said. "If I find a volunteer, I'll have Rashe bring her over in the speeder."

"Tell him to come in the back way. I'd rather no one knew anyone was here besides me."

Onca grinned. "You're thinking Qinta might do it, aren't you?"

"I was kind of hoping she would."

"So…you need a girl who can keep a secret *and* disappear?"

"Well, yeah," Aidan admitted. "That's about the size of it."

"The plot thickens. Rashe doesn't need to cloak the speeder, does he?"

A cloaked speeder could cause all sorts of nasty accidents, which was why such modifications were illegal. Onca's had come in handy a few times, but in this instance, using the cloaking feature would probably put the occupants in more danger than Sula's adventure, whatever it was.

"No. As long as they keep a low profile, they should be fine. Su"—Aidan nearly bit his tongue trying to keep from saying the rest of her name—"My *guest* would really appreciate the help—and the sooner the better. She's been hiking through the mountains for a while, and she's anxious to get cleaned up."

"Okay. Like I said, I'll ask around. If none of the girls volunteer, I'm sure Kim would be willing to lend a hand."

"Thanks. I really appreciate your help on this."

"No problem," Onca said. "You've helped us out plenty of times. I'm happy to return the favor."

Aidan had never accepted a paycheck for his work at

the orphanage, even though he'd done a fair amount of cooking and cleaning, not to mention catching some of the kids before they did something they would almost certainly regret. Because children's actions often originated from sudden impulses, such interventions were usually successful. Adults, with their tortuous thought processes, were another story. He might thwart one attempt only to have it repeated in his absence with even more serious consequences.

That was the best part about flying. Alone in the open sky where there were no fortunes to be told and no dire outcomes to contemplate, his mind was free and uncluttered. He was more himself during those flights than at any other time. Being with Sula had a similar effect, despite his constant concern for her welfare. She obviously intended to return to the mountains as soon as her leg healed, and the suspicion that she intended to do it alone filled him with foreboding.

It was times like these when he usually tried to divert his thoughts by volunteering at the orphanage. He could lose himself in menial tasks or explore his creative side by taking on some of the cooking duties.

Like I'm doing now.

After ending the call, almost without thinking, he'd pulled out the necessary ingredients for his favorite lemon spice cake. Simple, delicious, and quick, the cake was one of the most requested desserts at the orphanage, and he knew the recipe by heart. As he worked, it occurred to him that he'd never stopped to think about why he enjoyed cooking so much. Perhaps it was because food had no fortune to be told. He could focus on creating something delicious without fear of being pelted with premonitions about what might happen to anyone who ate it. Whether anyone would love or hate what he'd prepared also remained a mystery. Perhaps that was the reason he liked cooking for a crowd. It was one of the few times he could actually be surprised.

Sula's potential to surprise him was refreshing. He just hoped she wouldn't suddenly decide to take off in the middle of the night. Dismissing that eventuality as unlikely, he returned his focus to the task at hand.

The cake was baking, and he had just started on the korma sauce when the doorbell rang. The house computer had been programmed to play the first few bars of "La Marseillaise" to announce any visitors, a peculiarity Aidan had never seen fit to alter, mainly because he was usually the only person in the house whenever anyone came to the door. With Sula there to hear it, the melody seemed as pretentious as the house itself.

When he answered the door, he was confronted by not one, but two volunteers for the job, along with Rashe, a handsome Terran man from the Comanche tribe. Rashe and his wife also helped out at the orphanage, albeit on a more regular basis than Aidan.

"When they heard who needed help, we couldn't talk them out of it," Rashe said as Aidan glanced back and forth between the two girls.

Qinta inhaled deeply. "Oh my god. He's making the lemon spice cake."

"And chicken korma," Abuti added with a sigh. "We're just in time."

Aidan stared at them in disbelief. "You volunteered because of the *food*?"

"You bet we did." Qinta's vigorous nod sent her

mass of red curls tumbling over her forehead. Although similar in appearance to Terrans, Treslantis had the ability to blend in with their surroundings by projecting the scene behind them to any onlooker. The only things they couldn't mask were their eyes, especially Qinta's, which were a sparkling emerald green. "Nobody at the orphanage cooks as well as you do."

Somewhat taken aback by this, for a long moment Aidan couldn't think of a single thing to say.

Abuti broke the silence. "Besides, we figured if this lady has a broken leg, she might need two of us to help her to the bathroom and such. Or we could work in shifts. We'd be willing to split however much you were going to pay one of us."

"See what I mean?" Rashe threw up his hands. "I thought it might be because you're such a looker, but they insisted that wasn't the case."

Abuti snickered and waggled her sucker-tipped fingers at Aidan. "I might've lied about that part."

Qinta punched her cohort on her skinny, grayish-green arm. "Hush up, or you'll make him blush."

The Norludian girl licked her fishlike lips and fluttered her eyelids in an openly provocative manner. "I like the way he blushes."

With a cursory nod toward her companion, Qinta said, "That's another reason why we both volunteered. I didn't figure she could be trusted alone with you."

All of this was news to Aidan, even if he *had* noticed that every time he spotted Abuti, her bulbous eyes were usually aimed in his direction. Considering the amount of hype regarding the sexual prowess of Zetithian males, he wasn't surprised to discover that at least one of the girls had a crush on him. He just hadn't expected it to be a Norludian, even though they were a highly sexual species on the whole.

He was about to disclaim when the recollection that Norludian sex was exclusively oral made his cheeks prickle with the predicted blush.

"See what you've done?" Qinta exclaimed, giving her companion another punch. "Now he probably won't hire either one of us."

Aidan cleared his throat with difficulty. "I think we should let the patient decide who her caregiver will be."

"Good idea, dude," Rashe said. "Wouldn't want to make that decision myself, which is why I brought both of them."

"She's asleep on the sofa right now, but—"

"Hey, Aidan!" Sula's voice rang out from the front room. "If you've found a girl to help me, I need her now!"

Chapter 8

IN DESPERATE NEED OF A TRIP TO THE RESTROOM, SULA didn't care whether the female voices she'd heard coming from the kitchen belonged to her prospective caregivers or not. At that point, any woman would do, and only the most uncaring woman imaginable would've turned her down.

Unfortunately, the *slap-slap* of flipper-like feet on the hardwood floors heralded the approach of a Norludian.

Great.

She was in no position to be choosy. However, she was surprised when two girls and a Terran man who appeared to be a Native American entered the room along with Aidan.

The tall, redheaded teenage girl waved a hand, dismissing the two men. "You guys can skedaddle. Abuti and me, we got this. Just point us in the direction of the nearest bathroom."

Sula giggled. "How did you guess?"

"The urgency in your voice was a dead giveaway," the girl replied. "I'm Qinta and"—she pointed toward the Norludian—"this is Abuti. We're here for the job if you'll have us." Qinta's hopeful expression was accompanied by a broad grin from Abuti.

I'm probably gonna regret this…

"You're hired," Sula said with a decisive nod. As she sat up and swung her legs off the couch, she was pleased to note her lack of light-headedness. "I should be able to walk with one of you on each side."

Abuti laughed. "Hop, maybe, but I doubt you'll actually walk." She glanced at Aidan as she took Sula's hand. "Where's the potty?"

Aidan's expression hovered somewhere between amusement and dismay. "That way," he said, pointing. "First door on the left. You should have plenty of room to maneuver in there."

With the assistance of the two girls, who were both deceptively strong, Sula was able to stand. However, as Abuti had predicted, even with their assistance, all she could do was hop.

"If you guys want to make yourselves useful," Qinta said over her shoulder, "this lady needs a couple of nightgowns and a hoverchair to start with, and maybe some crutches for later on."

"Nonskid slippers too," Abuti added.

"You two act like you've done this sort of thing before," Aidan said with a hint of suspicion.

"When we were living on the street, we did lots of things you guys don't know about," Qinta retorted. She glanced at Sula. "Although this is the first time we've ever had access to the right equipment and been in such a nice house."

"Guess I'd better get more food while I'm at it." Aidan was starting to sound a little overwhelmed. "After dinner, maybe."

"I'll give you a hand," the Terran man said. "I'm Rashe, by the way."

"Nice to meet you," Sula said. She stopped short of introducing herself. "You all know my being here is a secret, right?"

"Mum's the word," said Qinta.

Abuti mimed zipping her lips shut. Sula didn't believe there was such a thing as a close-mouthed Norludian. However, at the moment, she was willing to believe almost anything if it meant not peeing down her leg in front of a bunch of strangers.

After traversing the rather lengthy hallway at an excruciatingly slow pace, Sula made a mental note to summon the troops before the need became imperative.

"He wasn't kidding, was he?" Abuti exclaimed when they finally crossed the threshold. "This bathroom is huge!"

Fortunately, the toilet was the nearest fixture, closely followed by a bidet, a whirlpool-style tub, and a double-sink vanity that seemed to go on forever. Everything, including the walls, was covered in gleaming dark-blue tile. The most significant feature was the space on either side of the toilet—easily enough room to accommodate her two assistants.

"You ladies arrived just in time," Sula said after several ecstatic moments. "I don't think I could've lasted another second."

"No problem," Abuti said. "If this is as bad as it gets, we're all good."

Sula nodded toward the shower stall that had to be at least three meters from her current position. "Is that a sonic shower?"

"Let me check," Qinta said. After a brief inspection, she returned. "Looks like it can do both. There's even enough room for the three of us."

Sula wasn't too keen on taking a shower with the two girls, although being Norludian, Abuti didn't wear clothing anyway. As shower companions went, she was probably the best choice.

Aside from Aidan, of course. If her upbringing hadn't left such a deep imprint of modesty on her personality, she might've welcomed a shower with him—although seeing him without a shirt was breathtaking enough. She would probably faint if she ever saw him completely naked.

She reminded herself that getting undressed wasn't a requirement for a sonic shower. In fact, a few minutes of the treatment would clean even the filthiest clothing, which was a definite advantage given her current status. "I'd like to try the sonic shower next. Aidan actually said I smelled too good, but I can hardly wait to feel clean again."

"That's probably because he's getting off on your scent," Abuti said with a knowing chuckle. "At least you're Terran. We Norludians don't smell good to Zetithians at all." This last bit was said with more than a trace of regret.

"Give it up, Abuti," Qinta snapped. "That hunky blond is not going to fall for a Norludian, no matter what you smell like."

Abuti groaned. "I know. But he is so totally hot!"

Any woman with a pulse would have agreed whole-heartedly. However, if Sula was going to be dealing with these two girls for several weeks, the very last thing she wanted was for them to tease her about Aidan. Perhaps her recent bereavement would protect her from their taunts.

"I'm sure he's very handsome," Sula conceded, keeping her tone as nonchalant as possible. "But so was Raj. We'd been together for over a year when he died."

"How sad," Qinta said. "You must miss him very much."

"I sure do," Sula said wistfully. "He was the love of my life. He died about a year ago." Sighing, she added, "Seems like yesterday."

To her surprise, the Norludian girl snorted with laughter. "After hanging around with Aidan for a week or two, that year is gonna seem more like six."

Even though Abuti was probably right, Sula remained firm in her denial. Unfortunately, she knew enough about Zetithians to know that they responded quite well to Terran females. One whiff of her "desire" would give him an erection. If that ever happened, she would make it clear that an eager body didn't necessarily guarantee a willing mind.

Besides, Aidan was probably used to fending off overzealous women, perhaps even those he passed on the street. If the orphanage truly was in the brothel district, the barrage of sex pheromones in the air would require him to pass by any number of artificially stimulated women on his way to work.

"What about the pheromones in the brothel district?" she asked. "Are you sure they aren't the cause of your attraction to him?"

Abuti shook her head. "Aidan doesn't need any help making girls fall for him. He does that all by himself. Besides, Onca had the 'advertising' turned off in the area around the orphanage a long time ago. He actually considered selling the building and moving the orphanage somewhere else, but it's such an awesome place, none of us who live there wanted him to do it. It's like living in a forest instead of a city."

"I'd like to see it sometime," Sula said. Sometime when it would be safe for her to venture out. For now, remaining within the walls of Aidan's house—however grandiose it might be—seemed the best choice. "But right now, if you ladies will help me up, I'm dying for that shower."

"Gotcha," Abuti said, sounding far more cheerful than the situation warranted.

With the girls' help, Sula limped into the shower stall. Any other time, she might've stopped to admire the crystalline fixtures and the large prism in the ceiling that directed sunlight throughout the room. For the moment, however, the only thing she wanted was to get herself clean enough that Aidan wouldn't pick up any scent from her at all, much less the scent of her desire—an involuntary response that would undoubtedly betray her at some point.

Hopefully not today.

Aidan watched Sula hobble off with her two aides, feeling more than a twinge of regret. This new arrangement was for the best, and he was okay with it, if only having Sula depend on him for her every need hadn't appealed to him on such a visceral level. He longed to be responsible for her—for her health, safety, happiness, and everything that commitment entailed.

A nudge from Rashe made his rather slack jaw snap shut.

"Chill, dude," Rashe advised. "Those two will take good care of her."

"I know. I can't help being a little"—he managed to stop himself before saying *jealous*—"concerned."

"Don't be. I'll make a few calls and pick up the things they suggested. Maybe a better splint too."

"Yeah. That one is kinda makeshift."

"I'm sure I'll be able to find something. All you need to do is get dinner on the table. They'll appreciate that more than anything."

As though in support of Rashe's suggestion, Aidan's stomach let out a loud growl.

"See what I mean?" Rashe patted his shoulder. "First things first. You know the drill."

Aidan nodded. He knew exactly what Rashe meant. Anytime a new kid showed up at the orphanage, getting a decent meal was always first and foremost in their mind. No doubt in Rashe's eyes, Sula was just another orphan.

Except she wasn't an orphan. She was an adult, and she was in danger. Not knowing where the danger was coming from made protecting her that much harder. He'd gotten the distinct impression that even she wasn't sure of the source. She might have suspicions, though, which was something he hoped to wheedle out of her eventually. To do that, he had to gain her trust, which meant letting her keep her secrets for a while. She might see things differently in a day or two. Might even let Giklor heal her leg.

Nah. Probably not.

After Rashe left, Aidan returned to the kitchen and picked up where he left off, increasing the amounts to accommodate the new arrivals. In one day, he'd gone from a rather solitary existence to being one of four people living under the same roof. He still wasn't clear on how he should behave toward them. Granted, he'd at least met Abuti and Qinta before, but Sula was a total stranger. Should he treat them like friends, long-lost relatives, or merely lodgers?

In the end, he realized none of that mattered, because either way, they still needed to be fed.

And he would do that to the very best of his ability.

"Not exactly like my mother used to make," Sula remarked when she'd finished her dinner. "But very good."

"Your mother made stuff like that?" Abuti asked. The Norludian girl had been the first to clean her plate, and the Treslanti came in a close second.

Sula shot Aidan a quizzical look before returning her gaze to Abuti. "Guess he didn't tell you where I was from."

"He didn't tell us anything about you," Abuti declared. "We don't even know your name."

"If you don't want us to know, we're okay with that, but we can be trusted." Qinta's eyes touched briefly on Aidan before reconnecting with Sula's. "With *your* secret, anyway."

"What's that supposed to mean?" Aidan demanded. "I don't have any secrets."

"The hell you don't." Qinta's tone was deceptively calm. "You're a walking, talking enigma."

Aidan gave an innocent shrug. "What you see is what you get."

Following a withering glance at Aidan, Qinta said to Sula, "Don't believe a word of it. There's a whole lot more to him than meets the eye."

Sula apparently knew more about her host than the two girls. However, she was good at keeping secrets herself. "You mean beyond being an extremely kind gentleman who is also a damn fine cook?"

"Oh, yeah," Qinta drawled. "There's whole a lot more going on in that head of his than he lets on. Don't let those blond good looks fool you into thinking he's nothing but a pretty face."

"He *is* rather pretty, isn't he?" Warmth flooded her body as Sula took another sip of her wine. Her leg still ached like the devil, but at the moment, she didn't care. Knowing she might end up spilling the beans, she'd been hesitant to drink any alcohol. Aidan hadn't insisted; the wine had simply been in the glass beside her plate when she came to the table. In a way, she was glad he'd provided it. She hadn't been this relaxed in a very long time. Still, she needed to guard her tongue. "I can't say I've detected any secrecy. I'm the one with the secrets."

"We know *you* have secrets," Abuti said. "We just can't figure out why *he* does."

"I'm guessing it has something to do with his Mordrial blood," Qinta said. "I've met his sister and his mother. They all have the same aura. Like they know things that nobody else does."

Sula studied the man in question for a long moment. She knew he could control the wind and had visions. What other talents was he hiding? And why? Whatever it was didn't strike her as being sinister. She prided herself on her ability to spot deception, yet she'd wound up in such a horrible mess. Perhaps she didn't know what she was talking about after all. Or maybe it was only the wine…

She took another sip of the sweet, potent vintage, feeling its effect in several places. Her head swam slightly, and somewhere down deep in her core, an ache began.

Oh no. Not now.

Numbness tingled her face. "Didn't you say there was cake?"

"Of course." Aidan pushed his chair away and rose from the table. "Lemon spice cake. I found the recipe online a while back. The kids love it. Seems odd, though. Lemons don't usually appeal to younger palates." He smiled at her in the most peculiar fashion. His face seemed to ripple as she looked at him.

"I may have had too much to drink," she blurted out. "I need some cake to counteract the wine."

"Cake counteracts wine? Never heard that one before," Qinta said. "I'll have to remember that."

Aidan chuckled. "Have you ever actually tasted wine?"

"Nope," Qinta admitted. "Couldn't afford it when I was on the street, and I'm too young to get it legally."

"Probably just as well," Abuti said. "You might disappear, and we'd never find you again."

"Very true."

Sula was watching the Treslanti as she faded into the woodwork behind her. "That is *so* cool. I've studied Treslantis, but I've never actually seen one of you do that before. I can still see your eyes, though."

"Yeah. That's the only thing we can't seem to mask," Qinta said as she slowly became visible again. She turned to Aidan so quickly, it was a wonder her head remained attached. "That's my claim to fame. What's your secret, Aidan?"

The barest hint of a smile lifted the corner of his mouth, partially revealing a fang. "I already told you. I don't have any secrets."

"I think he needs more wine," Abuti whispered to her friend.

"Being drunk won't make me tell you something about myself that isn't true," he insisted.

"Suit yourself," Abuti said. "We know you're hiding something."

"And we'll get it out of you eventually," Qinta added.

Aidan's gaze darted from one girl to the other. "Is that why you volunteered for this job?"

Qinta shook her head. "Haven't we already established that we're only here for the food?"

"Not sure I'd believe that," Sula advised. "They seem to have their own hidden agendas."

"Aidan's terrific cooking being one of many." Abuti giggled. "That and getting to gaze at him over the dinner table."

Aidan turned to Sula. "Did you give them any wine? I know I didn't, but it sure seems like they're both a bit tipsy."

In Sula's opinion, she was the only tipsy person present. Aidan showed no effects whatsoever, and his wineglass was no less empty than her own. Better metabolism, she surmised. Something about the larger muscle mass being able to handle the alcohol content better. At least she *thought* that was what the difference was.

Another wave of heat gripped her body, triggering the need to fan herself.

"What's the matter—whatever your name is?" Qinta asked. "Aidan isn't getting you all hot and bothered, is he?"

Chapter 9

"STRANGE MEN NEVER MAKE ME HOT AND BOTHERED," Sula insisted. "It's probably the wine. And if you must call me something, call me Sula. It isn't my real name, but it'll do."

"Hold on a second," Aidan said. "That's the name you gave me." He paused, scratching his chin. "At least I think you did. Maybe I imagined it."

Sula peered at her wineglass, which seemed miraculously to have refilled itself. She'd never heard that Mordrials were capable of teleportation, but combine that breeding with his Zetithian ancestry and there was no telling what might result. Or perhaps he was simply a magician practiced in the sleight of hand that had fooled unsuspecting people for centuries.

"That probably is what I told you, but 'Sula' is actually a nickname. My real name is quite a mouthful." Another glance at her glass proved it was empty again. Shaking her head to clear the cobwebs from it was a mistake. She pinched the bridge of her nose, hoping that would help. "Can I have some more lemonade? This wine is making me see things."

"Absolutely," Aidan replied. "Be right back."

He'd barely left the room when Abuti, who was seated to her left, leaned closer and whispered, "Seeing things, huh? Like super-hot Zetithian dudes? If so, believe me, you aren't imagining *anything*."

"That isn't what I meant." Although Abuti was right. Aidan was all that and more. Sexy. Kind. Charming. Plus, he could freakin' *purr*. As a Zetithian man, he was capable of many other delightful things, including myriad ways to make an unsuspecting woman—even one who was on her guard—do things she would undoubtedly regret.

But would she truly regret doing any of those "things" with him?

That one had her stumped. Maybe she only needed to let the wine do its thing and make her more receptive.

Wait a second. I might think he's pretty awesome, but is he interested in me?

Surely, she hadn't imagined everything. From the moment he'd come to her rescue, he'd been very attentive and had even accused her of smelling too good. That had to count for something.

Her overwrought nerves had barely begun to settle when Aidan returned with a tall glass of iced lemonade. "I should've given you this to begin with. I just thought the wine might help your leg feel better."

"It still pains me some, although the wine does make it less…" She stared at the wineglass, trying to recall the word she was searching for, which became more elusive by the second.

"Noticeable?" he suggested.

She frowned. "Maybe. I'm not sure." When she looked again, the wineglass seemed to have disappeared. Had he whisked it away that quickly, or was her brain simply too sluggish to notice what he'd done? "You're a magician, aren't you?"

He stared at her, mouth agape. "What makes you think that?"

"I dunno," she mumbled. "Call it a hunch." Perhaps she could make a deal with him, trading her secrets for his. The other option was to make it impossible for him to do anything *but* tell her everything.

How in the world could she do that?

She wiped her lips with her napkin. "Please forgive me. My brain isn't firing on all thrusters at the moment." Rather than being the logical, coherent organ she knew her brain to be, that seat of reason was currently embarking on numerous erotic tangents. She blinked hard, hoping to quell her rampant imagination.

Not surprisingly, her strategy didn't work. She found herself wishing she was capable of enough sorcery to be instantly naked and alone with him in his bed, wherever that bed might be.

He's going to smell my desire and get the wrong idea.

She gave herself a mental slap. *Wrong idea?* With respect to Aidan, there was no such thing.

On the other hand, there were two other females at the table. A Norludian's scent might not appeal to him, but a Treslanti's might. Unless he got very close to either of them, he might not be able to pinpoint the source. Or would he? She knew enough about Zetithians to know the acuity of their senses varied among individuals, the same way each Mordrial's powers differed in strength. Maybe he really was only a handsome face with weak senses and minimal powers.

She was about to console herself with this possibility when she recalled that the man could control the wind well enough actually to fly while carrying a passenger.

Nope. Nothing weak about his Mordrial side.

"I think it might be time to take you to bed."

Following a long blink and a slow, deliberate turn of her head, Sula's gaze connected with Aidan's, proving he had been the one to speak and also that there was nothing remotely suggestive in his expression.

Damn. "You might be right."

"Not yet!" Abuti protested. "You haven't had any cake. Trust me, it's worth losing a little sleep over."

Sula threw up her hands in defeat. "Okay. Cake first; bed second."

Alone, alas…

As he passed around the dessert plates, the only thing running through Aidan's head was the conviction that this had to be the weirdest day of his life.

Like any other turning point.

Funny how most people never recognized those moments for what they were. Having seen into a good many people's futures gave him a vantage point few others could claim. Upon observing each individual's timeline, he could've told any number of them which choices they ought to make. Unfortunately, his advice was so seldom heeded, he rarely offered it. On those rare occasions when he *did* voice an opinion, which was subsequently ignored, he'd never been one to say "I told you so" when calamity inevitably struck.

Any benefits from his gift seemed to have been balanced with the curse of skepticism. In the past, he'd been dismissed as an ignorant child who couldn't possibly know what he was talking about. More recently, any mention of eventual outcomes had been met with scorn. Perhaps when he was older, more people would

listen to him. He could envision himself as an elderly
hermit living in a cave high in the mountains, visited by
pilgrims who had traveled across the galaxy to benefit
from his wisdom.

Yeah, right.

In truth, his fondest wish was that, after years of
refusing to use his mystical talent—or at least act on the
information he received—he might eventually lose it.

I should be so lucky.

"You weren't kidding about the cake," Sula said,
interrupting his ruminations. "It's absolutely delicious."

"I'm glad you like it." Right on cue, his scalp tightened, and his face grew warm. Fortunately, Abuti was
looking down at her plate and missed his reaction. Today
had been a real eye-opener where she was concerned.
She liked the way he blushed? Seriously? Then again,
she *was* Norludian. Abuti wasn't the only Norludian
Aidan had ever known, and if any of them were even
capable of the blush response, he'd never witnessed it.
No doubt she considered his red face to be more of a
novelty than something to be admired. Nevertheless, he
waited for the warmth in his cheeks to subside before he
spoke again.

"There are three other furnished bedrooms in the
west wing of this floor, and each of them has its own
bathroom. You ladies can pick whichever you like best.
My housekeeping droid has already freshened them up."
The dome-shaped droid hadn't been this busy since his
sister's wedding when several family members had
stayed with him. Living alone and making very little
mess, he normally set it to run once a month.

Abuti leaned forward, elbow on the table and chin in

hand as she gazed longingly into his eyes. "And where do *you* sleep?"

"Here in the east wing," he replied. "I don't use the rest of the house very much. I hardly ever use this room, either. I usually eat in the kitchen."

The dining room was yet another of the house's more flamboyant features. Because the rococo-style window and crown moldings provided more than enough decorative touches, he'd furnished it with as few frills as possible. However, dining tables that could seat twenty-four did tend to be rather grand.

Sula looked up, a hint of alarm in her expressive eyes. "So that was *your* bathroom I used a while ago?"

"Yeah." With a shrug, he added, "It was the closest."

Her gaze softened. "Thank you, Aidan. I'm sure we'll be very comfortable."

Once again, a flush warmed his cheeks. "I hope so."

To his relief, Abuti didn't comment, seeming content to express her appreciation with a deep sigh.

Qinta remained focused on her cake, which was rapidly disappearing. "Dunno why I love that cake so much. It's just...perfect. Think you could teach me how to make it?"

"If you like," Aidan replied. "It's pretty easy."

"Unlike *you*," Abuti said. Turning toward Sula, she went on, "Twenty-six years old and he's never even had a girlfriend." She shook her head sadly. "Such a waste."

"It's only a waste if he lives to be old and gray and dies without ever finding love," Qinta amended, sounding like the old-sage-voice-of-reason Aidan the Hermit might be someday. How did she do that? Perhaps it was only a question of delivery. If he worked on sounding more like an oracle, he might be taken more seriously.

"How do you know he's never had a girlfriend?" Sula asked.

"Common knowledge," Abuti said with a casual wave. "Among the orphans, anyway."

"Only among the *girls* at the orphanage," Qinta stressed. "The boys don't give a damn."

Aidan had completely lost the thread of the conversation. "How did we go from talking about baking cakes to whether I'll ever find love?"

Qinta snorted. "Blame it on Abuti. Ever notice how Norludians tend to turn every topic into something sexual?"

"Yes, I have," Sula replied. "That's why I wrote my master's thesis on Norludians. I theorized that their sex hormones don't have peaks and troughs the way those of most other species do." She grinned. "Turns out I was right. The average Norludian starts pumping out hormones at birth and doesn't stop until the day he or she dies. What's even more astonishing is that no one ever bothered to research it before."

"No kidding." Aidan had yet to run across a Norludian who wasn't obsessed with sex, although he'd always assumed the trait was as much cultural as it was physiological.

Abuti clapped her hands, sticking her fingertip suckers together before pulling them apart with a loud pop. "At last, we have scientific research on our side! Most other species find our preoccupation with sex annoying, even disgusting. Nice to know we can't help it."

"You could talk about it less, though," Qinta grumbled. "That much you *can* control."

Sula giggled—a throaty, musical sound Aidan found completely captivating. "That trait was the basis of another thesis. Turns out loquaciousness is also inherent."

"How in the world did they prove that?" Qinta asked.

"They found three Norludian children who'd been raised by parents of a different species, and they turned out to be as chatty as the rest of them. Not conclusive, of course, but strongly indicative."

Abuti seemed every bit as pleased with this revelation as she had been with the previous one. "Ah, vindicated at last." With that, she made quick work of her dessert and then asked for more. "We also tend to eat a lot," she added as she passed her plate to Aidan.

Having had some experience with the care and feeding of Norludian children, he couldn't help but laugh. "I knew that part," he said, even though Abuti's fondness for chicken korma was unusual, since most Norludians seemed to prefer fruits and vegetables over meat. "Good thing I like to cook."

Maybe it's the Indian-style sauce. If so, Abuti would undoubtedly be pleased if Sula were to take over the cooking chores. Not that he would let her—at least not for a while. He had to have *something* to do. Teaching Qinta to make the lemon spice cake would only take so long, and with the girls taking care of Sula and the droid keeping the house clean, he was already beginning to feel superfluous.

He reminded himself that they *were* staying in his house. Perhaps that was his only function, unless it was to provide entertainment. Keeping an invalid amused wouldn't be easy, despite the availability of the usual sources of electronic diversion.

Sula's yawn put an end to his musings.

"Ready to call it a day?" he asked, carefully avoiding any suggestive phrasing.

"I believe I am," she replied.

The two girls began to stir, but he was too quick for them. "I got this," he said, waving a hand to belay them. "The tour of the west wing will go a lot faster if I carry you."

Sula's grateful expression would've melted the heart of a much sterner man than Aidan had ever claimed to be. "Thank you. I wasn't looking forward to hopping that far."

"No need for that when I'm around." He didn't even attempt to mask his feelings, picking her up from her chair with tender loving care.

Once again, the combination of her arm around his neck and her sweet scent brought entirely different images to his mind. Carrying Sula to bed. Making love with her for hours on end. Getting lost in the depths of her eyes. Letting his fingers drift through her silken hair. His hands caressing the length of her delightful body. Her intoxicating flavor bathing his tongue.

The sudden realization that he might actually be reading scenes from her future gave him hope where there had previously been very little.

With an irrepressible smile, he carried her down the hall.

———

I could get used to this.

Sula couldn't recall ever having been carried by a man in her lifetime. Her father had surely done so when she was a baby, although her memory didn't stretch back that

far. Since then, her natural independence precluded such
an event, and that she'd never broken her leg before was
a given. She'd loved Raj very much, but he'd never carried her. Never made her feel quite so cherished.

Did Aidan truly cherish her, or did his Zetithian tem-
perament deserve all the credit?

Some, perhaps. Surely not *all*.

Nevertheless, as he carried her effortlessly from room
to room, describing the merits of each one, her mind
remained focused on the play of his muscles against her
side and the soft warmth of his gleaming curls where
they lay draped over her arm. His left arm embraced
her shoulders, but even more distracting was the arm
that cradled her legs and the light grip of his hand on
her thigh.

So delightful were these sensations, she allowed him
to carry her throughout the tour, lingering long enough
in each room for her to study the fabrics and furnishings
before making her careful choice.

"I think I'll take that first one," she said at last. "It's
closer to the rest of the house, and there's plenty of room
to maneuver around the furniture."

Actually, there was sufficient space in any of the
rooms, but being closer to the east wing also meant being
closer to where Aidan slept, a detail that appealed to her
more than any considerations of space and convenience.
To be honest, she'd much rather sleep in a bed *with* him
than in a room *near* him. Something about being as close
to him as she was now made her feel a million different ways, all of them good. Without her own unwashed
body to interfere with her olfactory sense, he smelled
even better than he had before. The weird thing was that

her response to him wasn't necessarily sexual. He made her feel comfortable in ways she'd never experienced, as though everything was right with the world and nothing could ever harm her. Like being safe and snug near a crackling fire while snow shrouded the world outside.

"Good choice," he said. "I've always liked this room. It has a nice vibe."

"And the others don't?" Abuti said, clearly aghast at the notion of staying in a room with bad vibes.

"Oh, you know how it is," Aidan said. "There are some places that just make you feel better."

Like being in your arms.

Had he been reading her thoughts? Mordrials were known to have some truly remarkable mental abilities, and telepathy was one of them. Aidan hadn't admitted to possessing that talent, but in view of the secrets he claimed to have, the possibility did exist. She probably would've kept quiet about it if she'd been the one to be blessed—or cursed—with the ability to read minds.

She'd never considered what it would be like to know what others were thinking. Even knowing the nice things might be embarrassing. The bad things…well, she would prefer to leave those thoughts strictly alone. But if Aidan really did know what she was thinking…

"You can't read minds, can you?" Sula blurted out.

Aidan didn't answer right away. Being held against his chest, she was well aware that he'd missed a breath or two, perhaps even a few heartbeats.

Qinta fixed him with a shrewd gaze. "I've wondered about that. Your mother can communicate telepathically with animals, and your sister is an empath. What can *you* do?"

Chapter 10

"Um...I can feel the vibes in a room?" Aidan knew it sounded a little ridiculous, but at the moment, that was the only mystical ability he was willing to acknowledge.

Qinta's coppery curls swung back and forth as she shook her head. "There's a whole lot more to you than that. C'mon, Aidan. Spill it."

He sucked in a breath. "You wouldn't believe me if I did."

The Treslanti girl folded her arms and tapped her foot in an oddly Terran manner. "Try me."

"Can we talk about this later?" he asked, feeling rather desperate. "Sula really needs her rest."

"Sure," Qinta said with a sardonic smirk. "You go right ahead and put her to bed. Then you can tell us why you nearly always catch one of the younger kids *before* they get into trouble."

Aidan winced. "You've noticed that, have you?"

"You bet we have. We've talked about it too. Some of us think you can read minds. Others are wondering if you're some sort of fortune-teller."

"I'm no fortune-teller," he insisted. "I can't read palms or tea leaves or see the future in a crystal ball."

"No," Qinta said. "I think your powers are more refined than that. You don't need props or gadgets to tell someone's fortune. Do you?" She studied him through narrowed lids. "I'm thinking it's more along the lines of flashes of insight into the future."

"He has visions," Sula offered. "He said he knew where I would be when I fell."

"Yes, but having visions is a Zetithian trait," Qinta pointed out. "I'm talking about his Mordrial side."

"Does it really matter?" Aidan asked. "Why do you need to know?"

"If you can read minds, I want to know before I *think* something I'll regret."

"I can't read minds," he said with some asperity. "Does that satisfy you?" Instead of putting Sula down, he held her closer to his chest as though she might be stolen from him.

Qinta still didn't seem convinced. "You're telling me the truth?"

Aidan would've crossed his heart if he hadn't been holding Sula, whom he had no desire to drop. "Yes, that's the truth. I can't read minds, and I have no idea what you're thinking."

She arched a brow. "Then you know the future?"

"No. Not like that." His anger threatened to flare as he glared at her. "This is the real reason you volunteered for this job, isn't it? You wanted a chance to"—he gazed upward, searching for the word he wanted—"interrogate me."

"I wouldn't put it quite like that," she replied. "But I'm understandably curious. We all are. None of us has been able to figure out why someone like you would be content to cook and clean for a bunch of orphans."

"Someone like me?" he echoed. "What's so special about me? And why wouldn't I want to help a bunch of homeless orphans? Onca and Kim do it, and so do Rashe and his wife. I have more money than I know what to do with, money I didn't even earn. This is just my way of giving something back, offering help where it's needed the most. Can you think of a better way to do that than by caring for homeless orphans?"

Qinta seemed somewhat mollified by this explanation, if not entirely satisfied. "Not really. But you're forgetting something."

"Like what?" Aidan snapped, annoyance making his query much sharper than he would've liked.

"We care about you, and we want you to be happy." Once again, her piercing green eyes sought his. "You aren't happy, are you?"

"If you knew half of what I know, you wouldn't be happy, either." Vibrating with anger, he carried Sula over to the bed, where he laid her down as gently as his trembling arms would allow. *She* could make him happy. At least he thought she could. But even she couldn't shield him from the onslaught of dreadful scenes he'd had no choice but to witness. The futures of people who were destined to live happily ever after in no way canceled out the bad endings that so many others were fated to endure. Thus far, the only ones he seemed able to influence were children, and even with them, he wasn't always successful.

Sula took his hand and pulled him down to sit on the bed beside her. "Tell me what you see."

Her touch steadied him. If there had ever been a person he could confide in, it was Sula. He had no idea why that was, but he knew it with absolute certainty, regardless of how much he hated to transfer any portion of his burden to someone who was rapidly becoming very dear to him.

"Terrible things," he whispered. "I shake someone's hand and see images of their future. Sometimes immediate and sometimes more distant."

The concern in her eyes was like a balm to his jangled nerves. "Is it always bad? Never anything good?"

"Oh, there's some good thrown in with the bad, but its effect on me is brief. The awful things…I never forget *them*. They haunt me like malevolent spirits."

She squeezed his hand. "That's why you fly, isn't it? To escape?"

He nodded. "Sometimes it works, and sometimes it doesn't. Cooking also quells those memories." He paused, frowning. "I've never found anything else that works as well."

"You've never been in love, have you?" Her tone suggested that love might be the best and most obvious cure of all.

No. Although his lips moved, no sound came from them. He cleared his throat. "I think that would hurt even more. I couldn't love someone without seeing bits of their future, and it would be wrong of me even to hint at what I know. That sort of knowledge can be very disturbing."

The sensuous curve of her lips captivated him as they formed a smile. "You're probably right. If I'd known I was going to break my leg, I might not have climbed up on that plateau, and I never would've found what I was searching for."

"Why *were* you there?" He didn't expect to receive a straight answer, but he asked her anyway. "I can't help wondering…"

She leaned back against the pillows. "I was trying to find proof that primitive peoples have been purposely infected with the Scorillian plague."

"Why would anyone do that?" Abuti asked.

"Because invading a planet to wrest it from its indigenous life-forms is messy and expensive," Sula replied. "Mass extinction by a plague that leaves nothing behind except dust is much easier—something I witnessed firsthand on a planet called Ecos. How I managed to survive, I'll probably never know."

Aidan's eyes widened as comprehension struck. "You were the *only* survivor?"

"As far as I could tell," she said with a slow nod. "Only me. My boyfriend, Raj Arya, was among the first to die."

"And you're afraid whoever was responsible wants to shut you up permanently?" he asked as more pieces of the puzzle slid into place.

She nodded. "They've tried once already. While I was shopping for supplies in Damenk, a Terran man took a couple of shots at me. I managed to lose him in the crowd, and I've been in the mountains ever since, but now that I'm back in the city…"

"They might try again?"

"I'm afraid so," she replied. "I should've told you sooner. Should've known you could be trusted." Long dark lashes fanned out over her cheeks as she lowered her gaze, then slowly rose to frame eyes that swam with tears as she looked up at him. "What future do you foretell for me?"

"I see nothing of your future," he replied. "Not the good or the bad. Just…nothing."

She smiled again. "I'm so glad. Knowing the answer

might make me despair or become overconfident, and I refuse to allow anything, especially my own complacency, to prevent me from doing my utmost to bring these atrocities to light and ensure that they never happen again."

"You know, Aidan," Abuti drawled, "if you can't see her future, she'd be the perfect mate for you."

In a few short moments, he'd all but forgotten that he and Sula weren't alone. And now they'd both revealed their deepest, darkest secrets with a Norludian in attendance.

He was about to caution her, but Qinta got there ahead of him. "If you breathe one single, solitary word of this to anyone, Abuti, so help me, I'll—"

Abuti drew back, waving her arms in protest. "Are you kidding me? No freakin' way would I ever tell anyone about this! I've never been on a secret mission before, especially with a guy who can see into the future and fly—that is, if I understood you correctly. This is *so* cool." Her eyes alight with enthusiasm, she asked, "What's our next move?"

"*Our* next move?" Aidan snorted. "You girls are in enough danger simply from being in this house. You will not be going on any missions, secret or otherwise."

Qinta burst out laughing. "You know what they say, keep your friends close and your enemies closer. The only way to keep an eye on Abuti and make sure she doesn't tell everyone in the quadrant what you're doing is to take her with you." Her gaze darted back and forth between him and Sula. "When do we start?"

Sula would never have guessed that finding willing cohorts would be so easy. There was just one problem. "Um, when I'm able to walk again?"

Abuti's expression of frank dismay nearly made Sula burst out laughing.

"We've got to get you on your feet, like, tomorrow," the Norludian girl declared.

"I don't think so," Aidan said. "It'll be several weeks before she can walk on a smooth surface. Climbing mountains will have to wait a while longer."

"So, you found what you were looking for in the mountains, huh?" Once again, Qinta displayed an immediate and rather uncanny grasp of the situation. "What was it?"

Sula didn't bother to disclaim. "A cave with drawings on the walls and a few primitive tools. Right here on Rhylos."

Qinta whistled softly. "You think that's what happened here? The indigenous people were wiped out by the Scorillian plague?"

"That or some other disease," Sula replied. "While it's true that a mass extinction could've occurred naturally, after what I saw on Ecos, I have some serious doubts."

"Terra Minor has a similar history," Aidan mused. "Claimed by a consortium and then sold off in parcels after being rendered habitable. Makes you wonder what that rendering entailed, doesn't it?"

"I'm guessing it involved removing every trace of the previous inhabitants and their culture," Sula said. "Even if the Rhylosian natives died out without any help from the plague, given what we found, they appear to have been cave dwellers. I've explored dozens of habitable caves, and that's the only one that contained any artifacts whatsoever. I'm no archaeologist, but finding evidence only in one relatively inaccessible cave strikes me as highly unlikely."

Aidan nodded. "Evidence *you* wouldn't have found if you hadn't fallen through that crack in the plateau, and a cave *I* wouldn't have found if I hadn't had a vision and been able to fly like one of the condors."

"Kinda makes you believe in fate, doesn't it?" Abuti remarked. "Which means you two obviously belong together." Rubbing her hands together, she cackled with glee. "A dangerous secret mission and a sizzling romance. It just doesn't get any better than that."

"One thing I don't understand, though," Qinta began. "You were on a planet—Ecos, you said—and everyone died of the plague except you. The vaccine for that disease has been around for a long time. The people of Ecos obviously wouldn't have been vaccinated, but I can't believe Raj wouldn't have been."

"Me neither." Sula didn't dare look Aidan in the eyes to gauge his reaction to the "sizzling romance" comment, and she was thankful to Qinta for providing a diversion. "I did some research after escaping from Ecos. They had a really tough time developing a vaccine, because it took years to figure out how to culture the causative agent. Before that, the spread of the disease could only be controlled by the use of very strict isolation protocols. What if someone has developed a new strain that will even kill those who have immunity to the old one?"

"If so, that would be enough to get them locked up for the rest of their natural lives. Plus, you may have the potential to be the source of a new vaccine." Aidan's calm tone took on a note of dismay as he added, "And someone is trying to kill you—the one being in the known galaxy with a natural immunity to a new strain of the most dreaded disease in history."

"I'm also the only witness to an act of planetary genocide," Sula said. "Which makes me wonder why they only sent one guy after me. Considering what's at stake, I'd have sent an army."

"Scary stuff." Qinta shuddered. "I feel like I should disappear for good."

"None of that, now," Abuti chided. "We must think positively. After all, they don't know we know what they're up to." She stuck a contemplative fingertip onto her chin, then pulled it off with a loud pop. "Actually, the more people who know about this, the better. I mean, they can't kill all of us, can they?"

Aidan barked out a laugh. "After destroying the entire population of at least one planet—and possibly three, if you include Terra Minor—I doubt they'd hesitate to drop a bomb on this house."

"Okay, okay," Abuti said grudgingly. "So secrecy really is important." She turned to Sula. "Any idea who these someones might be?"

"Maybe," Sula replied. "Raj and I were sent to Ecos by the anthropology department of Dalb University with the intention of studying the people and their culture. My doctorate advisor, Professor Dalb, is the one who suggested us for the project, but we weren't the only candidates. Several other faculty members had a say in the decision, and they certainly knew where we were going."

"Professor Dalb of Dalb University?" Qinta echoed. "What, does he own it or something?"

Sula smiled. "You'd think that, wouldn't you? Granted, he *is* a distant relative of the university's founder, but he isn't even a department head, much less the chancellor."

"So whoever's in charge may or may not be the bad guy," Aidan said. "Anyone who knew of your mission could've infected you and let you go to Ecos as carriers of the disease."

Sula didn't have to think long before making the obvious connection. "Raj and I both received vaccinations and immunological boosters. We could've been injected with the disease then, but the incubation period for the plague is pretty short. We were in space for weeks before we reached Ecos. We should've been dead before our ship ever landed."

Aidan was silent for a moment, his eyes narrow with evident concentration. "What if the germ was encapsulated in such a way that it wouldn't be released into your system until after you were on the planet?" He met her gaze at last, albeit with an ominous furrowing of his brow. "And maybe *your* encapsulated germs haven't been released yet."

An icy chill gripped her heart and then seeped into her bones. "Meaning I might still be a carrier?"

"Possibly," he replied. "We ought to run a scan on you. There's a medscanner at the orphanage—a carry-over from the days when the guys scanned their clients before each session."

Sula didn't need to ask why. Anyone working in a brothel would want to be very sure a client wasn't going to infect him with something nasty, although she doubted they'd ever been at risk of contracting such a horrible disease.

"But we can wait until tomorrow to do that," he went on. "No need to rush over there tonight."

"Don't you want to know *before* you're exposed to the plague?"

"Considering how long you've gone without dying or infecting anyone, my money is on the immunity theory, which would make you very special indeed." His smile and the touch of his hand drove the cold from her body, immediately replacing it with soothing warmth. "Not that you need any help in that respect."

Snickering, Abuti gave Qinta a nudge. "Told you they were meant for each other."

"Oh, come on," Qinta scoffed. "Love at first sight or people destined for one another… That crap never happens in real life."

"Oh yes it does!" Abuti insisted. "Especially with Zetithians. It's a scent thing." Folding her arms in a rather smug manner, she aimed a nod toward their host. "Isn't that right, Aidan?"

Aidan looked as though he wanted to fade into the woodwork the way Qinta had done. "There's a little more to it," he mumbled. "And the less said about that the better."

Apparently, Abuti had no intention of abandoning the subject. "But it's still very important. You guys can't get it up for a woman who doesn't smell right."

Sula's burning cheeks reminded her that despite having learned about Zetithian mating behaviors during the course of her studies, she'd never expected to meet a Zetithian man, let alone become involved with one. At least not to the point where her scent mattered.

She wasn't sure she was involved with one now.

"While that may be true, it isn't an appropriate topic for young girls to discuss, especially when it causes embarrassment to a guest in my house." The authoritative note in Aidan's voice seemed at odds with his previous mumblings. However, Sula doubted silencing Abuti would be that easy.

Surprisingly, Abuti's apology was swift and unquestionably heartfelt. "Sorry, Aidan. But you can't blame me for getting carried away by so much excitement. Maybe we need to get out more often."

"Yeah, right," he drawled. "The thought of turning you girls loose on an unsuspecting public is one of Onca's worst nightmares."

"I know," Abuti said with a roll of her bulbous eyes. "And I can't blame him for that." She turned to Sula. "We were always in trouble before Onca and Kim took us in." Sighing, she continued, "I should try to remember that. It's hard, though. Life in an orphanage may be safer than living on the street, but it can be kinda boring sometimes."

"So is taking care of a woman with a broken leg," Sula said. "I doubt there'll be much excitement for a while yet."

"Maybe so, but at least there's a chance." Abuti's eyes lit up. "I mean, what if that dude comes gunning for you again? That would be *very* exciting."

Sula managed to suppress a shudder. "I'm sure it would be. However, I hope you'll pardon me if I don't wish for it."

"Oh, no worries there," the Norludian girl assured her. "Qinta and I can protect you." She nodded toward Aidan. "He's not bad in a fight, either. Don't let that pretty face fool you. He can handle a sword with the best of them, and he's a damn fine shot with a pulse pistol."

Sula doubted that demonstrations of that type were part of the orphanage's curriculum. "How can you possibly know that?"

Abuti giggled. "I've met his parents. Trust me, with him around, you'll be perfectly safe."

Chapter 11

AIDAN COULDN'T ARGUE WITH ABUTI ON THAT SCORE. As a child growing up with a bounty on his head simply for being a Zetithian male, he had been trained in every form of combat the adults aboard the *Jolly Roger* had ever heard of. Even though that threat no longer existed, he saw no reason to allow his hard-earned skills to fade from disuse.

"I've also seen him practicing with Onca," Abuti went on. "Onca's no slouch, but Aidan is nearly always the winner. Doesn't matter whether they're using swords, pistols, or their bare hands. He's *awesome*."

"Guess that's why he has such an incredible body," Sula muttered.

"I heard that," Abuti shouted. "And I couldn't agree more."

Aidan flapped his hands at the two girls. "Enough! You two run along now. It's way past your bedtime."

Abuti stuck out her tongue. "Sure thing, *Dad*."

"Don't give me that crap," he warned. "And don't make me sorry I hired you."

"For the record, *she's* the one who did the hiring," Abuti said, pointing toward Sula. "*You* can't fire us."

"Yeah, well, keep it up, and she might decide to fire you herself." Aidan hadn't had much practice trying to out-talk a Norludian—in fact, he was fairly certain it was impossible—but he suspected that Abuti was better than most when it came to talking someone to death.

"All right, all right, *all right*," Abuti grumbled. "You're no fun at all."

"I'm as much fun as the next guy," Aidan snapped. "Just not right now. This has been a very long day."

"Yeah," Abuti said with a sneer. "All that excitement must really take its toll on an old dude like you."

Aidan drew himself up to his full height and pointed imperiously toward the hall. "Bed. Now."

"Don't worry." Qinta curled an arm around Abuti's bony shoulders and steered her through the doorway. "We're leaving."

Once the two girls were out of earshot, Sula giggled. "Funny how you can go from *awesome* to *old dude* practically in one breath."

"That's a Norludian for you. But then, you already knew that."

"I suppose I did, although it's been a while since I dealt with one. They never cease to amuse."

Aidan grimaced. "Amuse isn't the word I would choose. I've always found Norludians to be more annoying than funny."

"That one sure knows how to pull your chain."

"I'll grant her that. She's a little easier to take when she's part of a larger group. This is the first time I've ever gone one-on-one with her."

"A formidable opponent, to be sure."

"She is that." Having exhausted the subject of Abuti, Aidan was at a loss for further conversation, and the awkwardness between them returned. "Guess I'll say good night." He hesitated before adding, "I've never needed this feature before, but the house is equipped with a voice-activated comsystem. Somehow or other, it identifies everyone and knows where they're located. Calling out a name will open a link between the two rooms."

"That's good to know. I wouldn't want to disturb you unnecessarily."

Meaning she probably wouldn't be calling for him during the night.

Damn.

He reminded himself that this was only the first night of many she would spend beneath his roof. On that cheery note, he made sure she was warm and comfortable before taking himself off to bed.

He hadn't been asleep long before wild, bizarre, outrageous dreams disturbed his slumber. Flying through the mountains, still searching for that one particular spot where Sula fell. Flying so high that his wings became scorched by the sun. Condors pecking at bodies that crumbled into dust. Predatory ships ripping great rifts in the atmosphere. Strange beings dying all around him while he was helpless to prevent their demise.

He awoke drenched in sweat, his bed sheets torn to shreds, presumably by his own fangs. He was alone in the room, yet the air around him reverberated with cries of anguish.

He rose from his bed, shaking the dregs of sleep from his mind and the tattered sheets from his body. Pausing to listen to the stillness, he heard only the sounds he should've heard in the middle of the night. The creak of timbers, the settling of the floorboards beneath his feet—and then a soft moan.

He stole from his room, his bare feet making no sound as he passed through the foyer and into the west wing. Sula's room was dark, but the door stood open.

Halting at the threshold, he listened once again and heard nothing except her deep, even breathing—until her respirations were interrupted by a gasp.

"Aidan?" Her whisper would've been missed by ears that were any less sharp than his. "Is something wrong?"

Strange she should ask that of him, rather than the other way around. "No. Are you okay?"

"I had the most awful dream," she replied. "I was back on Ecos, watching everyone die." Her sentence ended on a sob that would've melted the heart of the most ruthless bastard in existence—a description that didn't apply to Aidan in any respect.

In an instant, he was beside her on the bed with his arms around her trembling shoulders. Her tears trickled down his bare chest in miniature rivers until her weeping finally ceased.

"This is the first time I've cried," she whispered as she wiped her eyes. "I was fired up before—blazingly angry and determined to avenge the innocent victims, Raj most of all. I had plenty of time to grieve while I was alone on that ship, but I never did. Never allowed myself to waste a moment on anything other than my plans for seeking justice. Now, I have no choice but to lie here and feel the pain and suffering of those people as if it had been my own."

She raised her head slightly, peering up at him in the darkness. His exceptional night vision revealed not only her tragic expression, but also the reflection of his glowing pupils in her eyes. "This is what it's like when you sense someone's future, isn't it?"

"Yeah. I feel it all—the pain, the suffering, and sometimes even the remorse. It's strange the way so many heartless beings only feel regret at the end when the torment they've wreaked on others finally befalls them. Prior to that moment, they had no compassion whatsoever, not for anyone." He blinked back his own hot, angry tears. This was not the time for him to succumb. Not when Sula needed to be comforted.

"And right now, you can't even fly to avoid the sadness." A short laugh escaped her. "Or cook anything. I can't do either one."

"Those are only my means of coping. You must have a few of your own."

"I suppose I do," she admitted. "But for the life of me, I can't remember what they are, although I do like to read."

"I can help you with that," he said, eager to do whatever he could to alleviate her suffering—or at least distract her from it. "I have a library link pad with access to every book ever written and every song ever recorded."

"I might have to borrow that from you."

"I probably should've given it to you sooner." He hesitated, recalling one of her previous comments. "A while ago, you asked if I'd ever been in love. Did being in love make things easier for you?"

"Sometimes," she replied. "Having someone to love gives you a sounding board, someone with whom to share ideas and"—her voice dropped a notch in volume—"secrets."

"We've done that, haven't we?"

"I believe we did."

In another place and time, he would've kissed away her tears and made love to her until nothing existed to come between them—no secrets, no uncertainty, no mysteries.

He'd never done that with anyone. Never felt free

enough to allow himself the luxury of falling in love, or even engaging in meaningless sex. Zetith's tragic history was quite enough to keep him from spreading his seed—or *snard* as it was called in his native tongue—indiscriminately. That sort of thing had been attempted before, with disastrous results. *Snard* was more than mere semen; it was as sweet and addicting as the euphoria it induced.

Sula knew that. Or at least he assumed she did. *Snard* was, after all, the cause of his species' downfall and might've eventually resulted in their extinction had events played out differently—more than enough to earn a mention in any textbook on the subject.

Shifting in his embrace, Sula cleared her throat. "You should get back to bed. I've kept you up long enough."

"Don't give it a thought." He released her with even more reluctance than when he'd laid her on the bed. "After all, I'm not the one with a broken leg."

"Maybe not, but your life has certainly been turned upside down today."

He smiled. "My life *needed* to be turned upside down. Something tells me this is going to be a change for the better."

―――

If it hadn't been for her broken leg, Sula would've counted this among one of the best days of her life. She'd made two new friends, found the evidence she'd been searching for, and, of course, she'd met Aidan.

Aidan, who was currently sitting on her bed in the middle of the night, gazing at her with the shining eyes of a cat waiting to pounce.

She tilted her head. "A change for the better... Would that be foretelling your own future?"

"No," he replied. "I've never been able to do that. I can only predict other people's futures, which means that stopping off in the casino district would leave my pockets as empty as any other hapless visitor's."

"Not much of a gambler, then?"

"Not really. I've never seen the attraction. Oh sure, winning would be great, but it's such a rare event."

"You have better things to do?"

"Something like that."

Sula could think of several better things, starting with discovering what it was like to kiss a man who sported a pair of rather sharp-looking fangs. Would it hurt to kiss him? Or would she even notice the fangs? She also longed to learn how it felt to kiss a man who, if she remembered correctly, wouldn't have any beard stubble to scratch her face raw.

Without thinking, she raised a hand to stroke his cheek and found it to be as smooth as her own. "You guys don't grow beards, do you?"

"Nope. We don't have to shave our faces, and we hardly ever cut our hair."

"I didn't think you did." Smiling, she lowered her hand. "Please forgive my curiosity. I find your species... fascinating."

The golden glow emanating from his eyes burned brighter for an instant. "Only my species?"

"And you, of course. You're the only Zetithian I've ever met." She studied his eyes for a moment. "I didn't notice how different your eyes were during the day, but at night... I'd almost forgotten about the glowing vertical pupils."

"Just another part of our charm." Judging from his light, mocking tone, he didn't take himself or his exotic feline eyes too seriously.

"You certainly have plenty of that." What he didn't appear to have was even the slightest hint of conceit. She thought it strange that such a handsome and apparently wealthy man would be so humble, although that was also reputed to be a common trait among Zetithian males.

Excellent lovers and fighters, her professor had announced to the class. *But not an arrogant alpha male among them.* Apparently, he had believed this, for his statement had contained no derision whatsoever. Having finally met a Zetithian man, Sula was inclined to agree.

"Do I really?" Aidan's voice sounded strangely muted, until a louder rumble captured her attention.

He's purring.

He'd done it before, more as a means of soothing her than an attempt at seduction. This time, she wasn't sure what he meant by it.

"Is that another part of your charm?" she asked.

"What, you mean my purring?" His voice deepened along with his purr. "Yes, I suppose it is. Do you want me to stop?"

"Not particularly. I like the way it sounds—and the way it makes me feel."

"How *does* it make you feel?" he asked. "Or is that something you'd rather I didn't know?"

"I wouldn't mind telling you if I knew myself." She'd told him it was comforting before. Now, it was... "Pleasant, perhaps?"

"Pleasant is good." Once again, fire blazed in his eyes. "I'll be able to tell when that changes."

Time to play dumb. "How so?"

"Your scent will become more...enticing." He blinked slowly, as though lowering the shades over his gleaming eyes. "But you already knew that."

Nodding, she traced the inner edge of her lips with the tip of her tongue. "I wanted to hear you say it."

"Why is that so important?"

"It helps me understand more about the nature of your"—she deliberately avoided using the word *desires*—"intentions."

"My intentions?" If the room had been completely dark, she might've missed his heart-stopping smile. "Entirely honorable, I assure you."

"I can believe that." By all accounts, Zetithians were nothing if not honorable, and Sula had yet to discover any reason to suspect Aidan of deviating from the norm.

I still want to kiss him.

The effect her scent had on him remained a mystery. However, his delightful aroma or aura or whatever it might be was certainly affecting *her*. Her mouth watered, and she swallowed with a surprising degree of difficulty. How could she encourage him to kiss her without actually asking him? Flirtation had never been her strong suit, and she'd already wet her lips once. What more could she possibly do?

In the end, all she did was sigh. "I guess we should both try to get a little more sleep."

His eyes dimmed slightly as he nodded. "Without sufficient rest, your leg won't mend as quickly as it should."

For a few precious moments, she'd almost forgotten the pain in her leg. "My mother would say the same thing." With a quiet laugh, she added, "Only she would've used kisses to hasten the healing process."

"I can do that."

"I'm sure you *can*. The question is whether or not you *will*."

"Completely willing and entirely able," he whispered. "Where should I start?"

Despite longing to simply tap her lips with a fingertip, she opted for the obvious reply. "My toes?"

Without hesitation, he pulled back the blanket and leaned over, pressing his lips to her right great toe.

"Wrong foot," she chided.

"I know." With a wicked grin, he switched to her other foot, scattering warm, wet kisses from her toes to her knee, even dropping an achingly gentle one over the break where her flesh was the tenderest. Her skin tingled from his touch, the wave of goose bumps traveling up her leg to the point where her thighs met. Heat flooded her core as desire crashed through her body. Her nipples tightened almost painfully, as did her clitoris.

After placing yet another kiss on her knee, Aidan rolled up onto his hands and knees and began crawling toward her, his low, rumbling purr more pronounced than ever. The radiance from his eyes cast shadows on her rumpled clothing, highlighting her erect nipples. She'd been embarrassed when they'd strained against her T-shirt a few hours earlier. Now they stood like beacons, hopefully luring his beguiling lips to hers.

As his gaze swept upward to linger on her face, he drew in a deep breath that was immediately followed by a sharp, explosive purr. He crawled toward her so slowly, she wanted to scream in frustration. She knew exactly what he was doing. He was giving her every opportunity to push him away. A single word would've sufficed, yet she remained silent. His hair hung down on either side of his face, tickling her arms as he advanced. Grasping his golden curls with both hands, she pulled him down and kissed him.

The pressure of his lips on hers deepened in infinitesimal increments as his purr sent passionate vibrations rippling throughout her body. No longer able to deny her hunger for him, she longed to yank up her shirt and expose her bare skin to his gaze, his touch, and most of all, his lips.

Releasing her grip on his hair, she let her hands glide across his shoulders and down his back, stopping only when she reached the edge of his loose-fitting trousers. If she were to slide her fingertips beneath the waistband, she might get more from him than a simple kiss. And yet, as his tongue slipped past her parted lips, her clit tightened, and her core began to ache with need—sensations she never dreamed she would ever experience again.

Arching her back, she pressed her breasts upward and shifted side to side, rubbing their taut peaks against his chest. Shocking, delightfully erotic images flowed through her mind: his cock gliding over every erogenous zone in her body, its firm warmth against her lips, in her mouth, and plunging deep inside her. Passion nearly overcame her better judgment, and she fought the urge to reach for his cock. She could almost feel her inner muscles clasping his stiff shaft as he thrust into her again and again and again. She could scarcely wait to taste his *snard*, to revel in its sweetness, and to bask in the cloud of euphoria it would create. Only Zetithian men produced the marvelous secretions that made practically every woman in the galaxy wish the men of their species could do the same—something many of those men undoubtedly wished themselves.

Sula had only known Aidan for less than a day, and already she'd been captured in a spell cast by his powerful sexual magic. What would happen when she finally surrendered to her desires? Receiving the full force of this man's sexuality would undoubtedly bind her to him for life. Once that occurred, would she abandon her quest for the shelter of his arms, or would he fight alongside her as her most valiant ally?

Chapter 12

THE WOMAN HAS A BROKEN LEG SO SHE CAN'T EVEN RUN AWAY from me, and I only met her a few hours ago. What in the world am I doing in her bed?

The same thought must've occurred to her because Sula stiffened in his arms.

Aidan sat back, thankful he hadn't followed his inclination to tear off her clothes with his teeth. "Go ahead," he said ruefully. "Tell me to get my ass out of here before I do something stupid."

She grimaced. "You mean before *I* do something stupid, which, I might add, I was just about to do."

He was dying to know what she might've considered stupid, but he was also a little afraid to find out—especially if she'd been fixing to slap the hell out of him, which was no less than he deserved. He couldn't blame her for kissing him. After all, he'd been the one doing the purring.

Still, she was Terran, not Zetithian. If she hadn't *wanted* to kiss him, purring wouldn't have made her do it. Come to think of it, purring didn't guarantee success, even with a female of his own species.

Cheered by this realization, he rose from the bed, hoping her night vision wasn't sharp enough to spot the incredible boner her scent had bestowed upon him. No doubt a few breaths of fresh air would cause it to subside, but it felt so damn good. He would've preferred to stick around and enjoy it for a while.

Not tonight.

"Okay. I'm leaving. For the record, you weren't about to kick me in the nuts or anything of that nature, were you?"

Sula didn't answer him right away, which wasn't too surprising. Laughing one's ass off tended to make coherent speech difficult, if not impossible.

"No," she finally said, her voice still quaking with mirth. "Nothing like that."

"Glad to hear it."

"Good night, Aidan. Sleep well."

"Good night, Sula," he said and—because he believed it would've been rude of him not to—bent down and kissed her cheek. "Sweet dreams."

The mention of dreams gave him plenty of food for thought as he made his way back to his room. To hear her tell it, they'd both had similar dreams. That she would dream about people dying on Ecos wasn't unexpected, but for him to have the same dream seemed odd. Was he so in sync with her that they shared dreams?

With that question to ponder, by the time he reached his bed, Aidan's erection was history. However, having done it to him once, the chances she would do it again were excellent. Too bad they weren't alone in the house. From now on, he would have to stay upwind of Sula anytime her caregivers were present, which was much easier said than done—unless she could control her desire a whole lot better than he could.

Women were like that. Their desires didn't run quite as rampant as those of men, or so he'd been told. Nevertheless, it didn't pay to generalize, especially when it came to feelings. No two beings were alike in that respect, and he had his empathic sister to thank for that insight.

No two people can witness the same event and react exactly the same way, Althea had said. *It's always personal.*

He'd certainly taken that kiss personally, and he'd felt it all the way to his dick.

Sula's kissed me twice now.

With that in mind, he was still smiling when he finally drifted off to sleep.

―――∿∿∿―――

The following morning, Aidan was already in the kitchen fixing breakfast when Rashe arrived with a hoverchair piled high with groceries. After handing Aidan what appeared to be a nightgown, he maneuvered the chair over to the stasis unit. "Dude, did you know there's a creepy-looking Terran hanging around your neighborhood?"

"Seriously?" Aidan's first thought was that Sula's would-be assassin had somehow discovered her where-abouts, although he couldn't fathom how anyone could possibly know she was staying in his house.

"Yeah, and if looks could kill, I'd be pushing up daisies for sure."

"Was he armed?"

"Not that I could see." He set a bag containing four loaves of bread on the table. "But he probably saw me unloading this stuff, so he knows you've got company. Might not know who, but you get the idea."

Aidan gritted his teeth. "Dammit! I'll swear no one saw me bring her in here. Even if someone saw Abuti and Qinta arrive, they wouldn't have any reason to assume the girls were here to take care of a woman with a broken leg—or who that woman was."

"One thing for sure, nobody at the orphanage could've ratted on her. None of us knew her identity, much less who to tell about her." Rashe dumped a sack of fruit on the table. "I got that splint kit you asked for. Ever used one before?"

"Not personally, but I've seen it done. Aldrik broke his leg falling off a tower at the spaceport on Traxus Five when we were kids. Mom had him walking again in a couple of days."

"You Zetithians and your restorative sleep," Rashe said with a snort. "Wish Terrans healed that fast." Grinning, he added, "Wouldn't mind acquiring a few of your other attributes, either."

"Yeah, right," Aidan grumbled. "You and everybody else."

Rashe shrugged. "Just sayin'."

Aidan was still trying to figure out how anyone could've found Sula while he put the finishing touches on breakfast. A tracking beacon was a possibility, but if that were the case, whoever was after her would've caught up with her long ago.

"We really need to do a scan on Sula," he said, finally giving voice to his ruminations. "If she's carrying around a beacon of some sort, we need to get rid of it."

"A little late for that, don't you think?" Rashe said. "I mean, if the dude already knows she's here."

"We don't know that for sure, but we can't take any chances. Sula said some Terran guy was gunning for her in Damenk several months ago. She was able to lose him in the crowd, but the man you saw could be the same one."

"Hmm... Not much of a beacon if he couldn't trace her after that," Rashe commented.

"I agree. It would help if we knew how or when she might've been tagged. She was inoculated a while back, and the injection could've contained tracking nanobots, but if so, she'd have been caught long ago."

"Nanobots don't always show up on a scan," Rashe reminded him. "They don't have much range, and they don't last forever. Most of them quit transmitting after about a month."

The timer dinged, and Aidan pulled a pan of sweet rolls from the oven. "Maybe they *did* know she was in the mountains and didn't see any point in tracking her until she came back to town. She would've posed very little threat to anyone out there in the wilderness. Or maybe whoever was tracking her was too lazy to go looking for her, preferring to wait for her to come to them."

"What exactly does she know that's worth killing for? No, wait"—Rashe put up a hand—"if it's one of those 'If I tell you, I'd have to kill you' things, I really don't want to know."

"*I* wouldn't kill you," Aidan said. "But anyone tracking her would have to assume she's confided in us. She didn't until last night, and I'm sure there's more to it, but—"

"Meaning you're *all* going to be targeted, including the girls?"

Aidan grimaced. "I'm afraid we might be. And you've been here twice—"

"I've seen that guy too." Rashe sighed. "You might as well tell me everything. Wouldn't be the first time someone was after my blood."

"Hopefully it won't come to that." Aidan picked up a piping bag and began icing the rolls. "Besides, the man you saw might have nothing to do with Sula." If he told himself that enough, he might actually believe it. "Although in all honesty, he probably does. Guess I'd better fill you in."

He had just finished giving Rashe a brief rundown of Sula's background and current predicament when the rousing strains of "La Marseillaise" sounded from the foyer. "Who the devil would be ringing the bell at this hour?" he snapped. "I'll never get breakfast ready."

"If it's that creepy dude, want me to take him out?" Rashe actually looked hopeful. "Haven't seen any action for a while now. Might be time to put on some war paint and dust off my tomahawk."

"Let's not go that route yet." Aidan peered at the front door camera display and groaned. "I should've known."

"Who is it?"

"Giklor," Aidan replied. "He's probably sensed that there's a broken bone somewhere in the house and is just dying to fix it."

"Hey, it's what he does, dude. He can't help himself."

"I know. But Sula doesn't want to be healed by a Zerkan, and I can't say as I blame her."

"Yeah, well, you know Giklor." Rashe scooped up a stray dollop of icing and popped it in his mouth. "He'll probably talk her into it."

"If you're right about the 'creepy Terran dude,' she might agree. Having her mobile would certainly be helpful if we need to disappear in a hurry."

Qinta strolled into the kitchen and snatched a sweet roll from the pan. "You guys talking about me?"

"Nope," Rashe replied. "You aren't the only thing around here that can disappear." As if to prove his point, he made a sweet roll vanish in less than three seconds.

Qinta savored hers more slowly. "Oh, yum… Why don't you ever fix breakfast at the orphanage?"

"Because I don't like getting up that early." Aidan wasn't sure he wanted to be up now. He was still trying to figure out why he'd left Sula's bed when he could've been kissing her all night long. "La Marseillaise" played again. "Guess I'd better see what Giklor wants."

"Is that the Zerkan healer?" Qinta asked.

"They're *all* healers," Rashe said, helping himself to another roll. "Must never be anyone sick on their planet if they have to leave home to find people to cure."

Aidan had never been to the Zerkan homeworld, but if the Zerkans he'd met on other planets were any indication, Rashe probably had the right idea. With any luck, he could get rid of Giklor before he got wind of Sula's predicament.

"Nope," he muttered as he entered the foyer. "Probably not gonna happen."

"Greetings, my friend!" Giklor said when Aidan opened the door. "I sensed the need for my services, so as you can see, I have come!" Without so much as a "by your leave," the little Zerkan hopped over the threshold, his teardrop-shaped eyes glowing red with excitement. "Where will I find this unfortunate lady?"

"Mother of the gods!" Aidan growled. "How could you possibly know—"

"I do not question *how* I know. I simply *do*." He rubbed his hands together with such vigor, Aidan feared he would rip the pearly skin from his fingers. "Now, where is she?"

"Still asleep in her bed," Aidan said without much hope. Deterring Giklor from a healing mission was like trying to stop a volcanic eruption.

"She's awake now and ready for breakfast," Abuti announced from the west wing hallway. "I just need help getting her out of bed, unless you want me to take her food to her on a tray."

"Rashe already brought the hoverchair, so she can eat wherever she likes," Aidan said. "He also brought a splint kit. We can redo her leg after breakfast."

"Give me a few short moments with her, and she will need none of those things!" Giklor insisted.

"She won't need breakfast, either," Abuti said darkly. "I've seen what you guys do to people. She'll be sick as a Keldrak on a three-week bender."

"Any nausea is very short-lived," Giklor said. "And recovery is rapid and uncomplicated."

"Except for the red eyes," Aidan said. "She doesn't want those."

Giklor dismissed this objection with a casual wave. "I will explain that to her and allow her to choose."

"She's already made up her mind," Aidan said firmly. "She said no."

"That was before the enemy infiltrated the neighborhood," Rashe said, coming up behind him. "She needs to know about that before she can make an informed decision."

"We don't know that for sure," Aidan reminded him. "That man might have a perfectly valid reason for being here. Besides, any worthwhile assassin would make damn sure you *didn't* spot him."

"I think we've already established that he's no great shakes as a hit man," Rashe pointed out.

"What hit man?" Abuti demanded, her bulbous eyes wide with apparent fascination. "Did you get a good look at him? Would you recognize him if you saw him again?"

"Probably," Rashe said, albeit without much conviction.

Abuti stomped a flippered foot. "Probably isn't good enough. What did he look like?"

"Creepy," Rashe replied.

"You should've taken his picture," Abuti said, then glared at Aidan. "I don't think we want him on our team."

"Team?" Giklor echoed. "What sort of team? Do you need a healer? Oh, of course you do. Every team needs a healer. I hereby volunteer."

Aidan took a moment to massage the growing ache in his temples. "Why don't you all head into the dining room while I go get Sula? Then we can have some breakfast and talk this over."

"Want me to bring the hoverchair?" Rashe asked.

"No," Aidan said, a bit more sharply than he'd intended. "I can carry her."

"Suit yourself, dude," Rashe said. "Giklor can fix your sprained back right up."

Giklor nodded vigorously. "Indeed I can. Just say the word."

At the moment, *scram* was the only word that came to Aidan's mind. However, all he said was "Be right back."

After what had passed between them during the night, Aidan was a little nervous about facing Sula, but one glimpse of her welcoming smile banished his fears.

"Good morning," she said. "I had the nicest dreams after you left last night."

"Thanks to you, so did I." When he scooped her up in his arms, the kiss she planted on his cheek felt so right, he was tempted to forget about breakfast and indulge in far more pleasant activities.

"Sounds like we have company."

"Rashe and Giklor," he said with a weary roll of his eyes. "Rashe said he saw some creepy Terran man hanging around the neighborhood this morning, so of course everyone thinks he might be your assassin. Abuti is pissed at Rashe for not taking a picture of the guy, and Rashe is talking about getting out his tomahawk and war paint. Giklor wants to fix your leg and join the team as our medic." He sighed. "Are you *sure* you want to go through with this?"

"If the man Rashe saw really is the same man, I don't think we have much choice," she said. "Bad help is better than no help at all."

"I dunno about that. Bad help might be what gets us all killed."

After Aidan left her the night before, Sula had given serious thought to abandoning her mission so she could instead explore the possibility of a lasting relationship with him. Not only had he made her feel safe, he'd reawakened her desire in a way that couldn't be ignored. She'd looked forward to spending the coming weeks with him while her leg healed, providing her with a much-needed break from her search for evidence in remote mountain caverns. Now, the report of a possible assassin in the neighborhood brought those pleasant dreams to an abrupt halt.

"Any idea how he found out you were here?" he asked. "We've talked about tracking beacons and injected nanobots, but there might be a simpler explanation."

"I can't think of one," she said. "Trust me, I've been trying to figure out how he tracked me down the first time. Nanobots make the most sense, especially given that Raj and I were probably infected with the plague using the same method."

"Yet another reason to run a scan. We'll head over to the orphanage after breakfast, although that scanner might not be sophisticated enough to detect nanobots."

"Not if they're the really good bots," she agreed. "It scares me to think what I might be carrying around inside me—plague viruses, nanobots, or something we've never even heard of."

"Yeah. I imagine it would be. I—"

"Ah, there she is!" A short, thin-limbed creature came scurrying toward them, followed closely by Rashe and the two girls. "Please allow me to examine—"

"After breakfast, Giklor," Aidan said sternly. "Don't be bothering her now."

"I understand completely." As the little being bowed low before her, Sula fancied she could see the underlying tissues through his pale, translucent skin. "Forgive my eagerness, dear lady. I am Giklor of the planet Zerka, and I have had tidings of your mishap."

Sula had seen pictures of his kind before, but this occasion marked her first face-to-face meeting with one. With the exception of their eye color—the males had red eyes while the women's were blue—Zerkans were as sexless in appearance as Norludians and, like members of that species, wore no clothing.

"I'm pleased to meet you, Giklor," she said. "I am Sula of the planet Earth."

"Sula…" Giklor tapped his virtually nonexistent chin with a rounded fingertip that appeared to lack any form of nail or claw. "Short for Sulaksha, meaning 'fortunate,' I believe."

Sula was too shocked to deny it. "How could you possibly know that?"

Giklor blinked slowly, his eyelids sliding sideways in a sly, secretive manner. "Who can say from whence such knowledge comes? I have traveled far and have seen much. But as for you, Sulaksha…no one believing in fate could have named you otherwise."

Chapter 13

SULA HAD NEVER CONSIDERED HERSELF TO BE VERY FORTU-
nate. Taking the good with the bad, she figured her luck
was on par with almost anyone else's. However, in light
of recent events, the name was beginning to make sense.
She'd survived when thousands, perhaps even millions,
of others had died, and she'd made it to Rhylos alone
on a starship. She'd somehow managed to elude an
assassin, and just when she'd found evidence to support
her theory, she'd been injured, only to be immediately
rescued by a man who could fly.

Had her parents given her that name hoping it would
protect her, or did they have foreknowledge of the
events that awaited her?

Sula wasn't a great believer in fate. Such beliefs
tended to make people reckless, because with the future
predetermined, there was no need to be careful. She'd
observed a similar effect in her own country. For herself,
she couldn't see the benefit in taking needless risks and
was therefore reasonably cautious.

"Sulaksha." Aidan whispered her name slowly, as
though savoring each syllable. "What a lovely name."

Still somewhat dumbfounded by Giklor's uncanny
knowledge, all she could say was "I'm glad you
approve." For the little Zerkan, she had no words.

Fortunately, Abuti had plenty to say. "Now that you've
got us totally weirded out, can we please have breakfast?"

"Oh, of course," Giklor said graciously. "I have no desire to interrupt your repast."

Abuti snorted. "Sure seemed like it to me. Listen, pal, I've been smelling those sweet rolls for the past hour and getting hungrier by the second. Your timing really sucks."

Giklor bowed again. "Ah, yes. You Norludians are such treasures. Always speak your minds, never leaving any doubts as to where you might stand on any given subject."

Sula half expected Abuti to stick out her tongue, which was the Norludian equivalent of "Fuck you." Instead, she seemed content to do a sucker-tip pop with all ten of her fingers—a less obscene gesture that conveyed a similar sentiment—before heading back toward the dining room.

"Guess she told you, dude," Rashe commented. "Can't say as I blame her, either. These things are damned tasty." Having said that, he wolfed down the remainder of the roll he held and then licked his fingers.

"You'd better have left at least one for Sula," Aidan warned.

"I didn't eat *all* of them." Rashe grinned. "Haven't had enough time for that. How come you don't ever make these for the orphans?"

Sula would've thought the answer was perfectly obvious.

Aidan, however, chose to elucidate. "Do you have any idea how many I'd have to make to ensure that every child got at least one?"

"At the rate we're eating them, I'd guess at least five hundred or so," Qinta said.

"Exactly." He glanced at Giklor. "Have you had breakfast?"

"Why, no, I haven't," the Zerkan replied. "May I be permitted to join you?"

"Sure, no problem. What about you, Rashe?"

"I'm good with that," Rashe replied. "All that shopping made me hungry."

"I'll fetch some more plates," Qinta said before dashing off toward the kitchen.

Entering the dining room, Aidan put Sula in the chair to his right near the head of the table. "You'll have more leg room here."

Sula somehow managed to refrain from kissing him again as she thanked him. Abuti had enough fodder for teasing as it was. She saw no need to provide her with any more.

If anything, breakfast was a more sumptuous spread than dinner had been. In addition to the coveted sweet rolls, there was a platter of crisp bacon, a large bowl of scrambled eggs with cheese, and a fruit salad. To Sula's delight and astonishment, next to her plate was a stack of masala dosas, a jar of ghee, and three types of chutney.

"Oh, Aidan," she said with a sigh. "Do you have any idea how long it's been since I had a masala dosa?"

"As long as you've been climbing mountains?"

"And then some." After putting two dosas on her plate, she spread them with ghee and chutney and took a bite. "These are absolutely perfect. Even better than Mom used to make."

Abuti, who sat in the chair to Sula's right, leaned closer to sniff the dosas. "What did you say they were?"

"Masala dosas," Aidan replied. "The dosa is like a crepe made with a fermented rice and lentil batter. The filling is called aloo masala, or potato curry."

"Sounds weird," Abuti said. "I think I'll stick with eggs and fruit—and sweet rolls, of course."

Qinta helped herself to a dosa, then reached for the bacon. "Don't knock it 'til you try it."

"Can't stand that nasty bacon crap, either." Abuti popped a blueberry into her mouth with her fingertip. "Fruit is much better for you."

"So true," said Giklor. "However, I believe I'll have a dosa in honor of our new friend."

Sula smiled her approval while attempting to recall everything she'd learned about Zerkans. Try as she might, she couldn't remember what the typical Zerkan diet contained, although she doubted it was anything like traditional Indian cuisine.

Still, if what he put on his plate was any indication, their diet was mainly vegetarian. Giklor also eschewed the bacon, a circumstance that appeared to please Rashe and Qinta, who each devoured several slices. Norludians weren't entirely vegetarian; case in point, the relish with which Abuti had eaten chicken korma the night before. Why wouldn't she eat a dosa?

Sula puzzled over this inconsistency long enough to realize she was subjecting her tablemates to the same close scrutiny she would give a newly discovered species. Not only that, she was viewing them from the perspective of an outsider.

I'm thinking like an anthropologist.

Granted, they were all members of interesting species, but they were the sort of beings common to many cosmopolitan worlds, and Rhylos had the most varied population in the galaxy.

Perhaps her anthropology background had nothing to do with her attitude.

I've been alone too long.

Giklor had referred to her as a new friend. In the past, she'd been so focused on her studies and her career, friendships hadn't seemed important. If she and Raj hadn't been in so many of the same classes, she might never have paid him any attention. In truth, *he* had been the one to approach *her*. Prior to that, she honestly hadn't noticed him.

All work and no play makes Sula a dull girl.

Raj had changed that. Lively and fun, he'd encouraged her to engage in activities she never would have done if left on her own. He'd even convinced her to try rock climbing. Little had he known how useful that skill would become.

"You okay?" Aidan asked. "Leg hurting you?"

She shook her head. "Not too much. I was just thinking."

Thankfully, he didn't question her any further. Giklor, however, took the mention of pain as his cue to intervene. "About that broken leg, my dear Sulaksha. I can heal it with no side effects whatsoever."

Aidan viewed him with a narrow-eyed suspicion. "That isn't what you said a while ago."

"That was before I was able to assess her injuries. Because she has only suffered a broken bone in a limb, topical application should suffice. The bone will not mend as rapidly as it would if the healing fluids were ingested, but some concessions must be made for those not wishing to bear the mark of healing for the rest of their lives."

"Meaning the glowing red eyes." Sula stared at the Zerkan, suddenly realizing he looked like the ghost of a gingerbread man whose head was too big for the rest of him. She would've been laughing if Aidan hadn't mentioned the possibility that a hit man had caught up with her. Her presence put every one of these people in danger, and she had no desire to be responsible for the deaths of any innocent bystanders. "How soon will I be able to walk?"

"Internal healing, within perhaps one or two days. External, about two weeks."

Two minutes was too long to wait if there truly was an assassin lurking nearby. Still, either option was better than sitting around for six weeks. Glowing red eyes wouldn't be so bad. Aidan's eyes had a golden glow to them, and red and gold actually went well together.

She looked at Rashe. "How sure are you about the man you saw? You said he was creepy, but can you be more specific?"

Rashe shrugged. "Tall, mean-looking Terran dude with dark hair. Didn't notice what he was wearing, but he wasn't carrying a pulse rifle, if that's what you mean. I would've noticed *that*."

"Well, if he *is* the same man who tried to kill me before, we can't just sit around waiting for him to bump us off."

"What do you suggest we do?" Rashe asked. "Confront the guy or chase him away and hope he doesn't come back?"

"I don't know," Sula replied. "Maybe we could catch him and try to find out who's paying him."

"That works for me," Aidan said. "Not sure how we can do that, though."

"Set a trap with me as the bait?" Sula said this without much conviction. She already felt like a worm on a hook as it was.

"No way," Aidan snapped. "Anything but that."

Rashe rubbed his chin in a contemplative manner. "According to Aidan, you have evidence that suggests there were once intelligent natives of this planet. And you were there when the people on Ecos were wiped out. Plus, you've been targeted. Seems to me the best way to expose that sort of wrongdoing is to go public."

"We need to be very careful about this," Aidan said. "Once the existence of that cave is made public, what's to stop the bad guys from finding it and destroying the artifacts?" A cock of his head suggested a new idea. "It might be interesting to find out if there's any connection between Terra Minor, Rhylos, and Dalb University."

"Sounds like a job for Val," Rashe advised. "What's in the history books might not necessarily be the truth."

"Val?" Sula echoed. "Isn't he the Avian clone?"

Rashe nodded. "Awesome hacker. If you need to dig up dirt on someone, he'll find it."

"Yes, but involving Val would make him the hero of this story," Abuti pointed out. "Thought this was your baby, Sula."

"Does it matter who finds the evidence as long as the perpetrators are exposed?" Sula asked. "We're talking about genocide on a planetary scale. We can't just wait until they announce the discovery of Ecos as another uninhabited world and then tell everyone I've been there and know what happened to the indigenous people."

"We could—although I doubt they'd be calling it Ecos," Aidan said. "They'd at least change the name. We need to be able to pin this on someone specific. Someone in the university hierarchy who's been there for a long time."

"Or some group funding the research," Sula suggested. "Maybe a rich family?"

Aidan sat up straighter. "Now you're talking! Someone with enough wealth to be a donor or investor...someone who would benefit from the sale of a habitable world..."

Rashe snorted with laughter. "Shit, dude. Anyone would benefit from selling an entire planet. Especially if it was sold off in sections the way Terra Minor was."

"Not all of Terra Minor was actually sold," Aidan said. "Since it was designated as the new Zetithian home-world, much of the land has been set aside so that every surviving Zetithian could be guaranteed a place to live."

"Yeah, but there's so few of you, they could afford to be generous," Rashe scoffed. "Even the worst crooks try to put up a good front so they can at least appear to be respectable."

Aidan nodded. "Like the way Rutger Grekkor could hire mercenaries to destroy Zetith, deal in slaves and illegal drugs, and still maintain several legitimate businesses." His eyes burned brighter, like a bonfire that had been sprayed with oil. "Including the pharmaceutical company that manufactures the vaccine for the Scorillian plague."

"And who better to develop a new strain of the disease than the people making the vaccine?" Sula shuddered. "I'd hate to think they only did it so they could sell a newer, more expensive vaccine. However, if what I witnessed on Ecos truly was deliberate, I wouldn't be surprised if that were true."

Aidan's already grim expression hardened even further. "Grekkor may be dead, but he wasn't the only greedy bastard in the galaxy. Makes you wonder who's running that company now, doesn't it?"

Aidan would only have to meet that person to know their future and possibly their guilt. The trick would be getting close enough to do it.

"Then again, if we're right about all of this and both Rhylos and Terra Minor were 'cleansed' in the same manner as Ecos, this conspiracy would have to go back further than Grekkor's involvement. He may have been nothing more than a pawn."

As a man who would never have been born if Grekkor's vendetta against the Zetithians had been more successful, Aidan had no difficulty believing that an even greater evil existed.

"How can we ever hope to stop someone with that much power?" Tough, street-smart kids like Qinta didn't scare easily. For her to sound so horrified made Aidan wish he'd never allowed her to become involved.

"We'll need more help," he said. "But it can be done. All we need to do is find the right person and apply the appropriate pressure."

Qinta still seemed doubtful. "You make it sound so simple."

"The best plans usually are." He looked at Sula. "First of all, we need to get you back on your feet. Then we'll

head for Ursa Prime and see what we can find out there."
He chuckled. "I can't wait to see the look on your professor's face when you come strolling into his office."

Sula shook her head slowly. "I can't believe Professor Dalb would be in on this. It's so out of character."

"He might not know what's really going on," Aidan admitted. "But I'm sure they'll have found a way to keep him quiet. That's the first mystery we have to solve."

Giklor rubbed his hands together once again. "I take it my services will be utilized?"

"Since I can't heal myself overnight like a Zetithian, I don't see that I have much choice." She sighed. "I'm sure I'll get used to the red eyes eventually."

"Excellent!" Giklor hopped from his chair and rounded the table with astonishing speed. "You may feel ill or dizzy for a time, but that will soon pass."

"Yeah, after she's puked her guts out," Abuti said. "What a waste of a perfectly good breakfast."

"She will not lose her breakfast," Giklor said firmly. "None of those I have treated ever have."

"I might be the first." Sula already looked a little green around the gills, but she swiveled around in her chair to face Giklor with remarkable resolve. "Go for it, Giklor."

Although Aidan had never been healed by a Zerkan, he'd seen Giklor in action before, and the ritual was no less fascinating to watch than it had been the first time. As Giklor cupped Sula's cheeks in his palms, she stared blankly ahead as he fixed his gaze on hers. Soon, his own eyes began to change color, first going from red to purple, then blue to aquamarine. His forked, snake-like tongue protruded from his small mouth, growing in length as a ball formed inside it near the base. Sula never flinched as Giklor's tongue slipped through her parted lips. The ball began to slide down the length of his tongue, causing Sula to gag slightly as it continued on down her throat. Seconds later, Giklor's tongue recoiled into his mouth like a spring-loaded tape measure.

"There, now," Giklor said, appearing to be quite pleased with himself. "If you men will carry her to her bed and allow her to rest, she should be fully recovered in a day or two."

Aidan and Rashe both rose from their seats, but Aidan waved him off. "I got this."

Gathering Sula in his arms once more, he carried her unconscious form into her bedroom, where he laid her gently on the bed.

He was about to drop a kiss on her forehead when Abuti spoke from directly behind him. "That was one of the weirdest things I've ever seen." Moving closer, she touched a sucker-tipped finger to Sula's arm as though checking her temperature. "She seems okay. He never said he would knock her out, though. Is that normal?"

Aidan honestly didn't know for sure. His observation of Giklor's previous healings hadn't included the immediate recovery period. "Probably."

"I don't know about Qinta, but you can't get rid of me that easily."

"No one's getting rid of you," Aidan promised. "Not yet, anyway."

Abuti crossed her bony arms over her thin chest. "Sula will still need help until she's fully recovered. I'm staying."

"That's fine."

"I'm staying after that too," the Norludian girl went on. "Qinta and I would be in more danger if we went back to the orphanage now."

Aidan didn't quite follow her logic, but at the moment, he was too befuddled to understand why. "If you say so."

"She'll need me to help her walk, and—wait a second. You're actually saying it's okay for us to stick around?"

"Yeah." He stepped back from the bed, gazing down at Sula as she slept. Would the red eyes be the only change in her when she awoke? Or would she feel differently toward him?

He was almost afraid to learn the answer. He couldn't think about that yet. All he needed to do now was to get everything organized and be ready to go whenever she was able.

Straightening to his full height, he managed to give Abuti a smile. "The thing is, we won't be staying here for very long. What we need now is a fast ship." He searched his memory, trying to recall the most recent news he'd had of his siblings and the various "cousins" he'd grown up with. "I wonder whose is the closest."

Chapter 14

SULA HAD NEVER FELT QUITE SO STRANGE IN HER LIFE. Head spinning, she refrained from opening her eyes, even though she'd heard a variety of voices urging her to do so.

The last thing she remembered was falling under the hypnotic spell of Giklor's glowing red eyes. After that, everything was a blank.

Until now.

Beyond the dizziness, the first thing she noticed was the total absence of pain. While this was undoubtedly a good sign, the accompanying weakness and lassitude were not as welcome, nor was the appalling taste in her mouth.

As she lay there assessing her current status, somewhere in the back of her hazy mind, facts about another side effect of Zerkan healing drifted like a wisp of thought before coming sharply into focus. Her head now clear, she opened her eyes to find herself staring into Aidan's green and gold gaze.

"You didn't kiss me afterward, did you?"

He drew back in surprise at her accusing tone. "Was I supposed to?"

A shake of her head brought the dizziness surging back, with the result that several moments passed before she was able to mumble her reply. "Not unless you want to be bonded to me for life."

His own response wasn't nearly as long in coming. "I'm okay with that. Cat and Jack were bonded by a Zerkan."

"Cat and Jack?"

"They're sort of like my aunt and uncle, although not actual blood relatives. My family and theirs lived on the same starship. Cat is Zetithian, and Jack is a Terran trader who bought Cat in a slave auction years ago."

She managed a wry smile. "Sounds like an interesting story."

"It is, and if you ever meet Jack, I'm sure she'll tell you all about it. But right now, I'm guessing you'd like something to drink." He nodded toward a glass of fruit juice sitting on the nightstand. "Giklor said you'd have a nasty taste in your mouth when you woke up."

"Nasty doesn't even begin to describe how horrible it is." When she tried to sit up, she discovered her limbs were even less cooperative than she'd expected.

Without prompting, Aidan helped her to sit up and stuffed an extra pillow behind her.

"Sorry to be so helpless," she said.

"No worries. Giklor assured me that you'd be back to your old self in a day or two." He held the glass to her lips. "Meanwhile, he said for you to drink plenty of fluids and eat foods high in protein and calcium."

She took a long sip of the juice, savoring the sweet nectar as it soothed her mouth and throat. "Sounds like good advice for healing broken bones." As if on cue, her stomach let out a snarl. "How long was I out?"

"About a day and a half," he replied. "You woke up just in time for dinner."

Abuti came riding in on the hoverchair. "I thought I heard voices. Need a lift to the dining room?"

Sula giggled. "Sure. I'm guessing I probably shouldn't try to walk right away." She tossed back the covers, noting that the bamboo-and-bullwhip splint had been replaced with a clear polymer cast. "Did he say when—"

"All will be healed by tomorrow!" Giklor announced as he entered the room. "However, since we have access to a medscanner, I recommend a scan to ensure the break is fully healed before the cast is removed."

"Sounds reasonable," Sula said. "So…how red are my eyes?"

"Barely noticeable in daylight," Giklor said gaily. "Your night vision will be greatly improved by the treatment." He wheezed with laughter. "Yet another happy side effect."

She glanced at Aidan as she nodded toward Giklor. "Is he always this chipper?"

"He does seem more cheerful than usual," Aidan admitted after surveying his Zerkan friend. "Hasn't stopped smiling yet."

"Healing gives me such joy!" Giklor said. "Simply to abide beneath the same roof with one whom I have healed is a gift beyond price."

A quizzical look at Aidan yielded a barely perceptible nod. "A few more guests and we'll have a full house."

Abuti parked the hoverchair beside the bed. "Qinta and I have been practicing the stand-and-pivot transfer to the chair. It works pretty well. That is, if you're able to stand on one foot."

"I'm a little weak, but we can try it."

With Aidan's assistance, she was able to sit on the side of the bed and then stand without any difficulty.

Pivoting and sitting down was even easier. "No sweat," she said. "How does this thing work?"

After Abuti gave her a quick rundown of the controls, Sula zoomed out into the hallway and headed for the dining room. "This thing is a lot faster than I am, even on a good day," she remarked as the others followed in her wake.

Abuti took a seat at the table. "Yeah. We've been keeping ourselves entertained with it. Qinta can beat its top speed on foot, but not by much."

"We were hoping you'd be up by now," Qinta said as she brought in another place setting. "I was starting to get worried."

"There was never any need for concern," Giklor insisted. "As you can see, her recovery is nearly complete."

"I'll believe that when I see her walk," Abuti said.

Sula glanced around the table. "I take it Rashe went home?"

Abuti began scooping a generous portion of fettuccini onto her plate. "Yeah, he had other stuff to do." With a scathing glance at the Zerkan, she added, "Giklor obviously didn't."

Her blatant animosity toward Giklor was a little surprising, although without a patient to care for, the two girls would be back at the orphanage soon. Sula hadn't seen the orphanage, but she doubted it was large enough for each of the girls to have her own room. Aidan's house probably seemed like a luxury hotel to them. Sula felt that way herself.

"I will also be accompanying you on your journey to Ursa Prime," Giklor said. "On such adventures, a healer is a necessary part of the team."

"Aidan is a pretty good medic himself," Abuti said. "I don't think we'll need you."

Sula hid her smile. She wasn't entirely sure Abuti was needed, either.

"Ah, but what would happen if *he* were to be seriously injured?" Giklor countered. "You would certainly need me then."

"Good point," Aidan said. "Although I have no intention of becoming injured, we need to prepare for every possibility."

"Have you found a ship yet?" Sula asked.

Aidan nodded. "Curly's on the way. Should be here later tonight. He's the youngest of Cat and Jack's first litter—a little on the cocky side, and about as mouthy as his mother. Fantastic pilot too."

"I take it he has a fast ship?"

"Absolutely. Trust me, he wouldn't have it any other way. In fact, he insists that his ship is faster than the *Jolly Roger*. Of course, Jack disagrees"—he chuckled as he passed the pasta sauce to Abuti—"rather vehemently."

"I'm surprised they haven't held a race to prove it."

"That would be too easy," Aidan said. "Especially since their conversation consists primarily of recounting their various exploits. If they ever established which ship was faster, they'd have nothing to say to one another."

While this was probably an exaggeration, never having met Jack or her son, Sula could only trust Aidan's judgment.

"Handsome devil too," Abuti said. "Not as gorgeous as Aidan, but then, so few men are."

"Better not let him hear you say that," Aidan warned. "I'd never hear the end of it."

Abuti shrugged her bony shoulders. "Beauty is in the eye of the beholder, you know. I happen to prefer blonds."

Heretofore, Sula's preference had been for dark-haired men, although Aidan was enough to make her reconsider. He was not only blond, he was from another planet.

Never thought I'd find an alien man attractive.

Although if anyone were going to make her do that, she probably could've guessed it would be a Zetithian. She'd been as intrigued by their photographs as any of her fellow students. She'd just never seen one that was blond. "Say, does that Cat fellow have black hair and a scar on his cheek?"

Aidan nodded his somewhat puzzled reply.

"There was a picture of him in one of my textbooks," Sula explained. "We all used to drool over him."

Aidan's heart skipped a few beats on its way to his feet. "Curly looks a lot like him—minus the scar."

If Sula noticed his dismay, it didn't show. "I'd love to meet Cat someday," she said. "Although none of my classmates would ever believe me. Of course, that's assuming I'll live long enough to tell anyone about it."

Qinta held up her hand, spreading her fingers into a V between her second and third fingers. "You will live long and prosper."

Aidan rolled his eyes. "You've been watching old *Star Trek* episodes again, haven't you?"

"Yep." Qinta stared at him for a moment. "Did anyone ever tell you Zetithian dudes how much you look like Vulcans?"

"Only the ears and the eyebrows," Aidan said wearily.

"We certainly aren't as emotionless as Vulcans—or as logical. Plus, they don't have fangs or curly hair. Can't purr, either." Deeming it inappropriate in present company, he stopped before mentioning the *snard*.

Sula shook her head with apparent bewilderment. "I have absolutely no idea what you're talking about."

Aidan patted her shoulder. "Don't worry. No one else would understand unless they'd been around someone who'd grown up with Jack. She's always pushing to revive Old Earth culture. No one else seems very interested."

"Some of those old recipes are really good, though," Abuti said. "This puttanesca sauce is one of them." She stuffed a forkful of pasta into her mouth. "Thanks for making it, Aidan."

"You're welcome," he said. "Don't talk with your mouth full."

Abuti gave him a cheeky, fettuccini-laced grin. "Figured you'd get around to saying that eventually."

"You don't want Sula to think you've been raised in a slipshod orphanage, do you?"

"No. But to be fair, I haven't lived there my whole life. None of us have."

"True," he acknowledged. "There's a definite advantage to starting young."

"I wish I *had* lived there all my life," Qinta said solemnly. "Nobody ever gave a damn about me until I decided to go there. I had plenty of freedom while living on the street, but being on your own isn't everything it's cracked up to be."

Aidan had always suspected Qinta of being a runaway. To his knowledge, no one had ever questioned her origins, but they hadn't needed to. That she'd been abused was obvious to anyone who knew the signs. Although she'd improved during her time at the orphanage, while she seemed cheerful enough when spoken to, left to herself, her expression tended to grow pensive and, occasionally, angry. "We're very glad you came, and I'm grateful for your help with Sula's care."

To his surprise, the Treslanti girl actually blushed. "Don't be. I owe you and the other adults at the orphanage a debt I can never repay."

"Your continued health, safety, and happiness are all that's required." He glanced at Abuti. "And the same goes for you."

"Safety, huh?" Abuti said brusquely. "Does that mean you've already changed your mind about taking us with you?"

"No," he replied. "You were right about that. Leaving you here to be captured and possibly tortured by that assassin fellow isn't part of the deal. I just hope Curly has enough room for us on his ship. Otherwise, we may have to double up."

Abuti snickered. "I'll bunk with Qinta. That way, you and Sula can room together."

Aidan barely had time to register the surge of joy the prospect of sleeping with Sula gave him before Giklor lodged a protest. "What about me?" he demanded. "Don't I get a roommate?"

"Nope," Abuti said firmly. "Nobody wants to wake up with your creepy tongue down their throat. You can sleep on the couch."

"I never treat anyone against their will," Giklor said with an indignant tilt of his chin. "That would be unethical."

Abuti flicked her fingers in dismissal. "I'm still not sleeping in the same room with you, and I wouldn't wish it on anyone else."

"You don't care for Zerkans, do you, Abuti?" Giklor said sadly. "What a pity when we are such a useful, caring species."

"So are Norludians, but nobody likes us, either," Abuti shot back. "We have to have *someone* to dislike."

"Or we can each decide to treat others the way we would want to be treated," Aidan said. "Without bias or hatred or any preconceived notions."

"Tell that to the kids who pick on me," Abuti grumbled.

"Tolerance has to start somewhere," Aidan reminded her. "Let it begin with you."

Sula gazed at Aidan with increasing respect. He would make such a wonderful father. Funny how she'd never considered that when evaluating a man before—unless it was to judge the family life of a species she happened to be studying. She'd certainly never looked for that quality in any sexual partner—at least not intentionally. Come to think of it, that was another of the reasons her classmates had been so desirous of finding a Zetithian husband. Not only was their sexual prowess unsurpassed by the males of any other species, theirs had never been anything but an egalitarian society. Even on Earth, the taint left by patriarchal societies hadn't disappeared completely. Case in point, her parents' expressed desire to choose a husband for her. No doubt they would have approved of Raj, but Aidan? Probably not.

Still, her parents weren't omniscient, nor could either of them live her life for her. Aside from the physical impossibility, she simply wouldn't allow it. She'd come too far and seen too much to let anyone do that.

For now, however, she was content to let the conversation play out around her. Aidan chatted easily with the two girls, which prompted Giklor to voice his own restrictive notions regarding child-rearing. Sula's knowledge of Zerkans was negligible, mainly because so little was actually known about them. Having met Giklor, she doubted anyone would be capable of discovering very much, even if they tried. He seemed to enjoy being the sort of enigmatic alien common in old science fiction stories. Perhaps the entire species felt the same way, because if anyone had ever done any research into Zerkan healing fluids, they hadn't bothered to publish their findings.

"I'll never understand the workings of the human mind."

Sula glared at Abuti, who appeared to be the one who'd spoken. "What did you say?"

"You heard me," Abuti replied. "You're sitting there staring off into space while we're discussing the fate of the universe."

"The fate of the universe?" Sula echoed. "Oh, you are not."

"No? Then what *were* we talking about?"

"I have absolutely no idea."

"Stop it, Abuti," Aidan warned.

Abuti waved her hands in protest. "I'm not doing anything."

"I'm so tired. Can't cope…" Sula stared at her hands, which were quivering in a rather alarming manner.

When she shook her head and looked again, her eyes felt scratchy and dry, but her hands at least *appeared* to be normal. The way they felt was another story altogether. "What have you done to me? My fingers are numb, and all I want to do is sleep."

Aidan's face swam before her own. "What *did* you do to her, Giklor?"

"Nothing out of the ordinary," the Zerkan said firmly. "She should be fine now."

"Fine, hell," Aidan exclaimed. "She looks like a damned ghost—or at least like she's seen one." He tilted his head to one side and peered at her with his glowing, catlike eyes. As she watched him, his head seemed to change shape, becoming elongated and oversized, much like the people depicted in the cave drawings.

"There *is* something wrong with me," Sula whispered. "I think I'm—"

Asleep.

She awoke with a jolt that nearly gave her whiplash. "Sorry. Must've dozed off for a second."

"You were asleep a lot longer than that," Abuti declared. "The doorbell just rang. I'm guessing that'll be Curly."

Chapter 15

CURLY TSHEVNOE HAD ALWAYS BEEN COOL. BUT DURING the time since Aidan had last seen him, he'd somehow managed to up the coolness factor.

Exponentially.

Even as a kid, there'd been something of the swashbuckler about him. Now in his late twenties, he looked more like a pirate than ever. Tall and lean like most Zetithian men, he had his father's jet-black hair and obsidian eyes, but his personality was all Jack—right down to the pulse pistol strapped to his thigh. He stood on Aidan's back doorstep with his feet shoulder-width apart and his arms folded over a broad chest. His waist-length curls were braided back from the left side of his face—a style he'd adopted in his youth to prevent his hair from interfering with his piloting skills or his left-handed aim—leaving one pointed ear fully exposed. Clad in black leather from his jacket to his boots, one look at him had Aidan wishing he and Sula were already mated.

On top of that, if she'd needed someone to back her up in this adventure, Curly was far better equipped to help her. Not only was he an excellent shot, he had his own ship. Then again, Curly couldn't fly, control the wind, or predict the future.

We each have our own strengths.

Still, when he shook Curly's hand in greeting, he glimpsed a fate that, if he'd read it correctly, reassured him greatly. The love of Curly's life wasn't going to be Sula.

For the first time in recent memory, a reading hadn't filled him with dread or despair. This also marked one of the few times he'd been able to read the fortune of someone he'd known from childhood. He'd picked up a few things when they were kids—minor setbacks and the occasional schoolboy triumph—but nothing to suggest anyone's more distant future. Perhaps a separation period was all that was needed to enhance that ability. Or perhaps they'd both simply needed to grow up.

"Hey, Curly. Thanks for getting here so quickly."

Curly shrugged. "No sweat. Speed is my middle name, remember?"

Aidan couldn't help but smile. "How could I possibly forget?" Fortunately, if hearsay was to be believed, Curly wasn't too fast to satisfy the ladies. Rumor had it that he'd left more than a few broken hearts scattered throughout the cosmos, although Aidan suspected his lifestyle was more to blame for that than anything. Finding a mate who was willing to spend her life in space wasn't always easy, even for a Zetithian. Even giving a woman a sample of *snard* didn't always guarantee success, and there were several species that weren't affected by it at all.

Aidan waved him inside. "Still going it alone?"

"Nope," Curly replied. "I finally hired a navigator. He's also a damn good pilot. I have to sleep sometime. Dunno how Mom did it by herself for so long."

"Relied on the autopilot a lot, I guess," Aidan suggested.

"Probably so." Curly arched a brow as he glanced around the kitchen. "You said there would be other passengers?"

Aidan was a little surprised no one had followed him to the door. A giggle from a nearby corner made him realize that at least one of them had. "Come on, Qinta. Enough with the disappearing act."

"Aw, you're no fun at all," Qinta complained as she slowly reappeared. She took a moment to sweep Curly with an assessing gaze. "I'm guessing *he'd* be a good sport, though."

"Not always," Aidan said, recalling a few of their childhood rivalries. "Curly, I'd like you to meet Qinta, who will be one of your passengers. As you can see, Qinta is Treslanti."

Curly nodded and extended a hand. "Nice to meet you, Qinta."

Qinta wasted no time in responding with a vigorous handshake. "Pleased to meet you too. We've heard a lot about you at the orphanage."

Curly's narrow-eyed gaze was no less assessing than hers had been. "You must be one of the newer inmates. I don't believe we've met, and I certainly would've remembered you if we had. With that hair, you look just like Natasha, Warrior Queen of the Varbains."

Qinta stared at Curly in frank disbelief. "You play video games?"

"All the time," he replied. "Space travel can be super boring. Gotta have something to do."

Qinta still didn't seem convinced. "Are you any good?"

"Haven't lost a match yet," Curly said with a defiant lift of his chin.

"Oh, come on now," Aidan chided. "Your brother Moe has beaten you a dozen times or more."

"That's only because he can move his fingers almost

as fast as those orange toad people on Barada Seven," Curly insisted. "I'm better at strategy."

With a conspiratorial glance at Aidan, Qinta giggled. "He *is* kinda full of himself, isn't he?"

"A bit," Aidan agreed. "But he grows on you after a while." Motioning for Curly to follow, he headed into the dining room. "Come on in and meet the rest of the gang. We've been hashing out plans all evening."

———

If Sula had once suspected Aidan of being an angel, his friend Curly could've passed for the devil—as in devilishly tempting and dangerously handsome. He had an air of recklessness about him that was as exciting as it was frightening. Although to be honest, most Zetithians did look a tad scary. With their fangs and glowing eyes, anyone on the receiving end of their ire would certainly be shaking in their shoes.

Curly, however, seemed perfectly friendly as the introductions were made. Even so, she shuddered to think how he would appear to someone staring at him over the business end of his pistol.

"It'll be interesting to hear your opinion of our plans," Abuti said as she shook hands with Curly. "They seem too cautious to me."

"Do you have a problem with bringing everyone back alive?" Aidan asked.

"No," the Norludian girl replied. "But this sounds like a good way to fall into a trap. We can't just walk in and start accusing people of genocide."

Curly's nonplussed expression was priceless. "Genocide?"

Aidan nodded. "Seems someone's been using biological weapons to conquer planets without firing a single shot."

"Sounds illegal *and* immoral."

"That's putting it mildly," Sula said. "Although I'm still not sure who'll take responsibility for arresting the culprits. It isn't as though there's a galaxy-wide ruling body."

Sula had never been a student of politics before. However, this particular crime highlighted the need for some sort of galactic police force and judicial system. Most planets only prosecuted those who committed crimes on their own world. Crimes in space and on uninhabited planets tended to go unpunished. A few worlds had extradition treaties with others, but those were in the minority.

Qinta eyed Curly with concern. "No one saw you come in here, did they?"

"Not that I'm aware of," Curly replied. "I can see in the dark without any trouble. But I can't see through walls." He glanced at each of them in turn. "So...are you ready to go?"

"Right *now*?" Sula gasped.

"Sure." Curly helped himself to the one remaining crust of garlic bread and took a bite. "Even if you haven't plotted your strategy, there'll be plenty of time for that while we're in space. Ursa Prime isn't exactly nearby, you know."

Abuti giggled. "We can leave whenever you like. It's not like we have much to pack."

She was right about that much. Sula had little more than the clothes she'd been wearing when Aidan found her. Qinta had two outfits that Sula knew of, and Abuti and Giklor didn't wear anything at all. Of the five of them, Aidan probably had more to pack than anyone.

"Might want to bring along a few herbs and spices," Curly said to Aidan. "Jetoc and I don't do much in the way of cooking." He finished off the last bit of bread before adding, "Nothing as good as this, anyway."

"Jetoc?" Aidan echoed. "I take it that's your navigator?"

"Yeah. Totally worthless in the kitchen unless he's frying sausages."

Aidan groaned. "Don't tell me you hired a Drell."

Curly huffed out a breath. "I know it sounds crazy. I found it hard to believe myself. But he's certified on more navigation systems than Moe, and he's gotten us out of several tight spots. Of course, he was the one who got us into those tight spots in the first place, but—"

"What is it you do with your ship?" Sula asked, the mention of "tight spots" prompting her to interrupt.

"Fastest package delivery in the quadrant," Curly said with more than a touch of pride. "The most expensive too." With a wicked grin, he added, "But I'm worth it."

Sula was still a little puzzled. "What sort of tight spots?"

"Not everyone thinks those packages should be delivered," Curly explained. "At least not to the intended recipients."

"You mean you get attacked by thieves or space pirates?"

"Not often and never successfully. Most of them have learned to avoid us—the hard way. But every now and then, some crook gets wind of a particularly valuable cargo and tries to intercept us, which is why we're perfect for this job. If anyone tries to cut you off at the pass, I've got a fast ship and some really big guns. No worries. I'll get you to Ursa Prime on time and intact. Although if things get dicey, we may need an extra man on the weapons console." He looked at Aidan. "Jetoc is a decent gunner but not as good as you were back in the day. Think you still have that pinpoint accuracy?"

Aidan grimaced. "Let's just say I'm a little out of practice."

Seeming to take note of Sula's curious expression, Curly went on, "When he was younger, he could take out the weaponry or the stardrive on an enemy ship with very little collateral damage." He shrugged. "Mom always figured it had something to do with his Mordrial blood, but he swore there was nothing more to it than a good grasp of angles and trajectories." He aimed a searching glance at Aidan. "Which was even weirder, considering you were, what, ten or eleven the last time you fired a pulse cannon?"

Aidan cleared his throat in a rather self-conscious manner. "I was nine, actually. One of the last Nedwut ships to ever fire on us."

Curly nodded. "Crippled their stardrive and left them floating. My brother Larry sent them a com updating them on the defunct status of the bounty on Zetithians and then boosted their distress call." With a snort, he added, "He always was an old softie, even as a kid. Not that I hold it against him."

Sula was fairly certain that Jack was right: Aidan's Mordrial blood was *directly* responsible for that ability. However, he obviously had never admitted it to Curly or anyone else he'd grown up with. Would he admit to it now? Or did he know things about their futures he didn't wish to divulge?

Still, after an extended period of time spent aboard the same ship with their current cohorts, Sula had a sneaking suspicion that someone—her money was on Abuti— would let the truth slip eventually. With that in mind, she would advise him to come clean at his earliest opportunity, although she hoped he would do it without any prompting.

"Well then," Giklor said heartily. "Since we appear to have a capable escort, may I suggest we prepare to depart?"

—⁓—

Unfortunately, Aidan couldn't think of any reason *not* to leave right away.

So much for six quiet weeks at home with Sula.

"Sounds good," he said. "Let me throw together a few things, and we can get out of here. How long will it take to get to Ursa Prime?"

"Three weeks if we're lucky," Curly replied. "Jetoc was still plotting the course when I left. Should be ready by the time we get to the spaceport."

Rashe had come and gone with no trouble, but getting Sula out could be a problem. He studied her for a long moment. "You'll need a disguise."

Qinta nodded. "A *convincing* disguise."

Sula frowned. "What, a hooded cloak won't do it?"

"Maybe," Qinta said. "I was thinking more along the lines of making you invisible. I should be able to extend my projection to include you. Never tried it before, but I believe it's possible."

"Too bad we can't make you look like a Zetithian." Folding her arms, Abuti leaned back in her chair as she gazed at Sula. "That would really throw them off."

"That's assuming anyone will actually be watching us leave," Sula pointed out.

The drumming of Abuti's fingertips on her upper arms sounded like popcorn tossed into an open fire. "You think they won't?"

"Probably so," Sula admitted. With a glance at Aidan, she added, "Although you carried me in here without any disguise."

"You were essentially disguised even then," Aidan reminded her. "In that Indiana Jones getup, your own mother might not have recognized you."

"Yes, but your assassin fellow has undoubtedly seen that disguise—*and* seen through it," Giklor said. "Something completely different is needed. Either that or a diversion."

"I could take her in my speeder," Curly said. "They're looking for a woman with dark hair and eyes. All we'd have to do is make you over into a man with similar coloring. Or I could just stash you in the cargo compartment."

"I was dressed more like a man than a woman when Aidan found me." She paused, gaping at Curly. The cargo compartment idea was bad enough, but—"You're talking about cutting my hair, aren't you?"

"Seems the most reasonable choice, doesn't it?"

"No, it isn't," Aidan said firmly. "You are *not* going to cut her hair or stuff her into the cargo compartment. We'll think of something else."

"Actually, I think Abuti had the right idea," Qinta said. She turned toward Sula. "Your eyes already have glowing red pupils. We just need to make your eyebrows look slanted and curl your hair."

Sula appeared to give this some thought, then asked, "What about my ears?"

The Treslanti girl shrugged. "Your hair will cover them."

"You know, that might actually work," Aidan said slowly. "My housekeeping droid has lots of features I've never used."

"You mean it can do hair and makeup?" Sula asked.

Aidan nodded. "Those droids can do damn near anything. A makeover shouldn't be any problem. Jeeves might even be able to make your ears look pointy."

"Jeeves?" she echoed.

"The name was Jack's idea of a joke," Aidan said with a roll of his eyes. "Said he was like a gentleman's gentleman or some such thing."

Curly chuckled. "I remember that. She wanted to program him to speak with an English accent instead of communicating with beeps. And you told her to—"

"Never mind that," Aidan said hastily. "What about it, Sula? Want Jeeves to turn you into a Zetithian?"

"Sounds like an excellent idea," she said. "Let's do it!"

———

Aidan activated Jeeves and outlined the plan. Jeeves replied with a beep and proceeded to go to work on Sula. Almost afraid to watch, Aidan went off to make his own preparations.

He hadn't been on any extended trips in some time. But he'd spent most of his life aboard a starship. Knowing what to take and what to leave behind came naturally, although he couldn't recall his mother ever asking him to bring any herbs and spices aboard the

Jolly Roger. She'd always seen to that sort of cargo herself. He'd never flown with Curly before, either.

This should be interesting.

At least Sula hadn't seemed too taken with the dashing pilot, especially after he'd suggested a haircut.

He was zipping up his duffel bag when Sula came floating in on the hoverchair wearing a yellow tunic with matching trousers.

"This is so cool! I look like a real Zetithian! Jeeves fixed my hair and made me these clothes. He even made these for me." She held up a pair of jeweled sandals. "Of course I'll have to wait until I get this cast off to wear them, and the style is more Indian than Zetithian, but aren't they pretty?"

Her transformation was so complete, for a long moment, all he could do was stare. Her hair now fell in long spiral curls, and her eyebrows had somehow been given an upward slant. Her skin tone was lighter, and she even had fangs and pointed ears. The only thing Jeeves hadn't done was to reshape her round pupils into vertical slits.

"Very pretty," he said when he finally recovered his voice. "I keep forgetting Jeeves can do stuff like that. Never needed anything like it before. Wish I'd thought of it sooner. But you know how it is." *Stop babbling.* "You make a beautiful Zetithian, Sula. Although I believe I prefer the original version."

"Thank you," she said in a shy whisper.

He took a step back, studying her with a critical eye. "You know...from a distance, you could easily be mistaken for Onca's wife, Kim."

"You really think so?" Sula's glowing red eyes

were wide with excitement as she swept her hair behind her ears.

"Absolutely. As far as your would-be assassin knows, I might already have a Zetithian wife. You look very convincing." Persuading any onlookers that he was in love with Sula wouldn't require much acting at all. In fact, a stellar performance was practically guaranteed.

"I sure hope so," she said. "Qinta volunteered to act as a decoy. Wait 'til you see her. Jeeves made her up to look like me. We could almost be sisters. Curly was a little freaked out when he saw her. He said she looked great, but he really missed the warrior queen look." With a sly smile, she added, "We didn't tell him it was a wig."

Chapter 16

"Sula, Abuti, and I will head over to the orphanage in my speeder. Curly can take Giklor and Qinta and go straight to the spaceport." Given the possibility of being tailed and fired upon, Aidan thought the Zerkan might be of more use with the decoy.

"Good plan," Curly said. "Although I have no intention of being that easy to follow."

"I didn't think you would," Aidan said with a grin. "Feel free to throw in as many twists and turns as you like." He might not have flown on Curly's personal ship, but he'd been subjected to some wild rides with Curly at the *Jolly Roger*'s helm. If anyone could lose a tail, it was Curly.

Curly nodded. "My speeder is armored and can be cloaked, but I won't engage the cloak unless absolutely necessary."

"What do you consider an absolute necessity?" Even Qinta seemed a little nervous. Aidan didn't doubt Curly's ability to keep her safe, but she *had* volunteered for the most dangerous role in the scheme.

"I'll only use it if evasive maneuvers don't work," Curly replied. "We don't want that dude to track us to the spaceport. Plus, I can shoot back if needed." He turned toward Sula. "Are you sure there's only one guy?"

"That's all I saw in Damenk," Sula replied. "Although with so much going on, I might've missed an accomplice."

"He probably didn't have one," Giklor said. "Assassins tend to work alone."

"And how would you know that?" Aidan demanded.

The Zerkan gave him a wide, red-eyed stare. "Isn't that common knowledge?"

Aidan shouldered his duffel bag. "No, it probably isn't. Let's just hope you're right."

"This guy is probably pissed from having missed you before, Sula," Curly mused. "He might take your continued existence personally and be harder to discourage."

Abuti waved her skinny arms. "Hold on. Do assassins get paid up front, or only when the job is done?"

Curly arched a brow. "Hmm…I believe you'd have to at least make a down payment. Expensive equipment, you know. That, and they have to be able to travel."

The constant barrage of questions was beginning to grate on Aidan's nerves. "I'm not sure that's relevant right now, unless you're willing to capture the assassin and offer him more money to leave us alone."

"The idea has merit," Giklor said. "May I suggest—?"

"Not now," Aidan growled, herding the group toward the door. "It's dark outside, and at least for the moment, the coast appears to be clear. Let's do this."

It was dark inside as well. In an attempt to confuse anyone keeping the house under surveillance, they'd each gone to their respective rooms, pretended to go to bed, and then turned out the lights. The subsequent rendezvous in the dark near the back door wasn't as chaotic as it might have been had some of their number not possessed excellent night vision, but it was still fraught with anxiety, as evidenced by Sula's icy fingers when she grasped his hand.

"What if someone has put a tracking beacon on the speeders?" she asked.

"Not possible," Curly said before Aidan could reply. "Aidan's speeder is locked in the garage, and mine has an antispyware feature."

"Just checking," she muttered.

"Meet you all at docking bay ninety-four," Curly said. "Stay safe."

They left the house without a sound and climbed into their assigned vehicles. On Aidan's signal, the two speeders took off toward the street and then turned in opposite directions.

Moments later, the comlink on Aidan's control panel lit up. "Looks like our friend took the bait," Curly reported. "Anyplace you'd like me to lead him?"

"The nearest police station would be a nice touch, but that would only slow you down. Shake him if you can, and meet us at the spaceport."

"Will do," Curly said. "See you soon. Jetoc will be ready for you if I'm not there yet."

Aidan banked the speeder around a wide turn and onto a crowded thoroughfare. "The scan shouldn't take more than a few minutes. We'll be there as quick as we can."

Sula gripped his arm in a further display of concern. "What if the scan shows something…bad?"

"We'll have a better idea of what we're dealing with, but we'll keep on going no matter what. We can get rid of your cast after we take off."

A few minutes later, Abuti spoke up from the rear seat. "Um, Aidan…I think—"

"I see it," he said grimly.

"What's the matter?" Sula asked.

"We've picked up a tail."

Sula glanced over her shoulder. "How can you tell?"

"Nobody follows a speeder that closely." He swung the speeder sharply to the left, and the lights behind them duplicated their move. "See?"

"Oh no," she said with a groan. "What do we do now?"

"That's a very good question, because, unlike Curly's speeder, mine doesn't have armor, guns, or a cloaking device."

"Maybe not," Sula conceded. "But it does have a pilot who can tell the future and control the wind. Surely, there's something you can do."

"Maybe. I've never tried this in traffic before." Curly's reminder of his targeting ability brought back a skill Aidan hadn't used in some time. Focusing on the vehicles ahead, he sent his consciousness five seconds into the future, enabling him to anticipate their moves in real time. As other speeders changed positions, he veered into an open gap on the right, then decelerated sharply in the split second before the tail could follow suit.

"Nice move!" Abuti yelled. "See if you can stay behind him. Maybe we can figure out who he is."

The best Aidan could tell, there was nothing special about the speeder—at least nothing to indicate who might be piloting it. There weren't even any erratic moves to suggest he might be rattled by Aidan's evasive ploy. "At a guess, I'd say it was a rental, but that's about all I can see."

"Try pulling alongside and giving him a bump," Abuti suggested.

"Run him off the road, you mean? I can do that. Don't have to resort to bumping, though." Aidan accelerated until the nose of his speeder drew even with the thruster manifold of the other vehicle. After retracting the canopy slightly, he waved a hand. The ensuing gust of wind caused the rival speeder to swerve, nearly flipping it over.

"Aidan…" Sula began. "What about using the wind to lift us up like you do when you fly?"

Since speeders only hovered between one and two meters off the ground, flying any higher was something even the most well-equipped adversary couldn't do. "Even better," he said as he closed the canopy. "Unless he sees us do it, he won't have any idea where we've gone."

Sula grinned. "Almost like having a cloaking device."

"I dunno," Abuti said. "He's kinda busy at the moment. I don't think he'll notice what we do."

Abuti was right. In a desperate attempt to reenter the flow of traffic, their opponent's speeder had rammed another vehicle.

"Oh, you have *got* to be kidding me," Aidan said as blue lights began flashing and a siren began to wail. "He actually hit a police speeder."

Sula laughed. "You know, somehow, I don't think that was a coincidence."

"Yeah, well, let's hope Curly is as successful at getting rid of the guy chasing him."

"You mean you aren't going to make us fly up in the air?" Abuti sounded downright disappointed.

"To be honest, I've never tried that before," Aidan admitted. "Wouldn't you rather I practice it a few times without you and Sula as passengers?"

"Oh hell no," Abuti declared. "Where's the fun in that?"

"Hold that thought," he said. "The next time, we might not be so lucky."

———

Placing a hand on Aidan's knee, Sula leaned closer to him, grateful for having teamed up with a man whose luck was so uncannily good. Never in a million years would that scene have played out the way it did if Aidan hadn't been the one by her side.

I might actually live through this mess after all.

Sula had held plenty of doubts concerning her continued survival during the previous months. One by one, Aidan was putting them each to rest. However, she saw no need for complacency—or unnecessary risks. "We can try it another time, Abuti. Keep an eye out for anyone else who might be following us."

"No problem." Turning around, Abuti crouched in the seat, sticking her sucker-tipped fingers on the canopy to brace herself against any sudden moves as she aimed her bulbous eyes toward the rear.

"We'll have to be careful going in and out of the orphanage," Aidan said. "I can fly the speeder in through the rear entrance, but anyone observing my house might've followed Rashe here and be waiting for us."

"I hadn't thought of that." A chill crept up Sula's spine as they zoomed through the city. The way things were shaping up, she wouldn't have been surprised to see armed assassins lurking on every street corner.

And only a moment ago, I was feeling so lucky.

"It's unlikely," he went on. "We just need to be prepared."

Silence fell within the speeder. Sula knew the importance of her mission, but the thought of endangering so many others filled her with dread. "How much farther?"

she asked, wishing her tremulous voice hadn't expressed her fears quite so clearly.

"Should be there in another five minutes or so."

She nodded as she resumed her visual scan of the area. So many people were out and about—every species she'd studied along with some she didn't recognize—and any of them could've been the enemy. She felt as if their tiny band stood completely alone against the rest of the galaxy.

"We'll avoid any stray pheromones in the area by flying straight into the garage," Aidan said after a bit. "But some of them could get sucked in along with us." After clearing his throat, he lowered his voice slightly. "You might want to be ready."

Without waiting for her to comment, Aidan tapped the comlink pad. Following a brief conversation with Onca apprising him of their ETA, Sula was once again left alone with her thoughts.

She'd forgotten about the sex pheromones, and with the cast still on her leg, she would need Aidan's help getting out of the speeder. Being that close to him while the very air she breathed filled her with sexual desire could have significant consequences. In reality, *he* was the one who needed to be prepared. To anyone else, her raging desire might go unnoticed. Aidan, on the other hand, would undoubtedly get a woody he would never forget.

If he doesn't have one already.

She was frightened, yes, but being cooped up in a speeder with Aidan was having the inevitable effect. The man was irresistible. Add a few chemical stimulants to her reproductive organs, and she would be crawling all over him.

How embarrassing…

Especially with Abuti in the backseat.

Whether the visual cues were getting to her or some of the pheromone-laced air was seeping in through the air ducts, she wasn't sure. But her tingling nipples and aching core were telling a tale that Aidan's olfactory sense would soon detect. She couldn't help it. The next mental image was Aidan in a state of complete undress and arousal. She squeezed her eyes shut.

Unfortunately, closing her eyes only made the image of his penis clearer than ever—thick and long with a ruffled head dripping the orgasmic coronal fluid for which Zetithians were so renowned. Her pelvis tilted upward similar to the way it would to capture the full effect of his penetration.

Oh my God…

Panting with need, she didn't dare open her eyes or even turn her head in his direction. One good, long whiff of his delightful scent would surely be her downfall.

Aidan whipped the speeder around the next corner and threaded his way through the predominantly female foot traffic. "Don't worry. We'll be there in a few seconds."

Moments later, he brought the speeder to a halt inside the rear entrance of a nearby building. As the door closed, shutting them off from the outside world, Aidan released the canopy and hopped out of the speeder.

Her heart took a plunge as the thought that he was trying to avoid her scent took shape in her mind.

She only held the thought for an instant as he sprinted around to the passenger side. When he stooped to lift her from the speeder, Sula's response was automatic.

Flinging her arms around his neck, she kissed him squarely on the lips as he hoisted her into his arms.

With a loud, unmistakable purr, he returned her kiss with unabashed enthusiasm. Seconds later, he tore his lips from hers. "Bite my neck."

Sula didn't think twice, taking full advantage of the invitation as he tilted his head to one side. Too late, she remembered that Jeeves had actually given her fangs. The unexpected flavor of his blood on her tongue caught her as much by surprise as his explosive growl.

"I'm so sorry!" she gasped. "I had no idea—"

"Don't be." His voice was a hoarse, purring whisper. "Do it again."

Sula never got the chance as an urgent voice shouted, "Get inside, quick. Our surveillance cameras have spotted some suspicious characters hanging around the area."

Lost in the grip of a near orgasm, Sula's sex-clouded brain barely registered that the voice she heard was female.

"Wow!" the woman exclaimed. "Jeeves did one helluva job on her disguise. She looks just like me. Darker hair and probably a little taller, but—"

"Sula, as you may already have guessed, this is Kim." Aidan was no longer whispering, but the purr remained to roughen his voice. "Kim, this is Sula. Got the scanner warmed up?"

"Up and humming." Kim waved a beckoning hand. "Bring her on in."

With a few swift strides, Aidan carried her into an indoor forest populated with fabulous birds, enormous butterflies of every hue, and children of all ages and practically every known species. There was even a small stream winding across the grassy floor. "Oh my…"

"Beautiful, isn't it?" Abuti piped up from somewhere behind them. "They tell me it's like growing up in the forests of Zetith."

Up in the treetops, miniature lights flickered like fairies among the leaves. However, Sula was only allowed a glimpse of these before leaving the woods to enter a large lobby. Padded benches lined the perimeter, interrupted only by a door that presumably opened onto the street, and a full-sized medscanner that stood in the far corner.

"Will you be able to walk through the scanner?" Kim asked.

"I think so." Although to be perfectly truthful, Sula wasn't sure she could walk unaided even without the cast on her leg. Nevertheless, after Aidan set her on her feet, she was able to hop through the arched opening.

"She's perfectly healthy," Kim announced as Sula hobbled over to the nearest bench. "No disease, injury, or nanobots—at least none this scanner can detect. However, she is suffering from something you should be able to help her with, Aidan. Might not have the desired effect right now, but—" The inference was as clear as her suggestive tone.

"That's my fault for forgetting to close the air vents when we entered the brothel district," Aidan said.

"Forgot?" Kim echoed. "Sure you did."

"Whatever," Aidan said hastily. "No time for that now. We need to get that cast off her leg and get going."

Time?

In Sula's opinion, relieving her distress would've taken all of three seconds. Her nipples and clitoris were so hard, she could barely keep from touching them in a most scandalous manner. And if Aidan were to do the honors—

I can't think about that.

Abuti rubbed her chin with a fingertip. "Thought we were going to do that on the ship."

"If someone's watching this building, we need everyone to be as mobile as possible," Aidan replied. "The cast removal kit is in the speeder. Think you could get it for me?"

"Sure thing." Abuti was gone in an instant.

Taking Sula's hand, he smiled. "If you'll lie down there, we'll have you good as new in no time." With a glance at Kim, he added, "Might need to borrow Onca's speeder too. Something tells me this would be a good time for us to disappear."

Chapter 17

AIDAN WANTED TO DISAPPEAR, ALL RIGHT. OR RATHER, HE wanted the rest of the world to disappear so he could be alone with Sula—and not only because his response to her was surely noticeable by now. His trousers had plenty of ball room. However, his burgeoning erection wasn't quite so easily contained. Utilizing muscles he'd rarely needed before, he somehow managed to move it to an upright position against his abdomen, which created less of a bulge. Having neglected to don moisture-proof underwear as he prepared for their departure, the joy juice—as Captain Jack had so aptly dubbed a Zetithian man's orgasmic lubricating fluid—was much harder to control.

Sula tugged at his hand, returning his attention to their surroundings but also reminding him that if they'd been alone together, she might have been pulling him down onto the bench beside her. No further encouragement would have been necessary. Even now, he could've asked Kim to give them the room, but Abuti would return soon—too soon for the feast of delights in which he longed to indulge. He didn't care that Sula's scent was enhanced by the pheromones that were so prevalent in that district. After all, she'd smelled fabulous even when her scent had contained no trace of desire whatsoever. She was the one for him, and he didn't need a vision, a portent of the future, or even a scent to know it. He felt the truth deep down in his soul.

He drew her hand to his lips, pressing a kiss to her fingers. As his gaze locked with hers, her own desire shone beseechingly from her glowing eyes. She hadn't wanted Giklor's treatment or its inevitable side effect, but he was already becoming accustomed to that glow—a glow not unlike the light that emanated from his own eyes. Perhaps that sign of healing drew them closer together, made them more alike than they'd ever been before.

As if they'd needed anything more to bind them together. Not even being bonded to her by the Zerkan would've made any difference now. The gods had sent him to her in a vision, and her hand in his sent more warmth rushing through his body than a bonfire could have done.

He leaned forward until their foreheads touched. "You are so beautiful, and I want you so very, very badly. If we were alone right now, I would show you exactly how much you mean to me."

"But we aren't alone," she whispered. "I can wait—I think. Although I certainly don't want to." Catching her lower lip between her teeth, she closed her eyes and let out a groan. "Oh, Aidan…"

His heart sank as movement by his side advised him of Abuti's return.

"Here you go," Abuti said as she handed him the kit. "I also brought your shoes, Sula."

"Thanks." Releasing Sula's hand at that moment was the worst form of torture Aidan could imagine. Clearing his throat, he knelt beside the bench. "I just have to spray the dissolving agent on opposite sides, and it should come right off."

Abuti stood at the foot of the bench, regarding Sula's

leg with a critical eye. "Giklor did a pretty nice job on you. You don't even have any bruises."

"It certainly feels better," Sula said. "I'm glad I went ahead and let him do it."

Aidan's sexually stimulated brain wanted her to let *him* "do it." Right there on that roomy padded bench, and Sula's slow, secretive smile proved she would have welcomed him with enthusiasm.

"I came out of the scanner in pretty much the same state you're in, Sula," Kim said, giggling as she approached. "My first litter was conceived on one of these daybeds."

Sula gave her a bashful smile. "The pheromones were getting to you?"

"More like Onca was getting to me," Kim replied. "The pheromone effect wears off pretty quickly. The Onca effect never has worn off and probably never will."

The Sula effect was starting to seem permanent to Aidan. Terrans might not mate for life, but Zetithians certainly did, and there'd been enough Zetithian-male–Terran-female pairings to prove that the woman didn't have to be Zetithian for her mate to want her exclusively. Not only did those men not want sex with another woman, once imprinted with the scent of their mates, Zetithian men couldn't do it with anyone else.

Then there was the wild card of his own Terran— and Mordrial—blood. The gods only knew what might happen next.

Abuti cackled with glee. "I'm thinking it isn't just the pheromones with you, either, Sula. Trust me, Aidan does that to a lot of people."

"Oh, hush up," Aidan said, albeit without a single

ray of hope. Any attempts at silencing a Norludian were generally futile, and Abuti was no exception.

Focusing on the task of removing the cast from Sula's leg was only moderately successful in tamping down his raging desire. Sure, having her mobile would be a definite plus, but he would no longer need to carry her, a prospect he couldn't help feeling a tad ambivalent about.

After a quick spray on each side, the cast fell from her leg in two perfect halves. Aidan groaned as Sula wiggled her toes, wanting nothing more than to start kissing her there and work his way up. Instead, he waited for her to sit up before helping her to slip on her sandals. He'd never given much thought to a woman's feet before, but her brown toes peeking from beneath the jeweled straps were positively captivating.

A light caress of his shoulder drew his gaze to her face once again, a sight his eyes would never grow tired of seeing, not even if he lived to be a thousand years old.

"Thanks, Aidan," she said. "I should be able to walk now."

"What? Oh…right." He backed off slightly and stood, noting that her scent had already undergone a subtle change. Having spent sufficient time away from the brothel district's pheromone-laced atmosphere, no doubt the effect was beginning to fade.

Dammit.

A deep inhale proved her desire wasn't completely gone.

Perhaps her intoxicating scent wasn't artificially induced after all.

Taking her hand, he helped her to her feet, feeling a moment's disappointment when she failed to sway enough to require assistance. Still holding her hand, he urged her to try taking a few steps.

"No pain at all," she reported. "I could probably even dance."

"You could," Onca said as he came through the doorway. "But you'd be better off trying to run." He nodded toward Aidan. "Better take my speeder and cloak it before you leave the garage. Our loitering alert has been going off every ten minutes since you left home." With a glance at Sula, he added, "Somebody really wants to catch you."

"They won't," Aidan said firmly. "Not while I'm around."

―――

Just when I get used to being around one *of these guys, I have two new ones to deal with.*

Sula was kidding herself if she thought she'd gotten used to Aidan. On the other hand, Onca was as attractive as any Zetithian male—tall, lean, and handsome, with auburn hair and green eyes. He was older, though, and not quite as gorgeous as Aidan. Neither was Curly, although she did concede she might be slightly prejudiced in Aidan's favor.

"I'd keep it cloaked until you're out of this district," Onca advised. "Just don't let anything run into you."

"Easier said than done." Aidan sounded rather grim.

Sula couldn't blame him for being leery of piloting a cloaked vehicle, although he might be able to anticipate the moves of other speeders better than most other pilots, Onca included. He'd certainly done a great job of maneuvering in traffic earlier. She started to say as much when she recalled that Aidan had kept his powers secret in the past. Onca and Kim probably had no idea what he could do. Since that was his secret to keep or to tell, she refrained from commenting.

"I'm not worried," Abuti said. "Aidan is an awesome pilot."

Sula held her breath, but amazingly enough, Abuti seemed content to leave it at that.

"Let's go, then." Aidan tugged on her hand, still not having released it. She didn't mind. Holding his hand was tantamount to taking one of the best antianxiety meds ever. Something about him triggered her safe-and-secure mode, if people could be said to possess such a setting.

She didn't even notice that walking was as effortless as it had ever been until they'd reached the garage. As she climbed into the speeder, all she could think about was how much she was going to miss having to depend on Aidan for practically everything, despite having always prided herself on her independence. And while she could probably rely on him for any number of other things, none would be as intimate as having him carry her from room to room.

Except for those greater intimacies in which they'd yet to indulge.

Their relationship was already undergoing a change, and plenty of things could happen now that she wasn't nursing a broken limb. Once they were safely aboard Curly's ship, sex with Aidan was a distinct possibility.

All they had to do was make it to the spaceport alive.

She'd already lost one lover. Surely, she couldn't be so unlucky as to lose another, especially since their affair hadn't truly even begun.

She wasn't completely sure she was ready to risk

giving her heart to someone else. A year had gone by, and although meeting Aidan had helped considerably, traces of the pain lingered. Before she could move on, she had to avenge Raj's death and the deaths of countless others.

Have I set the bar to my own future happiness too high?

As she buckled herself in, Aidan reached over and gave her hand a squeeze. No words. No other gesture. Not even a reassuring smile.

But it was enough.

One step at a time.

"Even when cloaked, your heat signature can be tracked," Onca cautioned. "And I'm sure I don't have to remind you that not all tracking nanobots will show up on a scan."

Aidan replied with a terse nod.

Onca thumped the hood of the speeder with his knuckles. "Be careful out there. Call me when you get to the spaceport and let me know where you left the speeder." Chuckling, he added, "And don't forget to leave it uncloaked."

"Gotcha. It should be at docking bay ninety-four, but that may change." Aidan fired up the engine and closed the canopy before engaging the cloak. Moments later, the garage door opened, and they flew out onto the street.

Speeder traffic was relatively light at that hour, and foot traffic was slow enough that Aidan didn't appear to have any difficulty avoiding the pedestrians.

They'd reached the end of the well-lit street when he glanced toward the rear viewscreen. "Have we got a tail yet?"

"Don't see one," Abuti reported.

"Good. I'm going to stop and open the canopy."

Sula gaped at him in disbelief. "What?"

Aidan grinned. "We're going to fly the rest of the way. They might be able to track us, but they'll never be able to keep up with us."

"Way cool!" Abuti shouted, bouncing up and down with excitement. "Let's fly this thing!"

Aidan steered the speeder down a deserted side street. "The trick will be keeping us level. Speeder wings aren't exactly designed for flight." He unbuckled his safety harness and glanced at Sula. "I'll need you to drive."

"Oh, you have *got* to be kidding me."

"Nope. You flew a starship back from Ecos, didn't you?"

"Yes, but I didn't fly it manually," Sula protested. "The ship pretty much flew itself. The only thing I did was tell it where I wanted to go."

"This'll be a little harder, but not by much. All you need to do is provide the forward thrust and control the direction. I'll be the one keeping us aloft." He hopped over the side of the speeder before fixing her with a quizzical gaze. "You *have* piloted a speeder before, haven't you?"

"Of course I have," Sula replied. "But this is... different."

"I have the utmost faith in you," he said. "Now, scoot over and fly this thing."

Abuti peered over the side. "Are we still cloaked?"

Aidan nodded. "From where I'm standing, you ladies look like a couple of disembodied heads. From below, we should be invisible."

With no clear idea how the cloak worked, all Sula

could do was take him at his word. Negotiating the center console took a little doing—something she never could have done with her leg in a cast—but she finally settled into the pilot's seat and buckled the safety harness.

Aidan jumped into the passenger seat, strapped himself in, and stuck his right hand out with his forearm parallel to the side of the speeder. "I'll try to do this as gently as possible."

"Gentle, hell," Abuti exclaimed as the speeder shot up into the air, albeit with a slight roll to the left.

"Just give me a second to balance the updraft."

"Does the wind come out of your hand or what?" Abuti sounded frightened but fascinated.

"I've never really been sure," he replied. "Sometimes it seems that way. Sometimes not."

"That was about as clear as Usbentian pond slime," Abuti complained. "Let me know if you ever figure it out."

"Will do," Aidan replied.

Sula couldn't tell that he was doing anything differently, but the speeder slowly assumed a level position.

"Okay, Sula," he said. "Full speed ahead to docking bay ninety-four."

"Wherever *that* is," she muttered.

He nodded toward the navigation screen. "It's that green dot. Keep it directly in your sights, and you can't miss it."

Sula was of the opinion that it would be quite easy to miss, but she slid her fingertip up the throttle control anyway. The speeder shot forward. A minimal adjustment in direction brought the green dot into the crosshairs. It wasn't quite as cool as flying with Aidan when he was wearing his wings, but the sense of freedom was breathtaking. As they flew higher, the city lay like a dazzling map of moving lights beneath them.

"Wow! This almost makes me wish I were a pilot," Sula exclaimed. "Incredible view."

"Hey, you can fly me anytime you like."

A quick glance caught Aidan's grin before he turned away.

"That sounded kinda suggestive to me," Abuti said. "If I were you, I'd take him up on the offer."

Sula smiled to herself. "I just might."

Excitement flowed through her body, making her nipples tingle and her clitoris ache. This adventure was *so* inconvenient. She and Aidan had better things to do than to outwit assassins and bring a genocidal maniac—or maniacs—to justice. Even with her gaze fixed firmly ahead, she could sense him sitting beside her, his entire tantalizing Zetithian self just waiting for her to pounce.

She'd never been so forward with a man before, although considering what she knew about Zetithian mating behavior, pouncing was precisely what she needed to do. She'd already bitten him. Funny how Kim and Onca hadn't commented on the blood on his neck. Were they only being polite, or had they actually not seen it?

Another stolen glance proved she hadn't been imagining things. Granted, he was no longer bleeding, and most of the blood had dried and flaked off, but she'd definitely tasted it. If he hadn't been Zetithian, the flavor wouldn't have been the least bit stimulating. However, she suspected that his blood contained an even more powerful chemical attractant than his alluring scent. And because sustained exposure seemed to increase her sensitivity, before long, resisting him would be impossible.

Sounds like a win-win scenario.

—m—

With Abuti giggling her head off in the rear seat and Sula sitting beside him, it was a wonder Aidan could control anything, let alone the wind. He'd had several reasons for leaving the canopy open, not the least of which was to allow Sula's intoxicating scent to dissipate. This was not the time to let his attention wander. Even so, he caught himself thinking ahead to a day when he could drink in Sula's scent and actually make love with her, reveling in the feel of his cock snug inside her wet warmth. Nothing else could possibly compare. He was certain of it.

When a sudden gust of real wind caused them to roll to the left and veer off course, Sula's gasp of dismay was followed by a prompt course correction. Abuti finally stopped laughing.

A tilt of Aidan's hand adjusted the attitude. "This is different from the way I normally fly. Being off-center makes it hard to keep us level. If I was in the middle of the backseat, I could stick a hand out on either side and get better balance."

"Wish you'd thought of that sooner," Abuti said. "Too late now."

"Yeah. Let's see if I can't fine-tune this a bit." In the past, he'd only had to maintain sufficient upward thrust to overcome gravity and allow him to glide forward using his wings. This method required a little more finesse. Extending his arm straight out to the side, he aimed his palm backward at a slight angle. The nose of the speeder dipped a degree or two and rolled a tad to the left, but they continued to move forward with even greater speed. A minor rotation in the other direction was like tapping the brakes. Using both hands, he could probably create enough forward *and* upward thrust to fly the speeder even without the engine.

Another gust threatened their stability. "How far to the spaceport?" he asked.

Sula peered at the dashboard. "Two point seven kilometers and closing."

Her lilting tone caught his attention. "You're enjoying this, aren't you?"

"I believe I am," she replied. "This is a whole lot more fun than flying a starship."

Aidan nodded. "There's just something about having the wind in your hair." He paused. "Less forgiving, though. There isn't much to run into in space. No gravity, either."

"Or wind." She shot a brief glance in his direction. "Are your arms getting tired?"

"Not yet," he replied. "I've flown a lot farther than the spaceport before."

"While holding up a speeder?"

"I'm not exactly holding it up with my own strength," he explained. "It's more of a mental power than a physical one." To be perfectly honest, he thought it might actually be a sort of sixth sense that was impossible to convey to someone who didn't possess the same capability. Another Mordrial might know exactly what he meant, but the concept would be out of context for anyone else.

I really should talk to Althea.

She would understand. Controlling the wind wasn't such a big deal anyway. Plenty of Mordrials had the same talent. It was the fortune-telling part he didn't want to reveal.

"Which means we probably shouldn't distract him." Once she'd stopped giggling, Abuti had shown no sign of starting again, anxiety having apparently won out over excitement. Sula, on the other hand, seemed to be thriving. She truly was special.

"Yeah," Sula said, glancing at the rearview display. "Especially since someone with similar powers seems to be following us."

Chapter 18

AIDAN'S HEART TOOK A DIVE, AND THE SPEEDER DIPPED along with it. "Let me see."

Sula angled the screen toward him. "Whatever it is doesn't seem to be as fast as we are, but there's definitely something behind us. A police flyer, maybe?"

There were plenty of smaller vehicles capable of actual flight—the police force had several compact flyers—but air traffic control was such a bitch that, like cloaked speeders, their use was severely restricted.

"Possibly," he said. "Although I wouldn't have thought we'd show up on any location systems. I mean, we *are* cloaked."

"Don't forget the open canopy and our heat signature," Sula reminded him. "They could also be tracking your comlink or my nanobots—which, despite what the scanner said, I'm convinced I must have. Nothing else could explain why they keep finding me so easily."

Each of those possibilities was as chilling as the next, although having had the presence of mind to power down his personal link, Aidan could rule out at least one of them. Until he remembered that the speeder's link was still active.

Damn.

Unfortunately, even if they shut down the speeder completely, there was no way to mask their own heat signatures. The nanobot theory continued to gain credibility.

"Whatever it is, we seem to be able to outfly it," he said. "If it starts catching up, I could blast it out of the sky, but I'd rather not endanger anyone else."

"Think you could slow it down?" Sula asked.

"Maybe. Although increasing our own speed is probably the best alternative."

Abuti leaned forward, peering at the screen from the rear seat. "I dunno...I don't think it's a police flyer. Looks more like a big bird."

Aidan studied the screen again. "Shit. It's Val." For a moment, the speeder slowed as his wind control faltered. "Why would he be following us?"

"Maybe he wants to join the team," Abuti suggested. "You know how dedicated he is to fighting for the downtrodden."

Aidan didn't have to ask why Abuti would think of the Avian in that light. As a member of Onca's gang in the battle to expose the use of kidnapped street kids in the sex trade, Val was one of the orphanage's heroes. This adventure was exactly the sort of cause he would find appealing.

"But I haven't talked to Val in weeks," Aidan protested. "He couldn't possibly know—"

"Maybe Rashe or Onca told him," Abuti said. "I got the distinct impression they both would've come with us if they hadn't been needed at the orphanage."

"You're probably right," Aidan said. "I should've recruited him myself, but I'm not slowing down to talk to him now. He'll have to wait until we're aboard Curly's ship. Can you tell if anything else is following him?"

"Not from here," Abuti replied. "Guess we should've brought along some binoculars."

"I have a pair," Sula said. "They're in my pack somewhere."

"I'll see if I can get to them," Abuti said.

"Don't bother," Aidan said sharply. "We're flying with an open canopy. I don't want you falling out."

"Have you ever seen a Norludian fall out of anything?" Abuti said with a heavy note of sarcasm in her voice.

"No, I haven't," he admitted, their sucker-tipped fingers being the obvious reason for that. "But I'd rather not start now. We're not far from the spaceport anyway. Your eyes are keen enough to tell a bird from a vehicle, so keep a lookout to the rear—and do *not* take off your safety harness."

"Aye, Captain," Abuti said. The subsequent sound he heard was undoubtedly the result of her popping a fingertip off her forehead in a mock salute.

"Save the captain crap for Curly," Aidan said. "He might be impressed by it. I'm not."

"Ooh, getting a bit testy, are we?"

Testy was an understatement. With his patience already stretched to the limit from trying to keep them aloft, level, and moving forward, the Norludian girl was getting on his last nerve.

"Drop it," Sula warned before Aidan could retort. "Unless you want him to let us fall out of the sky."

"Okay, okay," Abuti grumbled. "I'll try looking over my shoulder. It'll give me a horrendous crick in my neck, but—"

"Look, Abuti," Aidan said, "I'm sorry I snapped at you. I'm a little preoccupied at the moment."

"I know. I was only trying to lighten the mood."

"And I appreciate that. But silence would help more."

"Gotcha. Mum's the word. Won't say another thing. Until later. Maybe tomorrow."

To his surprise, Aidan caught himself chuckling. Even more surprising was the sudden increase in their altitude and speed.

Abuti cackled along with him. "See? Laughing helps, doesn't it?"

"Yes, I suppose it does."

"This is such a fantastic adventure," Abuti went on. "I feel like an intrepid explorer, off to find bizarre new worlds and weird alien species."

"That's what Raj and I did," Sula said. "Trust me, exploration isn't everything it's cracked up to be. If we get out of this alive, I may never leave home again."

Abuti's head appeared at his side. "You have a house?"

"No, I don't," Sula replied. "Figure of speech."

"Must be nice to have a home. I don't think I ever had one, even when I was little. Can't remember it, anyway."

"You have a home at the orphanage now," Aidan reminded her.

"Not the same," Abuti said, her spirits seeming to sink along with the pitch of her voice. "Besides, I'll have to leave it eventually. Not sure where I'll go when I do."

"Onca and Kim won't kick you out. They'll find you a job and a place to live when you're old enough." Aidan tried to sound upbeat, but the dimming of his wind power proved he hadn't been entirely successful, as did Abuti's rather lukewarm response.

He'd never noticed how much his mood affected his abilities before. A glance at Sula reminded him of yet another change his life had recently undergone. Was she also responsible for an increase in his strength? The flight from the condor's cave suggested she might be. He'd been unprepared for that powerful updraft. Had her effect on him been that immediate?

More important, without her by his side, would he have been able to lift the speeder? He hadn't grown up experimenting and honing his Mordrial talents, so he truly didn't know for sure.

I shouldn't have been so secretive. But with the wind control would come some form of telepathy or, as in Althea's case, empathy. She hadn't been able to control fire as a child. Perhaps he could finally admit to his ability with the caveat that it had been thrust upon him as an adult.

No child should have witnessed some of the things he'd seen.

Sula's voice not only interrupted his thoughts, it calmed his emotional response to them. "We're coming up on the spaceport. Any idea what we should do next?"

"I'll set us down somewhere nearby, then we can decloak and proceed normally. Too much traffic around the spaceport to remain cloaked."

Aidan hadn't been to the spaceport in over a year. Traffic had been heavy enough then. On a night like this, there would probably be even more. An active nightlife was, after all, one of Damenk's claims to fame.

"I should be able to predict a gap in traffic and set us down, preferably with no one behind us. If we're lucky, no one will notice when we decloak."

"What happens if we aren't lucky?" Sula asked.

"We'll be spotted by the police. Getting arrested for driving a cloaked speeder in the city would really slow us down."

Sula couldn't find any fault with his logic. The best she could hope for was a relatively smooth transition from flying to hovering at a normal level. But as she looked down upon the city lights with a seemingly continuous flow of speeders on every possible route, she had her doubts. "Maybe we should've landed a little sooner."

Abuti reached forward and gripped Aidan's shoulder. "Are we going to crash?"

"Not today," he said, sounding suddenly more cheerful. "I got this."

"Seeing into the future?" Sula asked.

"Sort of. Back off the throttle to about half normal speed."

Sula did as he asked, then had to bite back a scream as the speeder seemed to plummet toward the ground. The suspensor force kicked in with a slight jolt, and suddenly, the speeder was moving normally behind a long line of other vehicles. She was about to profess her amazement at such a smooth landing when Abuti beat her to it.

"I don't believe it!" Abuti yelled. "Woo-hoo! What a rush! Are we still cloaked?"

"Nope," Aidan replied. "Did that on the way down." Sula's sideways glance caught his grin. "Timing is everything." He tapped the control panel, and the canopy slid shut.

Sula had grown so used to the altitude and wind speed that her ears popped when the canopy locks engaged. Even with the canopy closed, the speeder continued to swing from side to side, requiring her to make constant course adjustments. Her first thought was that there might be a malfunction of some sort until a quick peek over her shoulder revealed Abuti hopping around in the backseat like some weird alien toad.

Apparently, Aidan noticed the same thing. "Put your safety harness back on and settle down, kid. We're conspicuous enough as it is without you rocking the boat."

Abuti paused long enough to speak. "The most fun I've ever had in my life, and you're telling me to settle down?"

"Yes, I am," he replied. "Sorry."

"Okay. I'll be good." To Sula's relief, the erratic swaying ceased. "Wouldn't want you to send me home now. I wouldn't have missed this for anything."

Sula was a bit breathless herself. However, she had other reasons for that. A closed canopy meant she'd be inhaling Aidan's aura or scent or whatever it was that drove her mad with desire. "I need a drink," she muttered.

"Curly's always been the most free-spirited of Cat and Jack's boys," Aidan said. "He probably has some booze on hand, although with a Drell on board, he probably has to keep it locked up."

In all the excitement, Sula had forgotten about the Drell. On the whole, Drells tended be terribly rude, and liquor didn't improve their manners. Hopefully, she would have very little interaction with him. "What did he say the Drell's name was?"

"Jetoc," Abuti replied. "And don't worry, I know how to keep Drells in line. You just have to swear at them, and they scurry right off."

"Hmm, well, since he is Curly's navigator, I wouldn't want him to scurry too far." She yawned. "What time is it, anyway?"

"Half past three," Aidan replied. "I don't know about you two, but I'm ready to call it a night."

"Same here." Sula glanced at the rear viewscreen. A few speeders that had been stopped at the previous traffic signal were catching up to them, but nothing unusual stood out. "We probably shouldn't relax just yet, though. Do either of you see anything suspicious behind us?"

Aidan peered at the viewscreen for a moment, then twisted around in his seat. "Not at the moment. What about you, Abuti?"

"I don't see anything out of the ordinary," Abuti replied. "Not even the big bird."

"If I had to guess, I'd say Val is flying somewhere above us." He leaned his head back and stared up at the sky. "He's fast enough to overtake a speeder in the city. With no stoplights or speed limits up there, he might even beat us to the spaceport."

Sula knew of several intelligent species that were capable of flight. As diverse as Damenk's population was, it was a wonder the air wasn't thick with them. She tried to remember how many there were—that had been a test question somewhere along the line—but recalling facts and figures wasn't nearly as interesting as Aidan's fully exposed arched neck. She could even see the spot where she'd bitten him earlier. With a difficult swallow, she returned her attention to the road ahead.

Would he bite her like that if they ever made love? She couldn't remember if Zetithian women enjoyed being bitten. She certainly didn't, nor did she possess a Zetithian's rapid healing ability or saliva that could stop bleeding. Her fake fangs would have to go, and the sooner the better. Multiple puncture wounds wouldn't be good for either of them.

The linkpad lit up. "What's your status?" Curly asked over the link.

"Almost there," Aidan replied. "We had a tail but lost it. You?"

"Ours is pretty much the same story," Curly said. "Just came aboard. I'll say this for our tail, he was persistent."

"So was ours. We had to cloak to lose him."

Aidan was stretching the truth ever so slightly, especially by not mentioning anything about having flown most of the way, and if the snicker from the backseat was any indication, Abuti had also noticed that omission.

Curly chuckled. "Amateur."

"I take it you didn't have to fire any weapons or engage your cloak." Aidan's tone was perfectly even. As tired as he had to be, how he kept from rising to the bait was a mystery.

"Nope. Just outmaneuvered him. It's more fun that way."

"I'm sure it is," Aidan said, still without even a hint of sarcasm. "See you in a few." He terminated the link with a tap on the pad.

While trying not to laugh, Sula had bitten her lip, which, of course, was a mistake. "Ouch!" She shot a sheepish glance at Aidan. "Forgot I had fangs."

He grinned. "One of the hazards of being Zetithian." He glanced toward the backseat. "You can laugh now, kid."

On cue, Abuti went off in a peal of giggles that lasted even longer than Aidan's conversation with Curly. "Thank the stars and planets!" she gasped.

"Outmaneuvered him, my ass. Bet he didn't fly the way we did. Dunno how you kept a straight face."

"Yeah, well, I've known Curly all my life," Aidan said. "He's a great guy, but talking to him without resorting to one-upmanship requires practice."

"And a will of iron," Sula added. "He reminds me of one of my cousins. Never mattered what your story was—you could be telling her about a good day or a bad dream—she would always find a way to top it. Sometimes I embellished the truth just to see what she would come up with."

Aidan, on the other hand, wouldn't need to exaggerate to top Curly's adventures on the way to the spaceport. Telling the truth would do it quite nicely.

"My take on it is to wait and see what he'll do when left to his own devices. Sometimes I even try to predict what he'll say."

Sula gave him a warm smile. "I'll bet you're good at that too."

He shrugged. "Sometimes I get it right. Sometimes not. Even a fortune-teller doesn't know every detail of the future."

"Must be freaky knowing any of it," Abuti commented.

Having reached the next intersection, Sula turned right. "Yeah. Like whether we'll make it to the spaceport or not."

"We'll make it," he said. "There was never any doubt about that."

"How do you know for sure?" He'd already told her he couldn't read any of her future—or his own. That left Abuti...

"Knowing the future doesn't mean you don't have to work at making it happen," he replied. "The future is always in a state of flux. Anything can change it, and when the stakes are high, it's best not to leave the outcome to chance."

Abuti folded her skinny arms and rested them on the top of Aidan's seat back. "Okay, then. Whose future have you been seeing?"

"Yours."

"Mine?" Abuti squeaked. "What did you see?"

"I can't tell you that," he said with a sly smile. "But you will get older, and if you survive this adventure, that means we probably will too."

"Wish I shared your optimism," Abuti drawled. "Not everyone involved in a speeder accident dies, you know."

"True, but none of us is going to die tonight." He gestured toward the left. "The docking bays are down that way."

Sula nodded, banking the speeder around the turn. She didn't need any directions at this point, but she recognized his change-of-topic tactic for what it was. Unfortunately, it didn't appear to work on a Norludian.

Abuti sat back and huffed out an indignant breath. "You really aren't going to tell me, are you?"

"Nope," he replied. "So don't even bother asking."

"Why not?"

"Personal policy," he said firmly. "Until recently, no one knew I could see into the future, so I've never been asked, but I make it a rule not to volunteer the information. Just because you know what I can do doesn't mean you're exempt."

"But I won't tell anyone!" Abuti exclaimed. "I promise!"

To his credit, Aidan didn't laugh at the idea of a Norludian making such a claim. "Even if you kept it to yourself, knowing what I've seen in the future may cause you to do something that changes it."

"You mean like crashing into a lamppost just to make sure we don't board that ship?"

He shook his head. "Doesn't have to be that drastic. Timelines are fragile, and it doesn't take much to alter them. Other futures seem to be inevitable, and while there are many different paths to the same end, I prefer not to influence those paths."

Sula couldn't help wondering what he'd seen. Did it involve other people aside from Abuti? Had he seen a specific event or random images?

Something told her his "personal policy" wouldn't allow him to answer those questions.

Like everyone else who lacked prescient abilities, she would have to wait and see how the future played out.

Chapter 19

AIDAN HAD ALWAYS KNOWN HE WOULD REGRET ADMITTING to his fortune-telling ability. He just hadn't known how much. Telling Abuti anything was tantamount to shouting it from the rooftops. And the scene he'd witnessed was something he really didn't want to mess with.

"In the meantime, you need to be watching our six," he reminded her.

"Our six?" Abuti echoed.

"Out the back," he replied. "Our tail end. To the rear. You know, like you've been doing."

"Yeah, yeah. I got it," Abuti grumbled. "I guess hindsight is the only thing I'm good for."

"At the moment, hindsight, as you well know, is extremely important."

"Where's bay ninety-four?" Sula asked. "Or am I still following that dot on the navigation screen?"

Aidan had been through the maze of the Damenk spaceport many times. If there was any rhyme or reason to the numbering system, he had yet to discover it. "Better keep following the dot. If we have to stop and ask directions, someone will try to sell us a ship of our own."

The worst part was that at least one of their group would be tempted to buy it. The subliminal advertising was so strong in this district, it was a wonder anyone made it out of there with any credits left to their name.

"I certainly didn't have any trouble selling the ship

I came here on," Sula said. "The trick was not turning right around and buying another one."

"What's the name of Curly's ship?" Abuti asked.

Aidan scratched his chin. "I honestly don't know. I haven't flown with him since he went out on his own, but it's probably something cleverly macho."

"Whatever it's called, we just missed it," Abuti said. "I saw a number ninety-four on that side street we just passed."

"I'm on it," Sula said as she made a U-turn that pulled at least four Gs. "That dot must be the central hangar."

As they zipped down the narrow street, Aidan spotted Curly waving at them from the open doorway of one of the towering docking bays. Sula brought the speeder to a halt next to the loading ramp and lowered the parking struts while Aidan called Onca.

"We're at docking bay ninety-four as planned," Aidan told Onca when he answered. "Any idea why Val is following us?"

"I thought you might need a good hacker, so I told him where you were going," Onca replied. "He said he'd try to catch up with you."

"Sounds good. I should've called him myself. Thanks again for the speeder. The cloak came in very handy."

"No problem," Onca said. "Try to stay out of trouble."

Aidan couldn't help but laugh.

"About time you got here," Curly shouted the moment the canopy slid open. "We were starting to think you'd gotten lost."

"If it weren't for Abuti, we would've been." Aidan hopped out and went to collect their gear from the cargo compartment. He'd already handed off Sula's and Abuti's bags to their respective owners when Curly sauntered down the ramp.

"How come you weren't driving?" he asked.

"Defensive strategy," Aidan replied, determined not to let Curly get a rise out of him.

With a skeptical lift of his brow, Curly motioned toward the open door. "Head on in, and we'll get out of here. The engines should be warmed up by now."

"I don't suppose you've seen Val, have you?"

Curly frowned. "Val? You mean the Avian clone guy?"

"Yeah. He was following us at one point. Thought he might've gotten here ahead of us."

"Haven't seen him," Curly said. "If he doesn't get here soon, he's gonna miss the boat."

Aidan's brief survey of their surroundings showed nothing out of the ordinary. "Seems pretty quiet. We can give him a few minutes." Shouldering his duffel bag, he followed Sula and Abuti up the ramp and into the cavernous building.

Granted, it wasn't important enough to warrant a peek into the future, or even a Zetithian-style vision, but he wasn't the least bit surprised to see the name painted on the side of the S-class Telageist starship.

Interstellar Express—when you have a need for speed.

"I should've known."

"Sweet, isn't she?" Curly said with undisguised pride. "Faster than Mom's ship, even though she won't admit it."

Aidan had heard that story before. Didn't believe it then and didn't believe it now. "Newer, anyway," he conceded. "The *Roger*'s starting to get a little age on her."

Curly nodded. "Mom had her in for an overhaul a few

months back. I keep telling her she needs a new ship, but she won't part with it."

"Can't say as I blame her," Aidan said. "That ship has been home for a long damn time."

"True. I used to think she and Dad might settle down somewhere, but I don't see it happening anytime soon."

"Neither do I." Aidan couldn't imagine Jack without Cat or the *Jolly Roger*. It was almost as if together, they made one composite being. The closest he could come to imagining Jack settling down would be if she were to park her ship somewhere and continue to live in it like some sort of souped-up mobile home.

The *Interstellar Express* certainly didn't fall into that category. The interior wasn't what anyone would consider posh, but it was a cut above the *Jolly Roger*'s rather Spartan décor. The main deck's lounge at least appeared to be comfortable with an assortment of armchairs and sofas scattered about.

"Ever carry passengers, or do you only handle freight?"

"Just freight," Curly replied. "Sometimes large crates, but mostly small packages. You're the first passengers we've ever transported."

"Transported?" Abuti echoed. "You make us sound like cargo."

"Right now, that's technically what you are," Curly said. "The only difference is we have to feed you." He hesitated. "Although come to think of it, we did haul a dozen Yerkatian cormorants once, but they were shipped along with enough dried fish to last until we delivered them. Noisy rascals."

"I'll bet they were," Abuti said. "Speaking of food, do you have enough to feed us?"

"We do if Jetoc took on supplies like he was supposed to. He's very susceptible to the subliminal advertising around here. To be honest, we're more likely to have too much than too little." With a glance toward Aidan, he added, "And if you'll do the cooking, you'll eat better. You know how Drells are about their sausages."

The best Aidan had ever been able to tell, Drells never ate anything else, unless it was crackers. "I can do that. Where are Qinta and Giklor?"

"Checking out their quarters, I expect," Curly replied. "Qinta wanted to get out of her disguise." His slightly disgruntled expression suggested that the wig ruse had already been resolved.

"Speaking of disguises, I need to get out of mine too," Sula said. "I'm okay with the curls, but I'd really like to lose the fangs."

Abuti swept her with an appraising gaze. "I dunno…I think they look great."

"I'm not worried about how I look," Sula insisted. "I'm afraid I'll bite a hole in my lip while I'm asleep. Don't think I want to try eating anything, either."

Having had fangs practically from birth, Aidan had never considered them to be a problem in either of those situations. "Can you put them back on if necessary?"

She nodded. "They're just stuck on with little sticky pads. Jeeves gave me more of those and some adhesive remover. Where does he get all that stuff, anyway?"

"The gods only know," Aidan replied. "But he seems to be able to manufacture almost anything. We probably should've brought him along with us." He frowned. "I wonder what happened to Val. He wasn't that far behind us."

A loud rumble shook the ship, nearly knocking Aidan off his feet. Abuti landed on the floor in a jumble of skinny arms, legs, and flippers.

Curly let out a growl. "What the bloody hell was that?"

A strange, lilting voice sounded over the internal comsystem. "Captain Curly, we are taking heavy weapons fire. I have closed the hatch. May I suggest immediate liftoff?"

"If those fuckers so much as scratch the paint," Curly snarled, stalking toward the main passageway, "I'm gonna make them wish they'd never been born."

"Shall I return fire?"

Curly stopped just short of the passageway entrance and took a deep breath, ostensibly to regain control of his temper. Twitching muscles in his cheek and neck belied the effort. "Yes, Laurel. But stun weapons only."

"Understood."

"Laurel?" Abuti's attempt to rise from the floor was thwarted by another blast. "You have a woman on board?"

"She's the ship's computer," Curly replied. "Nice voice, huh?"

"I suppose so." This time, Abuti didn't bother trying to stand. Instead, she crawled over to the nearest bulkhead and climbed the wall like a huge, four-legged spider. When the third blast hit, she was at least able to remain upright.

"Captain Curly," Laurel said gently, "we would appear to have acquired an ally—a tall man with long golden-brown hair and a pair of rather large wings is in the docking bay, firing on a group of unidentified hostiles."

"That has to be Val," Aidan said. "We can't just leave him out there."

Curly pulled his pulse pistol from its holster and tossed it to Aidan. "I'll open the hatch while you cover him until he gets inside."

Aidan adjusted the pistol, which was set to kill, for a wide stun beam. "Let's do it."

The two men ran to the hatch. "On the count of three," Curly said. "One, two, *three!*"

Aidan never saw who or what he was shooting at, but after firing twice, the attack stopped long enough for Val to come aboard in a flurry of feathers.

"Welcome aboard, Val." Curly closed the hatch and locked it. "Jetoc! Are we cleared for takeoff?"

"Yes, Captain," a rather gruff voice replied. "The atmospheric engines are already up to speed. The stardrive engines should be ready by the time they're needed."

"Then get us the hell out of here. I'll be there in two shakes." Save for the masculine timbre of his voice, Curly sounded exactly like his mother, including his choice of expletives and archaic figures of speech. Not to mention the Nedwut pulse pistol she'd probably given him.

That apple didn't fall far from the tree.

"Strap yourselves in," Curly yelled as he dashed from the lounge. "This is gonna be a bumpy ride."

They might have been the first visitors aboard Curly's ship, but the row of seats outfitted with safety harnesses along the interior wall proved the *Interstellar Express* was equipped to handle at least six passengers. Sula was buckling herself into the nearest chair when another explosion shook the ship, loosening Abuti's grip on the wall and sending her hurtling across the room to sprawl on one of the sofas.

"Think I'll stay here," Abuti said. "It's the softest thing I've landed on yet."

Giklor and Qinta came rushing into the lounge, both of them staggering as another blast rattled the ship. Qinta had taken off her wig but had only removed the makeup from half of her face, giving her a clown-like appearance. Neither of them seemed to notice the tall, extraordinarily handsome Avian who had just joined them. Sula, being the anthropologist in the group, couldn't take her eyes off him, and her fascination had very little to do with his full lips, square jaw, and cleft chin.

His enormous wings were the same golden brown as his wavy shoulder-length hair, but his eyes were his most striking feature. Crystalline blue and slightly larger and rounder than human eyes, they had no whites at all, and his huge round pupils reacted to light with all the dramatic effect of a hawk's. He also appeared to be remarkably fit. Even after flying across the city and then engaging in a firefight, he was barely breathing hard. And because he wasn't wearing a shirt—only the same kind of tight brown leggings that Aidan had been wearing when she first met him—the rise and fall of his broad chest was easily observed.

Qinta finally spared a glance for the newcomer. "Hi, Val. Nice to see you again. Anyone know what's going on?"

Aidan snatched Abuti from the couch and planted her in the seat next to Sula's. "We're under attack. Get yourselves strapped in before someone else breaks a leg."

"As I have already demonstrated, I am quite capable of healing broken bones," Giklor said, sounding rather indignant.

"Even when it's your own?" Aidan snapped.

Without another word, Giklor sank into the end seat and began adjusting the harness.

"Didn't think so," Aidan muttered. He turned to Sula. "You okay?"

"I'm fine. Although I thought I was going to lose it there for a second. Never considered how funny 'Captain Curly' would sound, especially coming from a lovestruck computer."

He chuckled. "She did sound kinda smitten." As though suddenly remembering his manners, he began introducing her to Val but was interrupted by yet another pulse blast. "Guess we'd better strap ourselves in first."

The liftoff was barely perceptible, but the way the ship shuddered as it took another hit proved they were airborne.

"Yo, Aidan!" Curly's voice rang out from a speaker somewhere above them. "Need you on the weapons console. I have a job for Val too."

"On our way." He dropped a quick kiss on Sula's forehead before he and Val took off running down the passageway.

"What's Val doing here?" Qinta asked.

"Apparently, Onca thought we might need him," Sula replied. "He was following us at one point. Then we lost him when we landed."

"Landed?" Qinta exclaimed. "You mean you were actually flying?"

Abuti giggled. "It was so freakin' cool. Aidan cloaked

the speeder and used the wind to lift us up to get away from the guy who was chasing us. It was super exciting. You should've been there."

"We had a little excitement of our own," Qinta said. "Curly made some crazy moves while trying to lose the speeder that was following us. After a while, they sort of seemed to give up. Apparently, no one fell for my disguise."

"Mine, either," Sula said. "If Aidan hadn't done what he did, I doubt we'd have made it to the ship." She gritted her teeth, pleased to discover that her fangs didn't interfere. "Damned nanobots."

"I thought the scan didn't show any bots," Qinta said.

"Our adversaries have tapped into your aura," Giklor intoned. "Such things are traceable, you know."

"Yeah, right," Abuti said. "I'm with you, Sula. My money is on nanobots."

Sula nodded. "Now all we have to do is figure out how to get rid of them."

"Need you to work some of your old magic, buddy," Curly said as Aidan and Val arrived on the bridge. "I thought it was just ground fire, but we've got a ship taking potshots at us now." With a grimace, he added, "Your girlfriend is really hot, and I don't mean that in the sense of how cute she is."

"I know," Aidan said. "I'm beginning to wonder why they didn't just blow up my house with all of us in it."

Curly's fingers flew over the controls as the ship veered to port and back again. "That would've been more effective. Right now, these guys are only annoying the crap out of me. My ship can take the pounding, but I'm guessing—hoping—theirs can't."

Aidan slid into the gunner's seat and buckled the safety belt. "I'll target their weapons first, then go for the engines once we're outside the atmosphere."

"Yeah. Don't want to hurt anyone except the bad guys, but we sure as hell don't want them on our six all the way to Ursa Prime."

"No shit." Aidan scanned the targeting screen and shifted his mind ahead by roughly five seconds. That advance had always worked like a charm in the past, but he soon discovered that Curly's evasive maneuvers had improved since they'd last flown together. Their flight pattern was so erratic, his first three shots missed. After another five-second leap, he began doing some damage.

"What do you need me to do?" Val asked.

"Man the comstation and see if you can block their transmissions or jam them or something," Curly replied. "Anything you can think of."

"Understood." Val perched at the communications console with his wings draped over the back of the chair.

"We've picked up another ship." Aidan hadn't actually spotted it yet, but he knew it would be there soon.

"What? Where?" Curly demanded.

"One at three o'clock and another coming up on our six." Aidan fired again. The pulse cannon on the port side of the ship at three o'clock fizzled and died.

"We are approaching the outer limits of the atmosphere," Jetoc reported. "The stardrive engines are online."

Aidan had almost forgotten about the Drell. A glance in the direction of the navigation console revealed a pile of hair in the shape of a miniature haystack sitting in the chair.

"Great," Curly said. "Course laid in to Ursa Prime?"

"Aye, Captain," the haystack replied. "Awaiting your command."

Aidan fired a pulse blast that sent their newest opponent spiraling off toward the Rhylosian Sea.

Raising his right hand, Curly swept it forward and down. "Engage."

Chapter 20

"THEY'LL NEVER CATCH US NOW," CURLY CROWED AS THE points of starlight on the main viewscreen stretched into light trails.

"I disagree," said Val. "We are transmitting a signal. Weak but detectable at close range. If our adversaries have any knowledge of our destination, they could proceed there and resume tracking us when we arrive."

Groaning, Curly slumped over the pilot's console. "Oh, you have *got* to be shitting me."

Aidan had suspected as much. "Let me guess... nanobots?"

"I believe so," Val replied. "Once I isolate the source—"

"I can tell you exactly where the source is," Aidan interjected. "Sula's been walking around with the little critters swimming in her bloodstream for at least a year, maybe longer. The medscanner at the orphanage didn't show anything, but I'm sure they're there."

A haughty arch of his golden brow demonstrated Val's opinion of the equipment they'd used. "That scanner is a relic, good for nothing beyond diagnosing children's illnesses."

"I'm with you on that score," Aidan said. "Nice to have our theory confirmed, though. Any way to get rid of them?"

Val nodded. "I should be able to get them to

congregate in one spot so they can be removed. Not an entirely painless procedure, but I'm sure Sula will be pleased to eliminate them."

"It'll make it easier to sneak up on the bad guys too," Curly pointed out. "Or we might be able to use them as a decoy that will actually work this time."

"We will have to find a medium to store them in," Val said. "Nanobots don't survive long when removed from their host, and they have a limited lifespan. Given the length of time you say she's had them, these should already be dead."

"Must have a rogue element to them," Aidan suggested. "Sula wasn't bothered the whole time she was in the mountains but started being followed anytime she was in Damenk. Any ideas why that might be?"

Val replied with a lift of his wings, his standard I-don't-know gesture. "Nanobot technology is constantly evolving. Keeping up with the newest advances is a full-time job. I prefer to focus on communication and data collection."

Aidan studied the Avian's impassive face for a long moment. "Speaking of communication, how come you didn't tell us you were coming?"

"I should have thought that was perfectly obvious," Val replied. "Anyone carrying a comlink can be tracked, and messages are easily intercepted. I prefer to remain invisible. Onca contacted me after you left the orphanage." The brow went up again. "Considering the amount of firepower at the spaceport, I suspect your communications were being monitored."

"That's possible," Curly conceded. "They sure seemed to know where we were headed—and which speeder was carrying the real Sula." He glared at Aidan. "How *did* you keep from being caught?"

Aidan blew out a heavy sigh. "We flew."

Curly's eyes narrowed. "In Onca's speeder? How?" A moment later, the light dawned in his eyes. "You can control the wind, can't you?" With Aidan's nod, he exclaimed, "Dammit, I knew you had to have some Mordrial powers. What else can you do?"

"It's...complicated." Aidan's powers were difficult to explain, partly because he didn't completely understand them himself.

Curly leaned back in his chair and folded his arms. "Try me."

His targeting ability was the simplest to convey. "I can project my mind into the future. Not very far—only a few seconds."

"That explains why you're so good at hitting moving targets." Curly's stern gaze never wavered. "Anything else?"

The next part was even tougher to reveal. "I have visions of the future."

"So? All Zetithians have visions."

"Mine are different. Whenever I meet someone— especially if we shake hands—I see significant events in their future. Sometimes their deaths."

"Bummer," Jetoc muttered.

"Tell me about it," Aidan said. "In some cases, it's satisfying to see someone get their just deserts. Other times, it's horrifying."

Curly's expression finally softened. "You've had to deal with all that without ever telling anyone. Am I right?"

Aidan nodded. "I've seen things that would give

anybody nightmares. And you're right, I don't tell anyone. It seems unfair that some people should know their futures while others remain in the dark. Plus, I'd rather no one came to me demanding to know how their lives or specific events will turn out. Like I told Abuti a while ago, timelines are fragile. Just knowing what's supposed to happen can change the outcome."

"That explains a lot," Curly said. "Especially why you're so hesitant to shake hands with people. I always thought you just didn't like being touched or had some sort of germ phobia. I've seen the look on your face when you've been introduced to some of Mom's shadier business contacts." His eyes widened as perhaps the most relevant question finally occurred to him. "What about people you've known forever?"

"I mostly pick up little things, and it doesn't happen very often, almost as though being around someone for extended periods makes me immune to any visions about them. Kids are different. Sometimes I know what they're going to do even before they do." He shrugged. "I only intervene when their safety is at risk. Otherwise, I let them learn from their mistakes."

Curly glanced at Val. "You knew all this, didn't you?"

"Only his control of the wind." A frown so brief Aidan might have imagined it furrowed Val's brow. "I can only be thankful your visions don't include glimpses of the past. Otherwise, you wouldn't be able to tolerate being in the same room with me."

"I doubt that," Aidan said. "You've always been a good friend."

"What I have seen and endured is the issue rather than my ability to be a friend." Val's gaze bored into him like a raptor zeroing in on its prey. "You've seen my future?"

"I've seen a lot of futures," Aidan said quietly. "Some are better than others. Yours is one of them. More than that, I can't say."

"Can't or won't?" Curly prompted.

"Both," Aidan replied. "To tell what I know would disrupt my future and the future of anyone whose life I've touched, which is why I've always kept quiet." With a weary shrug, he added, "I can't explain how I know this. I just do." He drew in a ragged breath as exhaustion threatened to sap the remaining strength from his body. "Right now, I'm so tired I can't even think."

"I'm not surprised," Curly said. "I don't see how you can deal with what you know without going mad."

"I volunteer at the orphanage. Cooking helps a lot, and when the future weighs heavily on me, I fly." Smiling, he added, "Val has given me some pointers on that. I have a pair of wings and use updrafts to get off the ground—although after flying that speeder, I have some ideas for improving my technique."

Curly seemed to take this in with very little reaction, which wasn't surprising given the Mordrial blood in the people he'd grown up with. "What about Sula? Have you seen her future?"

Aidan shook his head. "I can't read her. Being with her soothes my soul in ways I never imagined. It may be selfish, but I believe that in saving her, I will also save myself."

"Nothing selfish about that," Curly said. "Sounds pretty normal for a mated pair."

"I hope you're right."

Val's arrival took up the last free bed that would've given Sula the chance to have a cabin to herself. Once the Avian man had volunteered to bunk with Giklor, Aidan didn't have any excuse to sleep anywhere else, unless he opted for a sofa in the lounge or shared with Jetoc. Granted, Jetoc seemed cleaner than most Drells, but that didn't mean Aidan had any desire to room with him.

Sula was asleep when Aidan entered their quarters. Asleep or awake didn't seem to matter; her delightful scent and warm presence called to him anyway. He smiled to himself as he spotted his duffel bag sitting in the corner of the tiny compartment. As logical as he'd tried to make his choice of accommodations seem, Sula had apparently arrived at the same conclusion.

Still, it didn't do to make too many assumptions, and with that in mind, he donned a pair of shorts and a T-shirt before climbing the ladder to the unoccupied upper bunk.

As tired as he was, he figured he would fall asleep the moment he closed his eyes. Sleep, however, proved elusive. He could've listed any number of reasons why, but if his level of sexual arousal was any indication, Sula was having some incredibly steamy dreams.

After he'd turned over for the umpteenth time, she whispered his name.

"Sorry for waking you," he said. "I can't seem to get my brain to shut down."

"I know what you mean," she said. "I've been lying here for hours and haven't slept a wink."

"Same here." Small wonder her scent had affected

him so strongly. That she'd been thinking rather than dreaming cheered him considerably.

"Do you think…I mean, I know these bunks are small, but I was hoping we might…"

"Share?"

The breath she exhaled sounded as though she'd been holding it for days. "Oh yeah."

Aidan rolled over and jumped down, landing lightly on the floor beside her. When she scooted toward the wall and pulled back the blanket in a silent invitation, he lay down beside her, sliding one arm beneath her head and draping the other over her waist. Even without his superb night vision, he would've known her by the crimson glow from her eyes.

"I see you got rid of the fangs," he said.

"I thought it would be safer for both of us."

"No kidding." Her teasing tone and coy smile made him wonder, though. Was she only planning to bite him on the neck, or was she going to do something else? Something erotic and stimulating, perhaps?

The mere thought of what she might do to him sent a surge of excitement through his body. His cock was already so hard, it ached.

Then she kissed him, and every stroke of his heart seemed to be pushing even more blood straight to his groin. The kiss was better than anything he'd ever felt or tasted—even better than their previous kisses. Still, there were other parts of her he longed to enjoy. Her full breasts, her taut nipples, her warm, wet pussy.

He hated that word. It seemed so inadequate for something so wondrously luscious. There should be something else—perhaps the Zetithian word. He tried to remember…

Loresh—the source of a man's joy.

He would tell her that at some point. For now, however, he let the word play through his thoughts, teasing him with the glorious delights yet to come. He avoided biting her neck, choosing to tug at her earlobe instead, catching it between his teeth and tugging until it slid from his lips. Her soft hum of pleasure told him how much she enjoyed it.

Without a word, she ducked her head and bit him on the neck. Even without fangs, the shocking sensation of her teeth pressing into his flesh shook him to the marrow. Her tongue on his skin sent shivers down his spine as she licked the place she'd bitten.

Only in that moment did he realize he was purring. He might've been doing it sooner, but his mind only surfaced long enough to register that fact before submerging once again into the splendid essence of Sula.

He spared a brief thought to the consequences. She would have triplets if she conceived. "Are you in one of your fertile periods? If so, we should wait—"

A finger pressed to his lips silenced him. "I have a slow-release birth control implant. It should be good for another five years."

Suddenly, what Kim had said about sex not having the "desired effect" made sense. The scanner might not have detected any nanobots or disease, but it had apparently found the implant. "So you're okay with this?"

A slow smile curved her lips. "In body, mind, and soul."

With another kiss, he began purring again. The play of her tongue against his—soft, wet, and utterly delightful—made him purr even louder. She caressed his shoulder with a gentle hand before spearing her fingers through his hair. A tug on his shorts by her other hand reminded him that he was still dressed and so was she. She was wearing the nightgown Rashe had brought for her, which was much too lovely to rip with his fangs, even though that was precisely what he wanted to do.

However, he found that bunching her nightie up with his fingers gradually brought him into contact with her bare, silken skin. A fragrance like rain-drenched spring flowers filled his head, but even that couldn't begin to mask the enthralling aroma of her desire. With every touch, he seemed to absorb more of her essence.

He'd never asked his father what it was like for a Zetithian to mate with a Terran—possibly because his father's breeding was so different from his own—so he hadn't known what to expect. His eyes widened as her aura seeped in through his pores. He was only touching her with his hands and mouth. What would happen when they were skin-to-skin?

"Something about you intoxicates me," he whispered against her lips. "I can't explain it any other way."

"You do the same thing to me."

"I need to touch more of you." Releasing his hold on her, he tore off his shirt and tossed it aside. His shorts quickly followed.

She grasped the hem of her gown. "Help me get this off."

Delighted to comply, he pulled it over her head.

She stretched out on her side, gazing up at him with the most beguiling eyes he'd ever seen, and for what seemed like an eternity, all he could do was stare. Her long, dark hair fell loosely over her shoulders in soft waves that curled around her breasts, the dark areolas in sharp contrast to the lighter tone of her skin. Her full lips beckoned; the arch of her brow enticed. The line of her lovely neck sloped to her shoulder in a graceful curve. The rise of her chest dipped to her waist before flaring out to the lushness of her hip.

"I've never seen anything so incredibly beautiful in my life."

Her smile compounded her allure, something he wouldn't have believed possible. "Neither have I."

In the next instant, he was beside her again, pressing the full length of his body to hers. The intimacy was shocking, as though every cell in his body was somehow awash with her essence. Her flavor when he kissed her was even more delicious and powerful than it had been before. How could that be? Something about her connected with him on a molecular level, binding them together in a way he never expected, almost as if she were the Mordrial mystic instead of him.

She had other flavors to discover. He'd avoided her neck before; now he let his lips and tongue roam freely where his fangs should not. Nevertheless, the metallic tang on his tongue warned that a fang had grazed her skin, drawing blood.

"Sorry," he whispered. "I'll try to be more careful."

Her smile surprised him a little. "No worries. I'll live."

Her soft, warm skin grew more delectable as he progressed from her neck to her breasts, and the firm bud of her nipple yielded a taste sensation that burst on his tongue like a potent spice. Her hum of pleasure drove him further still, on down past her navel and over the soft swell of her belly until he reached the source of the most amazing scent of all. One taste, no matter how sublime, would never be enough to satisfy him.

A swipe of his tongue over her clitoris had her grasping the back of his head. "Don't stop. Please don't stop."

His own desire began spiraling out of control as her thighs gripped his head. Moments passed—or was it an eternity of pleasure?—before her breath caught and her tight nub surged against his tongue.

With her climactic cry, the need to mate overwhelmed him to the point that he could think of nothing aside from sliding his cock into her tight, wet heat. A subtle move brought him up over her again, bringing that thought to the brink of reality. As she opened herself to him, the lure of her *loresh* was like magic, drawing him effortlessly inside her. A slight withdrawal followed by a strong pelvic thrust was the only reminder that he still had control of his muscles.

A moan broke from her lips as her sheath tightened around his cock, undoubtedly responding to his orgasmic coronal fluid. "Oh, Aidan…"

The steady push and pull on the fleshy ruffle at the base of his cockhead threatened to drive him mad. Each stroke forced the level of ecstasy higher still. He gazed down at her in amazement. "How are you doing that?"

"You're the one doing it to me." She gasped as her inner muscles gripped his cock once again. "I never *dreamed*…"

In the next instant, his control snapped, and his eyes squeezed shut as Aidan reached the first climax of his life. Sensations hitherto unfelt flooded his mind and body as his testicles contracted, sending forceful jets of *snard* flowing from his cock. An explosive purr issued from his throat, and for one rapturous moment, his mind went completely blank.

His mind might have been blank, but his body was flooded with an ecstasy so complete, it rivaled perfection. Even though his eyes remained closed, a brilliant light engulfed his visual sense, astounding him with its radiance. Then, like the tide crashing on a rocky shore, the light burst into a swirling sea of colors before slowly receding into darkness.

When he opened his eyes, he found himself looking down at Sula's lovely face. Her eyes were open wide in a response so extraordinary, he could only gaze at her in wonder. Aidan thanked the gods—and Giklor—for the red glow from her pupils; otherwise, he might have missed the most beautiful sight he had ever seen or even imagined.

Mesmerized, he watched as her pupils dilated, growing steadily larger until her irises were reduced to thin rims, like crescent moons emerging from the shadow of their mother planet. Her lips formed a soundless O, and her skin seemed to shimmer in the light cast from his eyes.

In that moment, he was lost. At last, he'd made love with the one destined to be his mate. No prescient visions filled his mind to inform him that this was true.

His heart told him everything he needed to know.

Chapter 21

SULA BLINKED, HOPING TO RETRIEVE HER EYES FROM THE back of her head where they'd rolled. As her vision cleared, she locked her gaze onto Aidan's, still unsure what had just happened to her.

I've made love with a Zetithian.

No written account could have prepared her, because there were no words to describe what she'd felt.

Unless they were Zetithian words.

"What's the Zetithian word for orgasm?" she whispered, not trusting her full voice.

The few moments he took to reply might have signified either a search of his memory or a voice as unsteady as hers. Or both.

"*Orwanda*," he finally said. "Which would suggest that the 'Oh' reaction is universal."

"Multiple orgasms?" She'd certainly had plenty of those in the past half hour or so—yet another first.

"*Orwandai*."

"I think I like that better than the Stantongue version. We should make an effort to add it to the galactic lexicon. I know some linguistics professors who could help. I'm sure they'd be interested. Of course, they'd have to experience this for themselves." She frowned. "They're really old, though. The shock would probably kill them."

She knew she was babbling, but at the moment, she

didn't give a damn. She felt as though her entire body were swimming in whiskey. Even her cheeks were numb.

"Might be better to—" She pressed her fingers to her lips as an entirely different sensation washed through her. "I feel sort of hot in the small of my back. No, wait. It's moving out to my fingers and toes." She managed a grin as her muscles and cares melted like butter on the tongue. "Way cool."

The slow, wet kiss he gave her made her relax even more. "What you're feeling now is called *laetralance*. Sort of like afterglow, only better. Or so I'm told."

"I can vouch for that." Sex with a human male had never been anything like this—except for the obvious similarities of inserting Tab A into Slot B and the procreative function. Beyond that, there could be no comparison. *None*. "No wonder some jealous dude blew up your planet. After being with one of you guys, no human female would ever be satisfied again."

"Once you go cat, you never go back?" His chuckle sent a warm vibration through her, much as his purr had done. "That was the slogan for the Zetithian Palace brothel."

"For once, truth in advertising." She grimaced as a new thought struck her. "How many customers did they have at that brothel?"

"With Onca, Tarq, and Jerden working there for several years? Thousands, I suppose."

"How did those women ever walk away?"

"They didn't. Remember those daybeds in the lobby? That's where they went to recover."

"I get that part," she said with a touch of impatience. "What I want to know is how they ever managed to get on with their lives knowing such ecstasy was even possible."

Aidan rolled over onto his back, robbing her of his warmth. The blanket he pulled over them was a poor substitute. "At least one of them didn't. She killed the woman who provided the scent that enabled the guys to do women of practically every species. Tarq had already left by then, and Jerden retired after that. Onca kept going for another two years before he finally gave it up. Considering the danger, most of us have been more selective since then."

"Selective? How many have you—" Too late, she remembered what Abuti had said about Aidan never having had a girlfriend. She'd been skeptical at the time; she was even more so now. Knowing what he was capable of, she couldn't understand why there hadn't been long lines of women waiting outside his house on the off chance they might catch a glimpse of him.

"No one but you, Sula." Clasping her hand, he pressed it to his lips. "Only you."

Sula didn't know whether to be honored or afraid. Afraid because if he hadn't been saving himself for someone special, she might simply be his first, and honored because she might actually be that special someone. If this was indeed his first time, and she had no reason to doubt his word, he'd seemed to know exactly what to do. The basics, anyway—which, for a Zetithian, was sufficiently mind-blowing. Any more expertise and she would've remained in the *laetralant* phase for days. She was tongue-tied enough as it was.

"I-I don't know what to say."

"You don't have to say anything." He kissed her hand

again before placing it on his chest and covering it with his own. "But it's true. I've never felt like this about anyone else."

Sula allowed herself a measure of cautious optimism. "Could that be because you've never let your guard down before?"

He didn't answer right away. "Maybe. Although to be honest, until I met you, I've never even been tempted."

His heart beat strongly beneath her hand as she snuggled closer. "I'm glad you did."

"Me too." He rubbed his cheek against her forehead and gave her a quick one-armed hug. "Think you can sleep now?"

"Probably. I'm a little surprised I didn't conk out immediately. That *snard* of yours packs quite a punch." Even if she hadn't already been well on her way to loving him, sex would've hastened the process. As it was, she suspected it might have sealed her fate.

"So do you."

Warmth stole its way into her heart at his words. She skimmed her palm over his chest, ruffling the blond curls that dusted his skin. Once again, she didn't know how to respond. "You keep saying things that leave me speechless."

"I guess that makes us even." Turning his head, he kissed her somewhere in the vicinity of her temple. The location didn't seem to matter. No matter where his lips touched her, their effect was somehow magical— sensuous, caring, and surprisingly familiar, like he'd been kissing her for years.

How could he make her forget Raj so easily? If *forget* was even the right word. Raj had been dead for a full year. She hadn't forgotten him, nor had her fondness for him diminished. Was it simply time for her to move on? What was a reasonable mourning period anyway? One year? Two? She'd heard of people who never ceased to mourn the loss of a lover. Was falling for Aidan somehow inappropriate? Should she be chastising herself for being so fickle? For that matter, would she have felt the same way about Aidan if she'd met him when she and Raj were still together?

That last question was pointless; Raj was gone, so she would never know the answer. His body had crumbled to dust right before her eyes. The horror of those last hours had haunted her for months. Aidan hadn't banished those memories completely, but he'd certainly made them easier to bear. Recalling that Aidan had seen her accident in a vision helped her to regain her perspective.

Such portents were not to be taken lightly. Perhaps she should simply trust that fate, destiny, or some higher power knew what was best for her. Whatever the source of Aidan's insight, his intervention had been vital. Without her continued survival, she would never discover the truth about what happened on Ecos or bring the instigators to justice. She'd survived for a very good reason.

On that comforting thought, she finally fell asleep.

Hours later, Aidan awoke feeling more content than ever before. He took the time to savor the moment, knowing that Sula lay safe beside him. He only had to get up, fix breakfast, take a shower, and go back to bed if he wished. Making love with Sula for the remainder of the morning sounded absolutely fabulous.

He moved his head, noting that he felt rather strange. He'd rarely allowed himself the freedom to get drunk for fear of blurting out his secrets, but that was exactly how he felt. His vision swam when he sat up. A shake of his head only made it worse.

How odd.

Especially in light of his Zetithian blood. Zetithians might go to sleep feeling rotten, but they seldom woke up ill. If any of his brothers or friends had ever done such a thing, he surely would've heard about it—and remembered.

He lay back down with caution. Falling out of the narrow bunk would really make him look stupid.

Unless the new strain of the Scorillian plague was sexually transmitted.

He caught himself before allowing that thought to go any further. Sula might have given the plague to Raj that way, but none of the other inhabitants of Ecos would've contracted it.

Still, he was a Terran–Zetithian hybrid with Mordrial ancestry. Did this have something to do with losing his virginity?

He frowned, noting a peculiar scratchiness in his eyes. If his brother Aldrik's experience was any indication, becoming sexually active wouldn't have that effect.

A sweet flavor coated his tongue, like a potent wine that tasted strongly of raisins. He hadn't noticed it the night before.

He nudged Sula. "Do you feel okay?"

"Perfect," she murmured. "You?"

"I'm not sure. Try sitting up."

She rose in one swift, graceful movement and

stretched her arms as far as the limited space would allow. "I feel great. Don't even have a *snard* hangover."

"I'm thinking maybe I do. I've never heard of such a thing, but there's a first time for everything. I feel really strange. Can't see straight, actually."

Sula leaned closer. "Your skin color looks okay." Peering at his eyes, she retracted one of his lower lids. "Mucosa is nice and pink." Obviously noting his quizzical expression, she went on, "If you had the Scorillian plague, it would be very pale, and the whites of your eyes would be slightly yellowish. They both look fine to me."

"Thank the gods for small favors," he muttered. "Although I really wasn't afraid I had the plague. The medscanner at the orphanage might not be the newest model, but it isn't so old it can't detect a virus."

"Think Curly would have a scanner on board?"

Aidan shrugged. "He might. Jack likes to be sure her sons are equipped to handle any emergency, and she's had enough experience to know the sort of difficulties you can run into in space."

"Yeah. Like weird new diseases and broken legs." She placed a hand on his forehead. "You don't feel feverish—no hotter than usual, anyway." A smile threatened. "I mean, you're always hot, but not the kind of heat that can be measured with a thermometer." She pushed herself up on her hands and knees. "I'm getting up. Hold still while I climb over you."

Aidan was pleased that the ship's lighting was currently on the daytime setting or he might've missed the early morning treat of watching Sula get out of bed. Granted, he could see quite well in the dark, but a little ambient light didn't hurt.

Her hair still had a slight curl to it, and her breasts swayed as she straddled him briefly before swinging her other leg over to land on the floor.

"Where's my—" Her roving gaze stopped at the foot of the bunk. "Ah. There it is."

He was only given a few seconds to admire her lithe form before, to his infinite disappointment, she turned the gown right side out and dropped it over her head. Rashe had chosen a very pretty nightie for her, but unfortunately, it covered her from her shoulders to just below her knees.

She pulled her hair out from under the gown and combed through it with her fingers. "Stay put until I get back. I'm going to find Curly and ask if he has a scanner."

Aidan thought for a second. "Val was carrying a pack when he boarded. He might have brought along something of that sort. Just don't tell Giklor I'm feeling bad. You know how he is."

"Trust me, I haven't forgotten." She gave him a quick kiss, then hurried toward the door. In an instant, the door slid open, and she was gone.

Left alone with his thoughts, he tried to imagine any source of contamination and couldn't come up with a thing, unless he was allergic to Drells. He'd never had that problem in the past, but stranger things had happened, and a Drell allergy was something he figured he could live with.

Then a more devastating thought surfaced. One that, if true, would indeed be a tragedy.

What if I'm allergic to Sula?

Sula hadn't been given a tour of the ship, but she found the bridge easily enough. Without bothering with pleasantries—or even caring who was there—she blurted out, "Does anyone have a medscanner? Aidan isn't feeling well."

Curly swiveled his chair around to face her. "In the morning? Impossible."

She stomped her foot. "I'm not kidding. Trust me, he's as weirded out about it as you are. He doesn't have a fever. It's mostly visual disturbances." Using Aidan's own choice of words would've undoubtedly resulted in the kind of morning-after jibe she would prefer to avoid. Unfortunately, Curly's skeptical expression seemed to presage precisely that sort of comment.

Val sat perched on a tall stool at what could've been the comstation or the science station. She wasn't sure which. He glanced up from the console. "Any other symptoms?"

The Avian's arched brow and piercing stare made her want to kick herself for not questioning Aidan more thoroughly. "He just said he feels strange."

"I'm sure he does," Curly drawled. "Losing one's virginity will do that to a guy."

Planting her fists firmly on her hips, she fixed him with her best angry glare. "And how would you know that?"

"You slept in the same room with him, didn't you?"

"Well, yeah…"

Curly folded his arms and leaned back in his chair. "I rest my case."

Her palms itched to slap that cocky smirk right off his handsome face. "Have you ever known sex to affect a Zetithian man's vision before?"

"No," Curly replied, relenting a bit. "But you have to admit, the timing fits."

Clearly, Curly was going to be no help at all. She dismissed him with a wave and returned her attention to Val. "Do you have a portable medscanner?"

Val nodded. "Yes, I do."

"Thank you." With a sharp exhale, she aimed yet another glare at Curly. "All I wanted was a straight answer, not a load of schoolboy crap."

To her surprise, Curly actually laughed. "I'm beginning to understand why Aidan likes you so much."

Spreading his wings slightly, Val slid off his stool and started toward the door. "I shall retrieve the device and meet you in Aidan's quarters."

"Might want to scan Typhoid Mary while you're at it," Curly called after him. "What with the orphanage's scanner being such a relic and all."

"That's an excellent idea," Sula said, doing her best to mask her annoyance. "But first, we need to figure out what's wrong with Aidan." Curly would probably grow on her after a while, but at the moment, she found his brand of humor difficult to appreciate.

As she followed Val down the passageway, she couldn't help marveling at his wings. Aidan's wings were pretty cool, but they weren't real, nor were they anywhere near as beautiful. Val intrigued her in other ways too. His speech patterns varied from stilted formality to colloquial slang, and he seemed serious to the point of being chronically troubled, as though there were dark times in his past from which he had yet to recover. Aidan might've known about some of those episodes, but Val's demeanor suggested that he rarely shared his burdens. As with Aidan at the start of their relationship, Val seemed to have built a wall around himself, with the result that his life was probably as lacking in romance as Aidan's had been.

Still, there was a great deal to be said for a compatriot who stuck to business.

Aidan's eyes were closed when she entered the room but slowly opened as she approached. "What's up?"

"Val went to get his scanner. If Curly has one, he didn't volunteer that information." She huffed out a breath. "Is he always that irritating?"

"Not really. You just need to get to know him better."

She responded with a snort. "Sounds like loads of fun."

"Val's his exact opposite," he said. "Hardly ever says anything and rarely cracks a smile."

"I noticed that." She took a moment to study his face. He didn't look any different than when she'd left him before, but the urge to check his sclera again was strong.

Any further discussion was thwarted by Val's arrival. As she'd expected, the Zerkan hadn't been content to remain behind.

Giklor darted past Val and ran toward Aidan. "My dear friend, please let me heal you," he urged. "One dose of my healing fluids, and you will feel perfectly well in a trice."

Aidan put up a hand. "Let's do the scan first. I'd really like to know what we're dealing with before you try to fix it for me."

"As you wish." Giklor didn't sound the least bit contrite as he stepped aside. In fact, he seemed as hurt as he'd been when Sula first refused his services.

Val knelt at Aidan's bedside, a position that would've

been easy for anyone else, but Val had to spread his wings in order to do it. He held up a small, round device. "This portable scanner is state-of-the-art. With it, I should be able to determine the cause of your problem."

"Go for it," Aidan said.

Val activated the scanner, then directed the beam toward Aidan. After several passes, he consulted the display. "Interesting."

Sula waited several excruciating seconds before prompting him. "How so?"

"There is a foreign compound in his bloodstream that reads like an inhibitor of some sort." After a few moments, he aimed his predatory gaze at her. "An ovulation inhibitor."

Sula suspected that being peered at by Val would take even more getting used to than Curly's peculiar sense of humor. As a result, her voice was little more than a squeak. "Seriously?"

His expression was an accusation in itself. "Have you been given some form of birth control?"

"I have an implant that's good for several years." She gaped at him. "Are you saying that some of it has somehow gotten into Aidan's bloodstream?"

"So it would seem," he replied. "If you intend to continue as sexual partners, may I recommend its removal?"

"Oh, you have *got* to be kidding me," she protested. "I've never heard of such a thing. A man being affected by his partner's medication? It's impossible."

Val's wings rose in an apparent shrug. "You've never had sex with a Zetithian. I'm surprised it didn't inhibit his erection."

Her cheeks prickled with embarrassment. She wasn't

accustomed to such frank sexual discussions, even if Val did sound a bit like a doctor.

He stood without waiting for her to comment. "Where is it?"

She pointed to the underside of her left upper arm. "I don't understand. People have been using these for ages. Raj was never bothered by it."

Val continued to glower at her. "As I said before, you've never been with a Zetithian. They are very sensitive to such things."

Sula didn't ask how he knew that. Should she remove it and risk conception at such a precarious time? Or should she simply abstain?

Tough choice.

Before she could say another word, Val grasped her wrist and lifted her arm. Following a pass of the scanner over the area she'd indicated, he studied the display. "This is also the source of another of your difficulties." A flick of his brow was accompanied by a grim smile. "It's covered with hundreds of nanobots."

Chapter 22

"Take it out," Sula demanded. "Now. Then we can space it."

"Let's not be too hasty." Aidan sat up on the side of the bunk and rubbed his eyes. He still felt odd, but at least his vision wasn't jumping around like a Borellian grasshopper. "I'm guessing you got that implant just before you left Ursa Prime, right?"

"I've had it a whole lot longer than that." Sula closed her eyes and pressed her lips together for several moments before she took a deep breath and spoke again. "Are you saying I've been traceable during all that time?"

"Possibly," Val replied. "Although these bots may have been programmed to seek out your implant after they were injected. Most bots are filtered out by the kidneys and excreted in the urine. These would appear to be more sophisticated. Although if what I was told is true and you were supposed to die on Ecos, tracking you would be pointless."

For someone who had only joined the party the night before, Val seemed surprisingly well informed. Apparently, he'd been brought up to speed during the night by someone who hadn't been busy making love with their roommate.

"I've wondered about that," Aidan said. "It does seem"—he caught himself before saying *overkill*—"superfluous. Could you have been injected with them after you landed on Rhylos?"

"That's possible," Sula replied. "Except the injections Raj and I received weren't entirely painless. I'm pretty sure I would've noticed it." She glanced at Val. "Could I have swallowed the bots?"

"Yes," Val replied. "Although injections are more reliable."

"Think, Sula," Aidan urged. "Were there any seemingly chance encounters—someone bumping into you or a diversion that might've distracted you for a few seconds?"

Shaking her head, Sula plopped down beside him on the bunk. "You mean aside from being fired upon when I was buying supplies? No, not really."

"How long had you been on Rhylos when that happened?" Val asked.

"Only a couple of days," Sula replied. "I'd already decided what I was going to do long before I landed. Once I'd sold the ship and had credits to spend, I didn't waste any time."

"And yet you were able to escape an assassin who was presumably able to track you," Val mused. "That seems highly unlikely."

"True," Sula agreed. "Maybe after the attack failed, they just decided to keep an eye on me and see what I intended to do. When all I did was head for the mountains, they might've figured they'd scared me off."

Aidan stared at the floor in front of him, trying his best to stop it from appearing to move in waves. "Or maybe they chose not to compound one mistake by making another."

Turning her head, Sula stared at him in apparent disbelief. "You think what happened on Ecos was a mistake?"

He clasped her knee, as much to reassure her as to steady himself. "No. I think what happened with *you* was a mistake, not the natives. I can't imagine anything of that magnitude being accidental."

"I agree," Val said with a grave nod. "I have seen far too much evil in this galaxy to believe otherwise."

Sula's shoulders sagged briefly. A moment later, she sat up straighter, her eyes wide. "Wait a second. What if the bots have nothing to do with the Ecos mission? What if they're related to the sale of the ship?"

"That's a possibility," Aidan said. "Your shady ship dealers could have tagged you with bots so they could find you and steal back their money."

"That might explain why I was targeted. But left alone for months afterward? Surely, they wouldn't give up that easily." Her shoulders slumped again.

"Perhaps your attacker found you by chance the first time." Giklor had been so quiet, Aidan had almost forgotten he was there. "Perhaps you didn't acquire the bots until your most recent return to Damenk."

"That makes even less sense," Aidan said. "Unless there's a traitor in our midst. I don't even want to consider that possibility."

"Perhaps you should," the Zerkan advised. "Who among you should not be trusted?"

"I refuse to accept that," Aidan growled. "I—"

"Wait! I've got it!" Sula exclaimed. "I think the bots were injected before Raj and I left for Ecos, either as a fail-safe measure or a means of making sure we actually made it to Ecos. Afterward, until someone learned that the ship made it to Rhylos, we were both presumed dead. With the ship as evidence, they had to figure at least one of us had survived, so they started tracking me again."

"The signal is relatively weak," Val said. "Although it may have lost power over time."

"That could explain how I was able to escape from the assassin and hide out in the mountains. No one could've predicted where I would go after they lost the signal, but when I came back to Damenk, they were able to find me."

Aidan squeezed his eyes shut as his vision wavered once more. "That sounds reasonable. At least I think it does. Not sure my brain is a hundred percent right now."

"I'm amazed that contraceptives would affect you like that." After a moment's hesitation, she turned to face him again. "Does this mean we can't have sex without having a baby?"

"Triplets, actually. But you knew that." He rubbed the back of his neck, which didn't help any more than blinking had done. "Okay. The signal is weak, so they can't track you in space. But if we remove your implant—and the bots along with it—we should be able to use it as bait, maybe?"

"Bait for an assassin?" she suggested.

"Mmm, yeah. Doesn't sound very good, does it?"

"Not really, no."

Aidan opened his eyes wider, hoping that might fix the problem. It didn't. "Okay, then. Let's try this. We pull your implant, leave it somewhere, but you won't be anywhere near it, so you can go to the university and see who's the most surprised to see you."

"And the most disappointed," Val added.

"Too bad my sister isn't here," Aidan said. "She could tell you who was lying and who was really weirded out by seeing you, no matter what they say."

"Aidan, sweetheart," she began. "All we need is for you to shake hands with anyone we suspect. You'll get some sort of vibe from them, wouldn't you?"

"I hadn't thought of that."

The dumb blond is back.

No. Not dumb, just drugged.

Yeah, by the birth control implant from the one woman in the universe I want to make love with. The only woman I've ever made love with.

Such a dilemma.

He sighed. "You're right. Since they won't be able to track us, we can get close enough to do it without anyone knowing we're coming."

"Shall I remove it now?" Val asked. "I must advise you that removal probably hurts more than insertion."

"Doesn't matter."

Aidan gazed into the dark-brown depths of her eyes with every ounce of pleading he could pack into his expression. "Please don't even think about the other option."

"Abstinence, you mean? I probably should." A feather-like caress of his cheek conveyed her regret. "You're kinda hard to resist, though."

He certainly couldn't resist her. In fact, if Val and Giklor would get lost, he would be kissing her right that very moment.

"There are other ways to show affection without risking conception." A sidelong glance proved that pearl of wisdom had come from Giklor. "Shall I enumerate them?"

"Thanks, but that won't be necessary," Aidan drawled. "I'm pretty sure I know them all."

Giklor wheezed with laughter. "Oh, I doubt that. You've only been intimate the one time. I cannot imagine that you demonstrated any significant creativity."

"Don't worry, Giklor," Sula said. "Anything he doesn't know, I probably do." She glanced at Aidan, her eyes brimming with mischief. "I've been studying the *Kama Sutra* since I was in junior high."

Sula wouldn't have thought a winged computer hacker would've possessed any surgical skills, but after only a few minutes in sick bay, Val was able to remove the implant with minimal blood loss and very little pain.

"You missed your calling," she said as he repaired the wound with the Seal 'n' Heal that Curly had advised them to use. At a glance, the ship's medical supplies appeared to be fairly comprehensive. Considering the box of cast kits on the shelf beside the Seal 'n' Heal, most broken bones wouldn't pose too much of a problem.

"It is a minor procedure." Val held up the implant with a pair of tweezers, his gaze roving over its length. "Learning more about these nanobots will require expertise of a different sort."

"Are you sure they're all in there?"

"I will scan you again to be certain, but I believe them to have imbedded themselves in the outer surface of the implant. Any remaining bots loose in your body should be eliminated via the natural excretory process."

The sooner that happened, the better. "Have you ever heard of nanobots acting the way these do?"

"Only those that are used in medicine to seek out abnormal tissues and repair or destroy them. Trackers of this type sometimes attach to bone, but even then, they are not permanent. I have no idea why attaching themselves to a birth control device would have extended their lifespan, unless these are an entirely new breed."

She pulled her sleeve down over the nearly healed wound. "You're forgetting who sent me to Ecos. Dalb University is home to scads of scientific research projects. It's frightening to think how the data they've amassed there could be subverted."

"I am well aware of such subversion," he said quietly. "I was created from it."

Not born, not cloned, but created. She didn't know how to respond. Should she praise his creator's inventiveness or condemn the illegal use of the cloning process? "It's nice to know something good can come from a misuse of technology."

"Good?" His crystalline eyes met hers with a glare that would've made her take a step back if she'd been standing. "I have yet to decide whether my existence constitutes good or evil."

She studied his handsome face, his powerful form, and most of all, his astonishing wings. Granted, he wasn't entirely human, but as a humanoid male capable of flight, he was perfection itself.

He resumed his visual inspection of the implant, giving her a much-needed respite from his unnerving gaze. "Perhaps malevolence is imbedded in me, much as these bots have imbedded themselves in this device, and is only awaiting the right trigger to manifest itself."

"I doubt that. From my perspective, I see only good

in you." Sadness might've clung to him like a damp cloak, but no veil of evil shrouded him from the light. "Has Aidan seen your future?"

His lips twitched in what was almost a smile. "All he would say was that it's better than most." With another smile that never completely materialized, he added, "He only told me that last night."

"He seems to be fairly reliable in that respect," she said. "You might want to let that sink in for a while."

He shook his head. "My past still haunts me. I have difficulty seeing beyond it."

"You aren't alone in that." Sula had come dangerously close to allowing her past tragedies to eliminate the possibility of a brighter future. She knew better now. "We all need to remember to focus on the present and not let our ghosts and fears rule us."

"So much wisdom in one so young."

"I'm not *that* young," she protested. Val, on the other hand, seemed almost ageless. "How old are you?" The words were out before she could catch them.

"I've never been quite sure," he replied. "I had not reached full adulthood when I was freed from my"— his hesitation suggested he was about to say *creator* but thought better of it—"captor."

"And you've been free for how long?"

A blink momentarily shielded her from his disturbing stare. "Twenty-one standard years."

That much, he seemed to know without doubt. "Okay. Let's say you were fifteen then. That would make you about thirty-six." When he received this estimate without any reaction, she went on, "Do you even have a birthday to celebrate?"

Something in his manner made her wonder if anyone had ever asked him these simple questions about himself. However, he didn't appear to resent the intrusion. "I was assigned a birthdate when I arrived on Rhylos. It was determined by a similar calculation."

Heat flooded her face. "You should've stopped me sooner."

"If you had been incorrect, I would have."

A tiny laugh escaped her. "I was always good at math."

"You are good at other things as well. Despite his peculiar reaction to the medication in your birth control device, I've never known Aidan to be happier than he is now. I believe he would have continued to suffer the symptoms quite cheerfully knowing that the only way to recover completely was to give you up."

Val obviously hadn't missed Aidan's aversion to the very idea of abstinence.

"He won't have to give me up," she said. "Conceiving his children is a risk I'm willing to take. You might even say I'm looking forward to it."

"As long as our mission is successful," he cautioned. "If you were to abandon this quest simply to become a mother, you would not be the woman I suspect you of being."

"You're right. I've come too far to stop now. Although I don't believe our mission and my relationship with Aidan are mutually exclusive."

"One will follow the other, which is just as it should be," Giklor said as he entered the room. "Our friend Aidan is already improving." The little Zerkan shook his head as he heaved a sigh. "These Zetithians…they seem capable of recovering from almost anything."

Sula smiled. "If I didn't know better, I'd think you were unhappy about that."

Giklor waved his hands in protest. "Oh no. Although they do require treatment on occasion, the severity of injury or illness when they arrive at that point is too dreadful to contemplate. I would not wish such grievous bodily harm upon any of them."

"I'm glad to hear it." She looked up at Val, who was still peering at the implant as though it contained the secrets of the universe. "Are you going to scan me again now?"

"Yes. This will only take a moment." He dropped the implant into an open specimen jar and then screwed on the lid. After several slow passes of the scanner over her body, he switched it off. "I see no evidence of any residual bots."

"That's a relief," she said. "I'm glad you brought that thing with you. Although considering the amount of medical supplies on board, Curly probably has one stashed around here somewhere."

"If he does, I doubt he's ever used it. Most of these items don't appear to been touched for quite some time." To illustrate, he held up a dusty finger after sweeping it over the top of the specimen jar. "These jars were sealed, or using them would not be advisable."

"Any idea whether the bots will continue to function without a host?"

"No," he replied. "In fact, it would be best if they don't. Their potential use as a decoy is outweighed by our ability to land on Ursa Prime without our enemy's knowledge."

She hopped up from her chair feeling a peculiar sense

of freedom knowing that she could no longer be tracked. "Considering all the trouble they've caused, I'd still like to space them."

"I can't blame you for that." Val wiped the tweezers and scalpel with a disinfectant swab before returning them to a nearby drawer. "No doubt our captain will have some suggestions for their disposal. For now, however, I believe the stasis unit would be the best place for them."

Giklor was still lurking near the doorway. "Speaking of the stasis unit…"

"Yes?" Sula replied. "Did you need something?"

"Ah, yes," he replied. "You see, I find myself in a dilemma of sorts."

Somewhat taken aback, Sula eyed him curiously. "Which is?"

Giklor bowed his head and clasped his hands in front of him. "I don't know how to find the stasis unit. I would greatly appreciate it if you would be so kind as to help me locate it. I would have asked Captain Curly, but I haven't been able to find him, either."

"Why didn't you ask Jetoc?" Sula asked. "They can't both be off duty."

Giklor shuffled his feet, still looking toward the floor. "If you must know, I am afraid of Drells." A grimace gave Giklor's mouth a peculiar triangular shape. "They look like a Zerkan with hair." He shuddered. "We Zerkans find such copious amounts of hair very disturbing on any creature."

"I understand." Given how hard it was to keep herself from laughing, Sula thought if she were to look at Val, she might actually catch him smiling. "I can help you find the stasis unit—or perhaps Val could show you. But right now, I need to talk to Curly myself." She started toward the door, then stopped as another alternative occurred to her. "Wait a second. Why didn't you just ask the computer where the stasis unit was?"

"I forgot I could do that," Giklor said meekly.

This seemed unlikely, unless—"Do you mean to say you've never been on a starship before?"

"To be perfectly honest, I haven't," Giklor said. "I was born on Rhylos, and thus far, I have found space travel to be almost as unnerving as the Drell's hair. However, I shall now ask—what is the computer's name?"

"I am called Laurel, and I will be happy to direct you to the stasis unit," a feminine voice replied from above, her aggrieved tone suggesting she should've been Giklor's first choice rather than his last resort.

"Thank you, Laurel," Sula said. "While you're at it, can you also give me Curly's current location?"

"Certainly," Laurel replied. "He is in the ready room with Qinta."

"With Qinta?" That sounded odd. "Can you tell me what they're doing?"

"As a rule, Captain Curly doesn't wish to have his actions questioned, nor does he wish to be disturbed at this time." Laurel sounded rather prim. "However, Qinta has given me no such instruction."

"Okay, then. What's Qinta doing?"

"She is engaged in a form of entertainment with the captain."

"Entertainment?" Sula's heart skipped several beats as she imagined the various activities a computer might classify in that manner. Anything from watching old movies to—*Oh, surely not.* "Can you direct me to the ready room?"

"Certainly," the computer replied. "Follow the flashing green lights on the passageway floor."

"Got it." Sula took off running, and within a short time, the lights had brought her to a door, which, of course, was closed. "Laurel, are you sure Curly doesn't want to be disturbed?"

"Quite sure."

It worked before; therefore, it was worth a try now. "Would you ask Qinta if I could speak with her?"

"I believe that would be possible."

"Do it."

The light above the door illuminated. "What's up?" Qinta asked over the intercom.

"Can I come in?"

"Sure, why not?" Qinta's tone was innocent enough to have dispelled any concerns, but Sula still felt it was her responsibility to be sure.

As the door slid open, Curly spun around in his chair, game controller in hand and fangs bared. "If you make me lose this match, as the gods are my witness, I'm gonna charge you double."

Chapter 23

"DIDN'T REALIZE YOU WERE CHARGING US ANYTHING," Sula said. "I figured this was an avenging-the-innocent-victims-free-of-charge sort of mission."

"Hey, even the good guys have to get paid now and then," Curly said with a shrug. "Was there something you needed me for?"

"Yes," Sula replied. "But that can wait. Right now, I need to be sure you really are one of the good guys."

"No worries there. I'm getting my ass kicked." With a nod toward Qinta, he added, "She's a pretty tough opponent." He arched a brow. "Why the inquisition?"

Sula did her best to keep her voice level. "You close the door and tell the computer not to let anyone disturb you while you play video games with a teenage girl, and you wonder why I'm asking questions?"

For a long moment, the only thing he did was gape at her. "I just didn't want any distractions."

"We're cool," Qinta said. "I'm the one who challenged him." Her sly glance slid toward Curly. "So far, it hasn't been much of a contest."

"That's part of my strategy," Curly insisted. "Lulling you into a false sense of security."

Qinta rolled her eyes. "Yeah, right. Admit it. I'm better at Super Starburst Football Adventure than you ever dreamed of being."

Curly tossed his controller onto the coffee table and

threw up his hands. "Have it your way. It's a kid's game anyhow."

"Look, Curly, I'm sorry for doubting you," Sula said. "But you must admit it seemed a little...suspicious."

"Maybe," he admitted. "For anyone but a Zetithian. If you know anything at all about us, you should know that taking advantage of women—young or old—is completely against our nature."

Sula exhaled sharply. "Sorry. I should've realized that."

"Apology accepted." Curly jumped up from his chair and started toward the door. "Guess I'll head on back to the bridge. Feel free to play as long as you like."

"Will do," Qinta said, sounding a touch more smug than was polite.

Without another word, he shouldered his way past Sula and strode off down the corridor.

"Mind telling me what that was all about?" Sula asked.

"It wasn't *about* anything," the Treslanti girl replied. "I just thought he'd be a fun opponent." She frowned. "He got really competitive and defensive, though. I figured a Zetithian would be a better sport." After switching off the game console, she fell back in her chair with a heavy sigh. "Aidan and Onca aren't like that. Why does Curly have to be an asshole just like every other man I've ever known?"

"Asshole?" Sula echoed. "That's a little strong, don't you think?"

"Maybe."

Qinta sounded like a typical sulky teen, a behavior Sula hadn't noticed in her before. Was she developing a crush on the dashing pilot? Or was there more to her mood than teenage angst?

"I keep telling myself that all men aren't like my father, but—" She broke off with a shrug. "Doesn't matter. I'll get over it. Someday."

Sula sat down in the seat Curly had vacated. "You want to talk about it?"

"Not really. Talking never helps anyway. I figured that out a long time ago."

"What exactly do you want from Curly?"

Qinta picked at the hem of her shirt. "I dunno. Just wanted to see if we could be friends, I guess."

Even though Sula didn't know her well, Qinta had always seemed tough and streetwise, but deep down, she was still an insecure teenager. And if Sula read the clues correctly, she'd suffered some form of abuse— mental, physical, or both—her father being the most likely culprit.

"I don't think being friends is too much to expect," Sula said. "Even if he is a little on the cocky side. According to Aidan, he's more like his Terran mother than his Zetithian father. I'm guessing she isn't one to lose gracefully, either."

"I've heard about his mother. She must really be something."

Never having met Jack, Sula couldn't say for certain. "Speaking of mothers, would you rather I stopped acting like one?"

That drew an infinitesimal smile. "No. At least you cared enough to check on me. My mother never did."

So…abuse and *neglect*. Unless the mother was also a victim.

"Is that why you're living at the orphanage?"

She nodded. "I couldn't take being at home anymore.

Everyone at the orphanage has been so kind to me. It's their job, of course, but it's been nice to be treated that way for a change."

"I don't believe any of the staff see working at the orphanage as a job. From what I understand, Aidan doesn't even draw a salary. They volunteer because they honestly want to help." Sula wasn't sure how she knew that, but she would've sworn it was true.

Qinta appeared to consider this. "You're right. I have a hard time believing anyone would care about me that much. I'm trying to adjust, and I think I've done pretty well so far, but it's hard sometimes."

"I think you're doing remarkably well. You were so ready to help me when I needed it. I'm here for you. I want you to know that."

"Yeah. I believe you. You know, this mission of ours," Qinta said slowly. "It could get us all killed."

"True. But it's worthwhile. Think of the children born on that world who never got the chance to grow to be as old as you are. None of them asked for that any more than you did." Sula hesitated. "I won't ask why you left your home. Whether you talk about it is your decision to make. No one will pressure you in any way."

Several moments passed before Qinta finally spoke again. "It's funny. My father was my best friend when I was little. Then as I got older, he changed toward me. Never said why. Just one day, he started treating me more like a"—she stopped and looked down at her hands—"sex worker than his daughter. Like I was only there to satisfy his needs. I knew it was wrong, but I went along with it for a long time. Then one day, I finally realized I didn't have to put up with what he did to me."

She sniffed as her tears began to fall. "It's so much worse when it's someone you should be able to trust."

"You felt betrayed?"

"Yeah." Qinta slammed her controller onto the table. "That's *exactly* how I felt." Following her brief outburst, she sat quietly, staring blankly ahead. "Curly didn't make me feel that way, though. He was only being himself, with no hidden agenda. He's just…Curly. Maybe he needs a friend as much as I do."

"Maybe even more." Sula suspected Aidan needed someone in the same way Curly did. "These Zetithian guys…they don't seem to do very well as loners." Val was probably just as needy. Finding someone to love him would go a long way toward breaking through that stoic facade of his.

But that was a job for another day.

Sula got to her feet. "Speaking of which, I need to check on Aidan. What do you say to a visit to the bridge?"

Her mouth stretched into a mischievous grin. "To say I'm sorry for beating Curly at Super Starburst Football Adventure?"

Sula chuckled. "That's a start, but I don't think you should apologize. Gloating would be better. After all, it's what he would do."

"Kindred spirits?"

"Yeah. Something like that."

"Gotcha."

Aidan still felt a little strange, but at least he'd made it from the bed to a nearby chair.

I'm allergic to contraceptives.

At least, that was how he'd interpreted the matter. Was that common among Zetithians? If so, he'd never heard about it. Perhaps a trip to Terra Minor was in order. The entire Zetithian database was housed there. He could access parts of it from home, but going there might be best. Since it had been designated as the new Zetithian homeworld, there were more Zetithians living on that planet than any other. They might know something.

However, except for his siblings, none of those Zetithians had Mordrial ancestry.

We just had to be different.

"I don't need help," he muttered. "I'm perfectly willing to make love with Sula without the benefit of birth control. Babies are good. The more, the merrier."

He still had a problem with the triplet idea, though. Three babies at one time sounded like way more trouble than any new parents should have to deal with. His parents had had two litters. Cat and Jack had had three. They'd had each other's help and support. Second and third litters were easier because the older children were there to help out, which was reportedly the way it had always been done on Zetith. Spacing of litters seemed to be built in as well. Jack had tried to have more kids in between the litters she'd had, without any luck.

Why was he thinking about this now when they were on their way to Ursa Prime with the intention of solving what was probably the most far-reaching murder mystery of all time?

When put like that, one ship and a handful of rebels seemed totally inadequate.

Then again, this wasn't a war that could be won with an army. The best way would be to get whoever was in charge to confess. Too bad they didn't know who that was, let alone how to get to them. Sula had suspicions, but that was the extent of it. Unfortunately, getting an evil mastermind to talk about their exploits probably wasn't as easy as it was in the movies. Even if the villain believed he had the upper hand, it didn't necessarily mean he would start spouting incriminating information. In fact, if the villain was as smart as Aidan suspected, he and his friends would probably be shot on sight.

Aidan had never wished to be able to read people's pasts as well as their futures. In this case, however, that ability would be far more useful. Of course, mind reading as a means of establishing someone's guilt probably wouldn't hold up in court anywhere except the Mordrial homeworld, where there would be others who could corroborate that evidence.

In this case, however, Sula *was* the evidence, along with the cave she'd found on Rhylos. He knew he could find that cave again, but so could someone else. That sort of evidence had been destroyed before, although no one else could possibly know what she'd found or where it was located. Even if she was suspected of having found something significant, they'd have done better to capture Sula and try to extract that information from her before someone else stumbled onto that cave. Then again, with Sula dead, no one would have any reason to connect that cave with what happened on Ecos.

Or did she worry them for a completely different reason? She hadn't died from what was apparently a new strain of the Scorillian plague. Was that what made her such a threat to them that they would send assassins after her?

Aidan squeezed his eyes shut.

My head hurts.

A footstep at the doorway made him open his eyes. He was pleased to see that, despite his headache, Sula looked perfectly normal; there was only one of her, and she didn't appear to be shimmering.

"Hey, you," she said. "Feeling any better?"

"I would if I could get my brain to stop hounding me." He peered up at her. "You realize we have absolutely no plans for how to accomplish this mission, don't you?"

She nodded. "We do seem to have been flying by the seat of our pants so far."

"We have to do better than that if we're to be successful—and remain alive."

"In a way, I'm amazed we're all still alive at this point." She tilted her head to one side, as though considering this. "Maybe some higher power has decided it's time to put an end to the atrocities. Are you sure you haven't seen anything?"

"I think the vision that led me to find you is a pretty good indication." He gazed up at her. "You obviously weren't meant to die on Ecos or Rhylos. And I don't think the gods have saved you just so you could be my mate." A brief smile tugged at his lips. "Not that that's anything to sneeze at. At least not from my perspective. But you see what I mean, don't you?"

She nodded slowly. "Yeah. I do."

"You're a savior, Sula. I hope you realize that."

Her initial response was a snort. "A savior would've figured out how to stop them before so many of the Ecosians died."

"Think any of them survived?"

"I doubt it. The plague spread like wildfire—almost

as if they'd all been infected at once. Granted, I was only observing one small village, but any travel between villages would eventually contaminate that continent, if not the entire planet."

"Maybe you and Raj were only the first wave of the attack. We might be able to stop any further attempts."

"After a full year?" She shook her head. "I doubt Raj and I were the only ones sent there. We were given specific instructions for where to land. A coordinated attack would've sent other unwitting victims to a variety of regions. Plus, they've had a full year to put their plans in motion. I don't know how long it would take for the virus to die out completely; Ecos might still be unsafe for humanoids. Bots would be okay, though. At this very moment, thousands of them could be scouring the planet, destroying every trace of their civilization."

"A full-scale annihilation..." Even after what had happened to his own homeworld, he still had a hard time wrapping his head around the sort of twisted minds that could justify such evil. "Greedy bastards."

"No kidding. I've given this a great deal of thought. Considering how long it's been since Rhylos was first colonized, if we're right about this, we're looking at a conspiracy that goes back at least two hundred years. Dalb University has been a fixture on Ursa Prime for over three hundred."

Aidan nodded. "Zetith was destroyed by one very rich man's jealousy. Imagine what an organization like that could do over hundreds of years." His eyes widened as he considered the full scope of this crime. "How can we ever hope to win against something that big?"

"I don't know, but we have to try. Like you said, I

was spared for a reason." She was silent for several seconds, then gave a firm nod before continuing. "When we were talking about the cave on Rhylos, Rashe mentioned going public. Keeping the cave a secret was our best bet at the time, but if we could trick someone into confessing publicly, or record it secretly and release it to the media, we might stand a chance of succeeding."

"Val can help. He should be able to hack directly into the news feed and broadcast it before anyone could stop us." He thought for a moment. "What if you were to walk onto the campus like nothing had ever happened? It would be interesting to see who was the most surprised to see you."

"I'd probably have to wear my Zetithian disguise to get that far, even without my nanobots."

"That would probably work better," he said. "What if I were to schedule an appointment with your professor, or maybe the department head, saying I was concerned about faulty information being taught about Zetithians? I could say I wanted to help update the textbooks or something of that nature."

"That might work. My textbooks weren't what you'd call complete. I've learned a lot more from hanging around with you guys. And there's your reaction to my birth control implant. I'm pretty sure that's never been a problem with anyone else." Her eyes narrowed briefly before opening wide. "I've got it! You could say you were willing to fund a long-term research project concerning the effects of your planet's destruction on Zetithian survivors and their culture."

"Offer the greedy bastards even more money?" He grinned. "Sula, you're a genius."

Chapter 24

AIDAN HAD KNOWN THEY WOULD COME UP WITH A PLAN sooner or later. Deciding upon a course of action now would give them more time to prepare. "Of course, that would make concealing our identities even more important. Not only would you need a disguise, so would I—or we would at least need to arrive on a different ship."

"Got any more friends with starships?" Sula asked.

"Several," he replied. "But Curly's mother would be the best choice." He thought for a moment. "Her or Leroy."

"And who is Leroy?"

"Lerotan Kanotay," he replied. "He's an arms dealer." Sula giggled. "I vote for him."

"Jack has plenty of big guns too, most of which were purchased from Leroy, come to think of it. Jack would be the perfect person to push for research. She's the most vocal supporter of Zetithians in the galaxy, and she probably has a collection of Nedwut scalps to prove it."

"You aren't serious!"

"No, but to be honest, I wouldn't put it past her. She still refers to herself as the Zetithian Protection Agency."

"One person is an agency?" she asked.

He chuckled. "I keep forgetting you haven't met Jack."

"True. Although I *have* met Curly."

"Which amounts to the same thing," he said with a grin. "Curly's brother Larry would be a good choice too. He's a whiz at communications. If we manage to get a confession out of someone, he'd be the best one to spread it around. Either way, I'm thinking your idea to space that implant and its nanobot buddies might be the best tactic. We certainly don't want anyone thinking you're anywhere around."

Her brows knit together in a frown. "Seems like they'd still be suspicious of anyone showing up with that story, especially after the way we were chased to the spaceport."

"Unless we come up with a better plan, that's a risk we're going to have to take. We really need you to come face-to-face with the bad guy. Just seeing you will probably make him show his hand." Aidan grimaced. "We could use some other evidence to tie the university to the scheme, which is why Onca sent Val after us. He's the best hacker there is. Like Rashe said, if you want to dig up dirt on somebody, he's your man."

"I'm all for that," Sula said. "I might've done better to team up with him instead of clambering about in the mountains."

He shook his head. "They probably would've caught you if you had. I'm guessing they have alerts on their database and would know if anyone started hacking into it." He smiled. "No. You were meant to team up with us, just as you were destined to be my mate." He gazed into her dark, exotically glowing eyes. "Don't worry. Everyone leaves a trail, whether it's printed on paper, stored in a computer, or drawn on the wall of a cave. The evidence will be there somewhere. We just have to find it."

Sula had been staring at the communications console for what seemed like days when her stomach let out a snarl, informing her in no uncertain terms that it was high time for a lunch break. Every bridge station was occupied by someone trying to uncover something— *anything*—to tie Dalb University to the genocide she'd witnessed on Ecos. Even Qinta and Abuti had joined the search, working from a small table near the main viewscreen on a pair of portable computers Curly had provided.

She glanced up to see Curly standing at the doorway eyeing them with disfavor. "This is gonna put a serious drain on my data plan," he complained. Then he smiled. "Remind me to add it to your bill."

Aidan looked up from the weapons station with a roll of his eyes. "You wouldn't be that mercenary, and you know it."

Curly shrugged. "Had to say something. I'm feeling kinda useless at the moment."

"Same here," Aidan said. "Three hours, and I haven't found a single shred of useful evidence. I take it you haven't heard anything from Jack or Leroy."

"Not a peep," Curly replied. "Which probably means they're too far out to get to us in time."

"I don't know if we should be in a hurry or not," Sula said. "Chances are, there's no one left on Ecos to save."

"We don't know that," Aidan said quickly. "We have to assume there are at least some survivors, and even if there aren't, more planets are being discovered every day. The sooner we find a way to put a stop to this business, the better."

"I can't argue with that, but we still need as much

help as we can get." Sula worried her lower lip with her teeth. "Any thoughts as to where we might rendezvous?"

Jetoc came shuffling past Curly, carrying a large tray. "There are several possibilities between here and Ursa Prime. We can choose one as soon as we know who we'll be meeting. In the meantime, I have prepared lunch for everyone." He held up the tray, which was piled high with crackers and a platter of steaming sausages.

Suspecting that this feast represented the full extent of the Drell's culinary expertise, Sula at least tried to be gracious. "Wow, Jetoc. Those sausages smell delicious."

Abuti, however, curled her lip in aversion. "I thought Aidan was going to be doing the cooking."

"Not every meal," Aidan protested. "Can't we take turns?"

Abuti demonstrated her opinion of this plan with a frown and a peculiar drumming and popping of her fingertips on the computer desk in front of her.

"Yes, but you actually *like* to cook," Qinta pointed out. "I don't think anyone else does."

"Maybe so," he said. "But even I need a break sometimes."

Sula got to her feet. "Thank you, Jetoc. It was very kind of you to prepare lunch for us."

Apparently oblivious to anyone's disapproval, Jetoc set the tray on the ledge beside the captain's chair with a complacency that implied this was the normal spot for delivering food to the bridge. "I brought enough plates for everyone."

Sula stole a glance at Giklor. Given his attitude toward Drells and the way he'd avoided the bacon Aidan had cooked when they'd breakfasted at his house, she doubted he would touch any of it.

"What? No forks or napkins?" the Zerkan grumbled.

Turning toward Giklor, Jetoc blinked in about the only facial expression that would've been detectable by anyone aside from another Drell. "Why would anyone need those for sausages and crackers? I said I brought plates." His inflection suggested that, at least in his mind, providing individual plates was the equivalent of formal dining.

Sula reminded herself that a nonjudgmental approach to cultural differences hadn't been drummed into the heads of most of those present. About the best she could do was lead by example. Walking purposely over to the captain's chair, she picked up a plate. "I hadn't realized how hungry I was." Helping herself to two sausages and a small stack of crackers, she carried them over to her seat at the communications console.

Whipping out the pocketknife that experience had taught her never to be without, she cut the sausage into thin slices and put each piece on a cracker like a makeshift canapé. As she took a bite, the flavor seemed to burst in her mouth. "Oh my God, this is good. You know, I would've killed for a sausage when I was in the mountains. I didn't have any spices with me. Had to eat those damned rock rats without so much as a grain of salt."

Giklor would undoubtedly prove to be a much harder sell, but Qinta and Abuti took the hint, which wasn't too surprising. They had each lived on the streets of Damenk long enough to appreciate food of any sort without complaint.

Qinta was the first to fill her plate. However, instead

of returning to her station, she carried it over to where Sula was sitting. "Can I borrow your knife?"

"Sure." Sula placed the knife on the girl's outstretched palm.

"Sorry for acting like such a brat," she mumbled.

"I'm not the one you need to apologize to," Sula said, keeping her voice down.

"I know. I shouldn't have needed reminding. But thanks anyway."

"No problem," Sula said with a smile.

Qinta went over to where Jetoc sat and said a few quiet words to him before drifting back to her station. Val, whom Sula had guessed was vegetarian, took only crackers. The other men helped themselves to both. After everyone else was munching on their lunch, Giklor finally relented and took a helping of each. Sula's knife also made the rounds before Aidan brought it back to her.

"You know something? You are one smart cookie," he said. "You made the rest of us look a bit dim."

She frowned. "That was never my intention."

"I know. That's what makes you so smart." A smile quirked the corner of his mouth. "Did Val say how long it would be before you'll be"—he stole a glance over his shoulder—"*available* again?"

She didn't pretend to misunderstand him. "Not really. I figure we ought to give it a week and have him scan me before we try again."

His crestfallen expression was priceless. "A week? Don't know if I'll last that long."

"Sure you will," she drawled. "But in the meantime, I guess we'll have to stick to those *other* methods we talked about."

The glow from his pupils, which had been barely discernable a moment before, waxed brighter. "Almost forgot about them." He swallowed as though one of the cracker crumbs had gotten stuck in his throat. "Can't wait."

"Me either. Wish we didn't have so much research to do."

"We have at least three weeks…"

"Unless we have to rendezvous with someone before then," she reminded him.

Cocking a hip, he leaned against the console. "This fighting-for-a-righteous-cause stuff sure gets in the way of romance, doesn't it?"

She chuckled. "I've always wondered about that. Seems like none of the heroes of yesteryear ever had a wife or a lover along with them. At least none that I can recall."

"Maybe that's because they hadn't teamed up with someone quite as special as you."

A blush warmed her cheeks. "Sweet."

"Although I can certainly relate to the wish to keep loved ones safe at home."

"That's the difference in our case," Sula said. "I'm the one who attracts danger wherever I go."

"That's what we need to fix. Then we can have our happily-ever-after free of assassins and guilty consciences."

"We have a brief respite—at least for now."

"Yeah. Until we finish lunch."

She rolled her eyes. "Back to the research grind. You'd think after so many years in academia, I'd be used to it. Just wish we could get some sort of breakthrough." She glanced around the room. "No one seems to be overly intrigued by any of it. That's the way it is with research, though. Most of the time, it's boring as hell."

A gasp from the science station drew her eye.

With his wings spread wide, Val drew back from the console, his face frozen in an expression of speechless horror.

Sula jumped up and hurried over to him. "What is it? Have you found something?"

"Ilya Zolo," he whispered hoarsely. A shudder rustled his wings.

"Who?"

"My...creator. The man who cloned me." Val turned his birdlike gaze on her, his pupils larger than she'd ever seen them. "He was once a professor of applied genetics at Dalb University."

⁓

Aidan had heard the name before, and he understood the significance that name had for Val. However, he was unprepared for Val's terrified reaction. "Zolo? He's in jail, isn't he?"

That reminder appeared to calm Val to some extent, although he still seemed pretty rattled. "Yes, he is. Although he did not receive a life sentence for his crimes. One day, he will be released."

"One day, he will," Aidan conceded. "But not today. It's interesting that he was once a faculty member, though. Having had at least one known criminal on the university's payroll increases the likelihood that there are others."

"Not necessarily," Sula said. "However, I do like your reasoning." When she placed a hand on Val's shoulder, oddly enough, he didn't flinch.

Aidan had observed Val around others before. He didn't appear to like being watched or touched. Either he was too weirded out to notice, or Sula's touch was as soothing to Val as it was to him.

"Is there anything you can tell us about Zolo that might point us in the right direction?" she asked. "Anyone he might've mentioned as a patron or a supporter of his work?"

A few deep breaths probably settled Val's nerves a tad, but the shock clearly hadn't left him yet. "I will try to remember," he finally said. "But it is difficult. I have done my best to suppress many of those memories."

There were plenty of memories Aidan would like to block. So far, he'd been unsuccessful. Perhaps at some point, he and Val could have that conversation.

"Don't focus on it," Sula advised. "Let your mind do the work on its own. If there's anything there to remember, it'll come to you."

"I saw that name in the stuff I was reading," Abuti reported. "Didn't understand the significance. Says here he was once highly respected. The university board didn't fire him; he left of his own accord."

"He might have been asked to resign when they realized what he was doing," Sula surmised. "Lots of job terminations go like that—either quit or be fired."

"The Zolo I knew wouldn't have wanted to be fired," Val said quietly. "He was the most egotistical being I have ever encountered. Nothing mattered beyond his goals. Certainly not the comfort and well-being of his creations. He cared nothing for our pain and suffering."

"Sounds like a really nasty piece of work," Curly

said. "Right up there with Rutger Grekkor, except he created rather than destroyed."

"Not always," Val whispered. "When his creations didn't please him, he killed them without remorse."

Aidan was hearing things from Val that were entirely new but were no worse than he might've guessed. "I'm surprised those creations didn't turn on him."

"We certainly testified against him at his trial. Unfortunately, he could only be charged with illegal cloning and genetic manipulation. He couldn't be charged with murder, because clones are not considered to be real, sentient beings. At least not in the eyes of the law."

"That's changed, though, hasn't it?" Sula prompted.

Val nodded. "Yes. We have rights as citizens, but only on Rhylos, which is why we live there now."

"But that's...that's *horrible*," Qinta exclaimed. "How could anyone look at you and say you aren't a real person?"

Val's nonchalant shrug indicated he'd regained a modicum of control. With the breach in the wall now closed, any emotions roiling beneath his stoic facade would require an empath to detect. "We were created by illegal means; therefore, we had no legal rights."

"That doesn't make any sense," Abuti said. "But I'm glad they recognize you on Rhylos." She cast her eyes downward to where her flipper-like feet were splayed out on the floor. "There are plenty of planets that don't welcome Norludians, but we have the same rights as anyone else. At least I think we do."

"You do," Sula said. "This makes me wish I'd written my thesis on Avians instead of Norludians. It wouldn't have helped with our current predicament, but *still*..."

"We have a champion," Val said. "A lawyer named Anara Threlkind fought for us and was able to secure the only rights we have." He shook his head slowly. "I understand the legal concerns. As clones, would we own the same property as our original, be married to the same person, and so forth? Or are we separate entities the way a twin would be? Even if those issues were decided, granting us even basic rights would weaken the laws against the cloning of intelligent beings." He nodded toward Sula. "But you're right. None of this helps with our current situation. It is merely an unfortunate side effect. I will resume my efforts."

"Take a break if you need to," Sula urged. "With so many of us working on this, we're bound to hit on something eventually."

"I have no wish to be alone at this time." What Val's breathing gained in rate, it lost in depth. Clearly, his past suffering still affected him. "I would prefer to remain here, among friends."

Again, Sula placed a hand on his shoulder, giving it a squeeze. "I don't blame you, but I do think it's worth looking into Zolo's known associates—anyone he coauthored a research paper with, any social connections to others in the university, that sort of thing."

Qinta chuckled. "*Known associates*? You sound like a police detective."

"Right now, I wish at least one of us had those credentials," Sula said with a rueful grimace. "We're nothing but a bunch of amateurs."

"So were we when we brought down Rutger Grekkor," Aidan said. "It took a team of us working together, but we managed it. We can do this." For the time being, his motivation to succeed was personal, but in the greater scheme of things, there was so much more at stake than his own happiness. Even if no weapon was ever fired, the deliberate extermination of developing civilizations was a criminal act on every conceivable level. "We *have* to do this."

Chapter 25

THE REST OF THE DAY PASSED WITHOUT ANY FURTHER breakthroughs. Val's mood didn't appear to improve, and dinner was a tasty, if somber, affair. The only bright spot was going to bed with Aidan. At least this time, there was no pretense of sleeping in separate beds.

Sula scooted across the lower bunk until her bottom was up against the wall. "Just wish these bunks were a teensy bit bigger."

The bed she'd slept in at Aidan's house had been large enough for most forms of sexual acrobatics. Too bad they hadn't utilized it. Reminding herself that not only had she been a virtual stranger to him at the time but she'd also had a broken leg didn't change how she felt. Space travel had always seemed so confining. Unlike traveling on land, in space there were no roadside stands or other points of interest to break up the journey. After spending so many months in the mountains, the interior of a starship seemed more cramped than ever.

"Same here," Aidan said as he climbed in beside her. "I can't even sit up without bumping my head on the upper bunk."

"Rules out some of my favorite positions. But then, we won't be attempting any of those for a while anyway."

"What a bummer." Lying down, he stretched out his arm, inviting her into his warm embrace. "At least we know it was your birth control implant that was messing me up. For one horrible moment, I thought I might be allergic to *you*."

"Horrible is right." Snuggling closer, she kissed his cheek before resting her head on his shoulder. Even though she'd only slept with him once before, everything about the arrangement—the rise and fall of his chest as he breathed, the beat of his heart beneath her hand—seemed so natural, so right, so…perfect. "Good thing I'm not allergic to *snard*."

He cleared his throat. "You do know it has the same effect on any mucus membrane, don't you? Not the conception part, of course. Just the other effects."

"I kinda figured that. It's supposed to be sweet, right?"

"So I've heard," he replied with a chuckle. "Never tasted it myself. Don't believe I care to, either."

"That's good, because I'm not planning to share."

"Greedy woman," he chided, giving her shoulders an affectionate squeeze.

"When it comes to you, I am." This time, she kissed him on the lips, albeit briefly. "I hope kissing is okay."

"I'll let you know if I start seeing double. Although that might be something you would do to me in any case—which is a risk I'm quite willing to take. A guy can only take so much deprivation before getting testy, you know."

"I see." She thought for a moment. "So what you're saying is, you've been testy your entire life up until last night?"

Whisper-like sensations tickled the back of her head as he played with her hair. "Hmm…hadn't thought about it that way, but you may be right."

He'd been testy for other reasons that were even more valid than the dearth of sex. The horrors he must've seen—

I can't think about that right now.

As she saw it, her current mission was to make him forget the awful visions. He hadn't mentioned any recent fortune-telling episodes, which was strange given the number of people aboard the ship. Although he did say he didn't get many readings on people he saw on a regular basis.

She hadn't thought that keeping her own mind off his troubles would be a problem. Fortunately, Aidan was the best walking, talking distraction she could possibly imagine.

"We can't have you getting testy."

This time, the kiss lasted longer—a *lot* longer—and he was purring by the time she finished. She could spend her entire life kissing him. He tasted as good as he felt, and he had the most fabulously sensuous lips. His cock was probably as delicious as the rest of him—and his *snard* even more so.

Unfortunately, while she could savor him as much as she liked, to avoid ingesting any of her bodily fluids, he shouldn't do the same to her, a restriction that ruled out most of what he'd done the night before. That left his hands, which were probably every bit as capable as his lips and tongue.

Kissing him from head to toe seemed like the best way for her to begin. She left the delight of his lips with a great deal of reluctance and moved on to his smooth, beardless cheek. Five more kisses brought her to the luscious place on his neck where she'd bitten him with her fake fangs. She didn't draw blood when she sank her teeth into him this time, yet his growling purr told her everything she needed to know.

"You're making me crazy," he whispered. The thrilling combination of purr and whisper was something she would never tire of hearing.

She bit him again. "That's the idea."

"Not sure I have that much control," he admitted, although he urged her on with a tilt of his head that gave her better access to his neck.

"That depends on whether you consider a bit of pleasure now to be worth how bad you'll feel in the morning."

"Hey, I lived through it once before. I can do it again."

She nibbled his earlobe and was rewarded with another loud, purring exhale. "Yes, but spending long hours staring at a computer screen is bad enough for your eyes, and you do need to be able to do that."

"I also need to be able to cook breakfast. Abuti will have my head if I don't."

"Then hush up and let me suck your dick."

He gulped. "You're really gonna do it, aren't you?"

She drew back and gazed at him in surprise. "What else did you think I was planning to do?"

"I'm not sure. I figured you might use your hands. Although I think I should do that to you first."

He tried to sit up, but she pushed him back down. "Oh no you don't. It'll be hard enough to focus on what I'm doing with your orgasmic juice setting off fireworks in my blood. I don't need you to give me physical orgasms when the chemical ones will suffice."

"My, that sounds so…clinical," he drawled.

"Will you please lie still and let me do my thing?"

"Okay, okay." Waving his hands in defeat, he lay back down. "If you insist."

"I do." A glance at his cock told her everything was

going according to plan. "Nice and hard and drippy, just the way I like it."

His groan sounded testy and frustrated, which was also the way she wanted him to be. "I keep forgetting you've done this stuff before. It's still pretty new to me."

"That's about to change." One deep breath later, she sucked the head of his big, showy cock into her mouth, nearly climaxing simply from the pressure of it on her tongue. She drew back, tugging on the fleshy, ruffled flange before letting go with a pop. "Tastes even better than the rest of you. Can't wait to try the *snard*."

His breath hissed in through his teeth. "You won't have to wait much longer if you keep that up."

"No rush. I'm just getting started." She was about to go down on him again when her first orgasm detonated. "Hold on a sec." She gasped as her core contracted, doubling her over with ecstasy. Several pants later, she finally had enough breath to spare for speech. "Oh wow. That was a good one. They're *all* good, actually. Some might be stronger than others. Probably depends on how frequent they are. Maybe the first is always the best. I'll have to get back to you on that."

The only light in their quarters came from a transom above the door. Nevertheless, it was enough to enable her to see the shine on one of his fangs when he smiled. "Am I your latest research project?" Amusement colored his tone as he stroked the length of her arm with a fingertip. A wave of goose bumps swarmed in the wake of his touch.

"You're a whole lot more than that. Sorry if it seems that way. Guess I've been in college too long." Although being with him was easily the most exciting form of research she'd ever undertaken. "But don't worry. I'm not taking notes or writing a paper on Zetithian sex, even though it would make a terrific dissertation topic, certainly the most enjoyable." She shot him a wink. "Speaking of which, I believe I'm ready to try again."

He waved a hand. "Don't let me stop you."

"I won't." She settled down beside him, cupping his testicles with one hand while grasping his cock with the other. She was about to remark upon the crimson gleam where his joy juice ran down the thickly veined shaft when she remembered that the red glow came from her own eyes. Avoiding the orgasmic fluid, she ran her tongue along the vein on the underside of his cock, marveling at the firmness of the underlying tissue and the velvety softness of the skin. He really would make an excellent subject for research, although he would undoubtedly test her descriptive vocabulary.

"Tell me some more Zetithian words."

"Right *now*?"

"Yeah. For example, what's this called?" She gave his dick a tug.

"*Cockaj*."

"Oh, you have *got* to be kidding me."

"Nope. That's the word. The orgasmic lubricating fluid doesn't have a Zetithian name, which we've always considered to be a severe oversight. Everyone calls it joy juice."

"That works for me." She dipped a hand toward the juncture of her thighs. "And this?"

"*Loresh*."

"What about a woman's lubricating fluid?" If he said "pussy juice," she fully intended to smack him.

"*Loreshtai.*"

"Damn, those are great words. Not crazy about the word for semen—a name like *snard* doesn't in any way do justice to such a remarkable substance—but it's a cut above the usual vulgar slang, and heaven knows there's nothing remotely romantic about the correct anatomical terminology."

Laughter shook his chest. "I can't say I've had much experience with situations like this, but I'm guessing you're the first woman to ever use the words 'anatomical terminology' while engaging in sex with a Zetithian."

"Hey, it's who I am," she said with a shrug. "Not sure that'll ever change."

"I'm not complaining." This time, his smile revealed both fangs. "Simply remarking upon your inherent uniqueness."

"I'm good with that. You're pretty unique yourself." She gave his *cockaj* a quick lick and waited for the subsequent *orwanda*—delightful though it was—to subside before taking him in her mouth again.

The flavor and feel of him were truly delectable. Was there anything about him that wasn't appealing? If there was, she had yet to discover it. Perhaps she never would. Having evolved around the need to entice rather than subdue a mate, Zetithian mating behavior was very different from that of humans. Granted, human males were attractive, but no more so than the females—unlike, say, birds, where the males had brighter colors and showier feathers. In contrast, the only difference between the genders of some mammalian species was their genitalia.

Aidan certainly had some remarkable genitals. The overall size and structure were no different from that of any well-endowed human male, until you reached the head of the penis. She'd never seen anything quite like it. The base of the domed head had a fleshy, ragged edge with rounded points that appeared to be the source of the orgasmic lubricating fluid. She backed off and slid her tongue between the points, working her way around the entire circumference of the head.

While this was an interesting endeavor in its own right, what it did to Aidan was nothing short of astonishing. Fluid seemed to pour from the tips of the flange, as well as from the slit in the top of the head, and the sounds he made were gasps, moans, and purrs combined.

When the inevitable result of licking his dick occurred once again, she paused until it passed for fear of biting her own tongue. She'd assumed the intensity would diminish in time, but apparently two orgasms were not the upper limit. How many it would take before her body could no longer respond was a treat for another day. This day would forever be identified as the day she had her first taste of *snard*.

Despite the orgasms, her nipples still tingled with anticipation, and her clitoris remained amazingly tight and sensitive. There was no down time to allow her to relax and fall asleep; the need to mate with him had reached a peak and stayed there. Perhaps the *snard* would satisfy her, but until then, she didn't want to stop—couldn't even conceive of *wanting* to stop. Such was the allure of the Zetithian male.

Aidan wasn't just another Zetithian hottie, either. He was the only Zetithian she wanted. The attraction wasn't so nonspecific that any one of them would do. Curly was a handsome fellow, but she had no desire to suck his cock.

She lay with her head pillowed on Aidan's stomach, his big, ruffled cockhead pointed right at her lips. Stroking the underside of his long shaft with the palm of her hand, she caressed her cheek with the smooth head while the slick sauce coated her skin. She had somehow managed to get enough of his juice on her lips to set off another orgasm when she realized she wasn't the one doing the caressing.

Twisting around to stare at him, she demanded, "How are you *doing* that?"

"Another Zetithian specialty," he murmured. "Complete directional control." To illustrate, he rotated his cock in circles, swung it side to side like an overly enthusiastic metronome, then drummed it on his stomach. "I haven't had much practice. Some of us can move theirs so fast, it actually vibrates."

"Oh wow," she gasped as he made a creditable attempt at vibration. "You're showing me this *now*? When we've decided that actual intercourse is inadvisable?"

Sighing, he cupped her cheek and turned her face toward him. "I just love it when you get clinical."

Somewhat embarrassed, she averted her eyes. "Sorry about that."

He slid his fingers through her hair in an intimate caress. "Don't be. Your word choice and inquisitive nature are part of your charm."

"Glad you think so, because I have lots of questions."

"Such as?"

"For starters, what's the Zetithian word for sex? The verb form rather than the noun. Hopefully, one that doesn't start with *F* and end with *K*?"

He frowned as though thinking hard. "I'll have to get

back to you on that one. In the meantime"—he tapped her arm with his penis—"think you could pick up where you left off?"

"Sure. Although, as I recall, I was in mid-*orwanda* at the time."

"You've probably had long enough to recover from that one. A good, long lick should get you back to where you were."

"Promises, promises," she scoffed. However, his prediction proved to be correct as yet another climax rippled through her. "Was that a guess or are you catching glimpses of my future?"

"Let's call it an educated guess." He exhaled a loud purr as his lips curled into a seductive grin. "I can't see your future, Sula. Although I *have* seen evidence of your effect on others."

She was about to ask who, but her query died on her lips when he tapped her arm with his dick again. "You're right. We can talk about that later."

Resuming her position, she wrapped her hand around his cock and gave it a tug. "Since you can't think of the Zetithian version of the F-word, which I find very hard to believe, would you please fuck my mouth? These damned orgasms keep distracting me."

Aidan burst out laughing. "I can see where that might be a problem."

"Mind you, I'm not complaining, but apparently, I can't do this on my own."

"Gotcha. I'll supply the meat and the motion if you'll supply the pressure and friction."

"Deal." Gripping his shaft with her hand, she slid the head into her mouth. The angle was perfect as he began slow, rhythmic thrusts. Not too deep or vigorous at first, they gradually increased in rate and depth. Sula didn't have a drop of Norludian blood in her, but she felt a different kind of climax building simply from having his cock pumping in and out of her mouth.

As his breathing grew shorter and his purr increased in volume, his dick became unbelievably hard, so much so that the engorgement seemed to cut off the flow of his orgasmic fluid.

Trust Zetithian biology to have found a solution to every conceivable reproductive quandary.

Two thrusts later, his breath caught, and his purr became a snarl. Sliding her hand to the base of his cock, she cupped his balls. As they surged against her palm, jets of sweet, creamy *snard* flowed over her tongue. She only had a few seconds in which to savor it before the sheer volume of fluid made her swallow. As his cock slid down her throat along with the semen, Aidan went wild, clutching the back of her head as he ejaculated once more.

"Mother of the gods!" At least, that's what Sula thought he said. As garbled as his speech was, it could've been anything.

Sula couldn't have uttered an intelligible word even if she'd known what to say. With something the size of Aidan's cock down her throat, she was surprised she was even able to breathe. She was trying to imagine how she could unswallow him when the *snard* effect took hold. Her lips lost their grip, allowing his penis to glide from her throat. Heat welled up inside her core before billowing outward with an explosive force. Another swallow, and the heat became an inferno. Apparently *snard*, when ingested, packed an even mightier punch.

In the next instant, the flames subsided to warmth so soothing, she would've sworn even her bones relaxed. She was relaxed, yes, but lighter too, like a bubble floating along on a rapidly flowing stream. The head of his cock was still in her mouth, and oddly enough, seemed to be moving.

Raising her head, she stared at the organ in question. Despite the dim light, she was able to see that the coronal ridge was indeed moving in an undulating wave. "Does it always do that?"

His shout of laughter surprised her even more than his wavy cock. "Sula, sweetheart...this is only my second time."

"Yes, but is it *supposed* to?"

He nodded. "The prevailing theory is that it helps sweep the *snard* in the right direction."

"Makes sense." Fascinated, she watched as the wave completed one circuit and began another. "I can't imagine why I didn't notice it before."

"Too many other things going on, I guess."

That much was true. "I'll have to pay closer attention next time." Thus far, the wave showed no sign of slowing. An experimental touch of her fingertip had no effect whatsoever. "Any idea how long it lasts?"

"No clue." He chuckled. "You can time it if you like."

She arched a brow. "More research?"

"Absolutely. You could search the entire galaxy and never find a more willing subject." He pulled her into his arms, kissing her with such tenderness and passion that her eyes filled with tears. "Take as many years as you need. A lifelong study would suit me very well."

Chapter 26

AT THE END OF YET ANOTHER DAY IN A WEEK OF FRUITLESS detective work, Sula took her seat at the dinner table, anxious to try Aidan's spin on chicken shawarma, which would undoubtedly prove to be the high point of the day.

Abuti set a salad of fruit, nuts, and greens on the table before plopping down in the chair to Sula's right. "I'm starving!"

Curly flipped out his napkin and dropped it in his lap. "I've been thinking—"

"Which is dangerous in itself," Qinta interjected as she brought in an enormous bowl of rice.

He made a face at the Treslanti girl before continuing. "Short of spacing those nanobots, the meanest thing we could do is drop them off on a really hostile world."

As promised, Aidan came in from the galley with a huge platter of shawarma. "Where did you have in mind?"

"Remember that planet with the giant sandworms? Jetoc tells me it's not far from here."

In mid-foodgasm simply from inhaling the fabulous aromas wafting toward her, Sula was at least able to speak. "I thought those bots didn't have much range."

"Yeah, but anyone assuming we were en route to Ursa Prime might follow the same flight path and be able to detect them. JR-51 seems like a great place to lure a bunch of badasses. As soon as they sent a death squad out to kill you, the worms would eat their ship and strand them there."

"Feeling a bit bloodthirsty, are we?" Aidan drawled as he took the seat to Sula's left.

"Kinda," Curly replied. "Reading through two hundred years' worth of research grants and university payrolls has me feeling downright murderous."

Sula couldn't blame him. She'd been bored to tears while researching a term paper before, but sifting through endless streams of data was mind-numbing. If they'd had someone tailing them through space the way they'd been followed through the streets of Damenk, she'd have been tempted to stand and fight if for no other reason than to break the monotony.

She couldn't even do that research in the same room with Aidan. After two days of staring at his back until she drooled—even turning her back to him didn't help, because she kept peeking over her shoulder—she finally recommended that he do his share of the drudgery from Curly's ready room. As grateful as he'd been for the suggestion, she could only assume that he'd welcomed the opportunity to allow what must've been a constant erection to subside. They'd spent every night together, but even that didn't diminish her response to him throughout the day.

Zetithians had been labeled as addicting before, and she was living proof of the validity of that claim. She might not die without Aidan, but she certainly was uncomfortable. Would pregnancy alleviate the constant yearning? Or would she feel this way for the rest of her life?

Surely, the intensity of her desire would ease after a

while. Older people remained affectionate, but passion tended to wane as years passed.

Unless you happened to be a Norludian. In the course of writing her thesis, she had been unable to discover a mated pair of any age that didn't exhibit signs of marked sexual interest.

But she wasn't a Norludian, and neither was Aidan. She was simply a human female completely hooked on an alien male.

At least Giklor's healing fluid hadn't bonded her to Aidan, although it might as well have done. She'd read accounts of those who had been bonded. When they were separated, the one that had been "treated" underwent what amounted to a death and rebirth, after which they were actually able to visualize their mate's scent trail. That ability was interesting and undoubtedly useful. It was losing the will to live when the other partner died that had her bugged.

A sharp pang in the left lower quadrant of her abdomen brought her up short. Val's most recent scan had demonstrated the dearth of artificial hormones in her system, which meant that tonight, she and Aidan could actually enjoy sex in the fullest sense of the word.

Unfortunately—or was it fortunate?—she was quite sure she had just ovulated. Generally speaking, most women didn't notice such a subtle occurrence, but Sula had always been sensitive to that moment. Plus, if she remembered correctly, Zetithian semen acted like a fertility drug, causing multiple ovulations rather than the splitting of one fertilized ovum. If she were to have triplets with Aidan, they wouldn't be identical, and three ovulations happening at once would be hard to miss.

Wincing, she pressed a hand to the sore spot, a gesture of discomfort that didn't go unobserved.

Giklor reached a pallid hand across the table. "My dear Sula, are you unwell? Enough time has passed that I could heal—"

Abuti slammed her palms on the table. "Dammit, Giklor. Will you *please* give it a rest? Not every bellyache is life-threatening, you know."

Giklor snatched back his hand. "I am well aware of that," he said with a haughty sniff. "I merely offer my services should they be required."

Sula darted a quelling glance at Abuti before turning her attention to Giklor. "I'm grateful for your concern. But I'm pretty sure this isn't something that warrants treatment."

Unless Aidan was in the mood to offer a cure. She'd found that *snard* possessed analgesic as well as euphoric properties. Hours sifting through computer data had left her with a crick in her neck and stiffness in her right shoulder. A dose of *snard* relieved the pain and sent her to sleep almost immediately. Tonight, however, she suspected the more traditional effect of semen would come into play.

Was she ready for the possibility of bearing triplets? Was anybody?

She reminded herself that she'd only known Aidan for a very short time. But so much had happened in those few days, she felt as though she'd met him years ago.

She and Raj had been friends since their undergrad days, only progressing to a romantic involvement during the year before they embarked on their mission to Ecos. Her relationship with Aidan was so completely different, she couldn't even begin to make a comparison.

Aidan leaned toward her. "Something wrong?"

"Not really," she said quietly. "We can talk more later on."

"Do you really think we'll have much time to *talk*?" His emphasis on the last word recalled his jubilant reaction to the results of the scan.

"Oh, I think we can probably make time for this particular conversation."

His brow rose briefly. "Are you sure there's nothing wrong?"

"Absolutely," she replied. "Simply a new development to be considered."

Sula was gazing into his sexy feline eyes when they suddenly widened with comprehension. With a vague nod, he looked down at his plate. For a long moment, he didn't move a muscle; even his breathing ceased.

A nudge on her right arm startled her, drawing her attention to the bowl of rice Abuti held out to her. "What? Oh, right." She scooped a portion of rice onto her plate, then took the bowl and turned toward Aidan. "Rice?"

He appeared to have recovered sufficiently to serve himself without further prompting. "Thanks."

"That shawarma smells incredible."

Abuti stuck her fingertips together and then popped them apart. "He's made it for us at the orphanage before. Wait 'til you taste it. You won't believe how good it is."

"Probably not nearly as good as his—" Sula caught herself before completing that sentence. Her only excuse was that she'd been reading so much, her eyes hurt, and fatigue had made her a bit punchy.

Her bulbous eyes gleaming with fascination, Abuti turned toward Sula, resting her cheek on her palm and a bony elbow on the table. "His *what*?"

Sula didn't have to think back very far for her reply. "Um, last night's roast Mondavian duck?"

The Norludian girl shook her head. "The shawarma is way better than the duck. Trust me."

If his shawarma was better than the duck, did *snard* fall somewhere in between?

No possible way. Snard had to be at the top of *any* list.

"This I gotta taste." Jetoc parted his moustache and pulled several long strands of grayish hair away from his mouth. "The captain has never made anything that smells like that. Smells almost as good as my sausages."

Frowning, Curly scratched his chin. "Can't remember you ever making shawarma when we were kids, Aidan."

"New recipe." Aidan still seemed a tad shell-shocked, his vacant expression suggesting that his mind was occupied with something else entirely.

Was he willing to make love with her without the benefit of birth control? Or was he trying to come up with some other alternative? Condoms had been used in one form or another throughout the galaxy for centuries, although she doubted there was a condom in existence that could accommodate his ruffled cockhead. None of those made for humans, anyway. Given the effects of *snard* and joy juice, she doubted there was much of a market for condoms among the Zetithian population, even on Terra Minor. She certainly had no intention of asking him to use one.

Something else we need to talk about.

Abuti nudged her again. This time, she held the meat platter. "Better hurry up and take some of this before Jetoc goes back for seconds."

A glance across the table proved that the chicken did

indeed meet with the Drell's approval. Judging by the way he was shoveling shawarma into his mouth, the remainder was definitely in jeopardy.

Sula spooned some onto her plate and then held the platter for Aidan. "How did you make this without using one of those vertical rotisseries?" She'd eaten shawarma before—usually purchased from a street vendor—and she doubted the ship's galley was similarly equipped.

"Just baked it on a tray and then cut it into bits," Aidan replied. "Most of the flavor is in the marinade."

He sounded so normal. Like she hadn't just dropped a bomb in his lap. Had he come to terms with the idea already? Or was she the one who was weirded out by the thought of having triplets?

Despite the pressure to reproduce and replenish an endangered species, becoming a father had never struck Aidan as a likely occurrence. He'd always seen himself as a bit of a loner, something his Mordrial abilities seemed to dictate, perhaps even require. If he'd ever been in love before, he might have felt differently, but he'd never even come close. Throughout his life, he'd always imagined finding a mate and having children to be future events, never a part of the here and now.

And yet here he was, on the cusp of an entirely new phase of his life. He still had a choice. He could look into Sula's beautiful brown eyes and tell her he'd decided that having a family wasn't for him. She wasn't Zetithian. She could go on to find love with someone else, whereas being mated to her, he probably never would.

He wasn't completely sure how he knew she was his

mate. This feeling was entirely new to him, and yet it was unmistakable. He knew it through her scent and its effect on him. He could tell her precise location in a room even with his eyes closed. Being near her had a positive effect on everything about him—his mood, his health, his happiness, and his outlook.

Following his reply to Sula's question, she had simply gone ahead with her meal, taking a bite or two before complimenting him on the excellence of the dish. Others had voiced similar opinions, and he'd thanked each of them. As dinner progressed and the convivial chatter of mealtime—surely among the most sane and comforting sounds imaginable—surrounded him, what had happened between him and Sula seemed more sur-real than ever. How could he possibly have mated with her so quickly?

He wasn't making love with her at the moment; he wasn't even speaking with her. No shadowy portents filled his mind with prescient gobbledygook. But when he gazed into her eyes, he could almost see the future unfolding. Infants cradled in her loving arms. Her fierce maternal pride in their children's achievements. Her love for him even after her hair turned white and her soft, supple skin grew wrinkled with age.

Tears stung his eyes, and for an instant, even breath-ing was difficult—until her hand closed over his where it lay on his thigh. Air filled his lungs again as their fingers entwined. Turning his head, he smiled at her, somehow managing to keep his tears from falling and drawing unwanted attention to his revelation. She must've seen them anyway, for a quizzical expres-sion narrowed her eyes briefly, accompanied by a dash of concern and a twinge of doubt. He drew in another breath and used her hand to pull her toward him. Without hesitation, he leaned closer and kissed her, putting every shred of emotion into the joining of their lips.

Their bond was nearly complete, and only one step remained—a step he would take without misgivings or uncertainty but would embark upon with eagerness, confidence, and joy.

"Aw...would you look at that?" Abuti clapped her hands, prompting the others to join in and bringing the kiss to an unfortunate end. "I'd give him a kiss for that fabulous dinner myself. But alas, he is taken."

"He certainly is." Sula squeezed the hand she still held, sending her tender affection coursing up his arm to warm his heart. "I think I knew it the moment I first laid eyes on him."

Qinta laughed. "Yeah. Right before you fell and broke your leg."

"And then he saved me from the nasty condors." Sula let go of his hand to cup the back of his neck. This time, she was the one who initiated the kiss. "My hero," she murmured against his lips.

Abuti peered over Sula's shoulder, her lips forming a pout. "He's one of our heroes too, you know. You won't stop him from working at the orphanage, will you?"

"I would never do such a thing." As Sula combed her fingers through his hair, his scalp tingled at the root of every strand she touched. "That much, I'm willing to share." A smile twitched the corner of her mouth. "But I'm keeping the rest of him."

"Can I at least be a bridesmaid?"

Sula chuckled. "I don't see why not." Her gaze connected with his once again. "That's assuming we were to actually get married." She quirked a brow. "Do Zetithians have a ceremony?"

"We didn't on Zetith," he replied. "Since then, any ceremonies have been more for the benefit of friends and family than for the mated pair. Zetithians mate for life, with or without the legal bonds of marriage."

She acknowledged this with a slow nod. "Weddings are quite a celebration in India, and my sister's was no exception. The flowers alone were breathtaking."

"How long ago was that?" Aidan asked, pleased to discover that he could actually form words and thankful for a topic that wasn't quite so emotionally charged.

"It was the summer between my freshman and sophomore year in college. She was so beautiful, and she and Dev were so much in love. I never expected to be a part of anything like that—not as the bride, anyway."

Giklor, of all people, rubbed his hands together in gleeful anticipation. "I trust your wedding will be every bit as wonderful as your sister's. And you will certainly be a beautiful bride."

To Aidan's surprise, Sula laughed. "You guys are assuming quite a lot. The last time I checked, Aidan and I weren't engaged."

"I trust that omission will soon be remedied," Giklor said pleasantly. "It's a pity I didn't think to bond the two of you when I healed your leg. But then, hindsight is always blessed with greater acuity than foresight."

Aidan could've added a few choice comments regarding the fuzzy nature of foresight, but Giklor continued. "However, I don't believe additional bonding was necessary. You each possess an aura that complements the other remarkably well."

"You mean you can actually *see* auras?" Sula asked.

"Oh, but of course," the Zerkan said with a hearty chortle. "I rather thought that was common knowledge. For the life of me, I cannot imagine why the ability to see auras would be such a rarity. It's so useful."

Clearly fascinated, Sula leaned forward to rest her elbow on the table. "How so?"

Giklor appeared to be more than willing to expound on the subject. "Auras change with a person's mood, but everyone—at least, everyone I've ever observed, as well as every species I have encountered—has a unique resting aura. Mated pairs, as I have said, have complementary-colored auras that tend to reach out toward their partner and blend together when they are situated close to one another."

Aidan didn't know many Zerkans, but Giklor's uncanny ability to sense when someone needed healing suggested psychic abilities of some kind. However, if he'd ever heard about the ability to see auras, he'd forgotten about it.

The little Zerkan aimed his huge teardrop-shaped eyes toward Aidan. "Without that ability, it's no wonder so many beings have trouble finding a mate."

Curly let out a snort. "Sounds like you guys ought to include matchmaking along with the healing you do."

"That has been suggested," said Giklor. "However, the practice is frowned upon. Too much interference in relationships tends to make them less stable."

"Meaning it's better to find love on your own?" Aidan suggested.

"Precisely. Aside from that, our advice, like our healing techniques, is often ignored or ridiculed." Giklor nodded toward Val, who was seated to his left. "For example, I could tell you where to find love, but would you listen to me?"

Aidan had never considered just how terrifying one of Val's hawk-like frowns could be, especially when accompanied by a flap of his wings. "I have no interest in finding love."

Giklor merely shrugged. "Be that as it may, I could still point you in the right direction." He offered Aidan a sympathetic smile. "Your reluctance to impart your knowledge of the future is quite understandable. For the most part, you would not be believed any more than we are. You see, most beings discount the notion of auras, simply because they cannot detect them. Because others cannot see the future, they refuse to acknowledge that the ability exists."

"Giklor, my friend," Aidan drawled, "you just said a mouthful."

Chapter 27

"For what it's worth, I believe you," Sula said. "If you hadn't had that vision, I would've been condor food."

"Possibly," Aidan acknowledged. "Although that was a Zetithian-style vision. In order to tell someone's future, I have to be near or in physical contact with them. You and I had never met."

Giklor nodded. "A slight but highly relevant distinction. How remarkable to have the mystical powers of two separate species." He punctuated this observation with wheezy laughter. "I have always suspected there was more to you than meets the eye."

Aidan leaned back in his chair and smiled. "More than just a big dumb blond, you mean?"

Sula gaped at him in astonishment. Aidan's twinkling green eyes led her to suspect him of joking, but she had always believed the adage that many a true word is spoken in jest.

"Who says you're a big dumb blond?" Abuti demanded. "I'd like to knock them senseless and suck their eyes out with my fingertips."

"What a horrible thing to say," Sula exclaimed, although she wasn't sure which was worse—the slur cast upon Aidan's intelligence or Abuti's gruesome retaliation.

Abuti was the first to reply. "That's a Norludian expression. No one actually does that." She stuck a contemplative fingertip onto her chin. "At least I don't think they do."

Aidan looked a bit sheepish. "No one has ever said that about me. Not within my hearing, anyway."

Sula felt like stomping her foot. "Then why did you say that?"

"Oh, you know what people always say about blonds." He shrugged. "I was only kidding. I didn't mean it literally."

Sula peered at him, trying to decide whether he was being entirely truthful or covering up a slip of the tongue. In the end, she decided to give him the benefit of the doubt. "I've met a lot of highly educated people during my years at the university. Very few are as sensible as you. I don't know how much schooling you've had, but I would never call you a big dumb blond. Not even as a joke."

Her own vehemence shocked her a little. Was she defending herself? Had she said or done anything to make him feel stupid? She didn't think so, but it was difficult to know how she came across to people. What would offend one person might seem like nothing to another.

Aidan raised her hand to his lips and kissed the backs of her fingers. "I'm glad to hear it, but there's no need to get all bent out of shape."

"For the record, anyone who grew up aboard the *Jolly Roger* has had plenty of education," Curly said firmly. "He may be big and blond, but he certainly isn't dumb."

"Why, Curly," Aidan drawled, "I never knew you noticed."

Curly rolled his eyes. "All I'm saying is that we were taught by the same teacher bot, and we both passed the exams. If you're dumb, then so am I."

"Gotcha." Aidan pushed himself away from the table and stood. "Who's on cleanup duty tonight?"

Qinta raised a hand. "That would be me." She aimed a grin at Val. "And you."

"Simple tasks are a welcome change," Val said. "They help clear the mind."

Sula could think of several things that would clear her mind, and most of them involved Aidan. Naked. Wiping tables and washing dishes had never been high on that list. Yawning, she said, "I don't know about you, but my brain is pretty numb after staring at a computer all day. I think I'm ready to hit the sack."

Abuti cackled with all-too-astute perception and waggled her fingers. "Let us know how it goes tonight."

Shaking her head, Sula groaned. "No secrets around here, are there?"

"Nope," Abuti replied. "Not as long as we have Laurel to keep us informed."

That was a detail of life aboard a starship Sula had all but forgotten, although any computer-controlled environment would be the same. Her parents had always known what she was up to as a child. There was simply no escaping an observant computer—yet another aspect of life in the mountain wilderness that she missed. *No assassins, no nosy computers...* "I guess I'd better tell Laurel to keep her mouth shut about what happens in private."

"Oh, please don't," Abuti begged. "I've been deprived of Aidan. The least I can do is revel in the sexy details."

Sula's jaw dropped. "Exactly how much does Laurel tell you?"

"Not a lot, actually." Abuti's crestfallen expression proved the computer had exercised some degree of discretion. "She only tells me when you're, um, busy. And only if I ask. She doesn't give me regular reports."

Thank goodness for that. "How often do you ask?"

"About every fifteen minutes or so after we first go to bed." She frowned. "I think she's starting to get annoyed with me, though. Either that or Aidan isn't getting any."

Amusement bubbled up inside Sula and spilled over into irrepressible laughter. Still laughing, she rose from her chair, somehow controlling the impulse to run screaming from the room.

Thankfully, Aidan took over from there. "Guess that proves you can't believe everything a computer tells you."

Sula was about to second that when she was startled by a flap of Val's wings. The intensity of his glare suggested he found this conversation repulsive, but he only said, "It couldn't possibly be that simple."

With every eye in the room on him, he still took a few moments to reflect before elaborating. "I think I know why we haven't been able to find anything to incriminate the university. It's an encryption within an encryption. Anyone searching for records is directed to a perfectly legitimate site, which contains several layers of the same data. No matter how deep we dig, we keep looping back to the same place."

"Doesn't sound simple to me," Jetoc remarked. "Sounds more like a bunch of bull."

Val nodded. "That's because it *is* a bunch of bull—everything we've been looking at so far, anyway. I believe I know a way around it."

"Thank the gods for that," Curly exclaimed. "I know it's for a great cause and all, but I'm so sick of this shit, I could scream."

"Not exactly your style, is it?" Aidan said mildly.

"In a word, *no*," Curly replied. "Right now, I don't even feel like playing video games." He sucked in a breath. "To be perfectly honest, I feel more like shooting something. For real."

"You may get your chance," Val said. "I'll know more in the morning."

"You're not going to stay up all night, are you?" As tired as she was, Sula couldn't imagine starting over again now.

A rare laugh escaped him. "When I go to bed, all I do is sleep."

"Dude, we've gotta get you a girl," Abuti declared. "When I think of all that hunky man meat just going to waste, it makes me want to—"

"Want to *what*?" Folding his arms over his muscular chest, Val stood with his feet apart and wings unfurled, in perhaps the most challenging stance Sula had ever seen.

"I dunno," Abuti replied. "But I'd like to do *something* about it." She grimaced. "Not sure what I can do, though. Don't know any girls who look anything like you."

"That's because there *aren't* any girls like me," Val said. "Our illustrious creator only saw fit to clone males."

"What a pity," Abuti said. "He could've created an entirely new species if he'd made a few women while he was at it."

"True," said Val. "His motivations for creating us were always something of a mystery. I, for one, never saw any point in asking him. Not that he would have told me the truth." His piercing gaze met Sula's. "Much like some of the other members of the faculty."

Sula nodded. "I'm starting to wonder if any of them

weren't in on this plot. Participation might even be a stipulation for getting tenure."

"Now, there's a scary thought," Aidan said. "Makes you wonder how any of them sleep at night."

"There's probably a crooked pharmaceutical professor cooking up illegal sleeping potions on the side." Sula shook her head, overwhelmed by the scope of the conspiracy. "I sure picked a great place to go to college, didn't I?"

Giklor let out a breathy chuckle. "In view of what we hope to accomplish, I would say your choice was exceptionally fortuitous."

In the greater scheme of things, Sula was forced to agree. Even if they weren't successful in exposing a wicked conspiracy, that chain of events had brought her together with Aidan. She only wished so many others hadn't lost their lives along the way.

"Not what we *hope* to accomplish," Sula said firmly. "What we *will* accomplish. None of us will be satisfied with anything less."

No barriers—chemical, physical, or emotional—prevented Sula from making love with Aidan in a way she'd never expected to do with anyone. The question of whether to have a family had never even been broached between her and Raj. Never, that was, beyond the knowledge that such a thing wouldn't be possible as long as her implant remained functional.

But with the implant removed, she felt oddly freed by its absence, which was strange because most women felt freer knowing that conception was impossible. Similar to the way she felt when adjusting to the biorhythms of a planet, she was reacquainting herself with the rhythms of her own body.

She understood enough about Zetithians to know Aidan would never willingly leave her. The mating process had already begun, and she suspected that this night would bring it to completion. On previous nights, they'd fallen asleep in each other's arms, each of them having given the other as much pleasure as they deemed prudent at the time. Now, they could have it all.

Love filled the air around him until Sula was almost convinced she could see his aura as well as if she were Zerkan. If she'd been in a more scientific frame of mind, she would have concluded that the air surrounding him was filled with sex pheromones, luring her closer to him until she was hopelessly ensnared.

*Snare...Snard...*The two words were nearly the same. Perhaps they were as close in meaning as they were in spelling.

Aidan still hadn't told her the Zetithian word for sex, and she doubted that omission was because he didn't know the answer. She could've asked Laurel, but for some reason she wanted to hear it from him, as if sharing that secret was somehow more significant than a simple exchange of information.

Somewhere along the line, they'd each adopted a particular side of the bunk, her against the wall with him on the outer edge. Was he there to protect her from intruders or to prevent her from falling? Whatever the reason, that arrangement allowed her to watch him as he climbed in beside her. His glowing eyes fixed on hers as he advanced toward her, his long blond hair framing his face while the subdued lighting outlined the play of sleek muscles as he moved.

"Have I ever told you how much I love your hair?" she asked.

"I don't believe so," he replied. "At least not in so many words."

"Well then, I'm telling you now. It's beautiful, silky, and amazingly sexy."

"I'm glad you like it." He was purring as he bent closer. His deep, sensuous kiss robbed her of breath and sent desire swirling down to her core, compounding the yearning she'd felt for him throughout the day. "You smell incredible." He kissed her again, gliding his tongue into her mouth to entwine with her own. "Taste great too."

"How do you do that?" she asked, gazing into his feline eyes. "Make me want you even more when I already want you so badly I can barely stand to wait another second?"

"I could ask you the same question, but some mysteries are better left unsolved—an enigma to bind us together."

She traced the line of his cheek with a fingertip. The shape of his face, the rise of his cheekbones, the graceful curve of his ears where they came to a point all conspired to fascinate and entice. Making love with him in total darkness would've been lovely, but without being able to see him, the experience would've seemed incomplete, as though lacking some vital component. "It was a rhetorical question anyway."

Gliding her palms up over his shoulders, she pulled him into an embrace that pressed the full lengths of their bodies together, exchanging heat as well as touch. They'd long since given up the pretense of wearing any clothing to bed. Donning a nightgown was pointless when it would only end up on the floor.

Pushing him onto his back, she climbed atop him. She didn't have enough room to sit up and move as freely as she would've liked, but the scenery was certainly better when she leaned forward. Hanging around with other beings who had six or possibly seven senses sometimes left her feeling shortchanged to some extent. But not now, not when she was able to drink in the sight of Aidan, his blond curls spread out over the pillow, his fiery eyes heavy-lidded with desire. Coupled with his warmth between her thighs, he was a treat for every sense she possessed.

She bent down and nipped him on the neck. "Think we can get you where you need to be without using our hands?"

"Absolutely," he purred. "Hands-free sex is a Zetithian specialty." With a lip-curling smile, he added, "All you have to do is back up and sit down. I'll do the rest."

She crawled backward until her *loresh* bumped against his *cockaj*. His cockhead was already awash with orgasmic syrup, enabling him to tease her slit until he found the opening. Another backward move brought him deep into her core. Sitting down stretched her almost to the limit.

"Ohhh...perfect," she whispered. "That's what I've been missing." Rising up, she sat down on him again. "You." Another bounce. "Inside me." One more. "Where you belong."

"I couldn't agree more." Purring like a kitten, he began moving his cock inside her, rotating it to stimulate every corner of her sensitive passage.

Her head fell forward as she groaned with pleasure. "I wish you could feel how fabulous that is."

"Feels pretty great on my end." He changed the direction of rotation. "But I'm perfectly willing to let you have the lion's share of the ecstasy."

She was about to protest when an orgasm signaled its imminent arrival. Learning to recognize the early warning signal for what it was and focus on the subsequent elation had only taken a few days. Now she discovered there was a disparity between the cock syrup orgasms when the source of contact was vaginal rather than oral. Not surprisingly, the vaginal source was more satisfying, perhaps because her core was able to contract around his magnificent shaft. Having something to squeeze made all the difference.

His upward thrust as she tightened around him doubled the delight. "How's that?"

Opening one eye, she scowled at him. "You know exactly how good that was."

A quick smile and a wink proved her supposition was correct. "Just honing my skills. I have a lot of lost time to make up for."

"Take all the time you need. I'm not going anywhere." Wiggling her hips exposed her clitoris to the friction from his pubic hair, providing her with yet another wave of superb sensations to savor.

"A willing participant?"

She ran a fingertip down the center of his chest. "More like an enthusiastic research partner."

"At least you aren't a practice dummy."

A peal of laughter escaped her. "Thank you—I think." Although the mention of dummy reminded her of his dumb-blond remark from earlier that evening. "Neither are you."

He winced. "Still aren't convinced I didn't really mean that, are you?"

"I'm surprised you would even entertain such an idea." She tilted her head, studying his expression. This didn't seem like the best time for a discussion of that nature, nor was it a good time to let it lie. Perhaps he would be more forthcoming because they were alone rather than part of a group. "There's more to it, though. Isn't there?"

For a long moment, his only response was a sigh. "Even though the money each of us received from the trust fund is more than enough to live on, most of us have gone on to do something interesting and useful. I haven't done that, because I encounter new people and new futures wherever I go. Granted, not everyone's future is dismal, but it wears on me after a while."

She nodded slowly. "I hadn't considered that aspect. Your lifestyle is more a matter of self-preservation than a lack of intelligence or ambition. But you assume that's what everyone thinks of you, don't you?"

"Yeah. Like it's a good thing I have money, because being an idle rich guy is the only thing I'm capable of."

"But you weren't idle, were you?"

"No. But I do try to limit my contacts." He frowned. "It's stifling sometimes. I feel better when I'm at the orphanage with the kids, because what I sense of their futures is more immediate than long-term. Those sorts of readings are easier to handle."

Leaning forward, she pressed a kiss to his lips. "I think your choice of volunteer work is quite admirable."

"As is my choice of mates."

"I'm glad you think so. I made a damn fine choice myself." When she kissed him again, he responded with a passion that seemed out of place in the wake of such a soul-searching conversation.

But perhaps it wasn't inappropriate. Perhaps this was no longer a time for deep thoughts but a time to display the love between two beings destined to live out their lives together. She wasn't the slightest bit surprised when he wrapped his arms around the small of her back, pulled her close to him, and flipped her over onto the bed.

He licked his lips. "My delicious, beautiful, incredible mate."

When he followed that up with a series of pelvic thrusts that had her seeing stars, if he'd added *prepare to have your brains fucked out*, she might've been better prepared.

The lack of preparation didn't stop her, however. Crossing her ankles behind his back, she pulled him in even farther.

"Oh yeah." Purring, he raised his head, exposing his neck. "You know what to do."

"You bet I do." With a fervor that shocked even her, she sank her teeth into the succulent muscle at the base of his neck.

Growling, he rocked into her so hard, her head slid over the upper edge of the bunk. "We really need a bigger bed."

She tapped his shoulder. "I have an idea."

"Lay it on me."

"We could put the mattresses from both bunks side by side on the floor."

"I've said it before, and it's still true: Sula, you're a genius."

The enormous sense of loss when his cock slid from her sheath was quickly overcome by the treat of watching Aidan drag the mattress from the upper bunk. His engorged cock was simply the icing on the cake of the most amazing male body she could possibly imagine. She'd seen him nude before, but his fluid movements and effortless strength had her gaping like a flabbergasted blowfish. Nevertheless, she let out a squeal as he dragged the second mattress from the bunk frame without waiting for her to get up. She'd barely had time to recover her equilibrium before he pounced.

Scooping up her legs, he pulled them up onto his shoulders and sank into her with pinpoint precision.

"You're getting good at that."

He grinned. "Practice makes perfect. When I can do it in a flying leap from across the room, I'll consider the technique mastered."

Sula wasn't sure she wanted to be pounced on from across the room, but that was a discussion for another day.

Chapter 28

SULA LAY WITH HER ARMS SPLAYED OUT ABOVE HER HEAD, gazing up at Aidan as he thrust into her. No one but her had ever seen him from that perspective, a fact that made her feel unique and very, very fortunate indeed. If there was a more stunning sight to behold in the entire universe, she couldn't imagine what it would be, unless it was Aidan making love to her by candlelight.

Her mind's eye took that thought a step further, casting a golden gleam onto his blond curls and tanned skin, and she made a mental note to ask Curly if there were any candles aboard the ship. If not, she hoped their rendezvous point would have a shop where she could get a few. But like the pouncing issue, that was something that could easily wait for a more appropriate time.

The feel of his cock inside her went beyond excellent to exquisite. An orgasm hovered, warning her mere moments before it caught her in its net. As her body contracted around him, she caught a glimpse of his satisfied smile.

"I love watching you do that," he whispered.

"I love watching you do almost anything," she said when she was able to draw another breath. "But I especially love the way you look right now." His arm muscles flexing as he rocked into her, his blond locks swaying to and fro, the golden glow emanating from his eyes—everything about him was sheer perfection.

Another woman might not see him the same way. But then, no other woman could claim to love him as much as she did. Had she told him she loved him? She didn't think she had. Perhaps this was the time.

"We're truly mated now, aren't we?" she asked.

He nodded. "I believe we are. I'm mated to you, anyway. Humans don't bond the way Zetithians do, and they don't always mate for life."

"Sad but true," she said. "However, I can't think of any reason I wouldn't want to be with you forever. I love you, Aidan. I'm quite certain I always will."

His smile revealed the tips of his fangs. "You once asked me to tell you the Zetithian word for sex, and I told you I'd have to get back to you."

Puzzled as to why he would bring that up now when she'd just confessed her love for him, all she could do was clear her throat and say, "That's right."

"There's a reason I didn't tell you then. You see, in the Zetithian language, the word for sex is the same as the word for love." His thrusts slowed and deepened, compounding her enjoyment. "*Klie* is the fondness one feels for their friends or family. The word for the love between a man and a woman is *amorjiel*, which is also the word for the sexual act. The words are the same because Zetithians very seldom have one without the other. Humans have different words, because for them, sex is possible without love or even desire."

"And you wanted to be sure I was feeling both of them, right?"

He nodded. "I already knew how much I loved you. The way that vision kept repeating, I think I loved you even before I ever laid eyes on you. *You* were the unknown variable in the equation, not me. If I possessed my sister's empathic abilities, I could've read your emotions. But I can't." His wistful smile tugged at her heart. "I could've told you how I felt, but I didn't want to prompt you into parroting it back to me. The words had to come from you."

She reached up to caress his cheek. "Do you believe me now?"

"Absolutely." Turning his head, he pressed a kiss to her palm. "I never truly doubted you, although I may have doubted my interpretation of your feelings." A small smile lifted the corner of his mouth. "I've never done this before, you know."

"Your inexperience isn't all that obvious. You were made for love. Not only your body, but your beautiful soul as well." She closed her eyes, savoring his steady thrust and withdrawal, focusing on the added stimulus his coronal ruffle provided. "Although being amazingly well-equipped doesn't hurt."

His purr added a subtle vibration to his chuckle. "Some would say it gives me an unfair advantage."

"It might if there were other men vying for my affection. But there aren't, and I can't imagine there ever will be. I am totally and irrevocably yours."

He appeared to be pleased by this; his fangs flashed with his smile, and if possible, his penis seemed harder than ever when her orgasm detonated. His pace slowly increased, but his hip movement was very slight, resulting in short, purposeful thrusts that focused on her sweet spot. How he knew where it was located was a mystery. Nevertheless, his unerring strokes continued until what little control she had left deserted her completely. Even her legs no longer obeyed her commands, slipping from their perch on his shoulders like a pair of noodles. He leaned closer, resting his weight on his elbows while cradling her head in his palms. The kiss he gave her promised a lifetime of love and enjoyment amid the swirling mass of galactic chaos.

Or perhaps it wasn't chaos at all. Perhaps it only seemed that way because of the horrible things that happened too often to be tolerated. Did people have to be ruthless and unscrupulous to rise to power? Whatever happened to good ol' human decency? Compassion? Kindness? Charity? Tolerance? Forgiveness?

Those who had sent her to Ecos in the hope of destroying her, Raj, and the entire population of an unsuspecting world possessed none of those traits.

"Harder," she urged. "You aren't the only one who has seen things they wish they could forget."

"In this way, we help one another," Aidan said. "Hold on. I'm coming."

She almost laughed. Did he mean what she thought he meant?

His breath caught, and his purring ceased. With a feral cry, he arched his back, and his head snapped up, tossing his golden mane over his shoulders like a raging stallion. His *snard* filled her, its creamy texture allowing greater penetration than ever before. How could this moment be so different from the first time they made love? Had he gained that much skill, or was it simply because he'd dropped his guard completely?

She couldn't know for sure, but even the *snard* effect seemed enhanced. Heat flowed from her lower back, seeming to trace the paths of her blood vessels all the way to the tips of her fingers and toes. Her eyes were open, but she didn't see him. She saw the deep-green jungles and rocky mountaintops of Ecos, but what was even more significant, she saw its people happy and thriving as they had been when she and Raj first landed there. The image remained even when she closed her eyes.

How could that be? Had Aidan somehow shown her a vision of that planet's doomed people before the plague? Or was this the aftermath of a massive intervention to save their species?

And why in the world was she seeing it now?

Carried aloft on a gentle cloud of euphoria, the vision dissipated, becoming the field of stars and their ship cruising through them, never close enough to see anything of the planets or any people who might live on them.

Her mind cleared, focusing on yet another clue she should've spotted long ago. Along with indigenous intelligent life-forms, Rhylos had no native primates whatsoever. The plague had apparently killed them along with the cave-dwelling beings that had drawn pictures on the wall of the condors' cave.

The truth was so obvious now. She didn't know whether there were any monkeys or gorillas on Terra Minor, but that Rhylos didn't have a single, solitary native primate species was common knowledge. Had anyone ever questioned that lack?

Somehow, she doubted it, just as she doubted any archaeological digs had ever been proposed or approved. Humans had always been fascinated by their own history, even though much of it was bloody and shameful. Studying the evolutionary processes on a world with no humanoid species had probably been deemed unnecessary and, more important, unprofitable.

Had anyone ever proposed such a study? And if so, what reasons were given for denying the funds? Because they surely would've been denied. No one in power would ever want the truth to be uncovered.

As her mind drifted back toward the present and the reality that was Aidan Banadänsk, she couldn't help but wonder. Had this been a vision of some sort? Or was what she'd seen simply a moment of postorgasmic clarity?

Opening her eyes, she gazed up at him, noting that he hadn't collapsed on top of her. Nor had he rolled away. If anything, he seemed frozen in place, an expression of awe etched upon his handsome feline features.

"Aidan, are you okay?"

"I'm fine," he whispered. "But we have three children now." He paused, blinking rapidly as though searching his thoughts for more information. "One girl and two boys."

For the moment, Sula's vision was forgotten. "How can you possibly know that?"

He looked down at her and smiled. "I can see their futures."

—∽—

Not only could Aidan see their children's births and infancy, but a rapid-fire string of images whipped through his mind's eye, predicting—or was it documenting?—their growth and development into adulthood and beyond.

To be perfectly honest, he hoped he would forget everything he'd seen by the time those children were born. Watching lives unfold in a predicted manner would lose a large measure of the joy parents should feel as their offspring reached various milestones, along with the sadness when pitfalls were encountered. No one's life was so charmed that they never encountered a single setback. Besides, if it was all joyous, how could anyone understand the precious nature of happiness? Aidan had known a great deal of sorrow, and while a large measure of it was not his own, the feeling was still as real as if he'd experienced those painful episodes himself. Coming at the moment of conception, perhaps this was the one time he would ever envision such things. Again, he hoped that would be true. Knowing everything about a child's life long before they did was wrong on so many levels.

"Are they happy? You can at least tell me that." Sula's anxious expression wouldn't allow him to deny her completely.

"Yes, they're happy. But that's all I'm going to say. And I'm not going to tell them what I've seen, either."

She nodded slowly. "I'm okay with that. Knowing their future would either have them anticipating the good times or dreading the bad. Everyone needs a few surprises—even a child's parents."

"I'm glad you agree." If she didn't, he could definitely see trouble ahead—whether he was a Zetithian-Mordrial mystic or not.

"What about you? You'll know everything even before it happens."

He grinned. "That's why I'm going to try very hard to forget what I've seen. The images ran by so fast, I didn't catch most of it anyway." She hadn't said whether she was happy herself. Although come to think of it, neither had he. "What about you? Are you happy?"

"Of course I am," she replied, somewhat indignantly, he thought. "I just never expected to know immediately, much less that the father of my children would know I was pregnant even before I did."

"I probably could've kept quiet, but I would never want to be accused of keeping secrets from you." After a moment's reflection, he deemed it best to amend that a tad. "Secrets that involve you, anyway. I'm sure you don't want to hear about all of them."

"You know, sometimes it helps to tell someone else about the things that bother you. Sharing the burden makes it easier to tolerate."

"I'll keep that in mind," he said. "Speaking of burdens, I should get up before I squash you." A quick glance around their quarters as he carefully withdrew and pushed himself up onto his hands and knees proved he hadn't exactly done a stellar job of bed-making. Sula was lying across both mattresses, but the gap between the two was so wide, she could've easily slipped through it. Plus, the mattress from the upper bunk had somehow managed to lose its sheet. "So...do you want to stay on the floor or put the mattresses back where they belong?"

"As long as I'm with you, I'm okay pretty much anywhere," she replied. "The floor is fine. We'll have more head room, and we won't have as far to fall if one of us rolls off the edge."

"That was one advantage to the bunks. At least I knew you wouldn't end up on the floor."

"True, but I don't want you falling, either. You're my mate now—and the father of our children. I have a duty to protect you."

Recalling that Sula had lived off the land for nearly

a year armed only with a bullwhip and a pulse pistol, had escaped from a planet where everyone else died of a dreaded disease, and managed to elude what was presumably a paid assassin, he knew she could probably take care of herself and anyone else she loved.

"Nobody better mess with our kids," he said with a low whistle. "From what I hear, their mom's a real tiger."

Sula was glad she was already sitting at the dinner table when Curly delivered the news that they would be landing on Ursa Prime in his ship rather than rendezvousing with another vessel.

"I thought we decided that was a bad idea," she said, aghast at the thought of arriving in a ship the villains were at least keeping an eye out for, if not actually tracking.

Curly winced as though she'd slapped him. "Remember when you sent out the request for a ride to begin with? There was a reason no one but me replied. The others are so far out of range, we'd have to wait a couple of months before we could rendezvous with them. I don't know about you, but I have better things to do, packages to deliver, and lots of places I'd much rather be."

"Larry certainly would've been helpful." Aidan turned toward Val. "But you can handle most of the technical stuff. Right?"

"I believe so," Val replied.

Sula would've felt better had he immediately claimed to have that capability and more. However, given his usual stoic demeanor, this was probably as enthusiastic as he ever got.

"I can do that also," Jetoc said. "My skills aren't

limited to navigation. I am well-versed in the techniques required to tap into communication relays and such."

Sula did a slight double take when the Drell spoke. Throughout their journey, Jetoc had been relatively quiet, and he had yet to display any of the inherent rudeness of his kind. If he could tap into the communication networks *and* keep a civil tongue in his head, Curly had really lucked out in his choice of navigators.

"Sounds good," Aidan said. "If we can get even a hint of a confession, it needs to be blasted all over the quadrant. Preferably live."

"That can be arranged," Jetoc said.

Val's wings rose slightly, but he merely folded his arms and nodded his agreement.

"If we make it that far." At this stage of the game, Sula practically had to sit on her hands to keep from biting her nails. Two days out from Ursa Prime, and they had yet to agree on a definite plan. "I just wish there was some way to alter the ship's signature so they don't know it's us. I'd hate to think we were walking into a trap." She glanced at Aidan, somehow hoping for reassurance, if not a miraculous promise that all would be well.

"I've been thinking about that," Aidan began. "Walking into a trap might not be a bad thing, provided we have sufficient backup. If they're convinced they have the upper hand, the bad guys might get careless. They might even enjoy the opportunity to gloat."

Sula peered at him with suspicion. "You've seen something, haven't you?"

"Nothing specific," he said. "It's more of a hunch than a vision."

"A hunch?" Curly echoed. "You? Seriously? What

good is a Mordrial fortune-teller if the best you can come up with is a hunch?"

Aidan rolled his eyes. "Give it a rest, Curly. This is going to work. Trust me."

Curly drew in a breath as though about to retort but pressed his lips together instead. The twitching muscles in his jaw demonstrated how much it cost him to keep quiet. He was, after all, risking his ship and his life.

As it happened, he didn't have to say anything. Jetoc said it for him. "I believe the captain doesn't care for the idea of allowing his ship to be captured or destroyed."

"I never said we were going to *fly* into a trap," Aidan said, clearly unperturbed. "We'll be *walking* into it. They'll let us land, if for no other reason than to be sure their suspicions are correct. After all, letting us come to them is far easier than chasing after us. They've already tried that and failed." He turned to Sula. "Your Zetithian disguise should be enough to fool them at first, and without those nanobots, you won't be traceable. By the time they realize who you really are, we'll have already gotten them to show their hand, and it'll be too late to do anything about it."

"You don't really believe that, do you?" Sula demanded. To be honest, she didn't follow his logic at all. Sure, she might look like a Zetithian to a stranger, but Professor Dalb knew her well enough to see through the disguise, and there were others on the staff who knew her better than he did.

"We've already made the appointment and told them what we have in mind. I believe they'll wait until they have the credits I'm offering for the research grant before they do anything rash."

That appointment was another thing Sula had misgivings about. Sure, an offer of grant money would get their foot in the door, but it also gave the university people time to prepare their own defensive strategy.

Abuti giggled. "This is perfect! They think we don't know they know we're coming, and we already know they do. They don't know how big our gang is, either."

Sula turned a bleak gaze on the Norludian girl. "Our gang is nowhere near as big as theirs." She hated to admit it, even to herself, but she was getting cold feet. When hers was the only life at risk, she could be as fearless as anyone. She'd already cheated death a number of times. But she had babies to protect now. Motherhood in any stage made a huge difference.

"The size of our gang doesn't matter as long as they don't know exactly how many of us there are." Aidan aimed a pointed glance at Jetoc. "And there's at least one of us they've never seen. Nor do they know about that cave on Rhylos—or who we've shared that information with. We've got several aces up our sleeves. We just have to decide when to play them."

Chapter 29

WHEN THE *INTERSTELLAR EXPRESS* LANDED AT THE URSA Prime spaceport, despite long hours of sifting through data, they had found nothing to substantiate their suspicions. As a result, Sula walked down the gangplank with a significant amount of trepidation.

Nothing had changed in the past year. The control tower still shone with imposing brilliance, and the main concourse was filled with self-important beings from all over the galaxy, not one of whom gave their ragtag band a second look, unless it was to peer down their respective noses.

The reason Ursa Prime had been adopted as the planet's name was readily apparent to any observer. *Ursa* meaning bear, and *prime* meaning, well…prime. *Prime bear.* Although prima donna might've been more accurate. Clearly, the planet's—and subsequently, the university's—reputation had gone to its collective head. Small wonder that some of those affiliated with such an august institution felt that they had every right to play God, particularly a professor descended from the university's founder.

Ilya Zolo had certainly attempted to play God when he'd created the Avian clones. Poor Val. To owe his existence to such a heartless monster was enough to mess with anyone's mind. The surprising thing was that he was able to function at all.

Aidan had his own share of demons, which, according to Val, Sula had helped him come to terms with, at least to the point of allowing him to be happier than he'd been in the past. He had certainly brought joy back into her life. Joy had been traded for despair on Ecos, only to be replaced with grim determination during her journey to Rhylos. Now that the end was in sight, she knew that exposing any atrocities committed by the university heads would not be the best of her life's work. Granted, the other aspects of her life might not have as many far-reaching effects, but promoting Aidan's happiness and the happiness of their children were worthy endeavors in themselves.

Val and Jetoc remained aboard the ship to handle the communications aspects of the plan. Curly volunteered to be Sula's bodyguard, and Giklor came along as their resident healer and spiritual leader. Abuti and Qinta simply refused to be left behind. Curly had equipped everyone with Darconian comstones, which was something Sula had only heard about. The stones only worked over a relatively short range, but all you had to do was tap the stone and call out the name of another person carrying a stone. Their response forged the link, which would remain open until the stone was tapped again, terminating the link. Like several other varieties of Darconian stones, no one knew how they worked, but they had the beauty of appearing to be a piece of jewelry rather than a manufactured device.

Sula was wearing her Zetithian disguise again. Putting on the slanted eyebrows, pointed ears, and fangs was easy enough. However, since Jeeves hadn't given her any makeup to take with her, she'd left her skin tone unchanged. Without the nanobots, she couldn't be tracked anyway. No longer needed as a decoy, Qinta hadn't bothered with a disguise.

They hadn't gone far when Curly's voice sounded in Aidan's ear. "Hey, Aidan. Comstone working okay?"

"Yeah," Aidan replied. "I can hear you loud and clear."

"That's good," Curly said. "Because you're being followed."

"Why am I not surprised?"

"The guy doesn't appear to be armed, but looks can be deceiving."

Aidan tapped his comstone and said, "Val, what about you? Can you hear me?"

"Not very well," came the faint reply. "By the time you get inside the building, you'll be out of range. We may have to go with Plan B."

"Understood." Aidan tapped the stone and muttered, "You ladies get that? Implement Plan B."

"Acknowledged," Abuti said cheerfully. "I always liked that plan better anyway."

Aidan rolled his eyes. "Of course you would, mainly because it's riskier than Plan A."

"Which is why it's Plan B," Sula said. "I'm still not convinced it will work."

"Both plans have flaws," Aidan admitted, "which is why we're relying heavily on luck."

Abuti shook her head. "Not luck. We know this will work. You said I would get older, right?"

Aidan actually laughed. "True. But I never said how *much* older you would get."

Sula swallowed hard. This discussion wasn't exactly

filling her with confidence, aside from the fact that one of her fangs had developed a slight wiggle.

The attitude of people on the street changed as they approached the university campus, which was within walking distance of the spaceport. Instead of disdainful glances, they were now subject to curious stares. Sula held her breath as they walked toward a group of students, two of whom she recognized.

"I know a couple of those guys," she whispered. "If I can get past them, we should be okay." When they passed by without accosting her, she exhaled with relief.

Abuti snickered. "Unless Aidan gets mobbed by a bunch of Zetithian-crazy girls."

"I hadn't thought about that," Sula said.

"I am receiving several interested looks myself," Giklor said. "Have these people never seen a Zerkan before?"

"Probably not," Sula replied. "I've been a student here for several years, and you were the first Zerkan I'd ever seen. You'd think there might be a few of you around here, though, wouldn't you?"

"Not really," Giklor said. "We seldom go offworld for education since our university system is far superior to any found on other worlds."

Sula smiled to herself. Apparently, the denizens of Ursa Prime weren't the only conceited folks in the galaxy. "That explains it."

Passing through the ornate double doors barring the entrance to the administration building, Sula was once again reminded of the medieval castle vibe she'd always gotten from the architectural style. Aidan's house had nothing on this place for ostentation.

The interior smelled exactly the same, making her wonder if the scent of ancient manuscripts hadn't been concocted to enhance the atmosphere. Ursa Prime had also been colonized by humans, but its habitation went back at least five hundred years. Was this the first world to have its indigenous population wiped out by a plague? Or was this simply the birthplace of the dreadful practice?

As they entered the main hall, the superior attitude of the occupants was so pervasive, she was surprised she'd never noticed it before. Perhaps she'd been as awed as any other student back then. She viewed it through different eyes now, eyes that had seen firsthand what unrestrained arrogance could do.

As Aidan led them to the reception desk, a sideways glance revealed Curly and Qinta entering the building. A Vessonian woman whose graying hair was pinned up in a beehive shape sat at the desk.

"We have an appointment with Professor Dalb," Aidan said.

The woman raised a haughty eyebrow until it seemed to disappear beneath her forehead ridges. "If you will sign the visitor's logbook, the lift is over there." She pointed to her left. "And by the way, that would be *Dean* Dalb."

"Thank you for clarifying that," Aidan said as he signed the logbook.

"Dean Dalb?" Sula murmured to Aidan as they rode up to the twelfth floor. "He was only a professor of anthropology when I left here."

"Kinda makes you wonder who he had to bribe or bump off to get that position, doesn't it?" Aidan remarked.

Sula had to focus hard on not biting her lip as her

anxiety level had her adrenal glands working overtime pumping out epinephrine. Her hands were cold, and her chest felt tight, making breathing difficult. She took hold of Aidan's hand, comforted by its steady warmth.

At least *he* didn't seem nervous. Abuti was popping her fingertips on and off the wall behind her. Giklor said nothing, but his eyes seemed to glow even redder than usual. Perhaps it was only because of the dim lighting. She couldn't be sure, though. Perhaps her own eyes were glowing brighter too.

Aidan stepped off the lift and tapped his comstone. "Yo, Curly. It's a go."

Sula's trembling hand made Aidan wish there could be any way to avoid including her in the confrontation with Dalb. Not that he blamed her for being nervous. Even knowing what he did, he was a little anxious himself.

Halfway down the hallway, Sula suddenly stopped and clapped a hand over her mouth. "We're too late," she said in a horrified whisper. "If he's been promoted to dean, the Ecos mission must have been successful."

"Not necessarily," he cautioned her. "However, it'll be interesting to hear what he has to say." He chuckled. "Especially when he realizes who you are."

"I'm not sure I *want* him to recognize me. No telling how many minions he has working for him now."

Taking her hand, Aidan raised it to his lips. "You're forgetting we have minions of our own, and damn good ones at that."

"You're right. I just can't help remembering…"

"That isn't going to happen to us," he said. "Trust me."

"It isn't that I don't trust you, because I do. It's just that, well, you know how it is."

He kissed her hand again. "Yes, I do. But this is going to work."

Her dark eyes searched his. "You've seen the outcome?"

He shrugged. "Let's just say I've seen *one* outcome. But it's enough to inspire confidence."

"You aren't going to tell me what it is, are you?"

"Not yet. Afterward, perhaps."

Aidan had only seen one possible outcome. But he also knew there were variations on every theme, and knowledge of the future sometimes altered its path.

He only hoped *he* didn't know too much.

When they arrived at Dalb's office, the dean's shapely blond Terran assistant seemed even more impressed with herself than the Vessonian at the desk downstairs. She merely nodded and said "Have a seat, and I'll see if he's free" when Aidan gave her his name. Clearly, the amount of money he was offering to drop in the university's lap wasn't enough to impress her, although she might not know about the proposed grant. Somehow, Aidan doubted that.

Spotting a scanner arched in front of the doorway to the inner office, he palmed the comstones over to Abuti. With no pockets, she merely held onto them with her sucker-tipped fingers like some weird version of Norludian finger jewelry.

To his credit—or *dis*credit—Dalb didn't keep them waiting long, and for once, Aidan was actually looking forward to shaking the hand of a stranger.

"You'll need to walk through the scanner before you go in," the assistant said with a toothy smile that seemed even less genuine than her hair color. "Security, you understand."

"I'm not walking through that scanner thing," Abuti announced. "You can't make me."

Meanwhile, Giklor sidled up to the assistant's desk. "Please allow me to introduce myself. I am Giklor of the planet Zerka, and I am available for any healing you may require." He punctuated this last statement with a wave of his forked tongue.

Clearly repulsed, the blond turned away from him, although judging from the retching sound she made, she was only moderately successful at hiding her reaction.

When the outer door opened slightly, Aidan glanced at Giklor, who responded with the horizontal blink peculiar to his species.

As Sula and Aidan passed through the scanner and entered the spacious office, Aidan was immediately struck by the décor. Various weapons and other cultural artifacts decorated the walls. Dalb himself sat behind an antique wooden desk that probably outweighed everyone in the room combined. Shelves of books covered one entire wall, and an ancient shield and spear hung high on the wall behind the desk. He hadn't known what to expect, but Dalb himself was surprising.

For some reason, he'd expected the man to be Terran. However, the man he now faced was Edraitian.

Trust the gods to leave out that one pertinent detail.

If the gods were playing a joke on him, so be it. However, the man's species explained a few things, his presumed arrogance chief among them.

"Good afternoon, Mr. Banadänsk," he said, rising from his chair. Characterized by the blue skin and red hair of his kind, he held out a hand. He was as stiff-rumped as any Edraitian Aidan had ever met, from the crisp perfection of his dark tunic to the flattop crop of his bushy hair. "I'm very pleased to meet you."

Aidan gestured toward Sula. "Allow me to introduce my wife, Prisha Banadänsk."

Dalb stared at Sula as though unsure of what he was seeing. Had he expected her to be traceable and therefore unable to walk into his office without his prior knowledge?

The pause went on for several moments. Was he weighing his options? Or was he trying to convince himself that Sula really was a Zetithian and not the Terran woman whom he'd sent to her death on Ecos?

The hand Dalb held out seemed to shake ever so slightly. Sula, showing remarkable fortitude, grasped the man's hand as though she was actually pleased to meet him. Was it possible they'd been wrong? Had they walked in expecting a trap only to confront an innocent man? Then again, perhaps it was simply the shock from seeing her alive that had him so rattled.

Dalb muttered a greeting and then extended his hand toward Aidan.

With a deep, fortifying breath, Aidan prepared himself for the visions that shaking Dalb's hand would induce. The ensuing glimpses into the future were terrible indeed but highly satisfying.

An irrepressible smile tugged the corner of his mouth as he realized that none of their pursuers had ever gotten close enough to Sula to get a good look at her when she was wearing her Zetithian disguise. The most that could've been discerned from a distance was that she'd curled her hair, her Zetithian features not being obvious until seen up close. Therefore, their pursuers on Rhylos hadn't been fooled by her disguise because they were simply following the nanobots.

Dalb might wonder if Prisha and Sula were one and the same, but without the nanobots, he couldn't be sure. *Let him sweat.*

Still, if Curly was right and they'd been shadowed after leaving Ursa Prime's spaceport, Dalb's surprise was simply a ruse intended to make them believe they'd succeeded in fooling him. Aidan would've used the same ploy had he been in Dalb's shoes. He just wasn't sure he would have been quite as convincing.

"About the grant," Aidan said. "Zetithians are a highly resilient species, but we've become concerned that the loss of our homeworld has caused emotional problems for those of us that remain. The loss of home, family, and identity has been devastating to some." He was thinking of Onca, who'd been taken aboard the refugee ship as a baby. His parents, for whatever reason, had only passed on his given name. He didn't know any of his family or even the province in which they'd lived. Aidan's father had been an adult when he was captured and sold into slavery. At least he knew his own name and where he'd been born. So many of the refugees didn't. "In many ways, we're all orphans."

"You seem fairly well-adjusted," Dalb said smoothly. "I take it you aren't concerned for yourself." Whatever he'd been feeling only moments before, he had either moved on from it or had brought it under control. If Althea had been there, she could've told Aidan exactly what the man was feeling. Once again, he wished they'd been able to rendezvous with Althea and Larry before attempting this meeting.

"Not particularly," Aidan replied. "You see, there are those of us who know who our parents are and where we came from. It's the children who grew up as refugees that concern me. Some have adjusted well. However, I would've thought that an anthropologist would be interested in studying this phenomenon. It can't be that often that an entire intelligent species faces extinction, along with the loss of their home-world. Surely, there would be repercussions, making it worthy of study?"

"Won't you sit down?" Dalb motioned toward the two chairs in front of his desk before resuming his own seat. "As I understand it, most of the remaining Zetithians are currently living on Terra Minor."

"That's correct," Aidan said. "Sending a team to study them wouldn't cause the university a great deal of inconvenience. Not like sending a team to observe a primitive species where contact with outsiders is best avoided." He paused, letting that sink in for a moment before continuing. "They all speak the Standard Tongue, so interviewing them wouldn't be difficult. Especially given that there are so few of us left."

Dalb tapped his chin with a fingertip. "Your situation *would* make for an interesting study." He glanced at Sula. "Forgive me, Mrs. Banadänsk, but you bear an uncanny resemblance to a former pupil of mine, although she was Terran rather than Zetithian."

"Interesting coincidence," Aidan said.

"Yes, it is." Dalb said slowly. "She was originally from India and had the brown skin and dark hair

common among people native to that region. I wasn't
aware there were any Zetithians with that coloring."

Aidan stole a glance at Sula. She could disguise many
things—her hair, her ears and eyebrows, even her teeth,
but although she was fluent in the Standard Tongue, her
lilting accent and timbre remained. Dalb might not be sure
of anything else about her, but her voice was unmistakable.

"There are variations in skin tone among our kind,"
Sula said evenly. "Just as there are variations among
Terrans. But you are correct. My mother was originally
from southern India. I am a hybrid."

"Ah, then," Dalb said pleasantly. "That explains it."

"This student of yours," Sula began. "You speak
of her in the past tense, and you seem to have had an
emotional reaction to seeing me. Can you tell me what
became of her?"

Aidan would've sworn Dalb turned a deeper shade
of blue. "It is believed she died while working on a
research project for the university."

"Believed?" Sula sat back in her chair, her brow
wrinkled in a convincing frown. "Do you mean to say
you don't *know*?"

"I didn't know for certain," Dalb replied. "That is,
not until today, Sulaksha."

Chapter 30

"I NEVER THOUGHT TO SEE YOU AGAIN, SULA." DALB'S tone was soft yet menacing. "But here you are, pretending to be a Zetithian, of all things."

Sula snorted with mirthless laughter. "Considering how many times your people have tried to kill me, can you blame me for wearing a disguise?"

"Not really. But then, you always were a resourceful little thing. Flying a starship to Rhylos all by yourself, escaping that idiot we sent to dispatch you, living alone in the mountains for months on end." He shook his head slowly. "You should've saved yourself the trouble and died on Ecos along with the rest of the vermin infesting that planet."

"But I didn't," Sula said. "Nor did I see any reason to trust you after what happened there."

Dalb chuckled. "You and Raj were two of our brightest students, which was why we sent the two of you to that lovely world. Raj came to me some months before your departure, telling me his suspicions. He didn't know who was responsible, of course. He merely questioned how it was that so many habitable worlds had been discovered that harbored no intelligent life-forms—or primates—of their own. I suppose he mentioned this to you?"

Sula shook her head. "He tried to tell me something before he died. He said, 'It's happening again.' I didn't understand what he meant at the time, but I had plenty of time to think on the way to Rhylos." She couldn't believe how well this was going. He was falling right into their trap, almost willingly. Did he want to be exposed for the monster he was? Or did he believe that they wouldn't live long enough to rat on him? "Rhylos was the first, wasn't it?"

Steepling his fingers, Dalb tapped his chin. "Actually, Ursa Prime was the first. Would you believe there were intelligent bearlike creatures living here at one time? Hence the name." He smiled again. "One of my ancestors discovered this world and unwittingly infected the inhabitants with a disease that wiped them out entirely. Oh, not with the Scorillian plague—that virus only affects primates. It was a different disease, long since eradicated."

"And from then on, such exterminations were deliberate?" she prompted.

He shrugged. "There were those who deemed it necessary. You see, in this way, the greater good is served. Higher life-forms need room to multiply and grow. These primitives might have developed into dangerous societies, posing a threat to the entire galaxy. In this manner, the dominant species are protected. You must understand this."

"I'm afraid I don't."

"Be that as it may, you are as guilty as I, my dear. Even if you leave this room and spread tales about the university's involvement, you will be seen as being complicit in this heinous act of genocide. You must have been aware that you were inoculated against this new strain of the plague prior to your departure."

Sula's heart dipped slightly as she realized this scenario was possible. But why would they have done that when the plague would've killed her so neatly? She shook her head. "I don't believe that, nor can you prove it."

"No? You were given a variety of vaccines in preparation for your journey. How could you prove that you weren't given the plague vaccine with your full knowledge and consent? After all, it's your word against mine." Dalb's insolent shrug made Sula long to punch his lights out. Unfortunately, he was beyond her reach. "And who would believe a little nobody like you?"

She took a deep breath, doing her best to control her anger. Aidan was sitting perfectly still, but his barely audible growl betrayed his emotions. All she had to do was keep Dalb talking, and he would hang himself. In fact, he was nearly there already. "But I wasn't inoculated, was I? I somehow developed immunity to the disease on my own. That's true, isn't it?"

"Sadly, yes," Dalb admitted. "Ordinarily, that would make you a person of extreme interest. However, because a vaccine has already been developed, you are worth less than nothing." He rose from his chair. "You must understand that none of you can be allowed to leave here alive." He looked down his nose at Sula. "Your death has already been reported. Your family may remember you, but they no longer grieve." He held up a small dart. "You have somehow developed immunity to the plague, but he"—he nodded toward Aidan—"has not. It's a fitting punishment for your interference, I believe. You get to watch another one of your lovers die."

Sula wouldn't have thought a man his age would have such astonishing reflexes and agility—another of Zolo's genetic modifications, perhaps?—but the dart was thrown at Aidan with pinpoint accuracy, landing squarely in the deltoid muscle, precisely where any good nurse would've given an injection.

Sula's bloodcurdling scream could've been heard in the outer office, but Aidan barely reacted, except to pull the dart from his flesh and lay it carefully on the professor's desk.

"I may be doomed, but so are you," he said. "You see, we're recording this interview, which is being broadcast live everywhere on this planet and beyond. Soon, there won't be anywhere for you to hide. No one will help you for fear of being painted with the same tainted brush."

"Oh, I doubt that," Dalb said with a smug smile. "We control the media here."

"I wouldn't be so sure about that," Aidan said.

Aidan might've remained calm, but Sula was about to come unglued as memories of the carnage on Ecos flashed through her mind, chief among them the image of Raj as he took his last breath. "I've seen how quickly that disease can spread. You would risk everyone on this campus just to kill one man?"

Dalb let out a derisive snort. "Do you really think us incapable of controlling a disease we created? Everyone in this building has been inoculated. They don't realize it, of course, but"—he broke off with a careless shrug— "it is, however, quite true. This room can easily be irradiated to remove any traces of the virus." He spared Aidan a dismissive glance. "Just as the dust that you will soon become can be vacuumed up and thrown out with the rest of the trash."

Sula had heard enough. If she'd been armed, Dalb would've died where he stood.

Aidan, however, remained unmoved. He even smiled.

"Ah, but you see, I know something you don't. I have seen you behind bars, suffering a lonely, ignominious death. Regardless of what happens to anyone else here today, you will not go free."

"You have *seen*?" Dalb leaned forward and slapped his palms on the desktop. "Nonsense."

"My prescient ability is quite reliable, I assure you." Aidan's calm demeanor never wavered. "I saw your death the moment we shook hands."

Dalb's expression didn't change, but as before, his trembling hands betrayed him. "Again, that is utter nonsense."

Aidan's lip curled with disdain. "You're a professor of anthropology. Therefore, you must know *something* about Mordrials."

"But—but you're Zetithian," Dalb sputtered.

Aidan arched a brow. "So? Even Zetithians are known to have visions. How do you think I found Sula in the mountains of Rhylos just as she fell into a cave—a cave filled with artifacts that will prove that an intelligent civilization once thrived there? I found that cave once. I can find it again."

"No, you won't." Dalb squared his shoulders, seeming to have regained some of his composure. "You'll be dead."

"You know something? I believe you're wrong." For a man who had just been exposed to the most dreaded disease imaginable, Aidan seemed freakishly composed. "You see, in seeing other people's futures, I've had glimpses of my own influence. I don't think your poisoned dart did anything more than annoy me."

Sula wasn't so sure. "Aidan..." She took a deep

breath, hoping to steady her voice. "You know there's no cure once you've contracted the disease."

"Unless I'm already immune."

"Immune? How?"

"Think back. Your contraceptive didn't bother me after that first time—even though I wasn't entirely successful at avoiding contact with your bodily fluids—which leads me to suspect I wasn't reacting to any type of medication." He smiled at her. "As you may recall, I scratched you with a fang. When I tasted your blood, I became imprinted with your essence." His brow rose, signaling the most important detail—one that she was already anticipating and praying was true. "And acquired your immunity to the plague."

Although momentarily heartened, Sula remained doubtful. "You don't know that for sure."

"Oh, but I do. Do you remember when I told Abuti that I knew she would survive because I'd seen her when she was older?"

"Yes, I remember," Sula said, although she was still puzzled. "But what does that have to do with you? How could that possibly mean you wouldn't die from the plague?"

"Because what I didn't tell you was that she was walking along a grassy pathway with crowds of people on either side. Nor did I tell you she was being escorted by my brother Aldrik, and most important, she was wearing a sari—the type that would be worn by a member of a wedding party." His smile stretched into a dazzling, fang-revealing grin. "Now, with those two as attendants, whose wedding do you suppose that would be?"

"Ours?" Once again, she cursed her voice for devolving into a high-pitched squeak.

He nodded. "I believe so."

"But how can you be sure?" she asked. "What if I married someone else?"

"Sometimes, I have to extrapolate the true meaning from what I've seen." He shrugged. "I'm not always right about the implications. I mean, it's possible that Abuti will marry Aldrik, although I don't think Norludians and Zetithians are genetically compatible. And even that doesn't explain why she would be wearing a sari. No, this time, I'm quite certain I got it right."

Still puzzled, Sula couldn't help but frown. Dalb might've been in another universe at that moment for all he mattered. "But you said Abuti would be older. Does that mean we won't get married for years and years?"

This time, he laughed—a rich, joyous sound Sula knew she would never tire of hearing. "As you may recall, I never said how *much* older she would be when I saw her future."

"A touching story," Dalb said with a menacing smirk. "However, neither of you will be growing older."

Sula's gaze landed on the pistol the professor now held in his hand.

"I should've used this to begin with," Dalb said. "Not as fitting, perhaps, but certainly more effective."

Aidan never batted an eyelash. "Just as I should have done this"—he swept his arm forward—"to begin with."

The wind Aidan created knocked Dalb off his feet and slammed him into the wall behind the desk. The ancient shield hanging on the wall fell and hit him on the shoulder as he fired the weapon: a laser pistol that burned a hole in the wall above the outer door.

"You know, you could get thrown in jail just for owning one of those," Aidan remarked.

The door flew open, and Dalb's assistant came dashing through it with Curly, Abuti, and Giklor hot on her heels. As snobbish as she'd been before, she was terrified now. "Shut up, Professor! Don't say another word. This conversation is being broadcast on every network in the city!"

Aidan brushed an infinitesimal bit of lint from his sleeve. "Better make that the quadrant."

"But they were scanned for weapons or recording devices before they entered." Dalb might've appeared momentarily dazed, but not so much that he couldn't aim the pistol at Aidan again. "Doesn't matter. You're both going to die anyway."

"Not today." Aidan summoned the wind once again, and the massive desk rose from the floor and crashed into the professor, pinning him to the wall and knocking the pistol from his hand.

Sula ran for the gun as the desk settled back to the floor. Snatching it up, she aimed the weapon at Dalb, although considering his condition, holding him at gunpoint was probably unnecessary.

Gasping for air, Dalb could only say, "How?"

"Like I said, I'm also Mordrial," Aidan said with a wink at Sula.

"B-but the broadcast…" Dalb sputtered. "Surely, you can't do that telepathically!"

"You didn't scan me," Qinta said as she materialized in the far corner, holding up a comlink. Grinning, she added, "You know something? I enjoyed that so much, I'm thinking of pursuing a career in cinematography."

Meanwhile, Giklor was hovering over Dalb's rather

inert body. "My dear sir, please allow me to introduce myself. I am Giklor of the planet Zerka. Should you require healing, I am at your service."

Dalb merely moaned in reply. He was finally beaten, and he obviously knew it.

Aidan shook his head in disgust. "You'll do anything to get your tongue down someone's throat, won't you, Giklor?"

"Healing is what we do," the Zerkan said with a shrug. "I thought you understood."

"I understand completely," Aidan said. "I just think he deserves a little pain for what he's done."

"Very true." Casting a contemptuous glare at Dalb, Giklor said, "I withdraw the offer."

Dalb's assistant began inching her way toward the door, a move that didn't go unnoticed by anyone, Curly in particular.

"Don't you even *think* about going anywhere near a computer," Curly snapped, waving his pistol. "No wiping memory banks or any crap like that."

Qinta's comlink chimed. "It's a text from Val," she said after a glance at the screen. "Says not to worry, he's got the files. He also says it looks like the plague outbreak on Ecos was limited to one relatively small area. Most of the natives remain unharmed. Apparently, they were afraid to push the project forward without knowing what happened to Sula."

Aidan burst out laughing. "Way to go, Val! Told you he'd dig up the dirt."

Sula pressed her fingers to her lips. Whether she could explain it or not, her vision of Ecos had indeed been a true one.

"Son of a bitch!" Curly growled. "Do you mean to tell me that after all the hours we've spent staring at five hundred years' worth of university payrolls, he finally gets it at the last second?"

"Val always did have a flair for the dramatic," Aidan said. "And he does his best work when he's left alone." He tipped his head to one side in such an endearing manner, Sula couldn't help but sigh. "Makes me wonder if he doesn't do it that way on purpose."

"I for one could do with a little less drama," Curly said. "I damn near had a heart attack when I heard laser fire." He glared at Qinta. "You might've warned me."

"What? And blow my cover? No way!" With an impish grin, she added, "Besides, one must be willing to make sacrifices for one's art."

Curly holstered his pistol. "Yeah, well, if it's all the same to you, I'd rather you didn't sacrifice *me* for your art."

Qinta stared at him as though not quite believing what he'd said. "I never had you pegged for being such a wuss."

"I am *not* a wuss," Curly insisted. "But when three of my friends are behind a closed door and I hear laser fire—knowing that none of them were even armed with squirt guns—I get a little antsy."

"He's an old softie like all the rest of us," Aidan said. "He'll never admit it, of course. He's a lot like Jack that way. Heart of gold, but prickly as hell."

Sula smiled. "I prefer my mate to be less prickly and more of an old softie." She peered up at him, somehow suppressing the urge to check his conjunctiva to see if it was turning yellow. "You're sure you feel okay? No symptoms of the plague?"

"I'm sure," he said.

She was momentarily reassured until another aspect of the past few minutes reared its head. "You've kept your abilities secret for your whole life. Now you've told the entire quadrant about them. Is that going to be a problem for you?"

"Not really," he said. "People can ask me to tell their future all they like. I just don't have to tell them everything."

"Like whether Abuti was wearing a sari, you mean?"

"Yeah. Stuff like that."

"Hold on," Abuti said. "What's this sari thing you're talking about? We Norludians don't ever *wear* anything."

"A sari is a traditional dress worn by the women of India," Aidan replied. "They're very beautiful."

If anything, Abuti appeared to be even more appalled than ever. "A dress? You expect me to wear a freakin' dress?"

"You don't have to," Sula said. "But if you want to be one of my bridesmaids, you probably should." Sula couldn't imagine her parents' reaction to having a Norludian in the ceremony, especially one who was essentially naked.

Abuti's bulbous eyes protruded even more than usual. "I can't be a bridesmaid if I don't wear a dress?"

Sula shook her head. "I'm afraid not."

"Well, crap." Abuti slapped the floor with a flippered foot and began popping her fingertips on her arms, nearly dropping a comstone in the process.

"If you'll recall, Aidan has already seen you wearing a sari," Sula reminded her. "I'm pretty sure it's going to happen the way he saw it."

Aidan took her hand and kissed the palm. "My, such faith you have in me."

"Faith? Of course I have faith in you. When have you ever let me down?"

"We've only known one another for a few weeks, but I think it's safe to say I've never done that. Not even when we were flying together."

"And I doubt you ever will." Sula flung her arms around his neck and pulled him close. As their lips met, soft and sensuous quickly became passionate and erotic, sending waves of desire flowing through her veins.

A groan from Dalb, who still lay crumpled on the floor, interrupted one of the best kisses of Sula's life.

This better be good…

Aidan aimed a scathing glance at the professor. "Something just occurred to me. I don't know why this university should get a grant when I already know an outstanding anthropologist who is perfectly capable of conducting a study of the Zetithian survivors."

Despite her momentary elation at the prospect, Sula frowned. "There's just one problem. I never finished my degree."

Aidan cast her protests aside with a wave of his hand, creating a stiff breeze that nearly knocked Qinta off her feet. "Doesn't matter. Although by the time the police have finished going through the evidence Val found, there might not be any faculty left to teach you anyway."

Sula looked up as several uniformed officers entered the room. After hauling Dalb to his feet, they handcuffed him and read him his rights. His bleached-blond assistant received similar treatment, after which they were both taken from the room. "You may be right about that," she said.

"I think you should get an honorary degree at the

very least," Qinta said. "Especially after finding that cave and all."

Giklor broke off his inspection of the spear that had fallen along with the shield. "I believe that would be considered archaeology rather than anthropology. But perhaps you should be granted two degrees."

Sula shook her head. "I really can't see that happening. A degree in anthropology is quite enough for me."

Qinta tapped Aidan's shoulder. "Um, by the way, Aidan. Was I part of that wedding vision?"

"I didn't see you," Aidan replied. "But that doesn't mean you weren't there."

Abuti waved her arms. "Okay, okay. I'll wear the damn dress. But no shoes! I have to draw the line somewhere."

Sula pointed at her own feet. "What about a jeweled anklet? Something like these sandals?"

"Maybe." Abuti's lower lip turned inside out in a gesture Sula recognized as indicative of extreme doubt. "It's just that I've never had anything touching my skin. Don't know how the rest of you can stand it."

"I have often wondered that myself," Giklor said. "Seems unnecessarily cumbersome."

"Until you've spent the winter on Nerik," Aidan said. "Trust me, even you two would want to bundle up there."

"I have never been to Nerik," Giklor said. "However, having heard that, I believe I'll pass."

"You might like southern India," Sula said. "It never gets cold there." She eyed Giklor's pale, translucent skin with misgiving. "Although it might be too hot for you during the summer."

"I will certainly come to the wedding, regardless of the climate," Giklor declared. "I take it the ceremony will be on your homeworld?"

Sula sighed. "You're getting ahead of us. Aidan and I are not yet engaged."

"I can fix that." Aidan got down on one knee and clasped her hands in his. "My darling Sula, you are already my mate and the mother of our children. Will you please do me the honor of becoming my wife?"

She gazed into his glowing feline eyes. Even without his wings, he still looked like an angel. Her green-eyed, golden-haired, pointy-eared angel. "You know I will. You've seen enough of the future to know that."

He shook his head. "Not really. I think I need to hear you say it."

Cupping his face in her palms, she kissed him again. "Before I give you my answer, I would like to know one thing."

"And that is?"

"Will our children be able to fly?"

Being irresistible to every species in the galaxy isn't all it's cracked up to be...

Read on for an excerpt from *Maverick*, the first book in the Cat Star Legacy series by Cheryl Brooks

Available now from Sourcebooks Casablanca

Chapter 1

LARSANKEN TSHEVNOE'S SHIP TOUCHED DOWN ON ONE of the two designated landing sites on Barada Seven, a world he hadn't visited since the age of six. Not much had changed in twenty years. The same thatched hut housed both the spaceport control center and the immigration office, although Larry was willing to bet the thatch had been replaced a time or two in the interim. The sky was still purple, and the land, what there was of it amid the vast ocean, was covered with a dense jungle, save for the coastal flats and a distant range of snow-capped mountains. Having turned over his pulse pistol—no weapons of any kind were allowed on Barada—he exchanged a few credits for triplaks, the local currency, and was given the customary cup of fuuslak juice, which tasted like a mixture of pineapple and tomato juice and had the reputation of improving the drinker's mood without inducing drunkenness or addiction.

The natives hadn't changed, either. They were still the same skinny, nimble-fingered, toad-like creatures he remembered, the only discernable difference between the sexes being that the females wore a bikini-style bit of cloth tied around their chests in addition to the tiny shorts that were also worn by the males. With mouths nearly the full width of their heads, forked tongues, and orange, wart-covered skin, Larry suspected they needed a daily dose of fuuslak juice simply to enable them to look at one another without vomiting.

Larry didn't have that problem. A lifetime spent aboard his parents' starship had introduced him to creatures far more foul-looking than these, some not nearly as pleasant-tempered or possessing such musical voices.

His mother, Jacinth—better known to half the galaxy as Captain Jack Tshevnoe of the starship *Jolly Roger*—had warned him about the Baradan natives' most peculiar attribute of all.

"Watch out when they start waving their hands at you," she'd said. "They use a form of mind control on damn near everyone. Tried it on me once." With a smug grin, she had added, "Didn't work, of course, but it still pissed me off. Might be why I haven't gone back there much. You might pick up some of that fuuslak juice while you're there, though. I've had a few requests for it."

To the best of Larry's knowledge, Jack had never returned to Barada, although he suspected that Althea had. He'd been listening to her wistful reminiscences of that world for nearly twenty years. "Such peaceful stillness," she'd said. "The sense of joy and harmony in the air...sublime."

And then one day, she was simply gone.

She'd left a message behind, of course. She was too fond of her family and her shipmates to leave them wondering. She only said she'd gone someplace where she could find peace.

Her parents, Tisana and Leccarian "Leo" Banadänsk, weren't surprised. "I've always known she would do something like this eventually," Tisana had said after reading the note. "She's descended from a long line of Mordrial witches. It's in her blood."

Tisana and her husband had been a part of Larry's life for as long as he could remember. Like Larry and his brothers, Althea was born aboard the *Jolly Roger*, along with her brothers Aidan and Aldrik. That set of triplets was a year younger than Larry's litter, and he'd known them all their lives, growing up in a closer relationship with them than most cousins enjoyed, despite the lack of blood ties between them.

Swallowing the last of his fuuslak juice, Larry paid for three barrels of the stuff to be delivered to his ship, set the empty cup on a bamboo tray, and left the office. He was perhaps a meter from the door when the inevitable junior guide approached him, albeit with a slightly different sales pitch than he might have expected.

"You are Zetithian, I see," the boy announced. "I am called Elvis. For three triplaks, I will take you to the Lady Althea."

Larry blinked. Clearly, any Zetithian who landed on Barada was expected to visit the one already in residence. "My, that was easy." He paused, frowning. "The *Lady* Althea, you said?"

"That is what she prefers to be called," Elvis replied. "She says it lets everyone know she isn't a native of this world."

How anyone could have mistaken a Zetithian for a Baradan of either sex was beyond Larry's comprehension, but if Althea wanted to set herself up as some sort of exiled noblewoman, that was her business.

He only needed to find her.

"Seems like her surname would do that well enough,"

Larry said. "I'm guessing there aren't many Banadänsks around here."

Elvis shook his head so fast his features blurred. "None at all. But many of our names *are* Terran in origin."

The fad of naming their children after Terran musicians was another aspect of Baradan culture that hadn't faded. Although if there had ever been a singer named Althea, Larry hadn't heard of her. Aretha, yes. But not Althea. That particular name was a reflection of her mother's expertise in herbal medicine.

"Three triplaks, you said?"

Once again, Elvis's head moved too quickly for even a Zetithian's eyes to maintain focus.

"I'll take that as a yes," Larry muttered. "Do you want payment before or after?"

"Before," Elvis replied.

Larry eyed the boy with a measure of suspicion. While he'd inherited his father's physical characteristics, his business acumen came from his mother, who rarely wound up on the short end of a deal. "How do I know you won't run off once I pay you?"

"You don't," Elvis admitted. "But we are a very honest and truthful people."

"So I've been told." Larry reached into the pocket of his khaki trousers, fished out three of the carved pebbles the Baradans considered valuable enough to use in trade, and dropped them onto the boy's outstretched palm.

"Thank you very much," Elvis said, mumbling slightly. "Shall I take you to the Lady Althea now?"

"Absolutely," Larry said with a grin. "Lead on."

—◆◆◆—

Althea glanced up from her botanical sketches to find Larry Tshevnoe staring at her. "That didn't take long," she remarked.

"Four years?" He shook his head. "I suppose not. Especially when you consider it took Mom six years to find her sister."

With a reluctant chuckle, Althea got to her feet. At first glance, she didn't think Larry had changed much in that time, although he might have filled out a bit. They were still almost exactly the same height with dark hair falling in spiral curls to their waists. Even though his mother was human, he was all Zetithian—from his pointed ears and catlike eyes, right down to his smooth, beardless cheeks. Despite the fact that her eyes were green as opposed to black, they'd often been mistaken for siblings. However, upon closer scrutiny, she could see that something had changed. A different aura, perhaps. "You look more like your father than ever."

Larry shrugged. "Minus the scars. Never having been a slave has its advantages."

"I'd imagine both of our fathers would agree to that." With a flick of her brow, she added, "Although it sure beats being dead."

"Maybe."

His complete lack of expression had her on alert. Too bad he was the one person whose emotions she couldn't sense. A mystery she'd never quite been able to solve.

"So, Larry...gonna tell me why you're here?"

"Isn't making sure you're alive and well enough?"

She drew in an unsteady breath, glancing at the

jungle that surrounded them. "Not really. You of all people should've known where I would go and that I'd be safe here."

"Okay. So I lied." Cocking a hip, he folded his arms across his broad chest. "I haven't been looking for you for four years. In fact, I came straight here." He nodded toward the trail to the coast. "With a little help from Elvis."

That much she could believe. "You still haven't told me why."

"I missed you, Al." A wicked grin revealed his fangs. "Or should I call you the Lady Althea?"

She flapped a hand. "Whatever." That look had always unnerved her, and she suspected he knew that.

"I'm going by Larsan these days, myself. Sounds more, I dunno…sexy? Manly?"

That last bit dragged yet another chuckle from her. "As if you needed any help in that department." Zetithian males hadn't been dubbed the hottest hunks in the galaxy for nothing, and Larry Tshevnoe was a prime specimen.

"More mature, then," he conceded. "Mom doesn't like it much, but you know how she feels about those crazy Zetithian names."

Althea nodded. Upon learning that the slave she'd bought was named Carkdacund Tshevnoe, Larry's Terran mother had opted to call him Cat, which was much shorter and more descriptive of a man with feline characteristics. Althea was grateful that her parents had gone with shorter names, and while Althea Banadänsk was still a bit of a mouthful, it had Larry, Moe, and Curly's full names beat all to hell and back.

"So why here and not Terra Minor?" he asked. "Or

do you enjoy the distinction of being the only Zetithian on the planet?"

"Not particularly," she replied. "And that isn't the reason I came here."

"I didn't think it was." His unblinking gaze remained riveted to her own. "You still haven't answered my question."

She should have been able to explain why some planets disturbed her more than others, but she couldn't. Not to him. Not someone whose emotions were so unreadable.

Even his facial expressions didn't always provide the right clues. With other people, she could feel their emotions and compare them to their facial expressions and body language. But there was something different about Larry. Something deeper. Something she'd never quite been able to fathom.

Truth be told, she'd never unburdened herself to anyone. Her own mother didn't know how her powers worked. She had an affinity with animals, although it wasn't the sort of two-way telepathic conversations her mother had with them. Her own communication was more subtle, like a suggestion or a request for a specific behavior instead of the mind-control techniques the Baradans used. She didn't have to wave her hands the way they did, either. The exchange was entirely mental. Her primary element was earth, and sometimes she was sure it spoke to her. Not in actual words, but with feelings, emotions. One thing she was sure of: land didn't like being moved or cultivated. For that reason, earthquakes were despised only slightly more than the plow. Barada Seven was different from just about every other planet in the known galaxy in that it had never been farmed. The inhabitants took what they needed from the jungle, living in absolute harmony with their environment. The ground still smarted from the few offworld-type dwellings that had been constructed there.

She lived in the trees like the Baradans, climbing a ladder made of vines up to her bedroom each night. Fruit was easy enough to come by. Some species produced year-round, and though others were more sporadic, there was always something available, although she questioned the edibility of a few of them.

"I like it here," she finally said. "It suits me."

"I see." That's what he said, but did he really mean it? Larry was an enigma when he should have been comforting. After all, knowing what everyone around her was feeling was exhausting, which was the main reason she'd chosen to live in relative seclusion.

"Think about it, Larry. This is the way my mother lived until my father came along. If it hadn't been for your parents tempting them with adventure and the chance to see the galaxy, they would probably still be living in a cabin in the woods of Utopia. I had my fair share of thrills growing up on a starship. I felt the need to settle somewhere."

"Geez, Al, you make it sound like you're in your nineties instead of your twenties. Sure, I left home and have my own ship now, but I'm not using it to hide."

"You're different. You don't have a thousand years of Mordrial witch ancestry telling you how to live. And I'm not hiding. If I'd been hiding, you wouldn't have found me." She couldn't be sure, but his expression suggested he would have found her anyway.

"Okay," he said. "So you're not trying to hide. Were you expecting someone? The first kid who pegged me as a Zetithian offered to bring me here."

"Elvis set himself up as my official helper, whether I actually need his help or not." Which she didn't. She didn't have to wave her hands to get a srakie to fetch bolaka fruit from the jungle's canopy, nor did she expect one of the little ratlike monkeys to ride around on her shoulder. They came when she needed them. "How much did he charge you?"

"Three triplaks," Larry replied. "Seemed reasonable enough." He glanced at the sketch she'd been working on. "So what do you do here besides draw plant pictures?"

Trust Larry to take a less-than-compelling interest in her work. "I'm compiling an encyclopedia of the local flora."

He arched a dark, elegant brow. "Wouldn't it be easier to take pictures?"

Unclenching her teeth, she exhaled sharply. "You're missing the point, Larry."

"Ah," he said with a nod. "I get it. Busy work. You'd be finished in an hour if you were using a camera."

Althea somehow managed to catch herself before letting loose with a full-fledged growl. "I'm starting to remember why I left home in the first place." Before he could say another word, she went on the offensive. "What about you? Why are *you* here?"

"Wondered when you were gonna get around to asking me that. I need your help."

"Oh?" To the best of her recollection, Larry had never needed help with anything, much less admitted it. "What's the matter? Your comsystem go on the blink and you need a telepath?"

"There's nothing wrong with my comsystem, and even if there was, I wouldn't need a telepath. There isn't a comsystem in existence that I can't fix. Besides, you're an empath, not a telepath." He stopped and shook his head. "Hold on, Al. You're changing the subject. You know how I hate when you do that."

"Best form of evasion ever invented," she said with a shrug. Still, if Larry Tshevnoe was asking for help, it was probably something important. "Okay. I'll tell you. I came here to escape all the mental noise. The racket on Terra Minor is awful, and Earth is even worse. Rhylos is almost unbearable."

"I, uh, take it there's less noise here."

"That's putting it mildly. Being here is like putting on noise-reducing headphones. Not entirely quiet, but close." And then there was Larry, who never *had* caused the kind of mental static that most people did. His presence hadn't altered the level in the slightest, which was probably why he'd been able to sneak up on her.

"Fewer people, I guess," he admitted. "Still don't get why you had to come here, though. There are places on Terra Minor where you'd be a thousand kilometers away from anybody."

"Tried that. Didn't help."

The brow went up again, which was a fairly significant expression on a Zetithian whose straight brows were already slanted toward their temples. "You're getting bad vibes from the freakin' mountains?"

"I have no idea, Larry. I just know it's there. I can't explain it any better than that. It's like the land is in agony." She pressed a hand to her forehead, half expecting the pain to put in another appearance. Fortunately, it didn't. "What is it you wanted?"

He sucked in a breath, seeming far less self-assured than he'd been mere moments before. "Look, I know you can't read minds, but you *can* read emotions. You see, there's this girl—"

This time, Althea didn't bother to suppress the growl. "Mother of the gods! You want me to tell you if this girl loves you for yourself or because you're Zetithian?"

"And rich," he said, frowning. "That's the part that's bugging me the most. I mean, if I was a *poor* Zetithian, like both of our fathers were, it would be different. But I'm not someone's slave. I've never been abused, and I've never missed a meal in my entire life—even if Mom did make us eat those cheap-ass Suerlin marching rations for months on end."

At the time, Althea had considered Suerlin food to be a form of abuse, so she knew exactly what he meant. Neither of them had been sold as slaves. They'd never had to fight for their lives, nor had they been orphans aboard a refugee ship for twenty-five years after their homeworld was destroyed. They'd had happy childhoods seeing the galaxy in ways most kids only dreamed about.

"Let me get this straight. You want me to go with you to wherever this girl lives and act as a lie detector?" Seconds later, her jaw dropped as the most important aspect of any relationship with a Zetithian man reared its dangerous head. "Wait. Have you had sex with this girl?"

"Well...no," he admitted. "You know how it is with us Zetithian guys. We're like a sex drug. One hit might not hook you for life, but women nearly always want more."

"Hmm... Maybe Terran women. Is she? Terran, I mean."

"Yeah. She's really pretty, and I like her a lot— maybe even love her. I just want to be sure before I do anything stupid."

"Once you do the deed, I doubt she'd ever leave you for someone else, if that's what you're worried about."

"I know that. But I want a woman to stay with me forever because she loves me. Not because I can wow her with my orgasmic joy juice."

Having evolved to entice their own relatively disinterested women, Zetithian males were irresistible to most other humanoid females, which, prior to the introduction of space travel to Zetith, hadn't been an issue. But once women from other worlds got a taste of them, the level of jealousy the men inspired had ultimately resulted in the destruction of their homeworld and the near extinction of their species. Larry, like most of the surviving Zetithian males, had apparently chosen to exercise both caution and self-restraint when choosing a mate.

Unfortunately, Althea suspected that the woman's emotions weren't the ones in question.

"You know, that whole 'I like her a lot—maybe even love her' part strikes me as your main problem. I can't help you with that, Larry. I can't read you. Never could."

"But you could read *her*, couldn't you? If your mother could read people instead of animals, I'd ask her, but she can't, and you're the only empath I know. Won't you at least try?"

"Can't you tell from her scent?"

"You'd think that, wouldn't you? Normally, I should

be able to tell the difference between love and lust. But her scent is...confusing."

As far as he'd traveled to find her, Althea really couldn't say no. Not to Larry anyway. She blew out a resigned sigh. "Where is she?"

He winced. "Um, would you believe she's on Rhylos?"

I should've known...

"Oh joy," she said with a groan. "You know, this would've been a whole lot easier if you'd brought her along with you."

Larry gaped at her with dismay. "I couldn't very well tell her why I was bringing her here, could I?"

"Well, no," she admitted. "Although I'm sure you could've come up with some sort of excuse."

"I would have, except she's really busy at the orphanage right now—did I tell you she works there with Onca and Kim? That's how we met."

"I see."

She did, actually. After Onca, their friend and fellow Zetithian, retired from the sex trade and married Kim, they'd turned the old Zetithian Palace brothel into a shelter for homeless orphans. Needless to say, the needs of those children far outweighed her own.

"Okay," she said. "I'll do it."

Acknowledgments

My sincere thanks go out to:

My loving husband, Budley.

My awesome sons, Mike and Sam.

My talented critique partners, Sandy James, T. C. Winters, and Nan Reinhardt.

My keen-eyed beta reader, Mellanie Szereto.

My long-time editor, Deb Werksman.

My fellow IRWA members for their enthusiastic support and encouragement.

My insane cats, Kate and Allie.

My sweet barn cat, Kitty Cat.

My trusty horses, Kes and Jadzia.

My peachy little dog, Peaches, who dearly loves to come along whenever I mow the pasture.

But most of all, I'd like to thank my wonderful readers who kept asking, "When will you write another Cat Star book? We need to know what happens to the kids!"

About the Author

A native of Louisville, Kentucky, Cheryl Brooks is a former critical care nurse who resides in rural Indiana with her husband, two sons, two horses, three cats, and one dog. She is the author of the ten-book Cat Star Chronicles series, the Cowboy Heaven series (two books and one novella), the Soul Survivors trilogy, the four-book Unlikely Lovers series, and several stand-alone books and novellas. *Mystic* is the second book in her Cat Star Legacy series. Her other interests include cooking, gardening, singing, and guitar playing. Cheryl is a member of RWA and IRWA. You can visit her online at cherylbrooksonline.com or email her at cheryl.brooks52@yahoo.com.

NIGHTCHASER

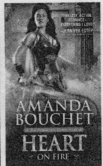

Also by Cheryl Brooks